TA
BREAT

BY
CARA SUMMERS

AND

NOT ANOTHER
BLIND DATE

BY
JANELLE DENISON
LESLIE KELLY & JO LEIGH

MILLS
BOON

Dear Reader,

St Valentine's Day has always been one of my favorite holidays, and I thought it would be the perfect backdrop for my fifth WRONG BED book. I love writing stories in which two people, who think they are so wrong for each other, discover (much to their initial horror) that they make a perfect match!

Special FBI agent Nicola Guthrie and Security expert Gabe Wilder share a common goal. They are each determined to catch a thief—namely the media celebrity who's been robbing Denver's socially elite and who only strikes on holidays. With St Valentine's Day a mere forty-eight hours away, the clock is ticking, and Nicola's prime suspect is Gabe. Of course, that doesn't stop her from falling into bed with him the first chance she gets...

For news about upcoming books, please visit my website, www.carasummers.com.

Happy Valentine's Day!

Cara Summers

TAKE MY
BREATH AWAY...

BY
CARA SUMMERS

All the characters in this book have no existence outside the imagination of
the author, and have no relation whatsoever to anyone bearing the same name
or names. They are not even distantly inspired by any individual known or
unknown to the author, and all the incidents are pure invention.

First published in Great Britain 2012
by Mills & Boon, an imprint of Harlequin (UK) Limited,
Eton House, 18-24 Paradise Road, Richmond, Surrey TW9 1SR

© Carolyn Hanlon 2011

ISBN: 978 0 263 89727 2

14-0212

Harlequin (UK) policy is to use papers that are natural, renewable and
recyclable products and made from wood grown in sustainable forests. The
logging and manufacturing processes conform to the legal environmental
regulations of the country of origin.

Printed and bound in Spain
by Blackprint CPI, Barcelona

Was **Cara Summers** born with the dream of becoming a published romance novelist? No. But now that she is, she still feels her dream has come true. She loves writing for the Blaze® line because it allows her to create strong, determined women and seriously sexy men who will risk everything to achieve *their* dreams. Cara has written more than thirty-five books, and when she isn't working on new stories, she teaches in the Writing Program at Syracuse University and at a community college near her home.

To all of my readers everywhere!
Thanks so much for your support.
Happy Valentine's Day!

Prologue

The day after Thanksgiving...

"I'M THINKING WHAT WE'VE got here is a copycat thief." FBI Agent Nick Guthrie kept his eyes steady on Gabe Wilder as he gestured to the Monet propped on the credenza to the left of his desk. In front of the cleverly forged painting lay a copy of that morning's *Denver Post*. The headline read: Priceless Monet Stolen on Thanksgiving Day.

"Don't you agree? He replaces the original with a very good copy. That's what your father always did. He's even signing your father's initials."

Gabe said nothing, letting the silence stretch between them. He'd been coming to grips with the fact that someone was imitating his father ever since Guthrie had called him to the crime scene the night before. At 6:30 a.m., the FBI offices were still empty, and Guthrie hadn't bothered to draw the shades on the glass walls that divided his office from the others in the White-Collar Crime Division.

"Well?" Guthrie prompted Gabe. "What are you thinking?"

"We're not dealing with a copycat." He shifted his gaze to the Monet.

"No?" Guthrie frowned. "The thief broke through one of the best security alarm systems available, one of yours. He has a detailed knowledge of the M.O. your father used. And it's a French Impressionist painting. Raphael Wilder was particularly talented at forging those. I say someone is deliberately imitating your father's style right down to signing the forgery with the initials, R.W."

"But my father never sent announcements bragging about his thefts," Gabe pointed out.

"Agreed," Guthrie said. "But everything else is the same."

Gabe couldn't argue with that. But why would someone choose to imitate the style of a legendary art thief and then deviate in a major way from his method? And why was this thief choosing to copy his father in the first place? Those were the questions that he intended to find the answers to.

"I had a chance to study the original painting when my company set up the security at the Langfords' house." Gabe nodded his head toward the Monet. "The forgery is a good one. It might have been years before the fake was detected."

Guthrie leaned back in his chair. "So why announce the theft?"

"Exactly. Raphael Wilder never would have." Then Gabe met Nick Guthrie's eyes. "That's why I'm not willing to agree that this thief is simply a copycat. There's more going on here. Why don't you come right out and ask *me* if I had something to do with stealing the Monet? The possibility must have crossed your mind. No one would know my father's methods better than I. His initials are on the painting. The Langfords were using *my* security system."

Guthrie said nothing.

"Perhaps I substituted the forgery when I installed the alarm system. That would eliminate the need to go back and break in later. I could sell the original and no one would be the wiser, perhaps ever."

"That's what your father would have done." Guthrie shot him a frown. "And maybe your involvement in the theft did cross my mind, but I dismissed the possibility. Raphael Wilder was a thief, a very good one, and if you'd followed in his footsteps, I imagine you'd have made a very good one also. But you haven't. We go back a long way, Gabe."

That much was true. The first day he'd met FBI Agent Nick Guthrie was the day the man had come into his home and arrested his father for grand larceny. That had been over fifteen years ago. And within a month of Raphael Wilder's conviction, he'd died in prison of pneumonia. Ever since then, Nick Guthrie had kept close tabs on Gabe. What might have begun as feelings of guilt or responsibility on Guthrie's part had evolved gradually into a friendship, one that ran both ways.

And Nick Guthrie had been one of the people who'd helped him stay on the straight and narrow at a time in his life when he might have chosen a different path. He owed other people, too, of course. Father Mike Flynn and the St. Francis Center for Boys had played a key role.

Nick Guthrie leaned forward. "I know about the promise you made your mother when she was dying. I was with you and Father Mike the day that you renewed that promise to your father in the prison infirmary. There's no way that you would break those vows by starting to steal paintings. You've built a business to protect people from theft and from harm. And you're doing a damn good job of it."

Gabe didn't smile, but the knot that had been in his stomach when Guthrie had asked him to come into the office that morning eased. If Nick Guthrie hadn't requested this meeting, Gabe would have insisted on one himself. He'd needed to know just how much G. W. Securities was going to come under suspicion because of his father.

Guthrie ran his hands through his hair. "Besides, if you were to take up a life of crime, I can't see you sending announcement cards. And why target one of your own security systems? I've known you since you were thirteen. You're not that dumb."

Now Gabe *did* smile. "So it really did cross your mind?"

Guthrie sighed. "Of course it did. I'm an FBI agent. I have to consider all the possibilities. But you didn't steal the Monet. And I'm not releasing any of the details about the thief using your father's M.O. to the press."

"Well, you're right about me, as it happens. I didn't steal the painting. But…"

Guthrie raised his hands, palms out. "I know. I know. You still think I was wrong about your father."

It was a discussion they'd had often over the years. Gabe was willing to admit that his father had been a thief, a brilliant one. And a reformed one. He'd never believed his father had stolen the Pissaro that Guthrie had arrested him for stealing. Raphael Wilder had denied the theft even on his deathbed. "My father made the same promise to my mother that I did. He didn't steal that painting."

Guthrie rose and walked to the window. Over the years they'd agreed to disagree. The first time they'd argued about his father's innocence, Gabe had punched the older man. He'd been thirteen and angry.

Guthrie had taken the punch and told him that he could take another. Anytime. But Gabe hadn't punched him again because it hadn't helped soothe any of the pain or the loss away. What had eventually helped was the time he'd spent at the St. Francis Center for Boys. At a crucial time in his life, Father Mike Flynn had helped him more than he could ever repay. Truth told, the priest was still helping him. He'd been the first person he'd called after he'd left the crime scene the night before.

"There was a time when I thought you might follow in your father's footsteps," Guthrie said. "But you've built a very different kind of life."

Yes, he had. And G. W. Securities was becoming known beyond Denver. Partly due to some consulting work he'd done for Nick Guthrie, he'd recently landed jobs as far away as D.C. and New York City. Gabe stretched out his legs and crossed them at the ankles.

"So why is someone imitating parts of your father's M.O.?" Guthrie spoke the question that was foremost in both of their minds.

As it hung unanswered in the air, Gabe's attention was distracted by the young woman who'd just stepped out of the elevator in the outer offices. Something moved through him as she strode purposefully toward a desk in one of the glass-walled offices and set her briefcase down.

Not recognition.

Or was it? He gave her another few seconds of his attention. There was plenty there to warrant a second look. The gray slacks and jacket did little to disguise the long legs and the curves in that neat, athletic body. The bright blue of the shirt drew his gaze to her face—also worth a second look.

This time he was sure it was recognition that flickered. He knew that short upturned nose, the stubborn chin.

"Who…?"

Gabe wasn't even aware that he'd spoken the question out loud until Guthrie answered, "That's Nicola, my daughter. She started working here a week ago."

Gabe registered the frown in the older man's voice, but he didn't take his gaze off of the woman.

"She didn't even tell Marcia and me that she was applying to the FBI, not until she'd been accepted at Quantico. She finished her training there last month and received the Director's Leadership Award. I had to pull a lot of strings to get her transferred here."

Nicola Guthrie. Of course. It was the hair that had thrown him. Now it fell straight as rain until it curved beneath her chin. Fifteen years ago a mass of curls had framed her face. He'd teased her ruthlessly about them and even pulled them a few times.

"I'm going to limit her to research on this case," Guthrie was saying. "She's smart, but she's not ready for field work. As long as she's in the office and behind that desk, I can be sure she's safe."

Gabe was about to turn his attention back to the Monet when Nicola Guthrie turned and her gaze suddenly locked on his.

The impact ricocheted through his system, coming into contact with every nerve ending. For a moment he couldn't breathe. Everything else faded, and all he was aware of was her. The sudden tightening in his gut was raw, sexual and compelling. Without any conscious volition, he rose from the chair.

"Gabe?"

Guthrie's voice came from a distance. Still, the sound might have been the only thing that allowed him to keep his feet firmly planted on the floor. The urge to go to her was so intense. He'd never felt a pull that strong. He couldn't drag his gaze away from her. He felt trapped. But he couldn't seem to summon up the will to fight his desire.

"What is it?" Guthrie's voice was closer now. Gabe felt

Guthrie's hand on his arm. But it wasn't until Nicola turned away that he was able to draw in a breath. Or gather a coherent thought.

"What's wrong?" Guthrie asked.

"It's this case." Gabe was surprised to find his voice worked. He was still looking at her as she picked up a file and leafed through it.

What the hell *was* wrong with him? No woman had ever affected him this way before. All that had happened was that their eyes had met. She was standing a good twenty-five feet away and she'd made him feel weak, winded.

What would she do to him when she was closer? When he kissed her? When he touched her? When he was inside of her?

No.

Ruthlessly, Gabe reined his thoughts in and turned to face the man he called a friend. "I want some answers. I don't have any idea why someone is using parts of my father's M.O." But there was a reason. He was sure of it.

"The announcement cards are easier," he continued. "This particular thief craves attention. Which means that he may strike again to get more."

"I wish we weren't thinking along the same lines," Guthrie said in a grim tone. "That brings me to the reason I asked you to come in today. I figure you're going to be working on this case and I'd like you to agree to share any information you come up with. My office will do the same. What do you say?"

Gabe managed a smile as he held out a hand. "I say two heads are always better than one."

Guthrie glanced toward the painting again. "I hope that we're both wrong about another robbery."

Gabe hoped so, too. But his gut told him they weren't.

As he left the FBI offices, he noted that more people had

reported to work. And in spite of his determination not to, he glanced once more in the direction of Nicola Guthrie's office.

Her head was bent over a file.

Gabe wasn't sure it was relief or disappointment he felt as the elevator doors closed and he descended to the street level.

1

Two and a half months later, February 12

"TURN LEFT IN point nine miles."

The calm voice of her GPS system had FBI special agent Nicola Guthrie gripping the steering wheel of her car and peering through the windshield into thickly falling snow. Easing her foot off the gas, she narrowed her eyes to study what lay in the beams of her headlights.

Not much. She was finding it more and more difficult to distinguish the narrow mountain road from the treacherous ditches that bordered it on either side.

The storm had been steadily increasing in intensity ever since she'd left Denver at 6:00 p.m. And her little Volkswagen Beetle convertible was not known for its winter weather capabilities. The one-hour drive to the church of St. Francis had stretched into nearly three.

And counting.

But it was going to be worth it. The moment that Father Mike Flynn had walked into her office and showed her the note, she'd gotten that tingling feeling deep inside of her—the same one that had guided every important decision she'd ever made. And it had never failed her.

Tonight, she had a good chance of finally identifying the art thief who'd been leading the FBI on a merry chase for the past three months. On each holiday since Thanksgiving, he'd relieved one of Denver's art collectors of a priceless painting. And if she unmasked him tonight, her father would finally have to relent and take her career choice seriously.

Nicola glanced at her speedometer. She could walk faster than this.

"Turn left in point five miles."

Not much longer. Her decision to join the FBI had not set well with either her father or her stepmother. Her father's tendency to be over-protective she could understand. Her mother had been an agent who'd worked with him, and she'd died in the line of duty when Nicola had been a toddler.

Her stepmother was a different kettle of fish. Marcia Thorne Guthrie had been born to wealth, and her ideas about a woman's role in society were slightly and almost lovably medieval. Marcia thought women should study art and literature, marry, run a lovely home and spread her largesse through the community by doing good works. *And* by throwing huge charity balls like the one Marcia gave every year at Thorne Mansion on Valentine's Day.

In fact, that's exactly where Nicola should be right now—at Thorne Mansion helping her stepmother make the final dessert selections for the ball.

The problem was Nicola didn't want to follow in her stepmother's footsteps. She wanted to follow in her father's. But she dearly loved both of her parents—enough to get a Masters in Fine Art degree before she'd secretly applied to the FBI. Throughout her life, her rebellions against her parents had ended in eventual victories, but they had always been hard-won. And actions had always spoken louder than words. Eventually, she'd win them over.

Which was why tonight was so important. If she could just catch herself a thief… And if that thief turned out to be who she thought it was? Well, her father would have to give her bonus points for that because he thought Gabe Wilder was as innocent as a newborn babe.

She didn't.

"Turn left in point three miles."

"Where?" Nicola frowned into the swirling snow.

Then she saw it—just the outline of the church steeple. Ahead and to her left. She might have missed it if not for the headlights of a vehicle parked nearby. When a sudden break in the wind gave her a better look at the silhouette of the parked car, Nicola's pulse jumped.

It was an SUV and it looked familiar. Could it be…?

The tingling sensation moved through her. She'd felt the same way when Father Mike had visited her office and shown her the note announcing that the statue of St. Francis was going to be stolen tonight. Gabe Wilder might very well be here.

"Turn left in one hundred yards."

One step at a time, Nicola. First, you have to find the driveway. Then the thief.

During the long drive from the city, her practical side had been cautioning her that a semi-retired Franciscan priest like Father Mike didn't fit the profile of the previous wealthy and socially prominent victims of Denver's well-publicized art thief. However, during the twenty years he'd served as the director of the St. Francis Center for Boys, Father Mike had certainly rubbed elbows with the movers and shakers of Denver.

And the thief always delivered a note to his next target

on the day he struck. Father Mike had received his note today. She'd read it.

I've always admired the statue of St. Francis—ever since I first saw it in the prayer garden at the St. Francis Center. I was so disappointed when you moved it to that isolated church. So, I've decided to take it off your hands. Enjoy Lincoln's Birthday.

The bragging tone and the specificity of the note were similar to the other ones in the file. The art piece and the holiday were always mentioned by name.

No one had expected the thief to make a move on Lincoln's Birthday, February 12. The press, the FBI and most of Denver's socially elite were expecting the thief to strike on Valentine's Day. A priceless Cézanne was going to be auctioned at the annual Valentine's Day Charity Ball—the one her stepmother was throwing—and the theory was that the thief wouldn't be able to resist it.

No one had given any thought to the possibility that the thief might target the statue of St. Francis. Truth told, she hadn't thought of it either. She'd been certain her father was right, and the thief would go after the Cézanne.

The small marble statue currently residing on a side altar in St. Francis Church didn't have the monetary value of the artwork previously stolen. But there were those who would testify that it was priceless.

The statue of St. Francis had been donated to the Franciscan order in Denver years ago by an immigrant family from Assisi, Italy. They'd claimed it had been sculpted in the image of the saint himself, and that it possessed special powers to grant prayers. Since its arrival in Denver, the reputation of the statue had grown to legendary proportions. Even in its original home in the small prayer garden next to the St. Francis Center for Boys, the statue had attracted crowds. Many thought that paying a visit to the statue and saying a prayer was like having a direct line to God.

There were no documented miracles. Yet. But there were plenty of people who'd testified to the fact that the prayers they'd said to the statue had not only been answered but had changed their lives. People had fallen in love, marriages had been saved and babies had been born to supposedly infertile couples. And almost everyone testified to finding peace.

The article published in last Sunday's edition of the *Denver Post* had included several of the stories. They ranged from recovering lost jewelry to improvements in health and relationships. There was even a local congresswoman who claimed she owed her latest election victory to St. Francis.

Nicola remembered a time when she'd believed in the power of the statue herself. She'd said a prayer, one she'd desperately wanted to be granted. But St. Francis hadn't been listening that day. She hadn't wasted another prayer on him since. But she was definitely in the minority.

When the St. Francis Center for Boys had been torn down and replaced by upscale townhomes as part of the city's urban renewal program, Father Mike had received permission to relocate the statue to St. Francis Church. Since then the pilgrimages to pray to the statue had picked up in numbers.

Nearly half the money that had sustained the St. Francis Center had come from visitors who'd left donations in the small prayer garden where the statue had stood for fifteen years. Currently the three masses Father Mike commuted to say on Sunday were packed, and at least twenty percent of attendees were people from out of state who'd come to say a prayer.

What was the value of a piece of art that could answer

your prayers? Nicola figured it might bring in a hefty price from some collector.

Evidently enough to have Father Mike hiring G. W. Securities, the premier firm in Denver, to protect it at its new location. That little known fact had also received quite a bit of play in the *Denver Post* article.

So if the statue of St. Francis was stolen, it would be the fourth piece of art snitched while under the protection of G. W. Securities. And to Nicola's way of thinking that made the company's owner, Gabe Wilder, a prime suspect. The fact that Gabe was the son of legendary thief Raphael Wilder added more weight to her suspicions.

"Turn left in twenty-five yards."

As Nicola peered into the snow, a blast of wind slammed into her car and the rear wheels fishtailed. Holding her breath, she eased her foot off the gas and kept her hands steady on the wheel. Her headlights shifted, briefly pinning the SUV, and Nicola's pulse jumped again. That was Gabe Wilder's car all right.

This time the tingling feeling racing through her was so strong that she nearly trembled. Then she felt her tires regain traction, and she shifted her attention to the road.

Her suspicion that Gabe Wilder had to be playing a key role in the thefts was the reason she'd spent the past few weeks tailing that SUV all over Denver during her off duty hours. Not that her surveillance had done her any good. Thanks to secure underground parking garages and the fact that he lived in an apartment above his office, she hadn't even been able to get a good look at the man himself.

Still, Nicola couldn't rid herself of her gut feeling that Gabe had to be connected to the thefts. Each time she'd tried to connect the dots in the case, he was the one who triggered that tingling sensation.

Beneath her, she felt her tires spin and slide to the right.

Focus, Nicola. When she peered through the windshield all she could see in the glare of her headlights was a whirling tunnel of snow. But the driveway to the church had to be close. The GPS lady was never wrong. She pressed her foot lightly against the brake. Surely that SUV would have left tracks. Any minute now she'd see the indentations in the snow. She slowed some more. But if she made a left turn without being sure, she'd end up in the ditch.

"Recalculating," her GPS system chirped.

"Damn." She'd missed the driveway, but at least she hadn't gone off the road. Not yet.

"Drive point four miles to Balfour Road."

"In your dreams," Nicola muttered as she eased her car to what she thought was the side of the road and stopped. That was when she saw the other vehicle. It was about fifteen yards ahead of her, just at the end of where her headlights reached. And it was tilting to one side in the ditch she'd been trying so hard to avoid.

Hoping that she'd left enough room for any possible travelers to get by her, she turned off the engine and then studied the other not-so-lucky car in her headlights. It was completely covered in snow, so it was impossible to figure the make or model—or even the color. It looked as if it had been abandoned. Just to make sure, she pressed the heel of her hand on her horn and gave three sharp blasts.

Nothing.

The church would be the closest refuge. She grabbed a flashlight out of her glove compartment, tucking it into the pocket of her coat. Then she turned up her collar and opened the driver's door. Fighting the wind, she climbed out.

Her first surprise was that the snow almost came up

to her knees. The second was the force of the wind that pushed her back against the car. Nicola shoved her hair back and managed to get the door closed.

Reaching the church ASAP had to be her first priority. Gabe Wilder had left his headlights on, which made it easier for her to see through the darkness. Assuming that *was* Gabe Wilder's SUV, he had to be here because of the statue. And she couldn't discount the possibility that who-ever had been driving that abandoned car was inside with him. If one of them was the thief, that didn't bode well for the other.

She shifted her gun from her holster to her coat pocket for easy access and moved forward.

2

HE WASN'T ALONE in the church.

Gabe had sensed that from the moment he'd found the door unlocked and the security alarm disabled. His conviction had grown steadily during the time it had taken him to walk quietly up the aisle to the side altar.

Since the storm had taken the power out, the place was as dark and cold as a crypt. The only illumination was provided by the three-tiered stand of votive lights in front of the altar. Nowadays, people didn't light real candles. Instead they donated money to purchase lights powered by lithium batteries. And they "burned" brightly enough for him to see that the statue of St. Francis was still there, enclosed in a shatterproof glass dome.

Inwardly, Gabe grinned. Turnabout was fair play. And very satisfying. The guy who'd had such smooth sailing so far must be feeling at least some of the frustration he'd been feeling for the past three months. There was no duplicate of the security system he'd created for the statue, not even a prototype out there, because he'd just invented it. It was very difficult to crack a safe or break through a security system when one had nothing to practice on.

Gabe started up the short flight of steps to the altar.

It was only as he reached the top that he saw it—the second statue sitting in the shadows at the foot of the altar. Crouching down, he examined it in the dim light, running his hands over it just to be sure. Then he welcomed the pump of adrenaline. It was a copy of the St. Francis, and that had to mean that his instincts had been right. The thief was still here.

Where?

In spite of the fact that all of his senses were now on full alert, Gabe was careful to keep the expression on his face perfectly neutral as he rose, narrowed his eyes and pretended to study the St. Francis that still stood beneath the glass dome.

The trap he'd set had worked. It was Father Mike who'd first suggested the idea that he might use the statue as bait, and the more Gabe had thought it over, the more he'd wanted to try it out. He'd called a friend at the *Denver Post,* and the resulting article in last Sunday's paper had not only highlighted the "priceless" reputation the statue had always had for answering prayers, but it had also mentioned that G. W. Securities had designed a premier alarm system for its protection. Evidently the combination of information had lured the thief into planning an attempt on the statue, just as he'd hoped.

The timing had surprised him. It was still two days until Valentine's Day, and the press as well as the law enforcement agencies had been expecting the thief to strike then. But the moment that Father Mike had called to tell him about the note, he'd sent the priest to the FBI office to update Nick Guthrie and he'd rushed up here.

Now, with the statue's help…

He mentally said a prayer, and then he just listened. There was nothing but the muted howling of the storm outside. His eyes had fully adjusted to the dim light, and he saw nothing in his peripheral vision that seemed out of place in the shadows.

His guess was that the thief had found a place to hide. His gaze went immediately to the door of the choir loft. It was open. Slipping quietly away from the altar, he moved along the side wall of the church until he reached the door.

For a moment, he paused and listened hard.

Nothing.

Then he heard it, the scrape of wood against wood, and he felt a draft of icy cold air. Pushing through the door, he ran into the room.

The blow caught him by surprise. Pain exploded in his head and icy water poured down the collar of his shirt. With stars spinning in front of his eyes, he stepped to the side and the kick aimed for his groin glanced off his thigh.

Off balance, he threw himself forward and took his opponent to the ground. They rolled across the marble floor, each struggling for an advantage. A table overturned and glass shattered. He was on the bottom when their bodies slammed into a wall.

Hands closed around his throat and cut off his air. Vision blurring, Gabe gripped his attacker's waist and bucked upward. The hands loosened around his throat, and Gabe reared up and butted heads with his opponent. Pain zinged through his skull, but it did the trick. He was suddenly free.

Scrambling up, he ran after his opponent. He would have been successful if his feet hadn't suddenly shot right out from beneath him. He fell backward, heard the crack as his head struck a counter. Then another explosion of pain blacked out everything.

NICOLA DUCKED HER HEAD and fought her way into the wind. Icy pellets stung her skin, and the boots that had been entirely appropriate for a day in the Denver office were no match for the snow that came closer to her knees as she moved forward.

Using her hand to shield her eyes, she checked on the SUV's location and adjusted her course. The headlights of the parked vehicle were all she could see now and they were helpfully aimed toward the long flight of steps that led to the front door of the church.

Everything else was totally engulfed in darkness and snow. When she reached the SUV, she leaned against it for a moment to catch her breath. Then she checked the license plate.

She felt a lot more than a tingle now. This confirmed it was Gabe Wilder's car. The plate numbers were as familiar to her as the details of the file she'd been compiling on him for nearly three months. She'd been right. From the first moment her dad had assigned her to gather research on the case, she'd been sure that Gabe had to be involved.

It wasn't just the fact that the thief was using his father's M.O., nor that Gabe's firm had handled the security for each victim. There was something about Gabe Wilder that just…fit. She knew what it was like to want desperately to follow in your father's footsteps—and to have to sometimes disguise that desire. But a person couldn't do that forever.

Just then the headlights went off. Was it one of those models where that happened automatically? Just to make sure…she felt her way along the side of the vehicle and pulled open the driver's door.

Empty.

He had to be in the church. Circling around the SUV, she pulled out her flashlight and headed toward the stairs. Finally, she was going to have a face-to-face meeting with Gabe Wilder, and she had no idea what he looked like. At least not anymore. The last time she'd seen him he'd been thirteen and she'd been ten.

As she gripped the iron railing and started up the long flight of stone steps, she let her mind return to those six months of her life when her stepmother had taken her every Saturday to the St. Francis Center. Charitable works were high on Marcia Thorne Guthrie's list.

The St. Francis Center had been located in a brick storefront building in downtown Denver. The first time she'd seen Gabe, she'd been standing in the small prayer garden that sat like a tiny oasis between the main building and a fenced in basketball court. He'd been tall with longish dark hair and scruffy jeans, and he'd had bad boy written all over him. At first he'd totally ignored her as he'd dribbled, jumped and sent the ball flying through the hoop again and again and again.

It had been Father Mike's idea for her to weed the garden while Marcia shelved donated books in the library. But she'd never gotten to the weeds. She hadn't been able to take her eyes off of Gabe Wilder.

Of course, she'd read all about his father, the notorious art thief, and how he'd died in prison. And she'd overheard her father speak about Gabe—about how hurt and angry he was. She'd known that he was at the center so that Father Mike could save him.

That's what Father Mike did—he saved bad boys. Most of the ones who came to the center shared Gabe's reputation. They came from all walks of life—some from the streets, some from the wealthiest Denver families—but as Marcia had put it: "Until they came to Father Mike, they were trouble with a capital *T*."

And that was exactly what Gabe Wilder had appeared to be. Trouble. She could see the anger and recklessness in the way he handled the ball. But she could also see a passion for the game. And it fascinated her. He fascinated her.

Suddenly he'd turned to face her. "What are you staring at?"

Nicola recalled that she'd swallowed hard and finally managed to blurt out, "You."

Bouncing the ball, he'd moved a few steps closer. "Why?"

A part of her knew that she shouldn't even be talking to him. She should be weeding. But she hated gardening and basketball looked like it would be so much more fun.

She drew in a deep breath and let it out. "Because you're great at basketball."

He turned and sent the ball whooshing through the hoop. Then he turned back to her. "You know how to play?"

"No." Basketball was not on Marcia's list of approved activities. Painting lessons, piano, ballet—those were.

To her utter amazement and delight, he'd sent the ball twirling on the tip of his finger. "I could teach you."

"No, I—I couldn't…" She knew very well that her stepmother hadn't brought her here to play basketball with one of the center's boys. But something in his eyes was tempting her, daring her.

"Why not?" he asked.

Why not indeed? It wasn't as though her stepmother was here watching her. And she did want to play. So much.

He bounced the ball again. "Look," he'd said, impatience clear in his tone. "I got friends coming in an hour. Want to shoot a few or not?"

Nicola could still recall the tingling sensation that had streamed through her whole body as she'd raced through the garden gate and onto the court.

"Ready?" Gabe had asked.

And when she'd nodded, he'd tossed her the ball.

After that, she'd played basketball with him every Saturday morning for an hour before his friends Nash and Jonah had shown up. That was always when Father Mike had come out to call her back into the center.

When Marcia had discovered what had been going on, she hadn't been pleased. Basketball was a boys' game. But Nicola hadn't ever regretted those Saturdays. Gabe had teased her, tormented her and endlessly critiqued her game. But she'd learned. Playing basketball had been her first rebellion against the kind of woman Marcia wanted to mold her into. In an odd way, she owed Gabe Wilder, she supposed. If it hadn't been for him, she might never have found the courage to take a stand in high school and try out for the basketball team.

Who knew? If it hadn't been for Gabe, she might not have rebelled against Marcia's and her father's wishes even further and become an FBI agent.

Having finally reached the top of the church steps, Nicola stepped into a portico that partially shielded her from the force of the wind. She hadn't seen Gabe Wilder for more than fifteen years—in spite of the fact that her last act on leaving the St. Francis Center for Boys had been to say a quick prayer to St. Francis that she would.

Some prayers went unanswered, and some bad boys couldn't be saved.

She'd just reached the door of the church when she heard it. A crash? It was muffled by the wind, but Nicola was certain she'd heard something. Glass shattering? She recalled the picture in the *Denver Post* of the statue of St. Francis standing in its supposedly shatter-proof glass dome.

As she pulled out her gun, she ran her flashlight over the door and saw that it stood ajar. After slipping through the narrow opening, she paused again. There was illumination that wasn't coming from her flashlight. Candles. She spotted the blur of light at the front of the church to her left.

She'd barely taken two steps up the center aisle when she heard another noise. This time there was no doubt about it—glass shattering.

After pocketing her flashlight, Nicola raised her gun and raced forward. As she neared the front of the church, she thought she spotted movement near those candles on the side altar. Then she saw it—a shadowy silhouette standing in front of the altar, its hands outstretched.

"Stop." She gripped her gun with both hands as she cut around the front row of pews. "FBI. Raise your hands."

A body rammed into her and she fell, landing backside first on the floor, then sliding into the first row of pews. Her head cracked against the wood and for a second, all she saw was stars.

"Stop." She scrambled to her feet and raced down the aisle after the fleeing shadow. Without breaking stride, she raised her gun again and steadied it with her other hand. "Stop or I'll shoot."

He kept on running.

She fired her weapon just as the darkness swallowed the shadow. Sprinting after him, she reached the front door of the church just in time to hear the motor of the SUV rev up. Then it lurched forward.

She ran out onto the front steps. As the wind whipped her breath away, she gripped her gun in both hands and took aim, but the tail lights dimmed as the vehicle gained speed. Then even those vanished into the falling snow.

A mix of anger and disappointment welled inside of her as she lowered her weapon. More than anything, she wanted to fight her way back to her car. But there was no way she could give chase. Not in this kind of weather. Even in that SUV, Gabe Wilder would be a lucky man if he could drive down off the mountain without spinning into a ditch.

But at least this time, she had proof that he'd been at the scene of the crime. He was connected to the thefts all right. She had to fill her father in. Pulling out her cell phone, she glanced at the time. Nine-fifteen—barely ten minutes since she'd left her car.

And the signal was dead. She looked back at the open door of the church. Hopefully, there was a landline inside. Wilder might deny being here, but she'd have more than a gut feeling when she talked to her father this time, and he'd have to listen to her.

And Gabe Wilder would have some explaining to do. She'd identified herself as FBI and he hadn't stopped.

Suddenly, Nicola frowned. Of course, she could only accuse Gabe Wilder of leaving a crime scene *if* there'd been a crime.

Hunching her head against the wind, she fought her way back to the open church door. Once inside, she pulled it shut, locked it and reholstered her gun.

She located a light switch, but nothing came on when she flipped it. Not surprising. The storm must have knocked out the power lines. That had to be why it was so cold. The moment she turned her flashlight on, she could see her breath in the frigid air.

She hurried toward the side altar. The statue of St. Francis was still there, standing on the narrow altar completely enclosed in a glass case just as it had appeared in the photo. So that hadn't been what she'd heard breaking.

Then she felt it—a prickling at the back of her neck telling her that she was not alone in the church. Pulling out her gun, she turned, listening hard as she scanned the shadowy darkness behind her. But Gabe Wilder couldn't have come back. Not this fast. And she'd locked the door.

Keeping her gun at the ready, she ran the beam of her flashlight over the floor. No sign of broken glass. It wasn't until she climbed to the top step of the altar that she spotted the second statue, and her heart skipped a beat.

After setting her gun and her flashlight down, she lifted it and set it on the altar. Then she picked up her weapon and ran the beam of light over both statues. They seemed to match perfectly. Both carved in beautiful Italian marble. The would-be thief had brought along an excellent forgery, but instinct had her gaze returning to the one under the glass dome. She was betting that one was the real deal. Though she hadn't seen it in over fifteen years, there was the same look on its face, the one that lured you into trusting...

Nicola gathered her thoughts. She still hadn't found any broken glass—or any explanation for the sounds she'd heard when she'd first entered the church. Turning away from the statue, she raised her gun, and moved away from the altar. No sign of glass anywhere. A brief fan of her flashlight showed a door along the side wall.

She moved toward it. The cold blast of air hit her just as she spotted the boots. Work boots, well worn on the soles and scuffed on the toes. As she stepped into the room, her flashlight caught the rest of him, and her stomach knotted. The man was sprawled full-length on the hard marble floor.

And he wasn't moving.

3

AS SHE DROPPED to her knees next to the man, Nicola absorbed other details. His legs were long and clad in black jeans. She noted the narrow waist, broad chest and shoulders. He wore a black T-shirt and an open Paul Bunyan-style plaid flannel shirt. It was rolled halfway up muscular forearms.

His face was cast in shadow. But the beam of her flashlight caught pale skin, dark hair, a strong nose and chin, a slash of cheekbones.

Recognition flickered at the edge of her mind, then faded when she saw the nasty-looking gash on the side of his forehead. Blood had already pooled on the marble floor beneath his head.

Nicola's stomach knotted again. His skin was too pale, his body too still. Setting down her gun, she balanced her flashlight to point upward. Then she slipped her hand beneath the collar of the plaid shirt and felt for a pulse.

She found one.

As it pushed strong and steady against her fingers, she let out a breath she hadn't even known she was holding. Whoever he was, he was still alive. And someone had worked hard to bring him down. The man was big. But his skin was cold and clammy.

And wet. So was his shirt. So were her slacks, for that matter. Then she noted for the first time the shards of broken glass and the flowers—a spray of red roses that lay strewn across the marble floor. The blood that had pooled around his head and shoulders was mixed with water from the broken vase.

Who was he? A janitor? The driver of that other car? Had he surprised Gabe Wilder when he was trying to steal the statue? But now wasn't the time to deal with any of those questions. When she glanced at him again, she once more felt a flicker of recognition, but she couldn't quite remember.

His cut needed attention. And if she didn't want him to go into shock, she was going to have to find a way to keep him warm.

Nicola took off her coat and tucked it as best she could around the unconscious man. It barely reached his knees. She slipped out of her suit jacket and pulled her silk T-shirt over her head. Folding it carefully into a square, she pressed it to the cut on the side of his forehead.

Finally, she placed her free hand on the side of his face and leaned closer. "Hey, can you hear me?"

No response.

She patted her palm firmly against his cheek. "You're going to be all right."

At least she was praying he would be.

Reaching for his hand, she drew it onto his chest and covered it with her own. Not an easy job. His palm was much larger than hers, his fingers long. They might have belonged to an artist, a pianist perhaps, except the backs of those long fingers were callused.

And they were cold. So was she. The draft of air she'd

felt when she'd first entered the room was growing more frigid by the second. Glancing around, she spotted the open window and scrambled up to close it. Then she returned to her knees beside the injured man and took his hand again. Squeezing his fingers, she raised her voice. "Can you hear me?"

His eyelids fluttered. She noticed for the first time how dark his lashes were, how long.

"Come on. Open your eyes."

He did. For an instant, as his gaze locked on hers, the punch of awareness and the flare of heat in her belly stole her breath away.

She'd seen this man before. He'd been in her father's office on the day after Thanksgiving. And he'd had the same effect on her then. Even through a glass wall, even at a distance of twenty-five feet, she'd felt the impact of his gaze like a punch. He'd made her lose track of everything.

"Cur...?"

The sound was little more than a gasp. *Cur?* It made no sense to Nicola. But it allowed her to shove the memory away and focus her attention on the injured man. She drew in a breath and felt her lungs burn.

"Head...hurts..." His fingers linked with hers and tightened.

This time when she met his eyes, she checked to see whether or not they were dilated. They weren't. Even in the dim light from her flashlight, she could distinguish clearly between the pinpoint of black at the center and the cloudy gray of his irises.

Then his lids drifted shut.

"Does it hurt anywhere else?" she asked. She had to find that out. And it was much safer to concentrate on that task than on what she'd just felt. Or what she'd felt that day in the FBI office.

But in the three months since it had happened, she hadn't been able to rid her mind of the memory. From the moment she'd walked into the office she'd been aware of him, but it hadn't been until his eyes had met hers that he'd registered fully on her senses.

And he'd registered *fully* all right. She was sure the impact might have been caught on a Richter scale—if there'd been one handy. Part of what she was feeling, she'd recognized—that tingling sensation that always told her something was just...somehow right.

But it had made no sense and it had never before made her feel as if the ground were dissolving beneath her feet. Not that she'd been able to feel her feet. All she could feel was him. And she'd wanted to feel more of him. Heat, glorious waves of it, had washed through her system. Every cell in her body had melted and yearned.

And when he'd risen to his feet in one fluid movement and taken a step toward her, she'd nearly run to him. Right through glass walls like some kind of superhero. The impulse had been so baffling, so totally insane, so verging on the irresistible that she'd finally found the strength to drag her gaze away from him.

And she couldn't, she wouldn't let him affect her that way again. Closing her eyes, she pulled in air, felt the burn in her lungs and then exhaled, and breathed in again.

Mental list time. When she opened her eyes, she checked the cut first and saw that the bleeding was slowing. After replacing the square of cloth, she slipped her fingers behind his head to check the back. The instant she touched the bump, he winced and made a sound.

So he'd suffered a double whammy to his head. No wonder he was woozy. Shifting her coat aside, she ran her hands on a quick journey from the back of his neck, down his arms. When he neither winced nor yelped again, she drew her palms from his shoulders to his waist, then from his hips down those long, long legs. The man was one solid wall of muscle.

And she still wanted him. There was no mistaking the heat that had flared to life deep inside of her as she'd run her hands over him. No controlling it, either. She knew what she was feeling. She wasn't stupid, so she'd pegged it the first time she'd seen him. Lust. Pure and simple. And incredibly intense.

Whoever believed that lightning couldn't strike twice was dead wrong. But wherever the lust had come from, it could just go back there. She had a job to do—a possible thief fleeing down a mountain, an injured man who was sliding into shock and two statues of St. Francis. Her plate was currently full.

She glanced down to where her hands still rested on his ankles. First step—she had to stop touching him. Releasing her grip, she was about to get to her feet when a sudden thought occurred to her. When she'd patted him down, she hadn't felt a wallet. But she checked his pockets just to make sure. She located a cell phone, but nothing else.

Had Gabe Wilder taken this man's wallet? Why?

She glanced back at his face. His eyes were closed now, and he looked even paler. She had questions, but he was in no condition to answer.

Fishing in her coat pocket, she located her cell and tried again.

Nothing.

Then she stared at the time. Nearly nine-thirty. Rising, she glanced around the small room and spotted the landline on a counter. There was no dial tone when she lifted the receiver. Even if she'd been able to call 911, it would take help some time to arrive. So she was on her own.

Grabbing some candles she found next to the phone,

she lit them. Then she located a pile of linen towels and mopped up the water around his head and shoulders. Finally, she dropped to her knees and took his hand again. It was so cold. "It's all right," she murmured. "You're going to be all right." As if to reassure herself of that, she lifted her square of T-shirt again and checked the cut. It was clean and not very deep. "You probably won't need stitches, and the bleeding has nearly stopped."

And she doubted he heard a word she was saying. But when she tried to pull her hand away, his grip tightened again—as if she were his lifeline.

"Statue..." he murmured.

"It's still here," she said.

"Both...?"

"They're both here." Curious about how much he'd seen, she leaned closer. "What happened?"

He didn't answer her this time, and a second later his hand went limp in hers. She felt the instant surge of panic and shoved it down. The steady rise and fall of his chest beneath their joined hands assured her that he was still with her.

For the moment.

"It's going to be all right. It's going to be all right."

And it was. It had to be. Step number one was to get him warm.

Shivering, she slipped back into the jacket she'd discarded earlier and buttoned it up; then she tucked her coat around him again. There had to be something in the closet that she could use to keep him warm.

Behind the first door she opened, she found choir robes hanging on hooks. Though they were a different color, they reminded her of the robe that St. Francis wore in the sculpture. She thought of the statue's special prayer-answering powers. In spite of the fact that she'd tried praying to him once before without much success, she decided to give him a second chance.

"Help me keep him safe and well until I can get him medical attention," she murmured. Then she started pulling robes off their hangers.

GABE STRUGGLED TO FIND his way to the surface again. He'd done it once, hadn't he? Or had he just dreamed that he'd seen Curls leaning over him?

Focus.

His thoughts were spinning like little whirlpools—just out of reach. There was something important, something he needed to take care of. The statue…the effort it took to remember had pain stabbing his head again.

Okay. For a moment, he gave up, letting himself drift. And he saw her again.

Curls.

The moment her image took shape in his mind, his headache eased, and the memory slid into place. He let himself drift with it. He'd been at the St. Francis Center shooting baskets, and he'd sensed someone watching him. Not his friends, Nash and Jonah, who never made it to the center until noon. And sure enough, there she'd stood in the small garden beside the basketball court, her hands wrapped around the narrow poles in the wrought-iron fence. She'd looked like a prisoner. Perhaps that's what had appealed to him, what had triggered a sense in him that they were kindred spirits.

Because at that time, he'd felt like a prisoner, too, trapped in promises that he wasn't sure he wanted to keep. He'd stood beside his mother's bed holding his father's hand as they'd both sworn their vows. He'd promised to never follow in his father's footsteps, and his father had promised to give up his lifelong profession.

But the promise hadn't done his father much good. Raphael Wilder had been falsely accused and convicted, and he'd died shortly after in prison.

So why should he bother to keep his promise? That was the question he'd been asking himself as he'd lunged, dribbled and shot basket after basket. And all the time she'd watched him. When he'd finally wheeled to confront her, it had been her eyes that had captured him.

He'd seen admiration and hero worship in them. Those had been balm to the raw, angry feelings of a thirteen-year-old who'd been newly orphaned.

So he'd taught her what he'd known about the game, and no teacher could have dreamed of a more responsive student.

The memory blurred for a moment. That wasn't what he should be thinking about. There was something else. Something important. Urgent. When he reached for it, pain pierced like a fiery arrow.

Curls.

This time when the image surfaced, it wasn't the child who had enchanted him, saved him when he was thirteen, but the woman who had gripped his hand and said that everything would be all right.

And it would be. He let out the breath he'd been holding and slipped under again.

TO PREVENT HER TEETH from chattering, Nicola clamped them together as she dragged the last choir robes out of the closet and added them to the pile at the injured man's feet. Thank heavens there'd been a generous supply. And they were heavy.

In spite of her efforts to keep her mind on the task at hand, she couldn't prevent herself from thinking about her reaction to the man. At twenty-six, she was no stranger to desire or lust. She'd had her moments and thoroughly enjoyed them. But those feelings had never flared quite so quickly or intensely before.

And she didn't seem to have any control over them. Each time she'd added to the pile of robes, she hadn't been able to prevent herself from looking at him. And each time she did, she felt that catch of her breath, that flare of heat.

There was no logic to it. There hadn't been from the beginning.

He was a stranger. But her heart was pounding. And in spite of her determination, her mind kept spinning back to those moments in her office and just minutes ago when he'd looked into her eyes and her thoughts had clicked off just as completely as if someone had thrown a switch.

Dropping the last robe on the pile, she drew in a deep breath. *Mental list time again.* She knelt down to check her patient. His pulse was steady, the bleeding on his forehead had stopped, but she knew he had to be very cold. She certainly was. Even with the window shut, the room felt like a deep freeze. Her feet had gone numb and she'd begun to shiver.

She had to get him out of the clothes that had been drenched by the vase of water. The Paul Bunyan shirt was easy enough. Placing his arms over his head, she tugged on the sleeves. Once they were off, she finessed the rest of the shirt from under him.

His T-shirt presented more of a problem, but it had to go. In the flickering light, she could see the wet stain covered his shoulders and ran in streaks nearly to his waist. She began by tugging the material free from the waistband of his jeans. But the moment the backs of her fingers brushed against his bare skin, she knew she was in trouble, and it deepened steadily as she eased the shirt up, uncovering the narrow waist, the broad chest.

Keep your eyes on the shirt. On his face. But not on his mouth. That was a definite danger zone.

By the time she'd pushed the T-shirt up to his armpits, Nicola was aware of two things. She had some control over her eyes, but none over what she was feeling as her fingers brushed against that smooth skin stretched taut over rock-hard muscles. The little flame of lust this man had ignited in her was being fanned brighter and stronger with each contact.

She kept her eyes steady on his face, on the dark slash of brows, the shadow of a beard on that strong angled chin as she moved behind him. But her mind wandered, wondered. So far the touching had been purely clinical. Almost. And one-sided. Definitely. Still, her throat had gone dry and her pulse was racing. What would happen if she ran her hands over him with the intent of arousing him, pleasuring him? And what if he touched her back?

Whoa.

Just thinking about it stopped her teeth from chattering and made her heart pound so loudly that she was amazed the noise didn't wake him up. She carefully maneuvered the T-shirt off one arm, then the other before she eased it carefully around the wound on his forehead.

Then her gaze slid to where it had wanted to be from the beginning. She sat back on her heels and simply stared, letting her eyes feast on what her hands had already gotten more than a hint of. The muscles in his shoulders and upper arms were well-defined; his chest was broad with a triangle of thick black hair that tapered down over equally defined abs. The man was built like a Greek god. She could imagine him in bronze or sculpted in marble.

She shivered then and shook her head. She had to get a grip. He wasn't a god. He was a man who might be in shock, who was in danger of slipping into hypothermia.

Moving quickly, she grabbed one of the robes, opened it up and tucked it along the length of him from shoulders to boots on one side. Then she did the same on the other side. A part of him would still be lying on the cold marble, but there was no way she was going to be able to roll him over.

The man was so tall she had to use two of the shorter robes to fully cover him. After she'd arranged them, she leaned down and patted his cheek again.

"It's going to be all right," she said.

His lashes fluttered. "C…c…old."

"I know. You'll be warm soon. I promise."

How soon? That was the crucial question. There were only two robes left. She'd had some idea of using them for herself.

She glanced at her coat. It was damp on the outside. And she was going to have to get out of her wet slacks and boots.

And then what?

Nicola very carefully avoided looking at the man. Because the answer was obvious. And it had been there lurking in the back of her mind ever since she'd started undressing him.

She was an FBI agent. She'd been trained in survival tactics, and the quickest, most efficient way to keep both of them warm—for the time being—was to share everything. Including body heat.

And the only reason she was stalling was because of the effect this man—this complete stranger—had on her senses. Annoyed—no, angry at herself, Nicola arranged the last two robes. They were both adults. And she was the only fully conscious one. What was her problem?

She tugged off her boots. If he tried anything, she could

handle herself. Shrugging out of her holster, she placed it next to her gun and the flashlight.

But what if you try something?

"Not happening," Nicola muttered as she wiggled out of her wet trousers. A little fantasizing, a little lust. She could handle it.

But she didn't look at him as she joined him beneath the pile of robes.

Every muscle in her body tensed when his arm snaked around her and pulled her close. Suddenly she was wrapped around him as intimately as a lover—her thigh across his, her head nestled into the crook of his shoulder. She might have objected if she hadn't felt a blast of warmth at each and every contact point.

Or if he'd moved another muscle.

But he didn't.

She waited, counting the seconds...five...ten...fifteen...twenty.

But the only thing that moved was the rise and fall of his chest beneath her palm. Still, she kept her eyes open, her mind alert as the seconds stretched into minutes.

But he lay there, still as a stone. And all the while the warmth spread, slowly, deliciously until she was certain she could feel it penetrate her muscles and even her bones. The instant she could feel her toes again and wiggle them, she considered moving. It would be the prudent thing to do.

And she'd always figured herself for a practical kind of woman.

He was warm now. She could feel the heat of his skin beneath her palm and along her stomach where her jacket had pulled open. It was probably safe to move away. It was probably safer to move away.

The yawn took her by surprise. Even more surprising

was the realization that at some point she'd relaxed fully against him. And she didn't want to move.

Not the most practical decision. She'd reconsider it in a minute. Just one more minute…

4

GABE SURFACED QUICKLY this time and began to orient himself. There was still pain thrumming at the back of his head and near his temple.

The fight.

The details were there, but he pushed them away for now, along with the pain. Both were secondary.

Primary was the flood of sensations storming through his system because of the woman. He was surrounded by them, trapped by them. The pressure of each one of the fingers splayed across his chest might have been a brand. The leg she'd thrown across him imprisoned his thighs and ignited an almost uncontrollable fire in his loins. His whole body was aroused, throbbing.

Who?

Opening his eyes, he shifted slowly until their positions were reversed. Her head lay in the crook of his arm, and it was his leg that held her prisoner now. Even as her eyelashes fluttered and then stilled, recognition streamed through him.

Nicola Guthrie.

What the hell was she doing here? He gave his head a shake, hoping to clear the fog. Pain stabbed. He shut his eyes against it and gritted his teeth as he willed details into place.

He remembered Father Mike's phone call about the note, the long drive through the storm. He'd arrived at the church, hoping to surprise the thief. Instead, he'd been the one surprised. He recalled the open window that had lured him into the choir room and the blow to his head. But it hadn't taken him out. He'd managed that on his own. The last thing he could dredge up was his feet flying out from beneath him. That's when the fireworks had exploded in his brain.

Moving more carefully this time, he glanced around the room. A flashlight and candles provided the only illumination. That and the howling of the wind outside told him that the storm hadn't let up. He should get up and check on the statue. But he was confident that his new alarm system had held, and his prayers to St. Francis had worked.

This time.

He glanced back down at Nicola. None of what he remembered explained why FBI special agent Nicola Guthrie was here, lying beneath him on the floor of the choir room.

Except...

He frowned as the image slipped into focus—her face filling his vision, her voice telling him everything would be all right. Assuring him that both statues were still here. He thought he'd been dreaming. Just as he'd dreamed of her too often in the past three months.

Because he'd known from the first instant he'd seen her in the FBI office that Nicola Guthrie spelled trouble for him with capital letters. When she'd met his eyes in that brief instant of contact, he'd felt everything else slip away until there'd only been her. The wanting had started that instant, and he hadn't been able to shake free of it.

So he'd avoided her like the plague for nearly three months. Although he'd consulted on the case, he'd never once set foot in the FBI office. Nick Guthrie was a good friend, one he owed. One he intended to keep. And the flare of hot, primitive desire he'd felt in that one meeting of glances with Nicola was the last thing he wanted to feel for a friend's daughter. Getting involved with her meant complications, and where women were concerned, he liked to keep his relationships simple. He'd even managed to avoid her during the past few weeks when she'd started tailing him during the evening hours. He had a pretty good idea why. Nick Guthrie might be convinced that he'd had nothing to do with the robberies. But it was a more than good bet that someone at G. W. Securities was up to his or her neck in them. So Guthrie had assigned Nicola to follow him—just to cover all his bases.

Gabe was fine with that. What he wasn't fine with was that having her on his tail had only increased the number of times she'd slipped into his thoughts each day—especially when he'd been working here at the church on the security for the statue.

He couldn't keep her out of his mind. That scared him. It ticked him off. It also fascinated him. No one, nothing had ever pulled at him the way she did.

And she was doing it again now. Without even trying. She was asleep, totally unaware of him. Like Sleeping Beauty, blissfully ignorant of the effect she was having on him. He should get up, move. But he couldn't seem to make his body obey.

Baffled, he studied her in the dim light, taking in the creamy porcelain skin, the sprinkling of freckles. Before he could prevent himself he brushed a strand of hair off of her cheek and behind her ear. At that simple contact of skin against skin, desire shot through him, a rusty claw in his gut.

He'd spent nearly three months being prudent and safe. Perhaps it was time to try a different tack.

One taste. That's what he told himself as he leaned closer and began to tease her lips apart with his. One taste. He rubbed his mouth softly over hers, then unable to stop himself, he sank in.

Her lips were soft. He'd imagined they would be. And warm. He'd expected that also. But when he finally slipped his tongue between them, he found a surprising mix of flavors. Cool and hot, sweet and pungent. Each flavor drew him, tempted him to taste and taste again.

She began to tremble. That, more than her flavors, undermined his resolve and he plunged in to take the kiss deeper.

IT WAS LIKE WAKING UP in the heart of a firestorm. One minute she'd been fast asleep, and the next, every nerve in her body was alive, burning, yearning. Before she could think, she wrapped her arms and legs around him and held on.

His mouth was so hot and nearly savage. The press of his body against hers vibrated through her right down to her bones. And the feelings he aroused in her were so vivid. So new. Desire had never been this sharp. Hunger had never gone this deep. Need had never been this demanding.

In some far corner of her brain where rationality hadn't been burned to cinders, she heard a voice telling her she had to think. The practical Nicola. But how could she pay any heed when her pulse was pounding in her head and his taste, ripe and rich, was pouring through her like a drug?

She wanted more. She had to have more. When he slipped a hand beneath her jacket and slid it up her bare skin to cover her breast, she arched, determined to get even closer to that hard, rangy body. Oh, yes, she had to have more. A sound, something primitive, clawed its way out of her throat.

As if in answer, he used his teeth, scraping them along her bottom lip before he moved his mouth to her neck. With sensations hammering through her system, she heard the practical voice again. This couldn't be right, shouldn't be right. But every nerve in her body tingled with the conviction blossoming inside of her that it was. Exactly right.

Stop. The word had become a chant in his head, but Gabe's body ignored the order. She was all wild flavors and silken textures, and she was driving him crazy. Wherever he touched or tasted, she responded with a huge unreserved pleasure that fascinated him. Captured him.

He'd thought about what it would be like ever since that first meeting of eyes. But any fantasies he'd entertained fell far short of reality. He hadn't wanted her to stir up this kind of primitive need. But hadn't he known she would? He slid his hands down to her hips, and when she arched up and tightened her legs around him, the only thing that kept him from taking what he was craving was that he was still wearing his jeans. His fingers were struggling with the snap when he recalled how he'd started this, kissing her when she was still asleep. He'd taken her this far without an invitation. Stealing a kiss without asking was one thing, but he wanted more...

He drew his head up then and brought her face into focus. She was awake now. He could see himself in those chocolate-colored eyes. She held him just as surely there as she did with her arms and legs. A warning bell sounded, but it was distant.

"You stopped," she said.

Her voice might have been a throaty murmur, but there was a note of accusation in the tone.

"Paused," he corrected. "And I won't stop if I kiss you again," he stated. "I wanted to make sure you were on board with that."

For a moment she said nothing. But she didn't move.

Neither did he.

In his mind, he might intend to play the gentleman, but his body hadn't gotten the memo. He was very much aware that they were pressed closely together, center to center, heat to heat, with nothing more than denim and her panties separating them. His body throbbed at every point a pulse could beat.

He rocked into her, saw the heat flare in her eyes, felt the shudder move through her body. One thread of whatever control he had left snapped.

"It would be a mistake." Her voice was barely a whisper.

"We're on the same page there." It would be a huge mistake. Hadn't he given himself that lecture countless times? But he'd also known that this moment was coming, that as hard as he might try, he wouldn't be able to prevent it from happening.

He ran his mouth along her jaw, then nipped at her chin. "What do you say?"

Say? She wasn't at all sure that she could form a word. But even as she desperately reached for one, she wrapped her arms and legs more tightly around him. The heat, the glorious blast of it was so intense, she felt as if she'd been caught in a sudden back draft of flames. There was pleasure pulsing through her in an endless stream until it was all she could feel. He was all she could feel.

And he felt so right. She was very aware of the hardness of the floor beneath her. His body was even harder and so hot that she wanted nothing more than to melt into him. She caught herself before she arched against him again. If she did, she might climax. She could feel it almost within reach.

"I should think…"

Had she said the words aloud? She must have because he drew back enough to meet her eyes, and there was a question in his. There was also a glint of something dark and reckless that ignited that familiar tingle deep within her. Her practical side might want to worry about mistakes and consequences, but something much closer to the bone ruled. Some mistakes were worth making.

"I want you so much," she said.

He kissed her then, and she felt that wonderful heat began to build inside of her again. She knew what happened when you played with fire. But she wanted the flash point. And she wanted it now. She tightened her legs around him and arched again.

He immediately gripped her hips and stilled her movements. Then he lifted his head.

She tried to move and couldn't. "You said the next time you kissed me you wouldn't stop."

"Protection." His voice was hoarse. "I don't—"

"We're good." She dragged his mouth back to hers and nipped his bottom lip.

"We're about to get even better," he promised. "But first, we have to get rid of the clothes."

"Oh…right." But she kept her mouth on his the whole time his hands slid between them to push down his jeans. Her clothes weren't an issue. He pushed the thin lace of her panties aside and slid a finger into her. "Now, come for me."

He gave her no choice. The climax that had been threatening erupted through her in wave after wave, each one sharper than the last. Helpless, she gave herself over to it and to the man who was giving it to her.

Her body was still quaking from the last ripple when he drew his finger out and pressed the head of his penis against the slick heat of her core. He wanted to go slowly, but her response, her surrender, were so much more than he'd imagined. How much further could she take him? Raising his head, he said, "Look at me."

She opened her eyes, and he watched them go wide and blurry as he thrust into her in one stroke. She was hotter and tighter than he'd expected. The feel of her muscles trembling and tugging urged him to go deeper. Hooking his arms around her legs, he lifted them so that he could push even more fully into her.

Her eyes went dark, then blind with pleasure. And for a moment he was sure his own did the same. He couldn't think of anything but the mating of their bodies. He couldn't even move. All he could do was sink farther and farther into her. The thought of withdrawing even a little, even to push into her again—he couldn't do it. This was where he wanted to stay. Where he belonged.

But as she continued to contract around him, the pulse of his own release tore through him. He tried to hold back, to hold her, to hold them both where they were right now. But as another climax radiated through her in little convulsions, his own pleasure overcame him, consuming him and finally overpowering him completely.

5

REALITY TRICKLED IN slowly. Nicola heard the sound of breathing, slightly ragged, but she couldn't tell if it was him or her. She could smell the faint tang of incense, and him—soap and water and something that was very male. She was still wrapped around him.

And he was still inside of her.

Without any hesitation, she grasped him, let go, then grasped him again.

"Ready?" He whispered the question in her ear even as she felt him grow harder inside of her.

"Mmm."

He gripped her hips and eased her into a rhythm.

Pleasure shot through her, but she managed to raise her head, just enough to meet his eyes. "I'm not…not usually. I don't understand…. It's you."

"Or you," he countered as his fingers dug into her hips and he abruptly increased the speed of his thrusts.

Then it didn't matter, not with his heart pounding against hers, beat to beat. Not with pleasure pummeling through her again and again with each thrust. She couldn't think, didn't want to. Not while she could take this wild ride to that place where there were only the two of them and only the intense pleasure that they could bring each other.

He cried out first as he drove into her one last time and the world around them shattered.

GABE WOKE TO FIND Nicola still sprawled on top of him. The steady sound of her breath going in and out signaled that she was asleep. And he could no longer hear the sound of the wind outside. In its place, he caught the closer clank of a radiator heating up, so the power and the furnace were back on.

Opening his eyes, he lay perfectly still, taking a moment to orient himself. The light overhead was also on. He lifted his arm to glance at his watch. After midnight. So roughly three hours had passed since he'd arrived at the church. When he turned his head, pain poked at his forehead, but it was manageable. The back of his head throbbed a bit, but his memory of what had happened was crystal clear. He hadn't caught the thief.

Instead, he'd caught Nicola Guthrie. Ready or not. He shifted his gaze to the top of her head. Her scent reminded him of spring flowers. And she felt right lying on top of him. The fact that he didn't want to move might have worried him, but his more immediate concern was that he was still inside of her. So there was a definite part of him that did want to move.

Just thinking about what it would feel like had him growing harder. It wasn't that he didn't want to make love to her again. He did. But he wanted to do it under different circumstances. A bed might be nice. Something with a little more room, a little more give than a cold, hard marble floor.

And wasn't this just the trouble he'd intended to avoid? Having her just this once wasn't going to do it for him.

He'd suspected that from the first time he'd looked at her through that glass wall.

Now there would be complications. Big ones. And he already had a lot on his plate.

Gripping her hips, he lifted her, then hoping not to wake her, he shifted slowly so that they were lying side by side. Her head was still tucked into his shoulder.

Progress. But not enough, especially when he wanted nothing more than to stay right where he was. This time it wasn't desire pulling at him, but a warmth that was even more seductive. Though he couldn't explain it, holding her close felt right. Against all logic and in spite of everything he'd done to try and prevent this from happening, it had.

Nicola had nearly protested when he'd shifted her. Instead, she continued to play possum for a few more minutes. It wasn't that she wanted him to make love to her again. Although if he made a move, she was pretty sure she would respond. She didn't seem to have any way to stop herself.

And this just wasn't like her. She'd never been so impulsive, so reckless with a man before. She had to break contact with him completely and get back to being FBI special agent Nicola Guthrie. She just needed another second to think of what she was supposed to do next.

What should she say? How could she explain what had happened, what she'd done, when she didn't understand it herself?

She'd been on duty. She'd been pursuing a thief who'd gotten away, and the man she'd just made love to…twice… might know something important that would solve the case.

Then there was her father. She had to find a way to contact him and let him know that Gabe Wilder had nearly stolen the statue of St. Francis. In short, she had a job to do, and snuggling under the covers with a perfect stranger, no matter how tempting it might be, could not be on the top of her to-do list. But how to get him off of it was the problem.

Back to business, Nicola. Move.

But it was the stranger who began to inch away.

Drawing in a deep breath, she opened her eyes and fastened them on his. She felt the impact of his gaze right down to her toes.

"You're awake," he said.

"I have been for a while," she confessed. "I was just trying to figure out what to say to you." She still didn't have a clue. And looking into his eyes wasn't helping. Dragging her gaze away, she fastened it on the cut on his forehead. "Your head. Are you all right?"

Guilt overcame her. She'd forgotten all about his injuries when she'd awakened the first time. The man had been unconscious and bleeding when she'd found him.

"I could use half a bottle of aspirin."

"I'm sorry. I'm so sorry."

His brows snapped together. "For what?"

"For...for...jumping you when you had clearly sustained head injuries. I checked your eyes to see if they were dilated—but I'm not a doctor."

"Are they dilated now?"

She studied them for a minute. "No." She raised her index finger in front of his face. "When I move it to the left and right, follow it with your eyes."

He did. "What's my prognosis?"

"Your eyes seem fine. But all of my medical knowledge comes from a mandatory first aid course I took. Or TV. You should definitely go to an emergency room." She started to move away, but he gripped her shoulders and held her in place. "For the record, the jumping was mutual. And I'm the one who took the initial step."

"You'd been unconscious. I should never have crawled under the covers with you… And you gave me a chance to stop things. I didn't."

And she wasn't moving away right now. In fact, if he gave her the least little bit of encouragement… No. She was going to move. Away. And she would have if he hadn't chosen that particular moment to smile. Her bones began to melt.

"Are you seriously trying to argue that you took advantage of me, Curls? I assure you that you didn't."

"Curls?" She blinked, then stared at him as fragmented images filled her mind the way they might have swirled into place in a kaleidoscope. She gave her head a shake. In denial? But the images didn't fade. She was back at the St. Francis Center playing basketball on the small streetside court. With Gabe Wilder.

He took a strand of her hair and tucked it behind her ear. "I miss your curls. Remember when I used to tug on them?"

The widening of his smile transformed the ripples of recognition that had been lapping at the edge of her mind into a full-blown wave. And she did remember. He'd often tugged her hair to push her into making a more aggressive play. She'd hated it. And he'd always called her Curls. She'd hated that, too.

"Gabe." She stared at him, hoping against hope that she was wrong. "You're Gabe Wilder."

"Guilty."

She closed her eyes. Perhaps when she opened them, she would find that it had all been a dream. But her practical side was reasserting itself with a vengeance, and she definitely hadn't dreamed what had happened. No way. Dreams never rocked your world. That was a job for reality.

So she'd deal. She would find a way to solve the problem. But when she opened her eyes, the only thing she wanted to deal with was right there in front of her. And she didn't want to move except to pull him closer and to feel his mouth on hers again.

"No. No. No."

That wasn't happening. And there was only one person she could blame for the fact that it ever had. Well, maybe two. When a tiny flicker of anger sprang to life, she finally found the strength to place her hands on his shoulders and push hard. Then she wiggled out from beneath the pile of robes.

The marble floor beneath her butt might just as well have been a block of ice. Her skimpy lace panties provided no protection. She felt around on the floor for her slacks.

"I can assure you that I am Gabe Wilder. I can even show you some I.D."

"No, you can't. I checked for your wallet before and it was gone." Then she made the big mistake of looking at him. He'd risen and was in the process of pulling his jeans into place. But before they got there, she got a good look at those long legs, the narrow hips and waist, and his... Her mouth went dry.

He checked his pockets, then frowned. "I'm missing my car keys, too."

"That's not all. The other guy took your car, too. Black SUV." She rattled off the license plate.

"He stole my car?"

"I saw him drive away in it. That's why I assumed *you* were not Gabe Wilder."

"Interesting."

"Interesting? It's more than that," she managed to say as

her brain cells began to click on again. "This whole thing is totally unfair. If I had known who you were, I never should have…we never should have…"

"Spilled milk, don't you think?"

"Think? That's just it. I wasn't thinking. If I'd known you were Gabe Wilder, I never would have…" She waved a hand. "Never. He…you were my prime suspect. I was sure that you were connected to the thefts. You had to be. I always get this feeling when I'm right about something."

"What things?"

"Applying to the FBI for a job, coming back here to Denver to work for my dad." Playing basketball with you when I was ten. But she didn't blurt that part out. "I'm not usually wrong."

When he walked over to her and squatted down so that he could meet her eyes, she stifled the urge to wiggle away. Instead, she lifted her chin and locked her eyes on his. She was going to figure out a way to handle him.

"You didn't recognize me."

"No." Since he was frowning, she frowned right back at him. "How was I supposed to? I haven't seen you since we were kids."

"Except for that one time when I visited your father. I saw you through the glass wall of your office. I wanted you that day. And you wanted me, too."

She swallowed hard, but she kept her eyes steady on his. "It's been fifteen years and you weren't wearing a name tag."

"Who did you think I was?"

Nicola felt the flame of anger inside of her grow. She hadn't been thinking then either. She'd just been feeling. "I assumed you were a client, someone who had business with the FBI."

He was interrogating her. And her butt was growing number by the second. Not to mention her toes.

"Not then. Who did you think I was when you crawled in with me?"

"Do you mind?" She would have gotten to her feet if she could have managed it without touching him. "I'm freezing here. I'd like to get dressed."

"Sorry." He picked up her slacks. "These are soaked from the knees down." After draping them on a nearby radiator, he took her hands and pulled her to her feet. Then turning, he picked up two robes and handed her one. "I'm sure Father Mike won't mind if we borrow these."

Nicola said nothing as she slipped into it. The material pooled around her feet. Gabe's robe, on the other hand, fell just below his knees.

"Your boots and socks are soaked, too," he said as he placed them on the radiator next to his shirt.

Then he turned to her. "Ready?"

"For what?"

Before she even had time to protest, he scooped her up in his arms and strode out toward the altar. "I want to check on the statues. Don't you?"

"Yes." Of course she did. That was what she should be thinking about, not... Then she was sitting in a front pew, her legs stretched out in front of her, and he was tucking the robe around her feet.

"Stay here. The thief didn't steal my cell. I'm going to see if it works."

"I couldn't get a signal earlier."

He tossed a grin over his shoulder as he climbed the steps to the side altar. "You've got to know where to stand to pick it up. When I was installing the alarm, I learned the only place to get a signal in the place is right here by

St. Francis. I'll update your father. He can put an APB out on my car."

Nicola frowned as she watched him push in numbers.

"Nick, it's Gabe."

There was a short pause, and then he began to fill her father in on what had happened. Clearly, Gabe wasn't having any trouble prioritizing what they should be focusing on. *He* was not only reporting to her father—something she should be doing, but he was trying to dry out their clothes and making arrangements for them to be picked up.

While her mind was still stuck on…him and what she was going to do. What she should do and what she wanted to do were miles apart.

Spilled milk. You cleaned it up and moved on. That was clearly his attitude. And perhaps she should take her cue from him. What was done couldn't be undone. Just forgetting about it and moving on was the practical solution. Except she wasn't going to be able to forget what had happened. What they'd done. She drew in a deep breath, gave her head a mental shake. She had to get her focus back on stopping the robberies, catching the thief.

"The road crews are out, but travel is not recommended." Gabe sat down in the pew and stretched one arm along the back. She felt the heat of it instantly.

"Your father is sending a helicopter for us. Its ETA is approximately forty-five minutes from now. So we have some time to kill."

Her eyes collided with his, and for a moment her brain cells shut down again. Worse, she didn't want to put any effort into resuscitating them. Everything inside of her yearned for him.

And he felt it, too. She could see that telltale gleam in his eyes and read the question as clearly as if he'd spoken it aloud.

Ready?

They weren't even touching, yet she was definitely ready. Ready to go anywhere he would take her. Ready to take that glorious leap into the world of sensation only he'd shown her.

But she shouldn't. They couldn't. As much as she wished she could.

Focus, Nicola told herself. Time to summon up a mental list that didn't start off with jumping back under the covers with Gabe Wilder.

It didn't help her concentration at all when he smiled at her and the effect sizzled right down to her toes.

She drew in a breath she wasn't even aware that she needed. "There's a thief out there that we have to catch." She said the words aloud for herself as much as Gabe. "I have a lot of questions. For starters, what are you doing here?"

"I'll be happy to answer that as soon as you answer two questions for me."

"Two?" She narrowed her eyes on his.

"I've already asked one of them. And then I'll answer two for you. Deal?"

Nicola studied him and thought of the Gabe she'd known when she was ten. He'd been a tease then, too, often tormenting her to get her to push just a little harder on the court. "What's your first question?"

"The curls." He lifted a strand of her hair and rubbed it between his fingers. "I really miss them."

"All you ever did was pull them."

"It made you angry and you played better ball."

Her brows shot up. "That's your excuse?"

He grinned. "And I'm sticking to it."

She saw the gleam in his eyes again, the one that had

fascinated her when she was ten. And the intervening years had only increased its effect.

He tugged on the strand of hair he'd been holding. "Where have they gone?"

"That's your first question?"

"Uh-huh."

The only thing that kept her from rolling her eyes was the fact that the quickest way she was going to get the answers to her questions was to humor him. "I use a flattening iron."

"Pity." Then the smile faded from his eyes. "Who did you think I was when you made love to me?"

That was the biggy, Nicola thought. And it was one she wanted answers to, also. But she was pretty sure she wasn't going to like them. "A stranger." Not good. "An injured man." Even worse. "I don't understand it. You were right. I wanted you that day when I saw you in the office. I haven't been able to stop wanting you. I didn't know you, and you were injured."

When he opened his mouth, she held up a hand to stop him. "And for the record, I don't make a habit of crawling under the covers with every hunky-looking stranger I meet. The problem was I wasn't thinking."

That was true enough. But it wasn't everything. And she needed to figure it out. If she could just get the right perspective, she could handle it. "You were lying on the floor and I had to bring you back to consciousness. The moment you opened your eyes, I recognized that you were the man in the office that day, and I wanted you. Just like that. I simply can't explain it."

"Yeah," Gabe said. "I think we're in the same boat, Curls."

For a moment neither of them spoke. She saw something flicker in his eyes and it triggered that tingling feeling inside of her. The one she'd felt when they'd been making love. That it was…just right.

She hurried on. "It never occurred to me that you were Gabe Wilder. Not then, and certainly not tonight. I'd just chased Gabe Wilder out of here. I'd even taken a shot at him, and he drove away in your SUV."

"Did you manage to hit the thief?" Gabe asked.

She shook her head. "I don't think so. I certainly didn't slow him down any."

"Wait here." She watched him rise and walk down the side aisle, his eyes on the floor. He was nearly at the end when he stopped and crouched down. "Blood. Your aim was on target, Curls."

Nicola felt her stomach knot, and she wasn't relieved at all by the grim expression on Gabe's face when he rejoined her in the pew. "Our thief got more than he bargained for this time."

When she said nothing, he reached out and covered her hand with his. "First time you've shot someone?"

"Yeah." As he linked his fingers with hers, she felt the knot in her stomach loosen.

"Why don't you take me through it? Everything that happened from the time you arrived."

She did. By the time she'd finished her narrative, Gabe knew three things. First, she had courage. But he'd already seen that when she was ten years old. Looking back, he could see that it had taken a good deal of it to accept his invitation to play basketball that day. Nearly as much as it had taken her to race up the aisle when she'd heard the sounds of a fight.

She was definitely a risk taker. And she had an excellent eye for detail. She'd spotted an abandoned car in the ditch that he'd missed and she'd seen the second statue. He didn't imagine there was much that escaped her notice.

Maybe she was just what he needed—fresh eyes on the robberies.

"That takes us right up until I crawled under the covers with you," Nicola wound up. "And none of what happened there pertains to the case."

"Indirectly, it does, Curls. I think by crawling in with me, you just may have saved my life."

She narrowed her eyes on him. "Don't get overly dramatic. In spite of your injuries, you don't seem much the worse for wear."

The dryness of her tone had him smiling. "Who knows how long it would have taken for someone to have found me? Hypothermia can be life-threatening. I owe you."

"For doing my job."

He raised her hand and skimmed his mouth over her fingers.

Just that brief contact had sensation flooding her system. "Don't," she managed to say. "We need to concentrate on the case. On catching the thief."

He had to agree with her on that one. But the pulse beating at her throat, the breathiness in her voice had him wanting badly to multitask. Reluctantly, he released her hand. "I still owe you."

Nicola glanced back up at the statues. "At least the thief didn't get St. Francis."

Gabe followed her gaze. "No chance of that this time. I designed a new alarm system, a prototype that isn't even in production yet. No one at G. W. has seen it. I called in a favor from a friend at the *Denver Post* and she wrote that feature article on the statue of St. Francis in last Sunday's paper. I was hoping it might lure the thief out here."

Nicola shifted her gaze to Gabe. "You set the statue up as bait? All of the other art pieces the thief has taken have been paintings. How did you know he'd come after it?"

"It was Father Mike's idea. He thought it might be helpful to involve the statue. Whoever is behind these robberies seems to have an affinity for G. W. Securities' systems. I was also depending on the statue's spreading reputation for granting answers to prayers. There are a lot of eccentric collectors out there who would pay a lot for that." He shrugged. "I also said a prayer that the trap would work."

"St. Francis evidently answered it this time."

"Except the thief came early and got away."

For the first time, she heard a hint of emotion in his voice. And she thought of the anger and frustration he must be feeling. He'd had his hands on the thief. She turned and met his eyes. "He couldn't have been happy when he didn't get the statue."

"That's probably why my wallet, keys and car are missing—to let me know that I was helpless to stop it. I think that's partly what the robberies are about—to let me know that G. W. Securities can't prevent them. At least we haven't until today."

He rose from the pew and paced a few steps away. "I've told your father that whatever is going on here, it's connected to me personally somehow. It's not just a coincidence that the thief uses my father's M.O."

"I've told him the same thing," Nicola said. "But I also suggested strongly the possibility that you were behind the thefts. He wasn't open to that."

"Don't worry. He'll arrest me if he can get enough evidence. That's the kind of man he is." He studied her for a moment. "Did he ask you to tail me?"

"No—how did you know I was tailing you?"

"Curls, my business is providing security. I spotted you the first day. I figured your father had assigned you just as a precaution."

"Ever since he had me transferred to his office, all he's

asked me to do is research. I wouldn't be here now if Father Mike had come to the office a half hour earlier. And when I made it up here and found your car parked outside the church, I was so sure you had to be the thief."

"Can't blame you." Gabe took a seat next to her again. "And now?"

She tilted her head and studied him for a moment. A tall man, broad shouldered, wearing a robe that didn't fit. Everything inside of her yearned for him.

Not good. "I'm not sure I can be objective anymore."

He smiled at her, then ran a finger down her cheek. "I'm that good, huh?"

Nicola raised an eyebrow, firmly ignoring the killer smile as well as the ribbon of heat that unwound through her veins until it curled her toes. "Evidently, *we're* that good. Your theory is that it was a mutual jumping, remember?"

"Yes, I do remember, Curls. Every detail. Want to talk about it?"

"No." She didn't even want to think about it. Though she would. She was sure of it. Later. "You said it was spilled milk. I agree. And I think we have more important things to discuss. Your turn to answer my questions. What are you doing here?"

He nodded in the direction of the statue. "I got a call from Father Mike the instant he received the note. I told him to go report to your father. And just to put it on the record, I'm not behind the thefts."

"Do you have any idea who is?"

The easy smile faded and his eyes turned cold. "The person or persons behind the thefts are either working for me or getting information from someone inside G. W. Securities. Or they're working in your office. That's why I didn't share any information on the prototype, not even with your dad. And one of the people involved is also intimately familiar with my father's methods."

"You think there's more than one person involved?"

"There has to be. There aren't a lot of thieves as multi-talented as my father was. He was a regular Houdini when it came to locks or safes, but he might have been even better at creating forgeries."

"You've examined the ones these thieves have left behind?"

He nodded. "They're excellent. And they match up in quality to the ones my dad did himself. Plus, he always signed his work with R.W. That detail isn't very well-known." He glanced toward the altar. "Let's see if this one is signed."

Nicola stayed right where she was as Gabe retrieved the statue she'd placed there earlier. There'd been both admiration and love in his tone when he'd spoken of his father. Her mind flashed back to the boy she'd first seen on that basketball court. He'd been orphaned, left alone, at thirteen. Within a very short time he'd lost two people he'd clearly loved. But he'd worked past that. And now fifteen years later, someone was digging up all those memories.

Even worse, it wouldn't be long before the press got hold of the details that would rake up Raphael Wilder's career and his connection to Gabe. The same details that had caused her to point the finger at Gabe Wilder as the prime suspect.

Gabe settled himself once more in the pew. "You won't be able to see it clearly in this light." He took her hand and rubbed her fingers along the base of the statue.

"Can you feel the swirl in the R and the W?"

What Nicola felt was a tingle, but she traced her fingers across the base again to make sure before she met Gabe's eyes.

"What is it?"

"I feel the W all right. But the other letter isn't an R. It feels more like a G."

Gabe immediately turned the statue over and examined it in the light. First he examined the base, running his fingers across the letters just as she had. Then he ran his hands carefully over every inch of the entire statue.

"Is the thief signing your initials now?"

Gabe met her eyes. "No. I signed this statue myself. Years ago."

6

"YOU SCULPTED THIS STATUE?"

Gabe shook his head. "No. The summer after my mother died, my father worked on it and some other pieces in her art studio. It was an old gardener's cottage she'd renovated and used for her own painting. I would sit on a stool and watch him. On this piece, he tried to teach me how to use the tools, and after I'd hacked up the marble, he'd smooth over my mistakes. I didn't inherit either his artistic talent or my mother's."

As the memories slipped into his mind, so did the mix of emotions that always accompanied those memories of his father. Gabe set the statue down in front of him and leaned back in the pew. "We finished the statue and I signed it just a few weeks before he was arrested and taken away."

And why in hell had he brought that up? He didn't talk about his father's arrest. It was a part of his life that he preferred to never revisit.

It was only as Nicola covered one of his hands that he realized he'd fisted his. When she said nothing, he spoke again. "He and I didn't have much time together. My parents met in Paris where she was studying painting, and it was love at first sight. But aside from their shared talent in painting, they couldn't have been more different. He was from the streets, and she came from wealth. Plus, he was already well on his way to becoming one of the most successful art thieves in Europe. After I was born, she brought me back here to Denver to raise me. She wanted me to have a normal upbringing, a quiet life, and he simply couldn't settle down. Stealing things, creating the forgeries to leave as replacements, running the cons—it was all a wonderful game to him, one he couldn't give up. But they never stopped loving each other."

"One grew up, the other didn't. They sound like Peter Pan and Wendy," Nicola murmured.

"That's not a bad analogy. I think they were very happy with the compromise they'd worked out. She'd inherited an estate and a small fortune from her parents, so she raised me here while he traveled the world. Until I was twelve, my father was someone I only saw on holidays. He never missed one. Then my mother became ill with cancer, and he came home to stay. He brought his friend Bennett Carter with him. When my mom became bedridden, Uncle Ben took over the running of the household and supervised the care my mother needed." Gabe's lips curved. "According to my dad, Uncle Ben used to work for one branch of Britain's Royals, and he was the best treasure Raphael Wilder ever nipped."

"Your father was especially talented at reproducing paintings, wasn't he? There was no mention of sculpting in the research I did on him."

"No." He was frowning when he met her eyes. "But I remember he had pieces of marble delivered to our home."

"Do you have any idea why he might have wanted to copy the statue of St. Francis?"

Gabe's frown deepened. "No. We spent a lot of time together after Mom died. One of the places we used to go together was the St. Francis Center. My dad would talk with Father Mike in the little garden while I played basketball with my friends."

"Jonah and Nash—the ones who always interrupted our games."

Meeting her eyes, he lifted a hand to tug at a strand of her hair. "Good memory, Curls."

"Do you know what Father Mike and your father talked about?"

"I assumed they talked about my mom. Father Mike visited the house often when she was ill."

Nicola let two beats go by. "Do you think your father was planning to steal the statue?"

"No." Then Gabe sighed at the vehemence of his tone. "He promised my mother on her deathbed that he would never steal ever again. I've always believed that he kept his word."

Nicola didn't argue, and when she squeezed his hand again, he linked his fingers with hers and felt some of the turmoil of feelings inside of him settle.

"When we started working on the piece of marble together, he never mentioned that it would be a copy of St. Francis. He said that the marble knew what was inside. It was our job to discover it."

"Well, one thing I can say. I'm beginning to be happier that I shot the thief."

"Why?" Her tone surprised him; so did the spark of anger in her eyes. Releasing his hand, she rose from the pew and, grabbing fistfuls of the robe, began to pace.

"You said that these robberies are personal, and you were right. If this guy had succeeded in taking the real statue and substituting that one, you might have been arrested. The press would have had a field day. And even when you were eventually released, the reputation of G. W. Securities would have been damaged. Badly."

For a moment, he said nothing. There were too many feelings running through him. He couldn't have even named all of them. She was only giving voice to the growing certainty he'd had ever since the first robbery. But having her say the words, knowing that she believed them, filled a space inside of him that he hadn't even been aware of. "A few hours ago you were entertaining the idea I was the mastermind behind the robberies."

She whirled back to face him. "I was wrong about that. But not wrong about the fact that you hold the key. And you may be at the center of it all."

"The center?"

She moved back to the pew. "What if the thefts aren't about the art? What if they're about destroying you?"

He considered it. If she was right, that did shift the perspective a bit. Opened up new possibilities. But… "Why?"

"That's the question we should be asking."

"The art has to figure in some way."

She nodded. "Sure. We've got a good forger in partnership with someone who knows his way around systems. But why are they using your father's M.O.—except to get at you?" She sat down and took his hands in hers. "I know I'm right. That's why I was so focused on you."

For a moment, Gabe couldn't speak because he was so focused on her. The instant she'd touched him, it was just as if someone had thrown a switch. Now he felt nothing but the torrent of liquid heat she alone had the power to set off in him. And nothing else mattered. Nothing else existed but her.

It was happening to her, too. Her eyes had darkened until her irises were only a shade darker than her pupils. And he felt each one of her fingers tighten on his hand. He could hear each one of the breaths she drew in and expelled.

His gaze dropped to her mouth. Her lips were parted, waiting. All he had to do was move a few inches and he could taste her again. If he did…

For a moment, he let himself imagine stripping her out of that robe and making love to her right there. He could picture her as she would look in the flickering light of the candles. He could touch her the way he hadn't been able to before.

There was a sound outside, not unlike the noise the blizzard had made at its peak. "I think that's our ride, looking for a spot to land," Gabe said.

"Clothes," Nicola muttered.

She led the way back to the radiator in the choir room. How she'd gotten to her feet or how she managed to walk on legs she couldn't feel was a mystery she couldn't fathom. If the helicopter hadn't been landing, they would have made love again—right there.

And that was *not* what she should be thinking about. Ruthlessly, she made a mental list. First, clothes. Then the thefts.

While she pulled on damp slacks, Nicola kept trying to put the pieces together like a puzzle in her mind. The robberies, the forgeries, and the holidays and Gabe Wilder. There had to be a way to make them all fit. If she focused on that, she wouldn't be tempted to look at Gabe. But when she heard his robe drop to the floor, she wasn't able to prevent herself from stealing one quick peek. And for an instant the puzzle pieces scattered.

His back was turned to her, and for a moment, she couldn't drag her gaze away from those broad shoulders, the skin stretched smooth over well defined muscles. Her breath caught in her throat, her heart began to pound and her palms itched to touch him again. She knew what that skin felt like beneath her hands—the warm, almost velvet texture of it in contrast to the hard muscles beneath. She hadn't had nearly enough time to touch him, to explore him.

And she wanted to have that time. ASAP.

What in the world had happened to the focused, driven Nicola who'd driven through a storm with the sole purpose of catching a thief? Namely, Gabe Wilder.

She felt a lot like someone had caught her. And she wasn't doing nearly enough to break free. A sliver of panic helped her to drag her gaze away and she moved to the pile of robes still lying on the floor. But just looking at them had her blood heating all over again. And suddenly she could feel him looking at her. Every nerve in her body tingled, and she simply couldn't prevent herself from turning to meet his gaze.

And then she wanted to run to him—just as she had that day in the office. The longing was so intense that she could hardly bear it.

The sound of the helicopter came again, this time closer.

"What are we going to do about this? We can't—"

The reckless gleam in his eyes told her that they could.

Trying desperately to ignore the thrill that moved through her, she said, "They're landing. We have to clean this place up."

When he simply nodded and bent down to gather some of the robes, she let out the rest of the breath she'd been holding. Quickly, she began hanging what he handed her in the closet and ruthlessly shifted her thoughts to what she should be thinking about. Maybe if she could keep her hands and mind busy...

"Your father has to play a part in it, too," she said. "But this thief or group of thieves is doing two things differently. They send warning notes and strike only on holidays. Why?"

"Warning notes are ego related. A look-at-how-smart-I-am kind of thing. Holidays make the thefts more of a challenge. More fun." Gabe located a broom and began to sweep up the broken glass and flowers. "Makes more of a splash in the press."

"And you said your father always visited you and your mom on holidays. That's another connection to you and your dad." She turned to him from the closet and met his eyes. "Who hates you that much? And how did they get hold of the statue your father made?"

"I don't know. For that matter, I don't know who hates my father enough to rake all this up. Whoever it is had access to a specific statue that was in my mother's art studio the day my father was arrested. There should be a way to trace what happened to it. And I'm pretty sure the person I fought with tonight was a woman."

Nicola's eyes widened. "A woman?"

"Yeah. I fell on top of her at one point."

She was thinking again. Gabe could tell by the little furrow that had appeared on her forehead. He could almost hear the wheels turning. It wasn't just fresh eyes she was bringing to the case; it was a sharp mind and good instincts.

He didn't like to make mistakes, but he was pretty sure he'd made one by avoiding her for the past three months. He not only wanted her, he wanted to work with her on catching the thieves. Plan A was shot to hell and it was time for Plan B.

"What are you thinking?" he asked.

"Any chance this woman is working at G. W.?"

He picked up the last robe, then joined her at the closet door to hang it up. "My second in command at G. W. is a woman—Debra Bancroft. She's been with me since shortly after I started the business. Earlier this evening she was doing a walk-through of the security we've installed for the annual Valentine's Day Charity Ball at your family's home. Your father will be able to vouch for her." He'd arranged for Debra to handle the meeting with Nick and Marcia Guthrie because he'd been sure that Nicola would be there.

"Mary Thomas, my father's administrative assistant, would know all the details of the case," Nicola said. "She's been with him for over ten years, and she knows everything my dad knows. And Mark Adams has worked right at my dad's side from the get-go on this case."

Surprised, Gabe tilted her chin up so that she had to meet his eyes. He hadn't expected her to mention anyone in the FBI office. "I'm going to take issue with something you said before."

"What?"

"You said you didn't think you could be objective. I think you can."

She raised a brow. "If we're being totally objective, how can you be so sure that I'm not the one who cleaned your clock and then had my partner steal your car while I came back in here to play nurse Nancy?"

"Oh, I can be sure of that," he said with a grin. "The person I wrestled with is taller and had a good twenty pounds on you."

This time the sound of the helicopter was closer and louder.

"Our ride is landing." Then Gabe did what he'd been aching to do. He leaned in quickly to steal a short kiss. At least that was his intention, but it changed when her lips softened beneath his and her hands gripped his shoulders. He sank into her then, absorbing her flavors—that honeyed sweetness with a surprising bite that lingered and lured. He changed the angle, nipping lightly.

She trembled, but she didn't pull away. Neither did he. As the moment stretched, he was no longer sure he could.

Nicola told herself that she had to put a stop to the kiss. But it was so different from the others they'd shared. There was no shock, no blast of heat. Just a warmth that was even more seductive. And she had to figure this out. She had to understand how he could do this to her. How could he make everything else fade to the background until there was only him?

No one had ever done that to her before. No one had ever been able to make her want this way. To need this way. And as he deepened the kiss slowly, persuasively, the soft, drowsy warmth slipped seamlessly into an ache that built and built until it penetrated, not merely her body, but her mind and soul as well. She felt parts of herself slipping away.

He eased the pressure on her mouth enough to whisper, "Nicola?"

She knew what he was asking. He wanted her to let go and to tumble with him again wherever the moment would lead. She wanted to and knew she couldn't. There would be people knocking at the door of the church any minute. But there was a part of her that just didn't care. For a moment longer, she hesitated, letting practicality and common sense teeter on the brink with passion and the promise of delight.

Then the pounding came, muffled but insistent.

She drew away. "I can't. We can't." But she had to fist her hands at her sides to keep from reaching out and pulling him back. She made herself meet his eyes. "We can't make love."

Not right now. Gabe didn't say the words out loud. But they formed a drum beat in his head. He felt as if he'd taken a fast ride down a roller coaster without being strapped into a cart. He'd known she'd be different for him. Now he was beginning to suspect that she might be everything. Something sprinted up his spine. Fear?

She turned and led the way out of the room and down the aisle to let their rescuers in. He'd been right about the complications. Not only did he have a very clever thief with a special vendetta against him, now he had to figure out what to do about Nicola Guthrie.

7

AT SEVEN-THIRTY the next morning, Gabe faced Nick
Guthrie across the wide expanse of a gleaming mahogany
desk. The only thing that lay on top of it was the morning's
paper with a headline that read: G. W. Securities and FBI
Join Forces to Foil Attempted Robbery of Famed Statue
of St. Francis.

"How's your head?" Guthrie asked, his gaze straying
to the Band-Aid that now adorned Gabe's forehead.

"Good. I had one of my men escort Nicola home, and I
stopped by a hospital where an old friend of mine works.
She checked everything out, and aspirin should take care
of any lingering effects."

Unfortunately, there was no such easy remedy for what
he was feeling about Nicola. Sending her home with one
of his men had turned out to be the most difficult decision
of the evening. He simply hadn't wanted to let her go. Oh,
he'd justified it rationally by telling himself that it was the
smart thing to do. Because if he'd gone home with her, he
wouldn't have let her go into her apartment alone.

And he'd needed to think, to sort through all the impli-
cations of what had happened at the church.

He'd done the right thing. But not all the rationalizing

he'd done had make it possible for him to stop thinking about her. And he hadn't once been able to rid himself of the desire to just throw caution to the wind and go to her. Even now, he was wondering when she'd arrive at the office, when he would see her again. He felt a bit like a teenager with raging hormones.

At the end of a long, sleepless night, he'd come to one conclusion. He wanted her to work with him on this case. Even though his motives weren't entirely related to catching a thief.

"You were lucky," Guthrie said.

Gabe met his eyes. "I might not have been so lucky if it hadn't been for your daughter's arrival."

"Nicola should not have been there. Neither should you." Nick Guthrie tapped a finger on the newspaper that lay between them. "Tell me that you did not have anything to do with leaking this story."

Gabe smiled. "That's a rhetorical question, right?"

Guthrie ran a hand through his hair and sighed. "Shit. Just tell me why. And while you're at it, tell me why you decided to use the statue of St. Francis as bait when we've put all our resources in place to catch this thief at the Valentine's Day Charity Ball tomorrow night?"

Gabe studied Guthrie for a moment. He was a tall, lean man in his late fifties who had the preppy kind of good looks that aged well. He knew that Guthrie's stellar record at the bureau had a lot to do with his being a meticulous planner. He always took the time to dot his I's and cross his T's.

The fact that Gabe hadn't filled him in on the prototype of his new alarm system and hadn't given him a heads-up on his hope that the thief might make a try for the statue was not sitting well with him. Gabe hadn't expected it to. Nick Guthrie didn't like to be thrown curve balls. Who did?

"You haven't talked to Nicola then?"

Guthrie frowned at him. "She's due in at eight. I'll see her after she types up her report."

A real I-dotter, Gabe thought. But he was beginning to get a clearer picture of Nick Guthrie's working relationship with his daughter.

"You still haven't answered my question," Guthrie said. "Why did you set up the statue of St. Francis as bait?"

"I wanted to rattle a cage or two. These thieves began by hitting us hard—a sort of one, two, three punch. Thanksgiving, Christmas and then New Year's. They'd stolen three pieces of art and broken through three of my alarm systems before I had an opportunity to analyze the problem fully. Then we had to wait a month and a half to see if they would strike on Valentine's Day. I figured the St. Francis might complicate their plans a bit."

"Why did you think they'd take the bait?"

Gabe shrugged. "The statue has a very high profile. There are plenty of people in the Denver area and beyond who believe in its prayer-answering power—and that makes it saleable to some collector. Plus, G. W. Securities installed the alarm system. I wanted to see if that would add to the temptation. I think it did."

"But in spite of the risks you and my daughter took, we still don't have anyone in custody. What if they're so *rattled* they skip the Valentine's Day Charity Ball? Where are we then?"

"Then we'll wait until St. Patrick's Day. Or Easter. But I don't think they'll skip the ball. They haven't missed a major holiday since this whole thing began. They even went for the St. Francis on a minor holiday. And failed. That's part of the reason why I leaked the story. After a well publicized failure, stealing the Cézanne that will be auctioned at the ball will be a matter of pride."

Guthrie rose and paced to the window. "I hope you're right."

"So do I. I miscalculated. I thought they'd wait until Valentine's Day to try for the St. Francis."

Guthrie turned and met his eyes. "You thought they'd go for both at once?"

"That's what I was hoping."

"And you would have been lying in wait at the church while everyone else was at the ball."

"Something like that. The security at the ball tomorrow night is tight. It's not going to be as easy as the other three robberies. Whoever is behind this is smart. They're going to protect themselves. We could end up preventing the theft but not catching anyone. I thought there might be a better chance of actually apprehending one of them at the church. But I didn't take into consideration that yesterday was Lincoln's Birthday."

"Hmmph." As Guthrie continued to stare out the window, the silence stretched between them.

And Gabe suddenly knew that Nicola had arrived for work. Every nerve, every cell in his body snapped to attention. He didn't bother to turn around. With the privacy shades drawn, he wouldn't be able to see her. But an image formed in his mind of that first time he'd spotted her stepping out of the elevator and striding purposefully to her office. She'd be wearing a neat business-like suit. And her hair would fall so straight into that slight curve. Neat. Way too neat. He couldn't help but wonder how many times he would have to run his fingers through it to tease back those curls? He hadn't yet had time to do that, and he badly wanted to.

"Earth to Gabe."

Gabe opened his eyes, shocked to find that he'd closed them.

"What are you thinking?"

Gabe quickly reined in his thoughts.

"Because I can tell you what I'm thinking. You and Nicola should never have gone into that situation at the church without backup."

"I sent Father Mike here to show you the note. When you weren't here, Nicola provided the backup I needed. She shot the perp."

"She shot the thief?" Guthrie strode back to his desk. "You didn't mention that when you talked to me last night."

"We didn't discover the blood until after I called you, and we'd already scheduled to meet this morning so that I could fill you in on all the details."

Guthrie sat down. "What the hell else haven't you told me?"

Gabe began the updates, starting with the fact that two men from G. W. that he trusted were on the scene at the church, getting a blood sample for DNA testing. One of them had even traced the abandoned car that Nicola had spotted in the ditch. It had been stolen and was free of prints. "Any news yet on my car?"

Guthrie shook his head. "I've asked the police to keep me updated. There were a lot of accidents last night, and attention has been focused on rescuing and treating victims. If your car was in one of them, I'll get a phone call. Eventually. Between the weather and the gunshot wound, our thief may not have made it back here."

"I've got a couple of my men running down gunshot wounds at the hospitals."

"Good." Guthrie met his eyes. "Anything else you haven't told me? You always save the best until last."

Gabe told him about his own signature being on the forged statue.

"Where is the forged statue now?"

"I have it safe at my place."

For a moment Guthrie said nothing, and when he spoke his tone was neutral. "So now we can be pretty sure that more than one person is involved in these thefts, and at least one of them is probably female. And the forgery this time has your signature on it. Where the hell did they get it?"

"The last time I saw that statue it was in my mother's art studio, the same place you found the Matisse that my father was arrested for stealing."

Guthrie frowned. "Any artifacts the FBI confiscated when they conducted their search were put in an evidence locker. Your mother's paintings were eventually authenticated and returned. The Matisse your father stole was returned to the museum."

The Matisse had been part of an exhibition that had been on a U.S. tour from a gallery in Madrid, and a year earlier, it had been stolen from an art museum in San Francisco. His father's initials had been on the forgery that was left behind. At the trial he'd denied both the theft and the making of the second painting. But the evidence had been overwhelming.

Nick Guthrie took a notebook out of his desk and picked up a pen. "I'll look into it."

After scribbling a few notes, he met Gabe's eyes. "And this forged statue with your signature makes you strongly suspect that someone in my office is involved."

"Whoever is behind these robberies had to have known that it existed and they also had to have access to it."

Guthrie leaned back in his chair. "That's the real reason you didn't fill me in on the prototype, and it's also why you requested to meet with me alone this morning before you filled me in on all the details. I have to be your prime suspect."

If there was one thing Gabe admired about Nick Guthrie, it was his ability to hide his emotions and keep his focus on the case.

"There's only one person I trust at this point," Gabe said. "Besides you."

"Who?"

Gabe had thought long and hard during the night about the best approach to take. Now, he chose the most direct one. "I trust Nicola, and starting right now, I want you to make me her assignment."

Guthrie leaned back in his chair and narrowed his eyes. "Why should I do that? She's an inexperienced agent."

"As far as I can see, she handled herself well last night. As for why you should assign her to this case—there are two reasons. First, someone is trying very hard to pin these robberies on me. The fact that they left that forged statue behind suggests that the St. Francis might have been on their to-steal list all along. If they'd been successful last night, you would have had to arrest me. So if Nicola watches me twenty-four-seven, you cover the bureau's ass—in advance. The second reason is the more important. She's already involved in this. The thief was not going to get the St. Francis. But she may have thought she could, given enough time. Nicola and I prevented that. And Nicola shot her. That news is bound to get out. Nicola's name is already in the paper. The fact that she shot the thief will be in the report she types up. Whoever is behind this is not going to be happy that a key member of their team is out of commission, and they may blame Nicola. These thieves haven't had much experience with failure up to this point. So far, everything has run like clockwork. Until we're sure how they're going to react, I say we take precautions."

"You think she's in danger?"

He met Guthrie's eyes very steadily. "I hope not. There's

been no violence yet. But I'd rather be safe than sorry. I don't want her out of my sight until this is over. Assign me to her and she'll be under the protection of G. W. Securities, and you have eyes on me. If I'm wrong, you still get eyes on me until we have somebody behind bars."

"Shit."

It was only the third time Gabe had ever heard Nick Guthrie swear. And all three times had been since he'd walked into the office this morning.

Guthrie ran his hands through his hair. "All right. Until this is over, you're Nicola's assignment." Then his eyes narrowed. "Promise me you'll keep her safe."

"Done." Gabe rose and held out a hand. "You won't be sorry." Then he said a quick prayer to St. Francis that he would make good on his promise.

8

NICOLA TAPPED THE PRINT BUTTON on her computer. It was 8:00 a.m., and she'd finished the report on what had happened last night at St. Francis Church. Through the glass wall of her office, she could see the papers shooting out of the printer that sat just to the side of Mary Thomas' desk.

Filing the report had been the assignment Mary had given her when she'd arrived a little after 7:30 to find that her father was already in a meeting behind closed doors. And in spite of the fact that he'd lowered the privacy shades, she was pretty sure she knew who was in there with him—Gabe Wilder.

She'd felt him right down to the marrow of her bones. Even right now, she was tingling in anticipation that she might see him again—much the way she'd felt on those long ago Saturday mornings when Marcia would drive her to the St. Francis Center.

At first she'd suspected that special agent Mark Adams was with them. But when he'd arrived at 7:45 and gone straight to his office, she'd felt better. At least she wasn't the only outsider. Mark was a tall, dark-haired man in his late thirties, and he'd been working with her father for nearly a decade. That meant he was a good agent.

She shifted her gaze back to the door of her father's office. When she'd told Mary that she should be part of the meeting, the woman had given her a sympathetic smile and explained that her father wanted her report on his desk ASAP. Then he'd see her.

So she'd written it up, and now she was back to square one.

She'd been so sure that last night would have made a difference. And if she'd caught the thief, it would have. But all she'd done was prove her father's theory that Gabe Wilder wasn't behind the robberies. But he was still at the center of it. She was sure of that.

And someone in this office might be involved.

Through the glass wall of her own office, she watched Mary stretch one arm gracefully to retrieve her report from the printer then place it neatly in her out-box.

Mary Thomas certainly fit within the parameters of Gabe's description of the female thief he'd wrestled with, but her father's administrative assistant gave no indication she was recovering from a bullet wound.

She figured the tall attractive brunette had to be in her late forties or early fifties, but she could easily pass for five or six years younger. And she'd been her father's trusted administrative assistant for almost fifteen years. In the three months since Nicola had joined the Denver office, she'd learned that Mary had a meticulously organized mind and ran a very tight ship. She also did yoga and tended to dress like a fashion plate.

Not that she had seriously suspected Mary Thomas of being the woman she'd shot last night. But the woman could be an accomplice—she knew everything that was going on in the Denver office's white-collar crime division. So could

Mark Adams. Her gaze drifted back to the man whose office was directly across from hers. And Debra Bancroft, Gabe's trusted assistant, could also be added to the list of possible suspects. If the robberies were a group effort, as Gabe was certain they must be, there could be more than one woman involved. After all, art theft and forgery were equal opportunity professions.

She glared at her father's closed door. So was the FBI. Supposedly.

Biting back a sigh of frustration, Nicola rose and paced to the window of her office. The sun was bright in the sky, and the snow had already begun to melt.

The instant she'd seen the headlines in the paper, she'd called Father Mike and left a message. Making the call had given her something to do. So had writing up the report for her father. And focusing on the case was the only way that she'd been able to get her mind off Gabe Wilder, however briefly.

She simply couldn't forget the kiss they'd shared just before they'd left the church and boarded the helicopter. In a way, that kiss had been more worrisome than making love to him. A onetime fling brought on by adrenaline and lust was almost understandable.

But the kiss had been different. There'd been a moment, however brief, when she'd felt as if she were coming home.

Talking about it had been impossible in the helicopter even if she'd wanted to. And Gabe had arranged for two cars to meet them at the landing pad. He'd said that he intended to stop by a hospital and get the cut on his head attended to.

She could hardly argue with that. But she'd wanted to. When the driver of one of the cars had driven her home and escorted her to her door, she couldn't help but wonder if Gabe had seen her to their door, would they have shared another kiss? Would they have gone inside and made love again?

And why couldn't she stop thinking about doing just that?

Seriously annoyed, Nicola strode to the counter behind her desk, opened a small refrigerator, and pulled out a caffeine-laden soft drink. Making love again with Gabe Wilder should be the *last* thing she wanted.

After twisting the cap off of the plastic bottle, she took a long swallow. He wasn't her prime suspect anymore. They should both be focusing on who was behind the thefts. Sending her home in a separate car had been an excellent move on his part. Obviously, they were returning to their first strategy—treating what had happened between them as spilled milk.

Fine. She was about to take another swallow of her drink when there was a knock at her door.

When she saw it was Father Mike, she set down her drink and hurried to let him in.

"You're all right." He took her hands in his. "Gabe assured me of that when he called me earlier, but when I received your message, I thought I'd come in person and see for myself."

"I'm fine." Nicola drew him toward a chair. He wasn't tall, and in spite of the fact that he had to be close to eighty, he moved with the agility of a much younger man. His hair was snow-white, and he had the kindest blue eyes she'd ever seen. When she'd first met him years ago at the St. Francis Center, she'd thought of them as Irish eyes because they always seemed to be smiling.

He drew a newspaper out of his pocket. "The statue is safe, but the thief got away. Gabe didn't give me much more than the paper has."

Quickly, she gave him a severely edited version of what had gone on in St. Francis Church the previous evening.

"Good thinking to use choir robes to prevent him from going into shock," Father Mike said.

Nicola could feel she was blushing. She'd of course deleted completely the part where she had decided to crawl in with Gabe.

Don't go there, Nicola. Stick to the case.

"Father, you've known Gabe for a long time, haven't you?"

"Since he was a baby. I was his mother's confessor."

She told the priest about her theory that Gabe was somehow at the center of why the thefts were occurring. "Do you have any idea of why someone would want to frame him for the thefts? Or to hurt him in some way?"

Father Mike leaned back in his chair and steepled his fingers. "Revenge is a powerful motivation. It's usually triggered by love or money. Sometimes both. A man in Raphael Wilder's profession—as good as he was—had to have made enemies."

She frowned as she thought about it. "A thirst for revenge that would extend from father to son…and then there's the money. Gabe says it's about the art, too."

Father Mike smiled. "You like him, don't you?"

Nicola frowned. *Like* him? Like seemed far too tame a word for what she'd come to feel about Gabe Wilder in the past twelve hours. "I haven't had time to think about that. Until last night at the church, I was sure he was behind the thefts."

"But you've changed your mind."

"Yes, he's not the thief."

"But he might have been if it weren't for you."

She stared at him. "What do you mean?"

"Fifteen years ago, you came into his life when he was at a crossroads."

Nicola frowned. "I was ten, and I let him tempt me into playing basketball instead of weeding the garden as I was supposed to do." And last night she'd let him tempt her again.

Father Mike beamed a smile at her. "Exactly. Teaching you to play and sharing his skill with you helped him to choose the right path." He tilted his head to one side. "And playing with him helped you also, I think."

"Perhaps." She met Father Mike's eyes. "You asked me if I liked him. I'm not sure I did like him when I was ten. But he fascinated me."

"And now?"

He still did, she realized.

Leaning toward her, Father Mike patted her hand. "If the two of you work together on catching this thief, you'll figure it out."

"Father Mike."

They both turned to see Mary Thomas standing in the doorway. "I buzzed Agent Guthrie that you're here, and he said to come right in."

Nicola rose when Father Mike did and walked with him to the door.

Mary said to her, "I'll check with him and see if he's ready to see you also."

Father Mike turned and took her hands in his again. "St. Francis will help you settle everything. You just have to have faith in his power."

For one long moment, Nicola stood in the doorway watching Father Mike disappear into her father's office. It didn't look as though working with Gabe on the case was going to be an option unless she figured out a way to make it one. And if she did, how on earth was she going to handle the intense attraction she felt for him? Still, she was debating whether or not to just follow Father Mike into her father's office when her phone rang. She hurried toward it hoping it was her father requesting her presence. "Agent Guthrie."

"Nicola, where are you?"

Nicola recognized the voice instantly. Her stepmother. And the call could only mean one thing. She was on Marcia's to-do list for the Valentine's Day Charity Ball. "I'm at the office."

"You have a meeting with Randolph Meyer this afternoon at 4 o'clock for a fitting of your gown. You can't miss it. You'll have to leave the office early."

Nicola didn't bother to argue that she *could* miss the appointment. The words would be wasted because Marcia, as much as she loved her, had a one-track mind.

"I want you to look perfect. Everyone who is anyone is going to be at the ball. I've had three people call today to ask if I can fit them in."

It wasn't nerves or annoyance that Nicola heard in her stepmother's voice. It was delight and excitement. Marcia loved to throw a party. And between the Cézanne that was being auctioned and the media buzz that an attempt might be made to steal it, the Valentine's Day Charity Ball had become a hot ticket.

"And Randolph is looking forward to seeing you again," Marcia said.

Meyer was *the* hot new designer that everyone in Denver's most elite social circles was using. Nicola also suspected that her stepmother had added Randolph to the list of eligible bachelors Nicola should be getting to know.

"Since you don't have an escort tomorrow night, I've invited Randolph to join our table."

Bingo, Nicola thought. Randolph Meyer would make

bachelor number four or five. She'd already lost count of the number of men Marcia had introduced her to since she'd returned to Denver.

"Yesterday, he stayed after my fitting and helped me make the decision on the desserts for the ball. Such a well-mannered young man. And so talented."

"What did you choose for the desserts?" Nicola asked, hoping to distract Marcia.

"Chocolate covered strawberries, chocolate cheesecake, crème brulee for those who avoid chocolate, and a selection of petit fours."

"Excellent. You always make just the right choices."

"But I won't be doing them forever, and you will have to step into my shoes. The charity ball has been held at the Thorne mansion for nearly a quarter of a century."

Nicola had heard the speech before, so she repeated her usual answer. "And that's where it will continue to be held. When the time comes, I'll step into your shoes, Marcia." She might not be able to fill them or meet all of Marcia's expectations, but she could certainly make sure that the annual ball went off on schedule.

"And you'll make the fitting with Randolph?"

To avoid answering the question, she lied. "I have another call coming in. I have to go."

She disconnected her stepmother and was replacing the receiver in its cradle when she suddenly tensed. Every nerve in her body began to tingle.

Gabe Wilder was here. She raised her gaze to meet his and just like that her pulse began to race, her nerves tingled.

He stood leaning against the door frame and she had to grip the arms of her chair to keep from going to him. He wore black from head to foot—slacks, turtleneck sweater and a leather jacket. And his eyes—at this distance—were nearly black, too.

Just looking at him made her want him. Desperately. It was that simple, that basic. That terrifying. No amount of common sense or practicality could control her instant and primitive response to just seeing him.

"Ready?" he asked.

She wasn't at all sure she was. Not for him. But there was a gleam in his eyes that tempted her just as it had when she was ten. "For what?"

"To take me on as your new assignment? I've convinced your father that someone needs to keep a close eye on me since the mastermind behind these thefts seems to be very intent on framing me for the robberies. The job is yours if you want it."

"I do." Snagging her purse from her desk drawer, she headed toward him. She wanted the job all right. Now all she had to do was keep her mind on it.

Gabe's cell phone rang.

"Wilder." Then he listened. She could hear the rumble of a voice on the other end of the connection, but she couldn't make out the words.

"I'll be there in ten minutes," he said as her father and Father Mike appeared in the doorway of his office.

"The state police just called," Nick Guthrie said. "They found your car in a ravine about four miles from Denver. The driver—a woman—was airlifted to a hospital several hours ago. They assumed the car belonged to the driver and didn't get around to running the plate right away."

"She's at St. Vincent's," Gabe said. "One of my men just tracked it down. They didn't discover the bullet until she was in surgery so it didn't get reported right away. According to my man, she wasn't carrying any identification."

There was a beat of silence as Mark Adams appeared in

the door of his office. Nick Guthrie turned to him. "Mark, I need to fill you in." Then he shifted his gaze back to Gabe. "The two of you go and check the woman out. Get an I.D. on her. I'll arrange for a police guard at the door, and I'll get on that other matter we talked about."

Nicola said nothing until they were out of the building and he was opening the door of a low slung black convertible parked at the curb. The car was certainly in Gabe Wilder's signature color, but it was a sharp right turn from the black SUV she'd tailed. "How in the world did you persuade him to assign me to watch you?"

He gave her a sideways glance as the engine leaped to life with a purr. "I appealed to what matters most to him. I told him I thought you were in danger. I do, by the way. And I promised him I'd provide you with the protection you need."

Nicola's eyes narrowed. "So *you're* really assigned to *me* and not vice-versa."

"Not at all." He smiled at her. "It's a mutual assignment, Curls. And a perfect arrangement. You get to prove yourself in the field, and I get to work with the best mind the Denver FBI white-collar crime division has."

Nicola felt the warmth steal through her right down to her toes. But as grateful as she might be to Gabe Wilder for making the "perfect arrangement," it didn't slip by her that she was dealing with a very smooth operator.

9

GABE STOOD WITH NICOLA and a male nurse just inside the room where a young woman lay hooked up to several beeping machines. Just outside the door, Pete Walters, a young man who'd been working for him ever since he graduated from college, was talking to the policeman that had just arrived.

The nurse's name tag read *Sid*. He was in his mid-twenties with brown curly hair and a cherubic face, and in spite of his youthful appearance, he ran a tight ship. He wasn't about to leave them alone with the injured woman, nor had he been overly generous with the details of her condition other than telling them it was critical.

"Five minutes," Sid reminded them. "Then I'll have to ask you to leave."

"She looks so young," Nicola murmured.

That had been Gabe's first thought when he'd seen her. It was hard to estimate her exact age because she had enough bandages wrapped around her head to make her look like a nun. But he was guessing late teens, early twenties. Except for a bruise that had darkened around one eye, her face was free of injury, and there were no wrinkles. She had delicate features and the high cheekbones of a model. And something about her pushed at the edge of his mind.

Not recognition. For he'd never seen this woman before. He was sure of that. Just as he was pretty sure that she was the same woman he'd fought with the night before. The hospital sheets were tucked tightly around a tall, athletically built body. Gabe stepped to the foot of the bed to get a closer look.

"That's far enough," Sid said. "I agreed to let you see her. That's all."

Nicola pulled a notebook out of her purse. "I'm going to make a sketch of her. The FBI has a program we can run it through. We may be lucky enough to get a match."

Gabe watched out of the corner of his eye as she moved her pencil skillfully over the page. The strokes were quick, competent. Either of them could have easily taken a picture with a cell phone, but the sketch might prove more useful. At the very least it was distracting the nurse.

"You're good at that," Sid commented, his eyes on her sketch pad now.

Gabe moved closer so that he, too, could take a look. Sid was right. She was very good. As he studied what was taking shape on the page, he once more felt the flicker of something, some memory. But it was too dim, too far away.

"Do you have any idea how old she is?" Nicola asked Sid.

"We figure she's in her early twenties," Sid replied. "Do they give lessons in drawing at the FBI?"

"I studied art in college," Nicola said. "She must have been badly hurt."

"Lucky for her Dr. Cashman was on call. He's one of our most skilled surgeons. She suffered severe head trauma in the accident, but he was able to relieve the pressure on the brain."

"She's going to make it?" Nicola asked.

"We're working on it," Sid replied. "The coma she's in is induced. The surgical team hopes to bring her out of it in a few days. Then we'll see if there's been permanent brain damage."

"There's a chance of that then?" Nicola asked, not glancing up from her sketch.

"Always. But Dr. Cashman is hopeful that he relieved the pressure in time."

"What do you think of the likeness?" Nicola asked, holding up her notebook.

"Very good," Sid said.

"Thanks." She shot him a smile before she flipped to a new page. "There was a gunshot wound also?"

"Dr. Cashman removed a bullet from her shoulder. No artery was hit, and it missed the bone. The pain and the loss of blood may have factored into why she lost control of the car, but there's a good chance the storm also played a major role. Our emergency room was filled last night with the victims of weather-related accidents."

She wasn't only good at drawing, Gabe thought. She'd also found a way to set Sid enough at ease, so that he was giving them the information they needed about the mystery woman's condition.

"That's why the policeman and that security agent are standing guard, right? Because of the bullet? Is she in trouble?" Sid asked.

"We won't know for sure until we know who she is," Nicola said. "Did she have any personal effects on her?"

"No wallet or cell phone," Sid said as he moved to a small closet. "Just this." Removing a plastic bag, he passed it to Nicola.

Inside was a bracelet. Nicola removed it and held it up to the light. The chain was thick, finely crafted gold and there was a flat gold disc hanging from one of the links. The engraved initials read D.A. Gabe felt something flicker at the edge of his mind again, but the memory was still out of reach.

Nicola slipped the bracelet into the plastic bag and said, "I'll want to keep this. It could help us with the identification."

When Sid frowned, Nicola hurried on. "Do you happen to know what color her hair was? That could be even more helpful than the bracelet. The last thing I'd want for her is to come out of that coma and not have anyone here for her."

"I'll make a call," Sid said and hurried out of the room.

"And while he's doing that, I'll get her prints." Gabe grabbed one of the plastic glasses and gently pressed the young woman's fingers to it. Circling the foot of the bed, he did the same with a second glass, tucked both into his briefcase, and moved to Nicola. "Great idea to make the sketch."

"It's the first time I've had any practical use for all those art classes my stepmother insisted on."

"Good job." He noted the flush that spread to her cheeks. "You're talented at drawing. You're also good at questioning people." And instinct told him that she hadn't heard a lot of compliments in her life. He'd have to do something about that.

"I like working with you, Curls." Then he made a mistake and did what he'd told himself he wasn't going to do, something he'd been aching to do ever since he'd walked into her office. He touched her.

Not the way he wanted to. All he did was tuck a strand

of hair behind her ear, but the simple act of brushing his finger over her cheek set off an instant chain reaction. Her breath caught, and he felt it like a punch in the gut. When the pulse quickened at the base of her throat, his own leapt to match it.

She raised a hand and placed it against his chest, and the pressure of each one of her fingers triggered a torrent of liquid heat so intense that the reality around him faded.

Neither one of them moved. He'd never experienced such an intense awareness of another person. In that moment, nothing else mattered. Nothing else existed except Nicola. The realization baffled him. It frightened him. And fascinated him.

"I want you. I have from the first moment I saw you in the office," he murmured.

"I know. What are we going to do?"

Run like hell. That's what he'd been doing for almost three months. But that wasn't what he wanted to do anymore. He was leaning toward her, closing the distance between them when a voice said, "Blonde."

They dropped their hands at the same instant as Sid entered the room. "She has blonde hair."

It was Nicola who recovered enough to turn and say, "Thank you so much, Sid. And we're going to get right out of your way."

Just outside the room, Gabe stopped to talk to his man, Pete.

Nicola listened to him fill the young man in, but she didn't speak again until they were in the car and Gabe had pulled into traffic. By that time her heartbeat had steadied and she could think again. But she didn't trust herself to look at him. Not yet. "We're going to have to do something about what's happening between us. The spilled milk strategy isn't working."

"Spilled milk?"

"That's what you said at the church. Ignore it and it will go away. It's not going away. We were in a hospital room with a woman who's in an induced coma. Someone who tried to steal the statue of St. Francis. And I lost track of everything when you touched me. *Everything.*" Just as she had in the church. Just as she had that first day in the office.

"It's a mutual experience, Curls."

She kept her eyes on the road but gripped the armrest when he took a quick right turn. "We have to find out who that woman is and how she's connected to what's going on. And there's a clock ticking on this."

"Agreed."

"We don't have time for...what's happening between us. We can't afford to..."

"Make love again?" This time he turned left and then swerved to pass the car directly in front of them. "We're going to. Because we both want to."

She should argue with him. Tell him they wouldn't, they couldn't. But she'd be speaking lies—not only to him but to herself. Instead, she said, "We shouldn't."

"Probably not." He took another sharp left turn and earned a long honk from an oncoming car.

Nicola glanced in the sideview mirror and noticed a blue sedan make the same turn. "Is that car following us?"

"I'm finding out." For a few seconds, he zigged and zagged through traffic.

Nicola noted that the blue sedan was still in her sideview mirror.

"You know, we're not exactly cut out of the same cloth, you and I," Gabe said. "And you're the daughter of a man who's been good to me. Who's trusted me. I've spent nearly three months avoiding you because that was what I felt I *should* do."

Nicola looked at him then. His eyes were on the road, but his knuckles had turned white on the wheel. "Do you always do what you should do?"

There was just a hint of recklessness in the smile he sent her. "Not always. But I try when it counts. My mother made me promise on her deathbed that I would live my life within the law, that I would never follow in my father's footsteps. So I've kept that promise. I'm not saying I did it on my own. Dad made Uncle Ben my guardian, and I had Father Mike, the St. Francis Center and good friends. Your father kept an eye on me, too. When I was first starting out, he called me in to consult on cases. That helped G. W. Securities build its reputation. I *should* have been able to keep my hands off of you. But you're different for me, Curls."

Her throat was dry when she tried to swallow. She hadn't been able to keep her hands off of him either. And she wanted them on him again. "You're different for me, too."

And what an understatement that was. But it occurred to her for the first time that maybe they weren't so different from each other. Whatever rebellions she'd had in her life—playing basketball, joining the FBI—she'd accepted the transfer to Denver partly because she'd felt it was what she *should* do. Sure her main goal was to prove to her father by her actions that she'd make a good field agent. That way he'd worry less about her job choice. But she'd also known it would please both of her parents if she returned to Denver.

Gabe made another left, and she noted that the blue sedan followed them.

She turned her attention back to him. "You know, when

it comes to doing what you *should* do, I could be the poster girl." But there was a time when you had to make a choice between what you should do and what you wanted to do. She'd made a choice when she was ten because she'd wanted desperately to play basketball with Gabe Wilder.

Want seemed far too tame a word for what she felt each time Gabe Wilder touched her. But she'd already made her choice. "We'll make love again."

"We will."

"But our priority has to be to catch the thieves. What's happening between us can't interfere. This case is too important."

"We couldn't be more in sync. We'll just have to juggle our priorities. Hold on to your seat."

She did and the right turn he took was so sharp it made the tires squeal.

She glanced in the sideview mirror again. "They're still with us."

"See? Neither one of us missed that. We seem to be juggling okay."

She glanced up at the tall building and recognized the parking ramp they turned onto. "You led them right to your office."

He pulled into a space. "I did."

She looked at him then. "I didn't notice them on the way to the hospital. Were they following us then?"

"No."

"Three people besides my dad heard you say we were going to St. Vincent's. Mary Thomas, Mark Adams and Father Mike."

"I wanted them to. The attempted theft has made the papers. The woman in the hospital hasn't checked in with her colleagues, so they'll check out St. Vincent's. I've got Pete, one of my best men, outside the door. The policeman is his backup. If anyone makes a move to contact her, we'll have more than we have now. And we need more than we've got."

"And one of the people in my dad's office may have sicced the tail on us," Nicola said.

"Our minds are running in tune. And that's more than we knew before, too. The important thing will be to make sure they don't follow us when we leave here later."

The grin he sent her reminded her so much of the boy who'd taught her to play basketball that her heart took a little tumble. She pressed a hand against her chest as he climbed out of the car and circled to open her door.

Making love with him was one thing. They were both adults, perfectly capable of deciding to indulge in a sexual fling. She was going to have to remember that anything more than that was not on her agenda.

10

WHEN THEY STEPPED INTO the elevator that opened off the parking garage, Gabe put a key in a slot and then punched in a code. "We'll go to the G. W. offices first. I need to check in with Debra."

State of the art was Nicola's first thought as she stepped into a hall that bisected a maze of glass-walled rooms. The place reminded her of the set of a Spielberg futuristic movie, and it seemed to fit the man walking at her side to a T. Smaller rooms housed individual desks with computer screens. About half of them were occupied.

Gabe led the way to the opposite end of the floor where a larger room offered a view of the city. Five people were seated around a glass-and-chrome conference table but Nicola's eye was drawn to the tall woman standing in front of a wall-size TV screen.

"That's Debra?" she asked.

"Yes."

The moment the woman spotted Gabe, she signaled to one of the men at the table to take her place and picked up a newspaper as she left the room.

Debra Bancroft was very attractive, but not in a flashy way. Nicola guessed her to be in her mid-forties, but she moved with the grace of a younger woman. She wore her blond hair pulled back into a bun. Her black jacket and slacks, which managed to look stylish and business appropriate at the same time, revealed a slender, athletic body. It occurred to Nicola that Debra Bancroft fit the description Gabe had given of his opponent at the church last night just as well as Mary Thomas had.

And neither one of them was the woman she'd shot. That young woman was currently in critical condition and tied up to tubes in an intensive care unit.

"Gabe." When Debra's glance shifted to Nicola, Gabe made the introductions. Then Debra held out the newspaper. "Have you seen this yet?"

Gabe gestured to the Band-Aid on the side of his forehead. "I was there." He gave Debra a brief rundown on what had occurred starting with Father Mike's phone call and ending with their visit to St. Vincent's and the condition of the young woman.

"You're all right?" she asked.

"Yes."

"We've thought from the beginning that there has to be more than one person involved. If this young woman pulls through, she may be able to identify the others. Do you want me to assign someone to stand guard?"

Gabe shook his head. "I've already arranged that, and the FBI has notified the police. There was a uniform on the door when we left the intensive care unit."

Debra's eyes narrowed as she absorbed what Gabe had told her. "So one of the thieves is already in custody."

"In a manner of speaking."

"I'm assuming we go forward with our security plans for tomorrow night even if they may be one man down."

"Yes. In the meantime, Agent Guthrie is assigned to me twenty-four-seven."

At Debra's raised brow, he continued, "The FBI wants to cover all their bases. We did install the security on the statue of St. Francis and the other art pieces."

"They suspect that we may be involved?"

"In their shoes, I would, too."

Debra glanced at Nicola, then shifted her gaze back to Gabe. "Could I speak with you privately for a moment?"

"Until this is over, the FBI and I have no secrets."

Something flickered in Debra's eyes, and Nicola thought it was impatience or annoyance.

"When I did the walk-through to check the security on the Cézanne, I noticed that you've installed a new alarm system, one that I'm not familiar with."

"Just as an extra precaution."

"I was surprised when I saw it."

"It's a prototype I'm trying out. I figured this was a good time to pull out all the stops."

There was a beat of silence before Debra continued, her tone noticeably cooler, "Should we consider making any other modifications to what we've set up for tomorrow night?"

Gabe gave her an easy smile. "I'll be working upstairs in my apartment reviewing that very question. If there are any changes, I'll let you know."

Again Debra's eyes flickered as Gabe turned away. This time Nicola thought it was definitely annoyance. She waited until they were back in the elevator before she said, "She didn't like the fact that you didn't fill her in on the prototype."

"I'm having that problem everywhere. Your father didn't much like it either."

Nicola couldn't prevent the smile at his slightly aggrieved tone. "You didn't tell her about the forged statue."

"I told her everything that she needs to know."

And everything Debra Bancroft could have discovered from other sources. If she was involved in the thefts. "So there are only three of us who know about the second statue of St. Francis."

"Outside of the thieves. I want them to wonder about it."

Right, Nicola thought, and then she was distracted by the space she stepped into. It was a large open area with skylights overhead and a wall of glass that afforded the same view of the city she'd glimpsed on the lower floor. The inside wall sported floor to ceiling bookshelves except for the space that held a theatre-size flat screen TV.

Her gaze skimmed over an L-shaped leather sofa and matching chairs. Beyond that she caught the gleam of a black granite counter framing a kitchen that her step-mother's chef might envy. To the left of the elevator, a wrought-iron staircase spiraled to a loft with more skylights overhead.

She shifted her attention to the work space to her right as Gabe moved toward it. The desk faced the windows, and if the rest of the apartment spoke of luxury and indulgence, Gabe's office was a testament to high-tech efficiency. But it was the floor to ceiling whiteboard behind it that surprised her. It looked like the "murder boards" she'd seen on TV shows.

Moving closer, she studied the series of photos pinned to it. From left to right were newspaper pictures of the art pieces that had been stolen so far. And the last one was a photo of the statue of St. Francis that had been in last Sunday's paper.

She glanced at Gabe to see that he'd already lifted the prints off the plastic glasses.

"Can you modify that sketch you drew? Take away the bandages and add blond hair?"

"Sure." Fishing her notebook out, she did what he'd asked and then handed it to him.

"I'll upload it into my computer along with the fingerprints and start a scan."

"What else can I do?"

"Take a good look at the whiteboard and tell me what you see. I need a fresh perspective." He didn't bother to glance up from what he was doing.

He was all business again, and Nicola, for the first time, was eager to follow his lead. The board intrigued her.

"Tell me your thoughts as you go along," Gabe suggested. "I'm at the point where I'm seeing the same things, thinking the same scenarios."

"I know just what you mean." She stepped closer to the board and studied the photo of the first piece of art.

Then she skimmed through the newspaper report. "The Monet was taken while the Langfords were having Thanksgiving dinner with friends, specifically my parents and me. Their house showed no signs of forced entry. Since the painting was still on the wall, they thought the note from the thief was a practical joke. Until they called my dad."

"Your thoughts?" Gabe asked.

"The thief either had the security code or possessed the skill to disarm the alarm system. The house was empty." She turned to face him. "Someone skilled at disabling alarms or someone who had access to the codes could have pulled this off alone. No inside man needed."

Gabe looked at the board and nodded. "I agree. They would have had to know that the Langfords had art worth the trouble and that they would be out of the house on Thanksgiving Day. But that's Research 101 for a good thief, and this one is very good. What about the next robbery?"

She turned her attention to the board. The photo was of

a lovely color print of a Degas that had been stolen from the Glastons. The newspaper headline read: Christmas Day Robbery in the Suburbs.

"The whole Glaston clan, twenty-four in all, was there eating dinner. The chef had hired in a catering service. At some point, the note was dropped through a mail slot in the front door. The painting was kept in a glass case with its own separate security system." She turned to Gabe, intending to ask about the alarm, but once she met his eyes the question faded away.

He was closer than she'd realized. So close that their bodies had nearly brushed when she'd turned. If either of them made the slightest movement, they would come into contact. And she could read the awareness of that in his eyes. What she should do was take a step away and put some distance between them, but when an ache in her belly blossomed, all she could think of was that if she stepped a little closer…or if he did…

His gaze lowered to her mouth and lingered for one long moment. The ache in her belly stretched into longing, and her heart began to beat so loud that the sound of it seemed to fill the room. Still, she didn't move. Neither did he.

"I really like your mouth," he said.

She was so close to him that his scent filled the air— soap and something so male, so right, that it made her mouth water. The temptation to step forward grew.

Still, she fought it. Making love again was not what they'd come here for. "You're interfering with my ability to think again."

"It's mutual, Curls."

The nickname had her frowning. "I don't have them any more. And you wanted my thoughts on the case."

"True."

They were in agreement, so why couldn't she make

herself turn back to the board? Or why didn't he? She had to get a grip on this.

"Maybe we both need a little something to tide us over." He leaned in quick and did what he'd been wanting to do, what he'd been aching to do since he'd left her the night before. He kissed her. Just a quick one, he promised himself. But the instant he covered her mouth with his, her response was so generous, her flavor so…necessary…that he was lost.

Sensations hammered at him, through him, until he was sure his blood began to sizzle. Her mouth burned on his like a brand, and the need inside of him built until it was so sharp, so jagged, it sliced right through to his soul.

He could feel parts of himself slipping away and fear slid up his spine. No woman had ever been able to do this to him.

Only this one.

It was that thought that gave him the will to set her away from him and step back. He drew in a deep gulp of air, but he wasn't sure he'd ever get his breath back again. And looking at her with her lips swollen, her eyes dazed, had desire cutting through him again. He clamped down on the urge to just grab her and finish what he'd started. "Well," was all he managed to say.

"Well," she echoed. She felt as if she'd been knocked flat and come close to being out for the count. He'd kissed her before. Shouldn't she have been more prepared? But once his mouth had touched hers, there'd been nothing else but him. Nothing.

No one had ever had that kind of power over her. Only this man. And she needed to think about that. Once her brain cells clicked on again. And she needed to think about something besides jumping him.

"The case."

They said the words together, and Gabe smiled at her. "Nice to know that our minds are as in tune as our bodies."

"It's our minds that we came up here to use." It gave Nicola some satisfaction that she was the first to break eye contact and turn back to the photo of the Degas. But it took her a moment to bring the picture into focus. "Because the family was at home, this job presented more of a challenge."

"But it still could have been a one-man job. My father could have pulled it off quite easily, I imagine."

"But your dad would have created his own forgeries. You don't think that's the case here."

"No. As I said, someone with my father's talent is rare."

"So, hypothetically, one person on the team is good at breaking through security, making the switch and then getting away. She may very well be the one who's lying in that hospital room. Another one is talented at French Impressionist painting. But is it a two-man team or are there more?"

"That brings us to theft number three," Gabe said.

Nicola turned her attention to it. The headline read: Third Holiday Robbery.

"The Baileys were celebrating New Year's Eve with three hundred friends, and they'd locked the Pissaro in a floor safe. The note was delivered to the front door shortly after midnight and the butler handed it personally to Mr. Bailey."

"I personally installed the safe and set up the security code a few days before the robbery. The Baileys wanted extra precautions taken. I also installed two cameras without telling the Baileys. The thief or thieves disabled them."

"Who did know about the cameras?"

"Your father was the only person I told."

Nicola frowned. "He didn't mention them to me, but he keeps meticulous notes, which means that Mary Thomas could very well have known about them. And Mark Adams has been working very closely with my dad on the case."

"Here at G. W., the technician I worked with knew about the cameras at the Baileys and so did Debra. Any professional thief worth his salt would have checked for them, but it would have taken time. And with all the people in the house, that would have raised the risk of discovery and failure."

She moved closer to the whiteboard. "So you think the New Year's robbery would have required an inside source, someone who knew what you'd installed."

"That kind of knowledge would have helped with all of them," Gabe said. "But for the New Year's heist, I believe there had to have been someone with access to detailed information about the security and the cameras."

Nicola narrowed her eyes as she looked again at the photos and the headlines and felt that tingle that always told her she might be on to something. "More than one inside source maybe."

"What are you thinking?"

She moved closer to the board. "These victims all travel in a very small world. And whoever the thieves are, they had to have a fairly intimate knowledge of the social calendars of the Langfords, the Glastons and the Baileys. The New Year's Eve bash would have made the papers, created lots of buzz, but the fact that the Langfords wouldn't be home for Thanksgiving or that the Glastons would be having a large family dinner on Christmas and would be hiring caterers... Someone who moves in those inner circles and doesn't work for either your office or mine might be providing information."

"I hadn't thought of that. Good job." Gabe settled his hands on her shoulders. "What else do you see?"

Nicola tried to ignore the warmth that moved through her at his words. He had an ability to reach her on so many levels. "There's obviously an escalation in the difficulty of the job and in the risk. The first one takes place in an empty house, but the homes get more and more crowded. And while the number of people and the chances for easier access are increased, there's also more risk of discovery. There will be close to a thousand people at Thorne Mansion tomorrow night."

"Your idea of escalation makes the attempt to steal the St. Francis even more of an anomaly," Gabe pointed out. "Its location was isolated. No one was supposed to be around."

"Yes. But you went out of your way to bring that to the thief's attention, making it very tempting."

"Anything else?" Gabe prompted.

She studied the photos. "Each piece of art is portable, and, St. Francis excepted, they're all French Impressionist paintings. Those were your father's specialty. Even though forgeries are left behind, the thief wants them to be discovered. Why? And why holidays? There has to be a reason for that, and I'm betting that connects to your father, too."

Nicola moved to the first picture. "Last night, she came for the St. Francis alone. And there's a possibility that she worked the first robbery alone. Why?"

Gabe narrowed his eyes. "Maybe she did it to prove something. To show herself and perhaps others that she could."

Nicola tapped a finger against the photo of the statue. "But that raises another question about why she went for

St. Francis alone last night. If they're a team by now, why did she decide to go solo?"

"She's young. Maybe being a team player isn't what she expected. And it's a good possibility because of her age that she's not the one in charge. And if the first robbery was a test she had to pass to show her abilities…"

Gabe took a step back and swept his gaze over the pictures again. "Maybe the first three robberies are all practice. Work out the kinks until the big job at Thorne Mansion on Valentine's Day. That would explain the escalation."

Nicola felt that tingling again. "If you're right, then the painting that's being auctioned tomorrow night may be just as important as you are. You said it was about the art, too."

"Your father says the Cézanne is the most expensive piece that's ever been donated for the Charity Ball."

"And my stepmother is expecting the biggest crowd she's ever entertained. Because of the other robberies, there is some expectation among the guests that they'll be on the scene when this thief is taken down. Or when a major piece of art is stolen."

She stepped closer to tap her finger on the photo of St. Francis. "And maybe the attempt on the St. Francis isn't an anomaly. Maybe it was part of the plan all along."

"How?"

She turned to face him then. "If the forgery with your signature on it had been discovered at the church, G. W. Securities might not be operating at the top of its game tomorrow night. You might well have been in jail."

For a moment, there was silence in the room except for the hum of the computers behind them. Then Gabe took her hands in his. "I like the way your mind works, Curls. I wanted to bring you here last night."

"You did?"

"Very much. But I thought I needed distance. Perhaps we both needed some distance. I didn't even dare drive you home myself because I would have asked to come in."

Nicola let out a breath. "I would have asked you in."

"As it was, I didn't find myself thinking clearly about the case. I couldn't stop thinking about you."

"I couldn't stop thinking about you, either. I don't understand it."

He raised her hands and brushed his lips over her knuckles. "I want you, Nicola, but I also need you working on this case with me."

This time she couldn't ignore the warmth, not when it streamed through her like a warm, slow-moving river. Her heart took that little tumble again. "We've got a long way to go."

"I think we do."

She narrowed her eyes as a little skip of panic moved through her. "I'm talking about the case. We've got some pieces, but there are pieces we're missing."

"I couldn't agree more. We have a ways to go on the case, too." Then to her surprise, he grinned at her, pulling her to him and swinging her around in a circle. "But we're making progress."

When he set her down, her head was still spinning.

He nodded his toward the humming computer. "We'll get there, Curls. Something will float to the surface. It'll happen when we're totally focused on something else. And I have an idea about what we could do."

Her heart thumped hard when he grabbed her hand again. She fully expected him to head in the direction of the spiral staircase. And she didn't pull back. She didn't even open her mouth to protest. Not even when she realized he was pulling her toward the elevator.

It wasn't disappointment she was feeling. Definitely not.

But she was beginning to think that he was much better at juggling their priorities than she was.

"Where are we going?" she asked as the doors slid shut.

"To focus on something totally different."

When the elevator dropped only one floor and opened onto a professional-size basketball court, Nicola's eyes widened. The honey-colored floor gleamed. Bleachers lined three walls, and scoreboards hung over the hoops at either end of the court.

"Wow!" She turned to face him. "You've come a long way since you played on that basketball court outside of the St. Francis Center."

Gabe grinned at her the same way he had that first day on the basketball court. Her heart took another little tumble.

"I'd say we've both come a long way, Curls. Want to play?"

"I'm not dressed for basketball."

"We can change. Locker rooms are to your right. I keep a supply of uniforms and shoes here for the kids. Some of them can't afford them, and there are always new ones showing up. I'll bet a boys' large or extra-large will fit you. And you'll probably find a pair of boys' shoes that will fit." Taking her arm, he steered her toward the locker room door.

"What kids play here?"

"When the St. Francis Center had to close down, Nash and Jonah and I started up a boys and girls club that operates out of a building a few blocks from here." He pulled a T-shirt and shorts off piles on a shelf, then located a few shoe boxes. "Try these for size."

"Sure," she said as he handed her shoes and clothes.

"Father Mike still helps out there during the week.

Sports are a big part of the kids' activity schedule, and since I already had this built, they play all their basketball tournaments here."

There were questions she wanted to ask, but she wanted to play basketball more. "I'll race you," she said before she turned and ran into a changing room.

SHE'D BEATEN HIM BACK to the court and was waiting for him at the far end holding a basketball in her hands. The borrowed T-shirt and shorts weren't a perfect fit, and she shouldn't look sexy in them. But she did—enough to dry his throat. He purposely took his time moving toward her so that he could take in the view, something he'd denied himself for nearly three months.

She wasn't tall, but what there was of her was mostly legs. He'd explored the length of them, experienced the strength of them wrapped around him. Even thinly disguised in borrowed high tops, her ankles were narrow, her calves and thighs shapely and slender. Watching them, watching her stride toward him quickly, purposefully, triggered something inside of him that was more than lust, more than heat. He felt both of those, but he also simply liked the look of her. And he liked seeing her here on his basketball court. Somehow she looked right.

"Ready?" she asked.

His lips twitched. It was the same thing he'd asked her on that first day. "For what?"

"This." She held up the ball and he braced to receive it. Then quick as a snake, she darted around him and sent the ball sailing. It tapped the backboard lightly and fell through the hoop.

"Good job," he said as he caught the ball on the rebound. He pivoted and streaked for the other end of the court.

She kept up with him, and when he was close enough to

try the shot, she dodged in front of him and stole the ball. By the time he turned, she'd raced away. Because she'd surprised him, delighted him, she had time to pause at the three-point line and sent the ball whispering through the hoop.

He ran right past her, snagged the ball as it fell, and ran with it. She was on him like glue. He sank his shot this time, but it was no easy thing.

She took the rebound and when he tried to block her, she turned into him and rammed her shoulder into his chest before running away.

"Foul," he called after her.

"I didn't hear a whistle." She executed another perfect layup.

He couldn't prevent the laugh, nor the admiration for her skill. Her guts. But he did play harder then. Sure he may have held back a little. And he may have let her get away with a couple of things that he definitely wouldn't have tolerated from his friends Nash or Jonah. But she could feint and fake as well as they could. Still, he was bigger, and he didn't want to send her crashing to the floor.

But overall, they were well matched, and she was a hell of a lot better at the game than she'd been when she was ten.

She was sneakier, too. Once, when he threw out an arm to block her, she ducked right beneath it and streaked away. Another time, he'd barely caught a rebound when she'd run in, leapt up and twitched it away with her fingertips.

She might have to take two steps to his one, but everytime he turned, she was there. And he wasn't the teacher anymore. Envy had streamed through him when he'd seen her take an over-the-shoulder hook shot.

Gabe lost track of time and eventually of everything but Nicola and the game. They were both panting when they finally stopped at midcourt to catch their breath. Air burned his lungs. And she still had the ball. He could tell by the look in her eyes that if he made a move, she'd be off like a shot. What a woman.

"I think...you won," he managed to say.

"I definitely...won." She straightened, drew in another breath. "But if there's...a question..." She turned, took one dribble, then sent the ball sailing. He watched it travel in a wide arc and then whoosh through the net.

"You're amazing. I'd like to think that I taught you everything you know."

She laughed then. Her face was flushed. Her hair, damp from sweat, had begun to curl. Hunger for her exploded inside of him. Though it had been thrumming through his system from the moment he'd stepped into her office earlier, it had never swamped him so quickly, so thoroughly before.

He moved in quickly, lifting her so that he could swing her around. By the time he'd turned in a full circle, she'd wrapped her arms and legs around him, and he felt every curve of her body mold perfectly with his. Their faces were aligned, their mouths a breath apart.

"I think this has to be a foul," she said.

"Thank God, there's no ref around."

He threaded his fingers into her hair and took her mouth with his.

11

GABE THOUGHT HE'D BE READY for her taste. But the moment her flavors exploded on his tongue, the blood drained out of his head so fast that he had to shift his feet to maintain his balance. Then he tore his mouth from hers and feasted on the skin at her throat. So smooth and salty with a lingering undertone of the soap she'd used. His hunger for her only grew.

The hitch of her breath, the sharpness of her nails—each sensation ignited a new craving. The voraciousness of his appetite stunned him. So did the very real fear that he might never get enough of her. That strong, slender body pressed against his felt so right. So necessary.

All he could think was more. More. He had to touch her. He ran one hand down her back and pressed her even closer. The heat they created exploded through him and nearly had him dropping to his knees.

Only then did he find the strength to pull back. She was still wrapped around him tight.

"I have a perfectly good bed upstairs." And hadn't he planned on using it? Hadn't he fantasized for nearly three months about using it?

Those glinting brown eyes met his. "I can't wait another second."

Neither could he. Yanking down her jersey, he fastened his mouth on her breast.

With an abandonment she'd never experienced before, Nicola arched against him, digging her fingers into his shoulders and calling out his name. She couldn't think. She didn't want to. All she wanted was to feel. She'd never wanted like this. Never needed like this.

Then they were on the floor, groping, grappling, fighting with clothes until they were naked. Fast and greedy, as if she were afraid that he might escape, she ran her hands over him, searching, seeking. And wherever he touched, her body burned with flames he not only set but stoked.

And none of it was enough. She had to have more. As if he'd read her mind, he used his mouth on her. Ravaging her breasts with teeth and tongue, then making a fast, torturous journey down her torso. She barely had time to absorb one sensation before another battered her system.

When he scraped his teeth against her inner thigh, she arched high. There was a tremendous ache building. And when his tongue pierced her center, so did a lance of pleasure so sharp, so consuming, that she lost her breath and some of her mind. As she spiraled slowly down from the peak, she was sure there couldn't be any more. But he showed her there was, building the pleasure again, pushing her higher and higher until a second climax dragged her over the edge.

Her breath was sobbing and he couldn't seem to catch his at all as he moved up her again. He could feel her trembling beneath him, but he saw only her eyes—just the dark glint of them watching him as he rose over her. Nothing else.

He wanted nothing else. Here was everything. The

thought pierced him as deeply as the pleasure when he thrust into her. She closed tight around him and for a moment neither of them moved. Sunlight streamed through the windows and dust motes danced. If he could have, he would have stopped time. More than anything, he wanted to hold her right here forever. When they began to move, it was together—rising, falling, sighing. Their breath mixed, tempting his mouth to take hers again and again as the tempo increased.

They made love then just as furiously as they had while playing basketball. Faster and faster until he felt himself surrender and slip over the edge. With his face buried in her hair, he let himself fall.

NICOLA DIDN'T WANT TO MOVE. And that didn't make any sense. They were lying on the hard wood of a gym floor, sweaty from sex and their game, and she'd never felt more comfortable.

But it was time to get back to finding the thieves, and it was high time that she became better at juggling their priorities. She drew in a deep breath, and when she smelled nothing but him, her thoughts very nearly scattered again.

Focus, Nicola.

She tried to move, but Gabe forestalled her by shifting so that they were facing each other, their bodies still tangled.

"Are you all right?" he asked.

"Yes, but I think that you definitely won the second round."

"It was my pleasure." He wound a strand of her hair around his finger. "I've always liked this room, but I'm never going to think of it in quite the same way."

Her lips twitched. "I may never think of basketball quite

the same way. My games don't usually end with wild sex on the floor. But it was fabulous."

He laughed, then gave her a quick kiss on the tip of her nose. "Agreed."

It took some effort, but she managed to sit up. Their scattered clothes looked like the aftermath of a war. "Well, I'd say we were very successful in shifting our focus away from the robberies. The question is, did it work?"

Neither said a word as they gathered their clothes. Nicola reviewed a mental list of everything they'd talked about while they were looking at Gabe's whiteboard.

"Sometimes the flash of insight doesn't come to me right away. It could come while we shower," Gabe said.

"Separate showers," Nicola said in a firm tone as she moved toward the locker rooms. "The scan may have produced some results. And I want to check out the Cézanne."

"Why?" Gabe asked.

She glanced back over her shoulder. "Because if our theory is right and the other robberies are a prelude to tomorrow night, I want to know everything about that painting."

A HALF HOUR LATER, Nicola once again felt that little tingle that told her she might be on to something. The Cézanne that was being auctioned off tomorrow night had a very short history of owners. An ancestor of the Robineau family in Denver had acquired several early works from the artist himself before leaving Paris and coming to the United States. But sixteen years ago, the Robineaus had lent their entire collection to the Denver Art Museum.

And there'd been an attempt to steal at least one of them.

"Bingo," she said as she brought up the newspaper story. Her stomach sank as soon as she noted the date.

"What?" Gabe asked as he turned away from the white-board.

"It may be nothing." And she wasn't sure how to tell him.

He moved behind her and scanned the screen. "An attempted robbery just after a gala launching the Cézanne exhibit…nearly sixteen years ago. After the party, the thieves concealed themselves in the museum, but set off a silent alarm. The police arrived on the scene, and when they made a run for it, one of them was shot and killed. Bedelia Bisset. At least one other got away in a van."

Nicola said nothing.

"You're thinking my father may have been her partner," Gabe said. "The one who got away."

"He was living here in Denver at the time."

"Yes. But in February 1995, my mother was still alive and very ill. And he'd made her a promise. That way of life was over for him."

She could feel the tension radiating off of Gabe in waves, and she could see a trace of pain in his eyes. He had to be wondering if it was a promise his father had eventually broken. Without thinking, she turned in her chair and took his hand in hers. His fingers gripped hers hard.

"He must have been questioned about the attempted theft of the Cézannes, don't you think? There's no mention of FBI involvement, but I could call my father and ask."

Gabe shook his head, then released her hand. "Not yet. There's someone else I want to talk to first. And we need to find out more about this Bedelia Bisset. I want to look at a photo of her."

"I'll get on that."

Just then the desktop computer stopped humming and gave a soft beep. They both turned to look at the split screen. On half of it the fingerprint scan was still running.

But on the other half was the driver's license of a young woman who looked very much like the sketch Nicola had drawn at the hospital.

"Claire Forlani," Gabe said as he tapped keys to print out a copy. Then he took out his cell and punched a number. "I don't want to turn this over to anyone here, so I'm going to have my friend Jonah Stone look into both Bedelia Bisset and this Claire."

Nicola heard the faint sound of the phone ringing.

Then Gabe said, "Jonah, I need a favor…"

Nicola studied him as he listened for a moment and then broke out into laughter. As the sound filled the room, she saw some of the tension leave his shoulders, and some of her own drained away with it.

Although they'd followed very different paths in life, it was clear to her that Gabe, Jonah, and Nash were still very close friends. She'd looked into both of them when Gabe had been at the top of her suspect list. Nash Fortune had left Denver to make a career for himself in the air force. He was currently stationed nearby at the Air Force Academy. Jonah now owned a string of successful nightclubs in San Francisco.

Nash's family was in Denver's social register. Jonah's wasn't. In fact, she hadn't been able to find any trace of family at all when she'd run the check on him. He'd been of special interest because he'd spent a few years helping Gabe establish G. W. Securities before he'd moved to San Francisco.

And if Gabe had been the thief and had needed a partner? Well, she'd figured Jonah might just be the man he'd choose…

Odd, she thought as she studied him. Gabe was sitting on the corner of the desk, his long legs stretched out and crossed at the ankles. Less than twenty-four hours ago, she'd been so sure that he had to be involved in the thefts. And he was, just not the way she'd thought. She glanced at the whiteboard again. The robberies themselves were turning out to be something other than what she'd thought, also.

But the tingle she'd felt a few minutes ago was telling her that there had to be a connection between the attempted robbery of the Denver Art Museum sixteen years ago and what was going on now. Was it just a coincidence that the Robineau family's collection of Cézannes had been on display in the museum and now one of their Cézannes would be auctioned at the Valentine's Charity Ball? She didn't think so. All she had to do was find more pieces to the puzzle.

"Okay, we'll have that weekend together. Just as soon as I tie up these robberies…no, I'm not going to mention any specifics over the phone. I'll send you details in an encrypted email. I do have some knowledge of how cell phones are tapped into."

As Nicola caught the sound of laughter on the other end, she rose and began to stroll down the length of the room. Curiosity drew her gaze to the books first. They ranged from bestsellers to the classics. She ran her finger down the spine of what looked to be a well-worn edition of the complete works of William Shakespeare.

There were photos, also. She moved toward the one of the Gabe Wilder she'd carried in her head all those years ago. He stood between a tall man who had to be his father and a fragile-looking woman. Her throat tightened. Then a flicker she caught out of the corner of her eye had her glancing at the two smaller flat screens on the far side of the big one. Each offered a different view of the offices below. Debra Bancroft was still holding her meeting in the large conference room, and several more of the smaller offices had filled.

She glanced back at Gabe who was now at the laptop, his fingers running over the keys. No, he wasn't a man to forget anything about security. Sending the names to Jonah in an email would be safer than discussing the case over the phone.

When he straightened, he glanced at her. "Ready?"

Her heart gave a little thump as she moved toward him. "For what?"

He tucked a strand of hair behind her ear. "Still the cautious answer. I told you I wanted to talk with someone before we fill your father in. So we're having lunch with an old and dear friend, my Uncle Ben."

The elevator doors slid open as they reached them. "I hope it's not too far. I'm starved."

"It's not far and the food is fabulous."

THE ONE THING SHE HAD to say about Gabe Wilder was that he was full of surprises. This time he'd made very sure that they hadn't been followed. Who would have thought to look for them in the beat-up truck he'd driven out of the parking garage? She'd been hiding on the floor of the front seat, and he'd put on another flannel Paul Bunyan shirt and some kind of cap that had been in the cab of the truck. Something very country was blaring out of the radio so loud she'd thought she might suffer some hearing loss.

It wasn't until they were speeding out of the city and into the hills that he'd allowed her to buckle into the passenger seat. She reached immediately to turn the volume down on the radio.

"Not to your taste?" he asked.

She shifted in her seat so that she could study him.

"You're enjoying this, aren't you? The disguise, the beat-up truck, the speed?"

He shot her a quick grin. "Yeah. Running G. W. Securities has gotten a bit boring lately. In the beginning, I got to do a lot of investigative work—insurance fraud."

"So you could put on a disguise and play a con?" she asked.

"Yeah. I guess that's why I could understand why it was hard for my father to give up the life he loved. I just try to keep my cons inside of the law."

"Did you inherit your affinity for Paul Bunyan shirts from your father, also?"

Gabe laughed, and Nicola found herself smiling at the sound.

"My Uncle Ben gives them to me for Christmas every year. It's his way of telling me that my wardrobe choices are too somber. I try to wear them whenever I visit him. I was on my way to see him yesterday when Father Mike called me and I headed to the church instead."

"This place is close to St. Francis Church?"

"It's about thirty minutes closer to the city. Uncle Ben lived in my mother's home until a year ago when he started having to use an oxygen tank. Then he announced he was moving out to this assisted-living home. The Eyrie. He's always been a gourmet cook, and he decided that if the oxygen tank was going to interfere with his ability to be creative in the kitchen, he was not going to give up eating gourmet food. I try to get out here when I can to share a meal with him."

"You think he might know something about this Bedelia Bisset."

"He might know if my father knew her."

Then she asked the question that had been in her mind ever since she'd found the information on the attempted theft of the Cézanne. "Are you going to be all right with what we find out about this?"

He glanced at her. "Yeah. I don't believe that my father had anything to do with that failed robbery at the art museum. If he had, they would have gotten away with it."

She said nothing.

"I don't believe he stole the Matisse that your father discovered when he searched my mother's studio. I think he was framed."

Framed. Nicola said nothing in reply, but she felt that tingle again. *Framed.* She turned the idea over in her mind as they drove farther into the mountains.

On the one hand, she could understand the unconditional belief in a loved one that would cause a boy of thirteen to insist on his father's innocence. But Gabe wasn't a boy anymore. He was smart, savvy—nobody's fool. And he had to have a very clear idea of what his father had been and what Raphael Wilder was capable of since he'd inherited some of those skills and honed them.

She put a hand to her stomach where the tingle was growing stronger. What if it wasn't wishful thinking or blind loyalty that made him so certain that his father had been framed? What if he was right?

And if Raphael Wilder had been framed for the theft of the Matisse, that might add another piece to the puzzle they were trying to solve now.

"Theoretically, how did they do it? Frame your father, I mean."

The look that he shot her held surprise. As he shifted his gaze back to the road, he said, "Your father's office received an anonymous tip telling them to check the Matisse at the museum in San Francisco. When they did, they discovered it was a fake and my father's initials were in the lower right-hand corner."

"The initials could have been forged."

"Yes. But the fact that they were there got your father the search warrant. And they found the real painting in my mother's art studio tucked behind some of hers. My father hadn't been able to bring himself to sort through any of her things yet."

"Did they discover when the Matisse was actually stolen from the San Francisco museum?"

"No. Whoever did it was good. The FBI's best guess was that the robbery might have taken place over a year earlier during Easter weekend when there'd been a small glitch discovered in the security system. But nothing had appeared to be missing. It might have been years before the theft was discovered—if not for the anonymous tip."

Nicola thought about that as Gabe made a right onto a drive lined with trees. A sign to their left read *The Eyrie*. "But your father never named anyone as a possible informant?"

Slowing to a stop in front of a long porch, Gabe shook his head. "Your dad let me read the file including all the transcripts of interviews with my father. He claimed to have no idea who might have called in the tip."

She turned to face him then. "No wonder you believe your father was framed. So do I."

He studied her for a moment. "Why?"

"Because it doesn't add up. If your father had stolen that painting, he wouldn't have brought it to your house. He especially wouldn't have hidden it among your mother's paintings."

"Your dad's theory was that he might have taken it before he'd promised my mother that he would give up his old life, and he was stuck with the painting. Maybe he was even planning on returning it."

Nicola couldn't help but wonder if her father had really

considered those possibilities or if he'd described them to comfort a thirteen-year-old boy.

"Or he was waiting for a certain time to pass after her death to go back to his old way of life," Gabe continued. "I don't believe that, but I can't prove it."

"If we find out who really stole that Matisse, maybe we can."

Gabe framed her face in his hands. He couldn't have named the emotions that she'd unleashed inside of him. The simple belief in her eyes and in her tone soothed away something that he hadn't even been aware of. "Thanks."

"For what?"

"For believing in my father."

"No. I believe in you. And the evidence. I researched Raphael Wilder. I read the file they had on him at Interpol. I find it hard to believe that someone with his reputation and skill would hide that painting where it might incriminate him. How hard would it have been for someone to plant it in your mother's studio?"

"Not hard at all if we're talking about the same person who got it out of the museum."

"It's connected to what's going on now. It's just got to be. Somehow. That Matisse had to be worth a bundle. If we're right, someone gave up a small fortune to put your father behind bars. And I think they're trying to do the same thing to you."

If we're right. The words sent a new flood of feelings through him. "I knew I needed fresh eyes on this." He leaned toward her then and brushed the merest hint of a kiss over her lips. "But I was wrong about that. What I needed was *your* eyes."

Her hands moved to his shoulders. His were still framing her face. And he was losing himself in her again. He watched her eyes darken, and in their depths he saw himself. Trapped. Hadn't he known he would be from the first time he'd looked into them?

Lord, he wanted to touch her. It seemed like forever since he had. His hands recalled the feel of her, the warmth of that skin, the silken texture. And his mouth recalled her taste, that mix of sweet and pungent flavors. And if he took her mouth now...

Just thinking about it had his whole body tightening because he knew now what her response would be—wild, free. And when her body was pressed fully to his, there would be that total yielding. That complete surrender. Then the world that was already dimming would slip entirely away.

He could feel her breath on his skin, feel it slip between his lips. It was his. She could be his. All he had to do was close that small distance.

The only thing that kept him from moving was the realization that if he did kiss her, he'd need more. And he might not be able to stop himself from taking more. His batting average in that direction was not good.

With a sigh, he leaned his forehead against hers. "I want to kiss you but I'm going to have to give you a rain check. Uncle Ben is waiting. We need a better place. A better time."

The breath she drew in and let out was nearly his undoing. "Rain check accepted. But finding that better place certainly hasn't been a priority for either one of us so far."

The hint of dryness in her tone had his lips curving. He drew back then and found the strength to drop his hands. "I'm going to have to put more effort into that."

THE EYRIE ASSISTED-LIVING facility lived up to its name. Like an eagle's nest, it was nestled right into the mountain.

The atrium boasted a lofty skylight and a glass wall that offered a stunning view of the surrounding mountains.

To Nicola, it resembled the lobby of a busy five-star hotel. One of the residents sat in a wheelchair in front of an easel. Others relaxed on leather couches reading books. Three corridors branched out from the circular space and at its center stood a white piano that might have made Liberace jealous.

"Uncle Ben." Gabe led her toward a tall man who was surrounded by women. When he turned and walked in their direction, Nicola could see why. Gabe's uncle was definitely a female magnet. He resembled Sean Connery, she decided. His height, his athletic body and his killer good looks were a stunning combination. And the oxygen tank didn't seem to slow him down any. It was one of those portable ones that he could carry over his shoulder.

The two men went into an easy, masculine embrace the moment that Bennett Carter reached them.

When they separated, Bennett let his hand remain on Gabe's shoulder for a moment. "You missed poker night last night. I'm assuming that whatever prevented your presence is connected to the Band-Aid on your forehead and that story in the paper this morning."

"Correct. It's fine. I'm fine. I'll fill you in on all the details after we eat. I want you to meet Nicola Guthrie. FBI special agent Nicola Guthrie."

Bennett took her hand and grasped it warmly. "He knows that I'm easily distracted by a beautiful woman. Is he fine?"

She smiled at him. "Very."

As he led the way into the dining room, he said to Gabe, "When I got your text, I reserved a table with a view and some privacy."

While they browsed the menu and made their decisions,

the two men talked on general topics. Nicola had ample time to study them. In spite of the age difference, which Nicola guessed to be about fifty years, there was an easy camaraderie between them that spoke of long acquaintanceship and family.

"Have you been back to the house lately?" Bennett asked.

Gabe picked up a roll, broke it and offered him a piece. "Too busy. Who would I visit at the house now that you're gone? Do you miss it?"

Bennett shifted his gaze to her. "He asks me that every time he comes here. And every once in a while, I do miss the peace and quiet." He winked at her. "But this place offers a lot of social networking possibilities."

"And Uncle Ben engineers most of them," Gabe commented.

As they continued to chat, Nicola turned her attention to the food, which had just arrived—a delicious tuna Niçoise that Bennett had highly recommended. Gabe had been right about it being fabulous, and Bennett had been right about the view. Through the wide glass window, the hills were crisscrossed by narrow, flat valleys. Patches of snow lay thick on the peaks and still blanketed the treetops in the green forests. The conversation lingered on general topics until the waitress brought their coffee.

As soon as she'd filled their cups, Bennett said, "How about those details now?"

Gabe filled him in on what had happened at the church the night before and everything they'd discovered since then. This time he left nothing out.

Bennett lifted his cup and sipped his coffee. "You want to know about Bedelia Bisset. That was the name in the newspaper coverage of the attempted robbery of the museum, but I knew her as Dee Atherton."

"Dee could be short for Bedelia," Nicola said. Digging into her purse, she pulled out the plastic bag that contained the bracelet she'd taken from the hospital. "The charm has the initials, D.A. Do you recognize it?" she asked as she tipped it onto the table.

Bennett picked it up and studied it. "Dee Atherton wore a bracelet like this. She told your father that her partner had given it to her."

"My father knew her?" Gabe asked.

"She worked with your father once in Paris, shortly after you were born. Your mother had already taken you back to Denver. Dee was very young, barely out of her teens, and she was very good at breaking through locks, safes, any kind of security. You name it, and she could get through it. Your father thought she had a real feel for it." Bennett met Gabe's eyes. "The same kind that you have. Except that you've used your talent on the other side of the law. Your father never worked with her again. He said she was impulsive, cocky, that she liked the rush almost as much as she liked to bag the prize. Your father, as much as he loved the game, was a meticulous planner, and something had almost gone very wrong during the job, something she hadn't warned him about."

Bennett raised his hands and then dropped them again. "I don't have any more details than that about Paris, but we ran into her four or five years later in Venice. She had hooked up with a new partner—an Italian, I think, and a very good forger. That was the first time I saw her wearing the bracelet."

Bennett sipped coffee before he continued. "She tried to convince your father to work with them. He turned her down."

Gabe studied his uncle for a moment. "What else?"

"She came to see your father again about a month before

the attempt at the Denver Art Museum. That would have been more than five or six years since we'd run into her in Venice. He spoke to her in your mother's studio. About a week later, she came back again, and she was carrying a long tube."

"Blueprints," Gabe said.

"That was my guess, too. It wasn't until the papers carried the story of her death that your father told me she'd come to ask him to help her steal one of the Cézannes from the collection. I'd surmised something like that. But he'd refused."

Bennett reached out and covered one of Gabe's hands with his. "He'd refused. He wasn't a part of it. He said he'd sent her away without looking at the blueprints. But he felt guilty about her death."

Gabe picked up the bracelet. "When I first saw this, it looked familiar to me."

"Makes sense," Bennett said. "After your mother died, you spent as much time as you could with your father in the studio. You may have seen her one of the times she came."

"There's more," Gabe said as he handed the bracelet back to Nicola. "I just can't remember it. Maybe I don't want to remember it."

Nicola studied Bennett for a moment, then asked, "Do you think Raphael Wilder stole the Matisse?"

Bennett hesitated.

Gabe covered one of Bennett's hands. "Uncle Ben isn't as sure about my father's innocence as I am."

Bennett met her eyes. "I'm not proud of the fact that I don't have as much faith in Raphael as Gabe does. And during that time frame when they believe the Matisse was stolen, Raphael was making some trips, tying up loose ends. What I do know is that he was determined to give up the life and settle down here. He loved Aurelia and Gabe very much."

"Uncle Ben thinks Dad might have stolen the Matisse as a last fling," Gabe said.

"He always denied it," Bennett said.

"It's all right," Gabe assured him. "I've always been the only one who believed in his innocence until I met Nicola here."

"Ah." Bennett reached for her hand then and gave it a squeeze.

"I have a question for you," Nicola said. "Why did Raphael take up sculpture?"

"That's an easy one. Aurelia, Gabe's mother, suggested it to him. She knew him very well. More than any of us, she realized what it would cost him not to go back to his old life. And he'd evidently toyed with sculpting while they were together in Paris. The next thing I knew he was ordering chunks of marble shipped over from Italy."

"Do you have any idea why he started with the St. Francis?"

Bennett shook his head. "I can't help you there."

Gabe took out his phone. "Jonah has something." He pushed a button, scanned a text. "Bedelia Bisset is an alias for Dee Atherton—Interpol's file on her lists her under both names. And he's sending a picture."

When he pressed the button, Nicola could see from his face that they had something. "What is it?"

"It's coming back to me. The memory has been tugging at me ever since we were at the hospital. I did see her when she came to the studio. And both times, my dad sent me out into the garden to play."

Gabe turned his cell so that both Bennett and she could see the picture Jonah had sent.

"That's Dee Atherton," Bennett said. "I'd swear that's her."

Nicola just stared at the image. Though she appeared to be older in the picture, Dee Atherton/Bedelia Bisset was a dead ringer for the young woman she'd shot—the woman who now lay in a coma at St. Vincent's.

12

AN HOUR AND A HALF LATER, Gabe drove through the gates of Thorne Mansion just in time for Nicola's fitting with Randolph Meyer. They'd spent most of the drive back to the city trying to process the information that Bedelia Bisset/Dee Atherton and Claire Forlani had to be related. That certainly would explain why they looked so much alike and why the younger woman had been wearing the older woman's bracelet. He'd already texted Jonah to start looking for a connection between Dee Atherton and an Italian in Venice, perhaps named Forlani.

The difference in age along with the resemblance and the bracelet argued that they were mother and daughter. Nicola had pointed out that they couldn't discount aunt and niece.

The call from her stepmother to remind her again of the fitting appointment for her dress had come just as they'd left The Eyrie. Nicola had been in the middle of making an excuse when she'd broken off, listened for a minute and then said, "Fine. We'll be there."

Her voice had been smooth, but he'd noted that her knuckles had turned white on the cell as she replaced it in her purse. Then she'd told him that her father was at the house and wanted to talk to him. She'd been frowning ever since.

"I take it that you aren't happy about the fitting," he said as he parked the truck in front of the sprawling front porch.

"I don't need another fitting. I just had one with Randolph last week. The dress is fine."

Turning in the seat, he took her hand and raised it to his lips. "It's more than the fitting. Tell me."

There was a mix of anger and hurt in her eyes when they met his. "It's the whole dichotomy between what I want to be and what they want me to be. Marcia wants me to marry well, step into her shoes one day, and throw charity balls. So does my father. That's not what I want—or at least not all that I want."

"And this dress-fitting thing symbolizes that?"

Her laugh was dry and lacking in humor. "You might say that. I've had four fittings for this dress because Marcia thinks that Randolph Meyer is just the kind of young man I ought to be seeing socially. Oh, he may not come from money, but he's definitely making his mark here in Denver. And he's invited to all the right parties. In fact, Marcia told me earlier today that he will be joining our table at the ball tomorrow night."

"She's matchmaking." He noted a bitter, coppery taste in his mouth. Jealousy?

"Yes. If I marry someone local, then I'll stay here in Denver. In fact, if your friend Nash Fortune wasn't always flying hither and yon for the air force, I'm sure Marcia would get it into her head that we were soul mates. She already invited him for dinner once she learned that he was stationed at the Air Force Academy, and he'll be sitting at our table tomorrow night, too."

Gabe had arranged for Nash to come in for the ball.

The fact that he was stationed at the Air Force Academy in Colorado Springs made it easy. Gabe was depending on his old friend to help out with security. Jonah was still tying up some business so that he could get away.

"You and Nash," he mused. "I guess I'll just count my lucky stars that my friend puts a high value on serving our country." There had been sufficient annoyance in her tone when she'd spoken of the Meyer guy and Nash to ease the jealousy he was feeling. "But the matchmaking isn't all that's bothering you. Spill it, Curls."

She took a breath and let it out. "Marcia said that my father's there and wants to meet with you. While I'm having this totally unnecessary fitting appointment with Randolph, you and my father will be in his office sharing information on what you and he have discovered so far. I'll be left on the outside just as I was this morning."

He studied her for a moment. "If you don't like what's going to happen in there, change it."

She blinked at him.

He shrugged. "They both love you, Nicola. And you love them. You're smart. You know what they want. That's partly why you accepted the transfer to your father's office after you finished your training. Have you tried telling them exactly what *you* want?"

Nicola opened her mouth and then shut it. She thought of that this very morning when she'd wanted to burst in on the meeting her father was having with Gabe and demand that he include her. But she hadn't. She didn't like to make waves. Temper tantrums had never been her style. She'd always tried to just forge ahead and prove herself by her actions. But maybe there was a middle road.

"Okay." She nodded at Gabe. "Okay."

"That's my Curls." He leaned in for a quick, hard kiss. As if someone had pressed the dimmer button on a stage light, everything around Nicola faded. Fire leapt along her nerve endings. Pleasure swirled through her body. And suddenly, she was drowning in him, sinking down to a place where the air was so thick, she couldn't breathe. Didn't want to.

Even as a nagging little voice told her to pull back, she framed his face with her hands and absorbed the sharp angle of his cheekbones, the strength of his jaw. She heard a sound, but she couldn't make it out over the thundering of her heart.

In what dull, little-used corner of his mind had he thought he could make the kiss a quick one? Not happening—not while she could make lights explode in his head and heat swarm his system. He scraped his teeth along her lower lip, absorbing the softness and the ripe taste of her surrender. Maybe it was that particularly addictive flavor that had him coming back for more and not being able to pull away. Or maybe it was just *her*.

She made a sound in her throat that vibrated through him. He wanted to hear it again. Had to hear it again. Lord, he wanted to touch her. But he knew that if he did, he wouldn't be able to stop. Why had he parked smack in front of the house? If he'd just pulled over a little farther back down the drive, he could have—would have—

He pushed the button on her seat belt and was about to grip her shoulders and pull her across the console when she lifted her hands and gave him a shove—as hard as a couple of the blocks she'd thrown on the basketball court.

It took a second for his brain cells to click on, another for him to pull in a breath. For a moment neither of them said a word. It gave him some satisfaction that her eyes were as blurry as he suspected his own were.

"That's the one bad thing about this pickup. No backseat."

She drew in a shaky breath and inched just a little farther away from him. "It's the parking location that's really bad. I have a feeling that the front seat would have proved more than adequate if I couldn't feel Marcia's eyes on me."

Gabe glanced up at the windows, and he saw one of the curtains twitch. "I'll be damned."

"No." She sighed. "But I probably will be."

"Good call, Curls. How did you know?"

Her tone went dry. "I grew up here. Every time a date drove me home, Marcia was on duty at that very window."

He grinned at her as he gripped her chin. "Ready to face the music?"

"Yes. Yes, I am."

THERE WERE THREE PEOPLE waiting to greet them as Nicola strolled into the foyer of Thorne Mansion with Gabe just a step behind her. Nicola's father and stepmother were joined by Randolph Meyer. Marcia came forward first to embrace her in a hug.

"Anna is waiting in your old room to help you change into the dress."

"In a minute." Out of the corner of her eye, she caught her father signaling Gabe to follow him.

"Dad?"

Her father turned to her.

"Before I do the dress fitting thing, Gabe and I need to talk to you, and I'd like to see the security setup for tomorrow night."

"But Randolph's on a schedule," Marcia protested.

"It's fine," Randolph said. "I'm more than happy to wait."

"Thanks." Nicola shot him a smile before she and Gabe

followed her father up the staircase and along the hall that led to Thorne Mansion's Grand Salon.

Her father pressed numbers into a pad on the door.

"How many people have access to the code?" Nicola asked.

"Gabe, his assistant Debra Bancroft, your stepmother and I have the code. Yesterday, G. W. Securities added a thumbprint to the access protocol. Marcia's, mine and Gabe's. Debra saw to the installation as part of the walk-through."

Nick turned to Gabe. "Marcia said that Debra stopped by earlier just to check on everything again."

"That sounds like Debra," Gabe said. "I've given her a lot of responsibility for this job."

Nicola studied Gabe, but she couldn't read anything in his expression. "Thumbprints can be lifted."

He nodded as they stepped into the salon. "My father once told me that there isn't a security system in the world that can't be breached—given the time. That's why the thumbprint was added yesterday. Working around it may slow the thief down a bit."

"Only slow him down?" Nicola asked.

"As you said, thumbprints can be lifted, and if I were the thief, I'd assume that your stepmother would have access. I'd come with her thumbprint and perhaps your father's. But only if I intended to enter through this door."

Together they entered the room. It was long and narrow. Late-afternoon sunlight slanted through the windows and glinted off honey-toned parquet floors. As far as Nicola knew, the salon was only used for the Valentine's Day charity auction each year. It was sparsely furnished to allow a maximum number of guests. Cocktails would be served here from 6:00 to 8:00 to allow time for guests to view the Cézanne and place their bids. Then everyone would exit to the upstairs ballroom for dinner and dancing. Marcia would announce the painting's new owner at midnight.

The Cézanne hung on a wall directly across from the access door. It was completely enclosed in glass, and there was another keypad with a thumbprint component. Next to it was a small green light.

"The glass is shatterproof," Gabe said.

"But the keypad looks the same as the one on the door," Nicola commented. "With the code and the proper thumbprint, this shouldn't take the thief long."

"I agree."

"They still have to get out," Nick Guthrie said. "We'll have men on the room."

"He or she won't use the door to exit," Gabe said. "This house is a historic landmark. The blueprints are on file. Any thief worth his salt will know how to get in and out without using the door. And to maximize time, they'll create a distraction in another part of the house to deflect attention from this room."

"Are you saying that the thief will get away with stealing this painting?" Guthrie asked.

Gabe smiled. "No, I'm merely saying that at some time tomorrow night, the thief will stand this close to the painting—and he or she will believe they're home free."

Nicola narrowed her eyes on the keypad again. Then she pointed to the green light. "The access code and the thumbprint won't be enough. You've installed the same new security system on this that you installed on the statue of St. Francis."

"You've got good eyes, Curls."

"Well, I'll be damned." Nick Guthrie bent close to inspect the light. "When did you install that?"

"Last week shortly after the keypad was installed."

"You weren't here last week. I've had men watching

the house since the painting arrived and we authenticated it. None of our alarm systems have been breached. I've personally checked the painting each day."

"What kind of a security expert would I be if I couldn't get past my own systems?"

Nicola smiled at the perplexed expression on her father's face. "That's exactly why Gabe was my prime suspect."

"How WOULD YOU GET the painting out if you were the thief?" Guthrie had postponed asking that question until he'd escorted them into the room he used as his home office and gestured them into chairs. Gabe figured by that time, he'd had a chance to mull over what he'd just learned.

"I'd come in the way I actually did—through an old heating air duct—after I bypassed the alarm system on the house," Gabe said. "I considered using one of the windows, but that would have required more time."

Guthrie narrowed his eyes. "I didn't know you were a second-story expert."

Gabe merely shrugged. "In my business I need to be. And I've had since New Year's Eve to try to get into the mind of the thief. The problem is—the person they're re-lying on to get through all the security is not going to be with them tomorrow night. So they'll have to improvise. That's why I'm thinking they'll definitely need to create some kind of a distraction."

"You don't think they'll call the whole thing off."

"No. Nicola has discovered some interesting informa-tion about the Cézanne." He turned to her. "Why don't you update your father?"

She met her father's eyes. "I was right when I told you that Gabe was at the center of this. No, he's not the thief. But he or his father or both probably are the motivating factor in why these thefts are taking place now."

Gabe leaned back in his chair and listened to as neat and concise a report on a case as he'd ever heard. Starting with the young woman who'd approached his father nearly twenty-five years ago in Paris, she wove a narrative including the attempted theft of the Cézanne collection sixteen years ago and ending with the theft they were expecting to happen the following night.

They'd discussed how the dots might connect on their drive back from seeing his uncle, but hearing it told in chronological order helped Gabe to see it all more clearly.

When she finished, she opened her purse and placed the sketch of the young woman they thought to be Claire Forlani on her father's desk; they added the printout of the driver's license. Gabe brought up the photo of Dee Atherton that Jonah had sent him on his cell.

Guthrie studied them for a moment. "The resemblance is compelling."

"I have my friend Jonah tracing the younger one. He's looking for a birth certificate that somehow connects to the Italian Uncle Ben believes partnered with Dee Atherton in Venice. The dates would be right, and we might have a connection. At this point I have a young man I trust guarding Claire Forlani's room at the hospital. He has orders to call me with updates on her condition and with any news about visitors. If she wakes up, we'll pay her a visit. I haven't informed the hospital of her identity. At this point, I'm not sharing anything I don't have to with my employees or anyone else."

Guthrie nodded. "I don't want anyone in my office working on it, either."

Guthrie included both of them in his glance. "So the two of you think that the Cézanne being auctioned tomorrow night may have been the object all along?"

"Stealing the Cézanne is part of the object," Nicola said. "Framing Gabe for stealing it is also a goal."

Guthrie shifted his gaze to Gabe. "They're trying to get revenge because your father didn't help this Dee Atherton-slash-Bedelia Bisset steal a painting from the Robineaus' Cézanne collection, and as a result, she was killed while she was trying to do it with her partner. I can perhaps buy into that. But why didn't they just get revenge on your father? Why are they trying to frame you for these new thefts?"

"Because Gabe was a major reason why his father wouldn't help in that original robbery. Raphael Wilder came home to raise his son. He made a promise to Gabe's mother that he was out of the business. They could believe Gabe shares in the blame for Dee Atherton's death."

Guthrie shifted his gaze to the photos again, tapping his fingers on the desk. "I still don't understand why they didn't just get revenge at the time—on your father."

"Maybe they did," Nicola said.

They both turned to look at her. "Maybe they got revenge on him by framing him for the theft of the Matisse."

Guthrie frowned. "Raphael Wilder stole that painting."

"He never confessed," Nicola pointed out.

"The jails are filled with people who claim to be innocent."

When he rose and strode to the window, Nicola followed. "If you step back and look at the whole picture, you have to admit it makes sense."

He turned to face her. "Then why didn't Raphael Wilder just tell me?"

There were several beats of silence while they thought about that. Gabe studied the two of them standing toe to toe, frowning at each other. They were very much alike.

Finally, he said, "Maybe my father didn't know who was framing him. If you think about it, the whole plan hinged on him not knowing. That way he had no way to defend himself."

"Pretty perfect," Nicola mused. "And cold. And that coldness is exactly what it would take to wait this long to get revenge on Gabe."

Guthrie ran a hand through his hair. But he kept his eyes on Nicola. Gabe could tell his old friend still wasn't buying it, not totally.

"Okay." Nicola waved a hand. "Take my theory about the Matisse being a part of this off the table for now. Let's just concentrate on what we know for sure. Dee Atherton comes to Raphael Wilder for help or advice on her upcoming job to rob the Denver Art Museum. He refuses to help, and she's killed. Her partner gets away."

"And he waits sixteen years to get revenge on Gabe?" Guthrie asked. "Why? And don't just give me that stuff about revenge being a dish best served cold."

For a moment, Nicola merely continued to frown, considering the question. Gabe waited for her to think it through and knew the instant she had it.

"Couple of reasons. Sixteen years ago, Gabe was just a kid. There's more to take away, more to destroy now. And Dee Atherton's partner was a forger. Dee was the one who could disable security systems." She glanced from Gabe to her father. "Perhaps the thief discovered at some point that Claire Forlani had inherited Dee's talents and then had to wait for her to grow up in order to fully take revenge. He may even have kept in contact with Claire over the years."

"I'll have Jonah check into that," Gabe said.

"Dammit," Guthrie said. "You're beginning to make sense." He turned to Gabe. "We need to find out who Dee

Atherton's partner was. I'll call Interpol, see if I can find out anything through channels."

Guthrie returned to his desk and sat down. Then he gestured Nicola back into her chair. "I've got something to report although it isn't nearly as dramatic. A statue of St. Francis was one of the artifacts that the FBI confiscated from your mother's art studio when we executed the original search warrant. It was signed out earlier this week a day after the article on the statue ran in the Sunday magazine section."

"By whom?"

"The name on the sign-out sheet was Mary Thomas. The clerk described a woman who might be Mary and swears she presented Mary's I.D. The signature was in Mary's handwriting. I checked the sign-out sheet myself. She wasn't in the office at the time."

"Have you spoken with her about it?" Gabe asked.

"No. If she's involved in this, I don't want to give her any warning until we have proof. You've already rattled their cages."

"And it isn't proof. We already know that one member of the team is a good forger," Nicola pointed out.

"Or Mary could have lent her I.D. to someone who was her height and weight," Gabe said.

"But the fact that the statue was signed out just before the attempt on the St. Francis," Nicola said, "supports my idea that framing Gabe is a big part of this."

"It would also mean that there's someone involved who would know or have access to a list of what was taken in that original search. That's likely to be someone in my office," Guthrie said. "If not Mary, then someone else."

Gabe didn't argue with him. Neither did Nicola.

Guthrie's frown deepened. "I didn't head up the investigation of the attempt at the Denver museum, but I do know that this Bedelia Bisset-slash-Dee Atherton's partner got away clean. There wasn't even a whiff of who he was. It was a couple of rookies who arrived first on the scene and neither one of them got the license plate of the van. I'll access the files first thing in the morning. Discreetly."

"There's another wrinkle in this that we ought to tell you about," Gabe said. "In addition to the strong possibility that this group might include someone working for you or me, Nicola thinks that they may have someone with access to Denver's very elite social circle feeding them information."

Guthrie thought for a moment. "It makes sense." He rose then, paced to the window. "We're making progress, but I don't like it. I don't like it at all.

"Why not?" Nicola asked.

He turned back to face them. "If you're right and revenge is a key element, and this elaborate plot was triggered by the death of Dee Atherton, aka Bedelia Bisset, then history is repeating itself in a way."

"What do you mean?" Nicola asked.

"Sixteen years ago, a woman was shot and killed during a failed attempt to steal the Cézanne collection," Nick Guthrie said. "Yesterday, you shot a young woman we believe is involved in planning and executing another attempt to steal one of those same Cézannes and she's currently in an intensive care unit."

Nicola swallowed hard. "If Claire Forlani doesn't pull through, then she, too, will have been fatally injured in a failed robbery."

"Exactly," Guthrie said. "If she's related to Dee Atherton and you're right about the fact that the mastermind behind this is hell-bent on punishing Gabe, then stealing the Cézanne tomorrow night may take second place to revenge. Both of you may be in mortal danger."

"THE DRESS IS PERFECT," Marcia said. "And it's so right for Valentine's Day. Randolph has such a good eye. Red is your color. Turn around so that you can see it from all angles."

Red, schmed. But Nicola didn't say the words out loud. The last place she wanted to be was closeted with Marcia in her room trying on a dress. She wanted to be with her father and Gabe so that they could bounce more ideas off one another. Her mind was spinning with possibilities. The whole series of thefts was beginning to remind her of an onion. Each time they peeled back a layer, there was more.

How much more? That was what they had to find out.

"Of course, you'll have to fix your hair. Smooth it back or better still, just let your curls frame your face."

Nicola bit down on her lower lip. Discussing her hairstyle was not going to get her downstairs any sooner. At least when Marcia had entered the library to drag her away, she'd first shooed the two men into the salon to share tea with Randolph Meyer. Her gut told her that her father's analysis was dead-on. Guarding the Cézanne wasn't the only problem they would have at the charity ball tomorrow night.

And that meant that the sooner they could get a handle on who they were dealing with, the better. "Randolph designs for a lot of your friends, doesn't he?"

"I've been recommending him to everyone. I like to do that when I see a young person who needs a helping hand. But I can't take full credit for the way he's caught on. I recommended him to Betsy Langford last summer, and she passed his name on to as many people as I have. Maybe more. She's very close friends with the Glastons. Randolph's designing several dresses for the ball, including Mariah Bailey's, and she only shops in New York or L.A.

But Randolph is catching on with everyone. Mary Thomas has been a fan of his for quite some time. And this afternoon when Debra Bancroft stopped by, she and Randolph discussed some of the changes he's made for her dress for the ball. She's working security, but she has to blend in."

Nicola felt her pulse actually skip a beat. Randolph had been in every single house the thieves had hit or intended to hit. Plus, he'd designed dresses for two of the people who were on the possible suspect list. She needed to talk to Gabe. "You're right, Marcia. The dress *is* perfect." She turned back to face the mirror. "Can you help me with the zipper?"

"You haven't even looked at it," Marcia said. "And Randolph will want to see it on you before he leaves. That was why he delivered it in person."

Biting back an inward sigh, Nicola faced the mirror again. And since she would have to fake it anyway, she really did look at the dress. It was the simplicity of the sketch Randolph had shown her that had appealed to her from the beginning. There was no doubt in her mind that he was a talented designer. From narrow straps at her shoulders, the material angled to a V neckline, then flowed smoothly along the lines of her body, stopping just above her knees.

"He's shortened it since the last fitting," she noted with a frown.

Marcia waved a hand. "That's because he noticed your legs. The benefit of working with a designer is that he tailors the clothes to your strengths."

Nicola gave the dress a second sweep with her gaze. As a child, Marcia had dressed her in ruffles and ribbons and pink had been her signature color. Probably as a result of that, Nicola tended to favor conservative tailoring and colors in her work wardrobe, and slacks were more practical than skirts.

While the dress couldn't be called flashy, it went a few steps beyond conservative. In her mind, she'd pictured it in black. Randolph was the one who'd decided that red would suit her better. And she supposed it did. Turning, she angled her head just enough to see that the hemline wasn't the only thing the designer had altered. He'd definitely lowered the back and taken in a couple of seams. It was a far cry from the party or prom dresses of her younger years.

And it made her think of Gabe. She definitely didn't look like an FBI agent in the dress. And she didn't feel like one either. She felt like a woman.

And the giddy idea of wanting Gabe to see her in a sexy red dress was the last thing she should be thinking about.

"I have a confession to make," Marcia said.

At her tone, Nicola turned to face her and was surprised at the sheepish expression on her stepmother's face. "What is it?"

"When I invited Randolph to sit at our table tomorrow night, I was hoping that you and he would hit it off. He seems so right for you. He loves art, you know. Last night, he couldn't stop talking about the Cézanne. He went to college with Celia Robineau, so he's familiar with the painting. I was so sure that you and he would hit it off."

Nicola smiled wryly as she took her stepmother's hands in hers. "I know why you invited Randolph to sit with us. You invited Nash Fortune to dinner for the same reason. You want to match me up with someone."

"It's that obvious?"

Nicola leaned in to give her stepmother a quick kiss on her cheek. Then she thought of Gabe's advice. "What's obvious is that you want me to be happy. I am. And I will be. It just may not be your vision of how I should be happy."

"But I never once thought of Gabe. I should have."

Nicola stared at her stepmother. "Gabe and I are working together on these robberies. We aren't…" What exactly weren't they? "It's not what you think…we're not…"

Taking her hand, Marcia drew her toward the door. "Nicola, I saw the way the two of you were kissing in the truck. You're definitely on to something. Your father has always had a special fondness for that boy. How long have you been seeing each other?"

"We haven't. I mean…" Less than twenty-four hours if she didn't count those Saturdays on the basketball court at the St. Francis Center.

Marcia patted her hand. "I was the same way when I first met your father. I couldn't seem to catch enough breath to get a complete sentence out. You'll get used to it."

No, Nicola thought as Marcia steered her out of the room. She was pretty sure that she wasn't going to ever get used to it. She didn't even know what "it" was.

13

When Nicola entered the salon with her stepmother, Gabe completely lost his train of thought. Tea sloshed over the rim of his cup onto his saucer. She was stunning. Had he ever thought of her as beautiful before? Attractive—very. Sexy—definitely. But in the red dress, she was breathtaking. It was simple, but it clung to every curve as if it had been designed specifically with her in mind.

And, of course it had been. Perhaps it was the lingering trace of jealousy that had his brain cells clicking on again. In any case it helped to shift his gaze from Nicola to the tall blond man with the athletic body and Hollywood handsome features. Randolph Meyer had taken Nicola's hand the instant she'd entered and he'd drawn the two women to the far end of the salon where a circle of bay windows let in the late-afternoon sunlight. The three of them were oohing and ahhing over the dress as if it were a work of art.

For Gabe it was the woman who made the dress and not the other way around.

"What exactly is your relationship with my daughter?"

Gabe spilled more tea. The question was not only unexpected, it made his stomach lurch.

Nick Guthrie took the cup from his hand and placed it on a nearby table.

"She and I are…" What? Lovers? That was a hell of a thing to tell her father. And wasn't this a big part of why he'd avoided Nicola for three long months?

"We're—" he began again and got no further. Seeing each other? Dating? Neither of those descriptions quite fit.

"I saw you kissing her in the truck when you drove up. All of us did."

"All?" Gabe turned to look at Guthrie then.

"Randolph, Marcia and I. We were all in the window when you drove up. The curtains are sheer."

"Sorry. I forgot where we were."

Guthrie set his own tea down. "How long have we worked together?"

Wary of the shift in topic, Gabe studied the older man. Then he said, "You called me in the first time to consult on a case six years ago. A safe deposit box that you wanted opened and you didn't want to destroy the evidence you expected to find inside."

Guthrie nodded. "See, you remembered that all right. In fact, I've never known you to forget anything. I'm going to try again. What is your relationship with my daughter?"

Gabe shifted his gaze to Nicola, then back to her father. "I'm trying to figure it out."

Guthrie studied him for a moment and for some reason Gabe couldn't fathom, he seemed satisfied with the answer. "The problem is, until you do figure it out, it's distracting you."

Gabe couldn't argue with that.

"Will it interfere with your keeping her safe?"

"No. I'll keep her safe." He kept his eyes steady on Guthrie's. "And I'll have help on that score. She's smart. We wouldn't have as much as we have right now if it weren't for her. And she's pretty good at keeping herself safe."

Guthrie glanced at Nicola and then back at Gabe. "I'll have to put my trust in both of you then."

The two women and Randolph Meyer chose that moment to start toward them. Guthrie spoke in a voice only Gabe could hear. "When this is over, I'm going to ask my question again. You'd better have it figured out by then."

BECAUSE IT WAS MUCH EASIER to think about the case than the look she'd seen in Gabe's eyes when she'd modeled the red dress, or the unsettling conversation she'd had with her stepmother, the moment that they'd made their escape from Thorne Mansion, Nicola filled Gabe in on what she'd learned about Randolph Meyer. "If Mary Thomas or Debra Bancroft are involved in these thefts, he could have provided very useful information to them."

"But you don't think he's the mastermind."

"Too young. I think that the person behind all of this has to be Dee Atherton's old partner—someone Dee might have told about your mother's studio and who might even have seen that statue of St. Francis you and your father worked on."

"Not a bad thought, Curls. If my memory is correct, we were working on that statue during the time when Dee visited my father."

"I think we ought to pay Father Mike a visit."

At Gabe's questioning glance, she said, "You said that one of the places you and your father spent time during that summer was at the St. Francis Center. You met Jonah and Nash and played with them while your father sat in the garden talking to Father Mike."

"And you're interested in what they might have talked about."

"Yes. He might have confided in a priest, things that he might not have told even your Uncle Ben."

Gabe dialed a number, pinned down the location of the priest, and twenty minutes later they knocked on the front door of the Franciscan monastery where Father Mike now lived. It was a huge building, Gothic in design.

"How much do you trust Father Mike?" she asked while they waited.

"He'd be right in there with Jonah and Nash, your father and you. Just what are you going to ask him?"

"Not sure yet. Just checking my parameters."

"You have none," Gabe said.

The door opened then and Father Mike beamed a smile at them, then led the way into a library.

The priest gestured them onto a sofa and took one of the chairs facing them. In front of him on a low table sat a crystal decanter and three glasses. "Would you care for some sherry? If you say yes, then I won't feel guilty about having one myself."

"Then yes," Nicola said. "It's been a long day."

When he'd poured the wine and handed out the glasses, he sat back in his chair and sipped. "You said you had some questions?"

Gabe gave her an *after you* gesture.

"The summer before Raphael Wilder was arrested, he brought Gabe to the center to play basketball with Jonah and Nash. And he spent time with you talking. We'd like to ask about those conversations if we could. If they're not protected by the seal of confession?"

Father Mike smiled at her. "Raphael wasn't Catholic. So I was never his priest in that sense. What would you like to know?"

"Do you know why he decided to sculpt a statue of St. Francis in marble?" Nicola asked.

Surprise and pleasure lit the priest's features. "I didn't know that he had. Was it a good likeness?"

"Nearly perfect," she said.

"He let me help him work on it." Gabe sipped his sherry before setting the glass on the table.

"I did know that he had decided to try his talent at sculpting," Father Mike said. "Your mother had suggested it. He was a talented painter, and she wanted him to find a new challenge. She was concerned that Denver might become a bit boring."

"Was he worried about that, too?" Gabe asked.

"A little. But your father was a resilient man. He loved you and your mother very much. If he had regrets about leaving his old way of life, it was that he hadn't left it sooner. I'd love to see the statue."

"I can arrange that," Gabe said.

Nicola studied the two men as Gabe went on to explain where they'd found the statue and that this wasn't the first time the thief had left a forgery in place of the art he'd stolen.

"Leaving a forgery behind—your mother told me that was what your father had always done," Father Mike said.

Nicola reached out and took Gabe's hand. "If the thief had succeeded last night in making the switch, I think Gabe would be in jail right now. Did he ever mention a woman named Dee Atherton or Bedelia Bisset?"

Father Mike frowned thoughtfully. "You're talking about that woman who was killed during the attempted robbery on the Denver Art museum. Your father called her Dee. She was the original reason why Raphael sought me out. He felt guilty about her death. He said he'd worked with her before, and she'd come to him twice here in Denver to ask for advice."

Father Mike set his glass on the table. "He refused both times and explained why he couldn't because of promises he'd made. He told her not to come again."

"He felt guilty because he hadn't helped her?" Gabe asked.

"Yes. She'd put him in a difficult position. If he'd helped her, he'd have broken a vow he'd made to your mother. But afterward, he couldn't help thinking that if he'd listened and given her advice, she might not have died. And, of course, the guilt only grew when he received the note."

"The note?" Gabe asked.

Father Mike nodded. "He received a threatening note a week after the woman was shot. It said, *You're to blame. You'll pay.* When he showed it to me, I told him to give it to the police."

"He didn't?" Nicola felt Gabe's hand fist beneath hers.

Father Mike shook his head. "He refused. They'd already questioned him about the attempt on the museum. He figured that if he showed them the note, there wasn't much chance they'd take it seriously. They might even take a harder look at him. He didn't have much use for the police. Then nothing happened."

"Until the Matisse was discovered in Gabe's mother's studio," Nicola said.

Father Mike narrowed his eyes. "You think that's connected to Dee Atherton's death?"

"She does," Gabe said. "And she's beginning to convince me she might be right."

"Interesting." Father Mike said nothing for a moment as he sipped his sherry. "St. Francis works in mysterious ways."

"How so?" Nicola prompted.

But it was Gabe he looked at when he spoke. "The real reason your father first brought you to the center was so that he could say a prayer to St. Francis. Your mother had told him about the statue's power. His prayer was that he wouldn't fail you or her. I've never believed that he did."

"WE'LL HEAD TO YOUR place next," Gabe said as he drove the truck away from the monastery. "You can pack what you need." He shot her a glance. "I promised your father that I would protect you, and my place has better security."

"I can hardly argue with that. My apartment isn't far. Take a right at the next light."

After making the turn, Gabe said, "Thanks."

"For what?"

"You did a great job of questioning Father Mike. I'd never thought to ask those questions before."

"You weren't so bad yourself."

He shot her a glance. "Looking back, I can see my faith in my father was mostly denial. I didn't want to look too closely at what had led to his arrest because I was probably afraid of the answers."

"You were the one who said he was framed. You're the one who started me thinking how that fact might shift the perspective on everything about this case."

"But I didn't pursue trying to prove his innocence at the time. Or since."

"You were thirteen. You'd lost your mother, but you had your father. A man who'd promised to stay with you, a man who'd only shared holidays with you so far. Then two months after he was sentenced, he was taken away also. And you're beating up on yourself because you didn't turn into a supersleuth and clear your dad? Instead, you kept your promise to him. You built a career, a life where you stop people from doing what he did."

The passion in her voice had something inside of Gabe easing. She had an ability to do that for him—to smooth away hurts that he hadn't even known were there.

"For what it's worth, the whole time that I was compiling research on this case, I never once questioned your father's guilt. Planting that Matisse was a perfect plan. And very cold. Most people who want revenge need for the victim of it to know. This person evidently doesn't need that. And he or she may just get away with it again."

"We're not going to let that happen."

They drove in silence for a few minutes. Then Nicola said, "Father Mike thinks the prayer-granting power of the statue is playing a key role in all of this."

"Yeah, I got that. I've certainly prayed to St. Francis a few times. And I have to admit I was hoping last night that the power of the statue would help me trap the thief."

"Take the next left," she directed. "Did you ever say a prayer to it back when you were at the center?"

"Sure. Father Mike made Jonah, Nash and me all say a prayer. It was the traditional prayer to St. Francis, the *Lord, Make Me an Instrument of Your Peace* prayer.

"Where there is darkness, let me sow light, where there is doubt, faith—is that the one?"

Gabe nodded. "But at the end he told us to add one more petition. He even told us what to pray for."

"What?"

"That we would find what we were supposed to find in life. Pretty general and pretty hard to figure out when or if he would answer it. I thought he had once I'd established G. W. Securities."

"And you don't think so now?"

He shrugged. "Lately, I've been…restless…thinking that there's something more."

"You could always give sculpting another whirl."

"Right. I'm pretty sure that's not the direction St. Francis is pushing me in." He glanced at her. "How about you? Did you ever say a prayer to the statue?"

"A couple."

"Have they come true?"

She turned to study him, recalling that long ago prayer she said when she was ten. "The last day I played basketball with you and my stepmother found out that's what I'd been doing, I prayed to St. Francis that I would see you again. I didn't think he'd answered me. But I guess he has."

"Father Mike used to tell us that prayers aren't always answered the way you expect them to be."

Nicola smiled. "There's a news bulletin. Oh, turn left on this next street. I live in the third building down on the right."

Gabe slowed in front of an old brick building, a renovated factory. Shops and restaurants were sprinkled along the street.

"I park in there." She pointed to a lot across the street and handed him her card to swipe.

"An underground garage would be safer," he said as he pulled into an empty slot.

"Then I'd be in an enclosed space. Here there are lights, traffic, a good chance of people strolling by. If I screamed, someone would hear me."

He got out of the truck and circled around to open her door.

"Besides, I have a doorman. Charlie keeps a pretty good eye on all of his residents." As they crossed the street, she pointed to the man standing behind glass doors and waving at her.

"You've given this speech before," he guessed.

"To both my mother and my father. Hi, Charlie," she said as they stepped into the building. "This is Gabe."

Charlie had a portly build and a friendly smile, but his gaze turned speculative when he looked at Gabe. "You'd be the one who sent the flowers? I sent the delivery man up and told him to leave them outside the door."

"Flowers?" They said the word in unison.

Charlie nodded. "For Valentine's Day. You have no idea how many deliveries there have been today. I couldn't keep up with all of them. When this guy came in with three huge vases, he asked if he could help out by taking them up. I checked the logo on the cards, and when I saw he was from the flower shop down the street, I sent him up. You'll find them right outside your door."

"Thanks, Charlie," Nicola said as she and Gabe stepped into the elevator. The instant the doors slid shut all the way, she pulled her gun out.

"Maybe they're from Randolph Meyer," Gabe said.

"Maybe."

"But you're not banking on it."

"I have a suspicious mind."

"I like the way it works." Gabe waited until the doors slid open again before he took his weapon out.

"You're armed," she noted in a barely audible voice.

"I run a security firm." He held up a hand and she listened with him. The muted rumble of a TV drifted from the far end of the hall. Otherwise, there was nothing. And there was no bouquet of flowers sitting in front of any door.

"Which one is yours?" Gabe whispered.

But she didn't have to give him an answer. The first one on their right was ajar. He moved to the far side; she took the near.

"Ready?" she mouthed.

At his nod, she booted the door open. He went in high, she low. Even as she scanned the debris, she knew there was no one there. Still she kept her gun raised, and Gabe covered her back as they checked the rest of the place out. She felt the rage and tamped down on it. Rage wasn't what she needed now.

The destruction had been thorough but selective. Nicola made a mental list of the damage as they moved through the rooms. It helped her focus. Her sofa had been slashed from end to end. So had the drapes.

And there in the middle of her coffee table was a huge arrangement of red roses and white lilies in a vase. Together, they moved past it to the kitchen. Her cereal and coffee grounds were scattered across the floor. Eggs had been tossed into the mix along with the contents of two bottles of soft drink and a wilted bunch of broccoli.

"Good thing I only keep the basics here," she said.

"Broccoli is basic?"

The question had some of the rage inside of her easing. "It fits into one of the essential food groups. I keep one in the fridge as a reminder."

"Ah."

It didn't escape her attention that he'd moved slightly in front of her since they'd entered, nor that he remained in that position and shielded her from the windows as they made their way to the bedroom. But there was no one here. Whoever had destroyed her apartment was long gone.

Her heart sank the moment she stepped around him to get a good look at her bed. She'd brought home a gallon of paint, intending to replace the bright yellow on the walls. The blue color she'd spent time selecting now decorated her mattress and a pile of clothes that had been pulled off hangers.

"You can get new clothes," Gabe said.

"Yeah."

He moved to check the bathroom. "Everything seems

fine in here. Nothing broken. He either got tired or ran out of time. Was anything taken?"

"I don't think so." *Nothing broken.* As she repeated the words in her mind, Nicola turned in the doorway and scanned the living room again. Her TV and stereo were fine. Her laptop untouched. No lamps overturned. "He didn't want to make any noise. I live on a street with shops and shoppers. Two or three hours ago, someone outside might have heard something."

"You'll have to add that detail to your spiel about the security here," he said as he joined her. "It definitely saved some of your things."

"Charlie may have been a surprise, too. He would have gotten suspicious if the delivery person had spent more time. And he may have a description. He has good eyes."

"What else do you see, Curls?"

She glanced back at the bedroom, then shifted her gaze back to the sofa. "Anger."

"I agree. Angry people make mistakes. Charlie may be able to describe him."

She allowed her eyes to settle on the flowers again. The arrangement screamed Valentine's Day, as did the large heart that dangled from a red ribbon. Gabe moved with her as she walked to the table. His fingers linked with her free hand when she reached for the heart.

Charlie had been right about the logo of the flower shop down the street. When she turned it over, she found the message card tucked into a pink lace pocket and pulled it out.

You're to blame. You'll pay.

A chill moved through her, but she also felt a tingle. "These are the same words as in the note your father received. This proves there's a connection between what's going on now and Dee Atherton's death."

"And whoever wrote them no longer cares if we put it together," Gabe said. "They want us to."

"Do you think they'll still go after the Cézanne?"

"Absolutely. That was the original goal and my father interfered with it by not participating, then Dee was shot. You've interfered in this one by shooting Claire."

She looked at him then. "You think my father is right—that stealing the Cézanne might not be only their goal anymore."

"I think we're no longer dealing with someone who will wait sixteen years to take their revenge."

14

TWO HOURS LATER, Nicola sat at the gleaming granite counter that framed Gabe's kitchen while he poured a dark red wine into two glasses. She'd had to file a police report, and while she'd answered questions for the two uniforms who'd responded to her initial call, Gabe had filled her father in.

It turned out that Charlie hadn't gotten a very good look at the delivery man's face because of all the flowers. He'd described a tall, lean man wearing black-framed glasses and a cap with a visor and ear flaps. It wasn't much to go on.

Gabe punched buttons on his microwave and set it humming.

"You don't cook at all, do you?" she asked.

He grinned as he set one of the glasses in front of her. "And you do?"

"It takes up time I'd rather spend doing other things."

"Exactly. That's what I always told Uncle Ben when he wanted to teach me." He placed a bowl of French bread on the counter between them. Then he lifted his glass, touched it to hers. "Here's to takeout and microwaves."

"And to state of the art wine coolers." She hadn't missed

the fact that he had one. As a highly trained FBI agent, she knew that people who invested in them tended to have very good taste in wine, and she wasn't disappointed when she sipped hers. The cabernet he'd selected was dark and rich and smooth.

"I forgot something," he murmured, setting his glass down. To her surprise, he located two candles and lit them. Then he moved to a wall and pressed a button. The muted sound of a bluesy sax floated into the room.

At her look, he said, "Just because I don't cook doesn't mean I don't know the elements of fine dining."

She laughed then. And though she couldn't explain it, some of the fear and anger that she'd been tamping down ever since she'd kicked in the door of her apartment eased.

She owed that to Gabe Wilder. He was taking care of her. Not in the hovering way that her parents often had. No, his technique was much more subtle. Back at the apartment, he'd never left her side while she'd called the police and reported the break-in. Earlier, when they'd first stepped out of the elevator on her floor, he hadn't tried to push her aside or go all protective male on her. She liked his style.

She wasn't used to it, but she was sure she could adjust to it. Quite easily.

And why did that scare her? Why did thinking about it tighten the knots in her stomach that had twisted there when she'd talked with her stepmother earlier?

"What is it, Curls?"

He'd reached to cover her hand with his just as the microwave binged. If it hadn't, she just might have told him. She might have simply asked the question. Where were they headed? She'd always known before. Sure, she might have taken some detours to please her parents. But with Gabe the territory was uncharted. Fear bubbled up again.

It wasn't the time to think about that. They needed to focus their attention on the case.

Mental list time. Once they'd caught the thieves and put them away, she'd deal with Gabe. She took another sip of her wine. She simply couldn't think about what she was going to do about him right now.

"I hope you like your chili hot."

"As long as it stops just short of cauterizing my vocal chords."

"You're my kind of girl." He was laughing when he turned back to her, but the moment he saw her, his laughter died. And he simply stared. There she was, sitting at his counter, sipping wine. And what he'd just said was true. As the realization struck him, he nearly dropped one of the bowls. She was exactly his kind of girl. It was that simple.

That terrifying.

He managed to get the chili to the counter and find spoons, napkins. When he sat on the stool across from hers, she met his eyes. There was a question in them, and he was pretty sure it was the same question that was hovering in his. He also saw a trace of fear. And he wanted more than anything to soothe it.

"You've got something on your mind. Why don't you just spill it, Curls?"

She frowned at him. "I wasn't looking for this. For you."

"Same goes," he said.

"And we don't have time for it. We have a thief to catch."

"I agree. But right this minute all we have to do is eat this chili and enjoy our wine."

She studied him for a moment. "Okay." Then she dug in. So did he.

He broke off a chunk of bread and handed it to her. "I'm sorry."

"For what?" She dunked a crust into the chili.

"For what happened to your things. I should have foreseen it."

She set the bread down and studied him. "Are you seriously thinking that you're somehow to blame for what happened at my apartment?"

He shrugged. "I should have put a guard on the place."

"You have two men guarding the St. Francis." She ticked that off on a finger. "Another one looking after Claire Forlani. And you're possibly running short of people who work for you that you can fully trust right now."

He picked her spoon up and handed it to her. "I have friends who don't work for me."

"Yeah." She shook the spoon at him. "One of them is digging up more information on Dee Atherton and Claire while we stuff our faces. And I imagine the air force intrudes on the other one's time."

"Besides Jonah and Nash."

She shook her head. "You have a problem, Wilder."

News bulletin there, he thought as he took another bite of chili.

"You're hung up on taking care of people."

He nearly choked.

"You've arranged things so that Father Mike can work in your Boys and Girls Club for as long as he wants. You've made sure that your Uncle Ben's social life is buzzing right along."

Gabe held up a hand. "Not guilty on that one. He does pretty well on his own."

"I don't doubt it. But besides a bevy of females surrounding him, he still has a poker night with the guys. And that's thanks to you."

"I like playing poker."

"And now you've taken me on. You persuaded my father to put me in the field by convincing him that I needed protection."

Gabe left that one alone. "From what I can sée, you take pretty good care of yourself." He lifted his wine and sipped it. "This whole thing started with you saving my life. So in the taking-care-of department, I think we're even. Are you finished with that?"

"No." She dug into her chili again as he took his bowl to the sink and rinsed it.

"I'm right about this. Your whole business, your career is devoted to protecting people and the things they love. I'd say that the prayer you said to St. Francis all those years ago was answered."

He sat down again at the counter and sipped his wine. "Any caregiver genes that I inherited came from my mom. I didn't realize it at the time, but she kept us together as a family. She made it so easy for my father to enter into our life when he came home on holidays. We used to mark off the days on the calendar until the next one. Then he'd arrive a few days ahead of time with presents and plans. We had celebration dinners. After a week or two, he'd leave."

"He came every holiday?"

"All of the major ones. Memorial Day, Fourth of July, Labor Day, Thanksgiving, Christmas. On Valentine's Day he always had a special dinner with my mom to celebrate their wedding anniversary."

She felt a tingle. "I've thought all along that there has to be a reason that this thief only strikes on holidays. There has to be a connection to your father. And he never worked on a holiday because he was always visiting you."

"What are you thinking?"

"The glitch in security in the San Francisco museum

when they thought the Matisse might have been stolen. It was on a holiday weekend, wasn't it?"

He narrowed his eyes. "Easter."

"If that's when the Matisse was stolen, it could very well mean that your father would have had an alibi for that robbery. He would have been with you. It's one more piece of evidence that we can look into."

"We'll do that," he said as he circled around the counter to join her. "But not right now."

He took her hands and lifted them one by one to kiss her palms. "You're not bad in the caregiving department yourself. I wanted fresh eyes on this case. Your eyes. You're helping me to think about things, to see things that I hadn't before."

"It's a two-way street."

"But I also wanted you, Nicola. I had very selfish motives when I convinced your father to assign you to me twenty-four-seven."

He leaned forward and brushed his lips across hers.

"I still want you." Just you.

Slipping her hands from his, she looped her arms around his neck. "I want you, too."

Forever? That was the question that hovered in the back of his mind, the question that he hadn't been able to acknowledge earlier.

They had now, he told himself as he took his mouth on a journey along her jaw to the soft skin beneath her ear. Now had always been enough for him. For a long time, it had been all that he had.

"Now," he murmured as he drew back.

"Now." She drew his mouth back to hers. But his lips remained soft and teasing on hers, sampling first one angle and then another. Her mouth offered darker riches, but he took his time. They hadn't had enough time yet, not nearly enough.

When she sighed, he slipped his tongue between her lips and sampled. There was the mellow flavor of the wine, the punch of the chili, and the heady, intoxicating taste of her. Gripping her hips, he lifted her off the stool and she wrapped arms and legs around him.

Heat flared immediately, and with it came the intense desire to lower her to the floor and take her right there. It would be so easy and it would finally ease the ache that was with him constantly now. But he wanted more this time. Tamping down on the need, he broke off the kiss and headed toward the stairs.

"Kiss me again," she murmured.

"First, I want you in my bed."

She nipped at his earlobe. "We haven't needed one yet."

"I need it."

"And I need a kiss."

"Be my guest."

She accepted his invitation, brushing her mouth over his and then tracing the shape of his lips with her tongue. He nearly stumbled when she nipped his bottom lip.

"I forgot I was dealing with an FBI agent."

"I'll try to be more gentle." She ran her tongue along his bottom lip to soothe the hurt, then pressed her mouth fully to his.

He did stumble then, nearly dropping to his knees on the top step of the staircase. He tasted hunger. His? Hers? It was so huge and filled him so completely that he forgot to breathe, forgot he needed to. When he drew back, his heart was pounding, his mind spinning, his vision hazy. He had to check and make sure where the bed was. And it took every ounce of his control to lay her on it and then settle himself at her side.

She reached for him, but he captured her wrists with one of his hands and held them above her head. "We have time, Curls. Let's take it. Do you know how long I've wanted you here in my bed?"

"No."

The moment he felt her wrists relax, he released them to run his fingers through her hair. "Ever since that day I saw you standing there in your office. I pictured you lying here with just the moonlight on your skin. And I thought of touching you."

She said nothing, merely watched him as he traced the curve of her cheek, the line of her jaw. But she began to tremble. And when he brushed a finger over the pulse at her throat it quickened. But he didn't dare kiss her again. Not yet.

"I wanted you naked from that first day." He began with her T-shirt, then her bra. It was plain and white and incredibly arousing. More arousing was the fact that each time his hands made contact with her skin, her breath caught and a new tremor moved through her.

"Your shoulders. So smooth and strong." He ran his hands lightly over them. Then he traced just the tip of his finger along the tops of both breasts. "And your skin is so soft right here."

And then because he simply couldn't help himself, he cupped each breast in his hands. "Just right." This time when she trembled, so did he.

As he fumbled with the clasp of her slacks, she tried to help him, but he brushed her hands away. Then he pleasured them both by drawing her slacks down her legs inch by inch and tracing the path of the flesh he exposed with his mouth. Her flavors, her scents, her textures enticed him, entranced him. And still his hunger for her grew.

He'd told her nothing but the truth. He'd dreamed of having her here in his bed from that very first time their eyes met. But he couldn't have known what the reality would be. There was so much to discover. Slowly, he eased her slacks down her legs, pausing to touch, then taste the newly exposed skin. Her pulse beat at the back of her knees. He lingered there to sample, to exploit. To savor. And her ankles—they were so slender and nearly as fragile as her wrists.

No, he couldn't possibly have imagined what the reality would be, nor what it would do to his system to hear her breath catch and release, catch and release.

How could he have known that in seducing her, she would so thoroughly seduce him?

She was sinking so fast. Her vision had blurred. Far away she could hear music. The sound thrummed quietly in her head as it blended with her sighs and the slowly quickening beat of her blood.

He'd showed her strength before. But this was different. Each brush of his finger, each scrape of his nail and flick of his tongue had her plunging deeper and deeper into a place where the air was too thick to breathe. Nothing had ever been like this. Pleasure had never been so intense. Needs had never been so huge. All she could feel was him. All she knew was him.

And then suddenly, he was gone.

"Gabe?" She opened her eyes and saw that he was getting out of his clothes. She held out a hand. "Come back. I want you. Now."

"First I need to do this." He knelt, straddling her as he stretched her arms out to the sides and linked his fingers with hers. Then he lowered his body to cover hers.

Finally they were flesh to flesh, eye to eye. Her fingers gripped his hard when he made a place for himself between her legs and she wrapped hers around him.

"Mine," she said.

"Mine," he agreed. Forever.

He slipped into her then and it was as if their bodies had never been apart. Though it took all of his control, he kept the rhythm slow. As he spun the moment out, the knowledge settled in his heart that this was where he belonged, where he wanted to be. And when her eyes clouded, when she arched against him and cried out, he was helpless to do anything but follow.

15

COFFEE.

Nicola firmly reminded herself of her goal when she stopped halfway down the circular staircase. She'd borrowed Gabe's robe and wrapped a towel turban-style around her hair. But she was tempted to discard both and go back up to the bathroom and jump Gabe. He was shaving. But he'd distracted her when she was showering, and turnabout was fair play.

Coffee, first. She glanced at her watch—nearly 9:00 a.m. She usually had her first shot of caffeine at 6:00 a.m. And they had a job to do. It was the practical Nicola who descended the rest of the stairs. But it was a different Nicola who did a little dance step on her way to the one-cup coffeemaker she's spotted among the gadgets on Gabe's counter.

As she made the coffee, she caught herself humming. And she *never* hummed. Nor did she begin her days with little dance steps. But she'd never before spent a night like the one she'd spent with Gabe.

A girl had to celebrate some way.

She was about to take her first sip when she caught the movement out of the corner of her eye. Then she nearly dropped her mug as two men stepped out of the elevator and into the room.

For an instant, all three of them froze as if someone had pushed the Pause button.

The only thing that got her heart pumping again was that she recognized one of them. Nash Fortune. It was little wonder that the man had been Marcia's selection as bachelor number one. In addition to a healthy inheritance from his grandmother, he had blond hair, handsome features, and a tall, lean body that looked as good in a uniform as it might have looked on a surfboard.

"Nicola." Nash was the first to move and he smiled as he reached her. "What a pleasure to see you again."

She could have hugged him for pretending not to notice that she was barefoot and wearing Gabe's robe.

"Coffee," the other man said as he dropped two bulging fast food bags on the counter and then circled it to commandeer the second mug that was filling in the small coffeemaker.

He had to be Jonah Stone. It had been fifteen years since she'd seen him, but the eyes were still that bottle-green color, and the dark, rough-edged good looks she'd seen in the boy had come to full fruition in the man.

He turned to smile at her. "Good thing I take this stuff black because Gabe is a real Mother Hubbard when it comes to filling up the larder. I'm Jonah, but the way. And help yourself to the food." He jerked a shoulder at Nash. "I brought plenty because pretty boy here only had girly food on his plane when he picked me up in San Francisco. Caviar, pâté, champagne."

"I don't stock my plane to please you, Jonah," Nash said as he opened one of the bags and began to divide it into four piles. "And you serve plenty of fancy food at your nightclubs."

Nicola took a deep swallow of coffee. "I'll just go up and tell Gabe you're here."

"No need." With one smooth move, Jonah blocked access to the stairs and motioned her toward a stool. "Take a load off. I texted him we were coming."

Nash took the mug from her and replaced it with a breakfast sandwich. "Of course, Jonah also told him that we'd ring and let him know when we arrived. But he has this deep-rooted need to show off, so he had to get through the security system without setting off any alarms."

"You helped," Jonah said as he bit into a french fry. "And I want Gabe to know that I'm still his best student."

Wary but oddly charmed by the two men, Nicola climbed onto a stool and retrieved her coffee.

"So what's up between you and Gabe?" Jonah asked.

Nicola tensed.

Nash sent her a rueful look. "You'll have to forgive Jonah. He's rude. What he's trying to ask is how long have you and Gabe been seeing each other?"

Nicola looked from one man to the other. "Jonah's question is more direct, and you look like two very smart men. I think you've figured out what's up."

They exchanged a look.

"*She's* smart, too," Jonah said.

"Holds her own," Nash added.

Then Jonah took the lead again. "What we're really wondering is what your intentions are."

"My intentions? You...you can't be serious."

"We think of Gabe as family," Nash explained.

"Are you just toying with our friend's affections?" Jonah asked.

"Toying with..." She set her mug down hard enough to slosh coffee. "That's...none of your business."

"Good answer," Nash said to Jonah. "Puts you right in your place."

"She has a bit of a temper, too." Jonah bit into his sandwich. "I can see why Gabe would like that."

Nicola narrowed her eyes. "Why don't you run a background check on me?"

"I already did," Jonah said. "Just as soon as Gabe said the two of you were working together."

She looked from one to the other as she tamped down on her temper. "Look, the two of you didn't like me much fifteen years ago, but if you—"

Nash held up a hand. "It wasn't that we didn't like you."

"It's that you were a *girl*," Jonah finished.

She fisted her hands on her hips. "Well, I'm a woman now."

"Exactly. And Gabe doesn't bring women here. He's very careful," Jonah said. "So naturally, we're curious."

"And rude." But she couldn't fault the way they cared for Gabe.

"She's right," Gabe said as he descended the stairs. "You are rude."

"Uh-oh," Jonah mumbled.

"Busted," Nash said. "You started it. You take the first punch."

"I took the first punch last time," Jonah complained.

"I have plenty of punches to go around," Gabe as he put an arm around Nicola's shoulders.

Both men raised their arms in surrender. "How about if we apologize?" Nash asked with his eyes on Jonah.

"I do," Jonah said turning to Nicola. "Sorry. We just worry about Gabe here."

"I think Gabe here can take care of himself," Nicola said.

Nash laughed then. "I like her." He turned to Nicola. "And I apologize, also. And if Gabe insists on punching us, I'll take it easy on him."

"If I were you, I'd quit while I was ahead," Nicola said.

This time it was Jonah who laughed. Then he held out his hand. "I like you, too. I'm pleased to meet you again, Nicola Guthrie."

She took his hand. "Likewise, I think."

"Pull up a stool," Nash said to Gabe. "Jonah was sure you were starving."

When Gabe had coffee in front of him, he said to Jonah, "You didn't have Nash pick you up and fly you here just to bring me breakfast. What have you got?"

Jonah dumped fries out of a bag and squeezed ketchup onto them. "I've got some background on Claire Forlani and on Dee Atherton. They're mother and daughter."

"You found a birth certificate," Gabe said.

"I found two," Jonah explained. "One in this country for a Claire Forlani. Mother—Susan Forlani, father—Art Forlani. But I couldn't dig up any more information on the parents. No birth certificates on them."

"Which means that whoever established Claire's background cover didn't go very deep," Nicola said.

Jonah met her eyes. "No, they didn't. In fact, other than the birth certificate, a driver's license and a passport which were both issued a year ago, there's no record of Claire Forlani even being in the United States. No college records, no high school records. She's a blank slate."

"I bet I know where you found the other birth certificate," Gabe said.

"Italy," Nicola guessed.

Jonah wrinkled his nose. "Do I get to tell this or not?"

Gabe waved a fry at him. "Go ahead."

"I tried looking in Italy, close to Venice, between 1990 and 1993 because those were the approximate dates you got from your Uncle Ben. And he was right. Dee Atherton had found a partner all right. Claire Forlani was born to Arturo Forlani and Dee Atherton on January 25, 1991. And there are school records there on Claire up until her first year in college. That would be about the same time she turned up in the States with a driver's license and passport."

"So she was raised by her father," Gabe mused. "What have you found on him?"

"According to a business partner of mine in Venice, Arturo Forlani was a respected businessman and a widower until his death a year ago. Claire was his only daughter of record. He didn't speak much English and he didn't travel. Interpol has nothing on him."

"It looks as though Dee Atherton's partner for the museum heist couldn't have been Arturo Forlani," Nicola said.

"I agree," Gabe said.

"Glad it's unanimous," Jonah added.

"Then who was her partner?" Nicola asked. "Bennett said when she met with your father in Venice, she had a partner, one who was excellent at producing forgeries."

"I'm still looking into that," Jonah said. "I've got my friend at Interpol looking for someone who would have been working in Europe during that time period. But I've got nothing back so far."

"My dad's looking for someone working in the States during the past fifteen years," Nicola said.

Gabe set his coffee down. "Nicola thinks the partner might have kept in touch with Claire over the years, perhaps to see if she inherited her mother's talents."

"Not a bad theory." Jonah sent Nicola a smile. "I'll check into it."

Nash wadded up empty wrappers. "What we think we've got is a forger and a security person, two people who combined had a chance to have the same kind of successful career Gabe's father had. And it must have been working because when Dee Atherton had a baby, she left the little girl behind with the father and went back to work." He shot the papers he'd gathered into the waste basket.

"Sixteen years ago—give or take—they came here and Dee sought Gabe's father out to ask for help," Nicola said. "Twice."

"Uncle Ben said she had blueprints. We're assuming she wanted help with breaking through the security of the Denver Art Museum, and the partner who got away was the forger."

"Then Dee was shot and killed, and the partner waited fifteen years to start up again?" Nash asked.

"Not exactly. We think the partner blamed Gabe's father for Dee's death and the failure of the robbery and got part of his or her revenge fifteen years ago." Then she filled Nash and Jonah in on the details of their theory that Raphael Wilder was framed.

"Revenge," Jonah said. "It's a powerful motivator."

"And it seems to have widened beyond my father and me." Gabe filled his friends in on the vandalism at Nicola's apartment and the note.

"So Dee Atherton's partner began his revenge with Gabe's dad and then waited all these years to finish the job?" Nash asked. "He or she had to have been doing something all this time."

Nicola looked at Gabe. "The whole thing about leaving a forgery behind is that it might never be discovered." She rose and began to pace. "Private homes are easier to break into than museums."

"I see where you're going," Jonah said. "You're thinking

the robberies here in Denver may have been going on for a while and the thief has only recently gone public."

"Yes," Nicola said.

"Still, a good forger has to have access to the pieces," Gabe pointed out.

"The Cézanne was on loan to the art museum the first time the attempt was made to steal it. My stepmother might know if the Longfords, the Glastons and the Baileys ever lent their paintings to the museum."

"Call her," Gabe said.

Then it was his own cell phone that rang.

"Wilder," he said. The expression on his face had Nicola's stomach knotting.

"It's Pete," Gabe said, "the young man I stationed at Claire Forlani's door. Someone has made an attempt on her life."

The three men rose at once.

"Wait." Nicola grabbed the towel off her head as she slid off her stool and raced for the stairs. "I need to get dressed."

"We'll wait," Gabe promised.

"Girls," Jonah muttered.

GABE STOOD IN THE HALLWAY directly outside of Claire Forlani's room in the intensive care unit. Once they'd reached the floor, the four of them had split up. Nash and Jonah had remained at the T in the hallway where they could keep the door to the waiting room and both ends of the hallway in view. Nicola had gone to the nurse's station the moment she'd seen that Sid was talking on the phone. He'd moved to talk to his man Pete. The young man had a bandage on his head and he was sitting on a chair on one side of Claire's closed door. A uniformed policeman stood on the other.

Through the glass window, Gabe could see the lights blinking on the machines Claire was hooked up to.

"I'm sorry I let you down, boss," Pete said. "It happened so fast."

"He didn't let you down all by himself."

Gabe switched his gaze to the uniformed officer, a man in his forties with thinning hair.

"The doctors had been through on their morning rounds, the floor was quiet, and I asked Pete if he'd mind covering while I went to get us both some coffee," the older man said. "I should never have left."

"What happened next?" Gabe asked Pete.

"One of the patients coded. The nurse's station cleared," Pete said. "When this guy in scrubs came along pushing a wheelchair, I thought he was here to transport a patient away for some procedure. The next thing I knew, something hit me in the side of my head. Hard. I blacked out for a couple seconds. When I came to and made it into the room, the nurse over there, Sid, was struggling with this guy. I pulled out my gun and told him I'd shoot. He shoved Sid into me and took off."

"It sounds like you did the job I hired you to do," Gabe said, putting a hand on the young man's shoulder. "Sometimes they get away."

"I'd say the two of them did a good job," the uniformed man said. "Sid said that the guy had a pillow over her face when he went in. And your friend here's still a little woozy."

"I'm fine," Pete insisted to the older guy. "Sid checked my eyes. I just need some aspirin."

"I'm familiar with the feeling." Gabe glanced over to where Nicola was talking to Sid. Since he figured she'd get what could be gotten of the young male nurse, he stayed where he was. "What can you tell me about the man who hit you?"

Pete frowned. "He was wearing scrubs—not the plain green ones, the fancier kind that a lot of the nurses wear. He was tall, lean. He was wearing gloves, and he had his hair covered with one of those shower cap things that they wear in the operating rooms on TV shows. He had a mask on, too."

"Could you tell the color of his hair?" Gabe asked.

Pete thought, then shook his head and immediately winced. "Glasses—he was wearing glasses. Black frames."

"Good job." After he gave Pete's shoulder a squeeze, Gabe walked over to where Jonah and Nash stood. "Observations?" he asked.

"It wouldn't be hard to get in here," Jonah said. "As long as you're wearing scrubs and something that could pass for an I.D. badge."

"Not a problem for someone who can copy a Monet or a Cézanne," Nash commented.

Gabe looked back at the room where Claire Forlani lay. "I should have taken more precautions."

"Too bad Nash and I didn't bring our violins to play."

Then he met Gabe's eyes. "There were two men on the door. One in your employ and one paid by the city. You were hoping someone would try to contact her. I can't see any way you could have predicted that someone would try to kill her."

"Well, someone definitely did," Gabe said. "Why?"

"My first guess would be to silence her," Jonah said.

"But if this thief framed your father and is now hoping to frame you for revenge, then we have to consider that revenge may also be the motivation here," Nash said.

"She failed to get the statue—therefore, she has to die? If that's true, then Nicola might be the next target."

"Or you," Jonah pointed out.

Gabe turned and when he saw that Nicola was standing at the window of Claire Forlani's room, he joined her and took her hand. Through the glass, the lights on Claire's machines continued to blink.

"According to Pete, her attacker was wearing black-framed glasses and had his or her hair covered. It could be the same person who delivered you the Valentine's Day flowers."

"Yeah. Sid also thinks it may have been a woman."

"Interesting." Keeping her hand in his, he drew her to where Jonah and Nash were waiting. "All we have to do is figure out who and make sure that the Cézanne doesn't get stolen."

"Unless the thief has changed the game plan," Nicola said.

Gabe felt his phone vibrate, took it out, and read the text. "It's from your father. Your stepmother just received a Valentine special delivery card, telling her she'll be relieved of the Cézanne tonight."

"Let's catch a thief," Nicola said.

IT WAS A WORKING LUNCH, but it was the oddest one that Nicola had ever participated in. The cuisine was Chinese takeout, but they'd never made it to the counter in Gabe's kitchen. Instead, she, Gabe, Jonah and Nash had gathered, cartons and chopsticks in hand, around the whiteboard in Gabe's office.

Jonah's contact at Interpol had nothing new. But Marcia had texted Nicola to remind her she was expected to arrive at the house by 5:00 p.m. so that she could dress and stand in the reception line. Her stepmother had also included the information that all three of the French Impressionist paintings stolen so far had been on display at the Denver

Art Museum over the past ten years, as had most of the
privately owned art in the Denver area.

"Who else do we need to add to our rogues' gallery?"
Gabe asked.

The newspaper articles and photos of the art pieces that
had formerly adorned Gabe's whiteboard had been replaced
by pictures of everyone who had close access to information about the thefts. Chewing thoughtfully on a piece of
Kung Pao chicken, Nicola swept her gaze over them. Mary
Thomas and Mark Adams lined the left side of the board.
Debra Bancroft, Claire Forlani and Randolph Meyer lined
the right-hand side.

While they'd been eating, Gabe and Jonah had run fi-
nancials on all of them. And they'd come up with nothing
suspicious on any of their current suspects. Right now they
were thinking of who they might add to the list so they
could widen the search.

"I don't think we should add anyone," Nicola said.

"Why not? We've come up dry on these." Jonah offered
her some rice, but she waved it on.

"Because, other than Gabe or my father, these are the
key figures." She pointed her chopsticks at the board.
"They're all close to the case and they all had access to
information that would help in the thefts. Anyone we add
to the mix like other employees here or at the FBI could
play a part in a minor way. But that won't get us any closer
to who's behind it."

Gabe set down his carton and moved closer to the board.
"She's right. We should be eliminating people instead of
adding them. If we're right in thinking the person behind
these thefts is Dee Atherton's old partner, then our mastermind can't be Claire. Though she might have a good
motive for avenging Dee Atherton's death, she couldn't

have been the one to frame my father. Fifteen years ago, she was a child."

"Based on age, we can also eliminate Mark Adams and Randolph Meyer," Nicola said. "That leaves Debra Bancroft and Mary Thomas."

"I hate to rain on this parade," Nash said.

"Liar," Jonah said. "You love to play devil's advocate."

Nash shrugged. "Maybe it's not either of them. Our mastermind may be keeping a low profile. Whoever it is has never shown up on the radar before. And they've managed to keep off of it for the past fifteen years."

Gabe removed the photos of the people they'd eliminated. "Yeah, but there's been a change in the game plan. Once you start delivering announcements and pulling your capers on major holidays, you're putting yourself firmly *on* the radar. I'm betting it's either Mary Thomas or Debra Bancroft."

"Me, too," Nicola said as she slipped her hand into his.

Gabe met her eyes. "If Nicola's right and our forger has spent some of the intervening time creating copies and then secretly breaking into houses and replacing authentic paintings with her work, she's needed inside information on the art collectors here in Denver as well as inside information on their security systems. So if it's between Debra and Mary, the cards are more heavily stacked against Debra. The person who was supposed to break through the security and switch the paintings won't be there, and Debra can get through everything but the last layer."

"We can't eliminate Mary completely because of the forged statue," Nicola said. "The thief had to not only know about its existence but also know where it was."

"I'm leaning toward Debra," Nash said.

"She has my vote." Jonah began to gather up empty cartons. "In any case, we need proof."

Gabe smiled. "That means we'll have to catch her in the act. And I've got a plan."

Jonah placed a hand on Nicola's shoulder. "Make sure you count the girl in. She's smart."

16

"GREAT DRESS," Nash said.

"Yeah." Gabe's eyes shifted immediately to Nicola. She stood with her father and stepmother greeting guests as they entered the salon. Even though he'd been given a preview of the red dress, it still very nearly made his tongue hang out. And the curls were back. Only they looked a lot sexier now than they had when she was ten.

At his side, Nash chuckled. "You've got it bad."

"What are you talking about?" Gabe asked.

"I mention a dress," he waved his glass of champagne. "And there are a lot of them here."

Gabe agreed. They were halfway through the silent auction part of the evening and the stream of viewers through the room had been constant. Currently, the place was glowing with silks and sequins. The scent of expensive perfume mingled with the food that was being offered by uniformed waiters. A string quartet played in one corner. The conversation was muted, and everyone was paying due homage to the Cézanne. Folded slips of paper containing the bids were accumulating in a silver bowl.

"But all I have to do is mention *one* dress and your eyes go directly to Nicola. You're stuck on her."

"Yeah," Gabe agreed as he looked at Nicola again. Each time he did, he felt the impact as if it were the first time.

"Jonah and I like her, for what it's worth."

Gabe shifted his gaze to where his other friend was circulating through the guests offering canapés on a tray. "I'm glad I have your approval."

"Have you told her yet?"

"Told her what?" He felt that same clutch in his stomach he'd felt when Nick Guthrie had been grilling him.

"That you're stuck on her." Nash tipped his glass in the direction of the door. "I wouldn't let the grass grow under your feet. You're not the only one who's impressed with your lady."

Gabe looked back to Nicola and narrowed his eyes when he saw Randolph Meyer raise her hand to his lips.

"Actually, the dress I was originally referring to is on our prime suspect," Nash said.

Gabe shifted his gaze to Debra Bancroft as she circulated through the guests. Her blond hair was smoothed back into a sophisticated twist, and earrings dangled to her shoulders. As far as Debra knew, they were following through on their original plan for tonight. Debra's job was to mingle with the guests while the other members of the G. W. Securities' team were working as waiters just as Jonah was. But Gabe had made a few additions to the plan.

Nash was assigned to keep tabs on Mary Thomas and Randolph Meyer. Both would be seated with him at the Guthries' table. Nicola was assigned to Mark Adams, who was also sitting with the Guthries. And when the wait-staff moved upstairs to serve dinner, Jonah would discard his uniform and return to the salon by way of one of the air ducts where he'd remain until he was needed. Gabe would stay behind in the salon with Debra, and then they would wait.

He didn't have a doubt that Debra would make a move. He'd thought out the various scenarios, and he was pretty sure with Jonah's and Nash's help, he had them covered. Hopefully, his prayer to St. Francis would ensure their success.

"That dress is not off the racks," Nash murmured as they watched Randolph Meyer cross the salon in Debra's direction. "My guess is that it was specifically designed for Ms. Bancroft and for the occasion. Perhaps by our designer friend."

Gabe ran his gaze over the dress again. It was black, sequined, and fell to the floor in a full skirt that swirled around her as she walked. "We know that Meyer designed it specifically for tonight. It wouldn't be difficult to hide a forged painting beneath that skirt."

When he reached her, Randolph Meyer took her hands and kissed them just as he had Nicola's. Debra did not look pleased.

"They look pretty chummy," Nash remarked.

"He may not be the mastermind behind the thefts, but he may have a role to play tonight. Keep very close tabs on him," Gabe murmured.

"On who?" Nicola asked as she joined them.

"Meyer."

Nicola turned to Nash. "I'm here on a mission. There's still a line at the door that goes all the way down the stairs to the foyer. Marcia would like you to start leading the way up to the ballroom for dinner. She wants you to escort Mary Thomas."

"My pleasure, and I'll convince Meyer to come with us," Nash said as he moved away.

As Nicola turned to watch the people, she spoke in a low voice to Gabe. "I'm also supposed to let you know that Dad has nothing to report."

"I recommend the shrimp," Jonah said as he offered them a tray of canapés. "And I do have something. My business partner called to say that the Forlani estate did have a semi-regular visitor over the years, someone who came specifically to visit the daughter, Claire. And I've got a description—tall, blond, attractive."

"Could be Debra," Nicola said. "The clues are piling up, but we need more."

"We'll get it." Gabe let his gaze sweep the room. Debra was checking in with one of the waiters, Mary Thomas was moving toward the door on Nash's arm. Randolph Meyer was following. "You both know what to do," he said.

Jonah moved away.

"Why is it that you and Jonah get to have all the fun while I have to watch over Mark Adams—Mr. Least Likely to Be Involved in this?"

Gabe met her eyes. "*Think* of him as involved. And there may be someone we haven't even thought of. Be careful."

She took his hands and squeezed them. "I'm going to be sitting at a table with Nash and two FBI agents. You may be down here for a time alone with someone who's already tried to kill someone today. Be very careful."

He gripped her hands more tightly when she tried to move away. "Nicola, after this is over, I want some time with you. Maybe we could go away."

She smiled at him, and he felt it again—that punch to the gut. "We're on the same page about that." Then she rose on her toes and brushed her mouth over his. "First, let's catch that thief."

CHANDELIERS GLITTERED, silver gleamed and music floated on the air beneath laughter and the buzz of conversation. Nicola Guthrie had to hand it to her stepmother. Marcia Thorne Guthrie knew how to throw a party. The ballroom at Thorne Mansion had never been this crowded, and from the looks on the faces of the guests, people were having a wonderful time.

The Valentine theme was present, but muted. Red ribbons were tied around small parchment favors that contained a print of the Cézanne. Red sweetheart roses floated in small heart-shaped crystal bowls in the center of each table.

Nearly forty-five minutes had gone by since dinner service had begun. Waiters were clearing the fish course and pouring red wine for the meat course. However, Nicola wanted more than the filet mignon. Time seemed to be dragging. What if they'd been wrong about who the thief was? What if it was someone who hadn't even made their list? Or what if the warning note had been a joke?

But each time the questions entered her mind, they were more than offset by the tingle of anticipation inside of her, which was growing stronger by the second.

Across the round table from her, Nash said something to make Mary Thomas laugh. Mark Adams sat directly to her right, Randolph Meyer to her left, and so far, neither of them had done or said anything in the least suspicious. The only thing she'd picked up was that the two men shared an avid interest in wine and thoroughly approved of the selections Marcia had made for the meal.

She might have joined in their conversation if she hadn't felt so wired. Something was going to happen soon.

As if she'd wished it, the chandeliers flickered overhead and went out. When they came on again, there was a sprinkling of applause. But Mark's voice was very soft and very clear in her ear. "In a few minutes, the lights will go out again, and you'll come with me. Make a noise or try to signal anyone, and Gabe Wilder dies. All I have to do is punch a button on my cell phone."

GABE TURNED TO DEBRA BANCROFT the moment the lights flickered in the salon. She'd glanced up at the overhead chandeliers. But she showed no concern as she shifted her attention back to the Cézanne.

"That's the signal, isn't it, Debra? You installed a timer on the main power switch for the house. Your plan is about to begin."

When she turned to face him, there was an icy coldness in her eyes he'd never seen before. And there was a small caliber gun in her hand. "When did you figure it out?" she asked.

The fact that she didn't attempt to feign innocence told Gabe that his time was short. Jonah would have had time to position himself in the air duct, but there was no way his friend could enter the room without drawing attention to himself.

Gabe figured his best strategy was to throw Debra off balance enough so that he could get the gun or Jonah could enter the room undetected.

"I've suspected ever since the second robbery that someone here at G. W. had to be involved. But it wasn't until I started working with Nicola that I finally concluded it was you."

Debra frowned. "What could she know? She wasn't even assigned to work on the robberies."

"She was assigned to do research and she came up with the theory that the thief—you—had two goals. To steal the art, specifically the Cézanne, and to ruin me."

"She couldn't have known that."

"She even has a theory about why you want to frame me for the robberies. You made a mistake when you sent Claire Forlani after the St. Francis. She left the forgery behind. That helped us put everything together."

There was a flicker of something in her eyes. Surprise?

Anger? Ego? Then they went cold again, and in the icy depths, Gabe caught his first glimpse of madness.

"I never make mistakes. Never. Other people do. You made the mistake of installing a new alarm system and then letting me see it. I've had time to adjust my plans. You'll have to pay now just like the others."

"Is that what happened to Dee Atherton? She had to pay for her mistakes?"

Gabe noticed the flicker in her eyes again. Definitely surprise this time. "It was the statue that allowed us to connect the dots back to Dee. I know that she came to my father sixteen years ago and that he refused to help her."

"It wasn't the first time he'd refused," she said, the anger clear in her voice. "We'd invited him to join us years ago in Venice and he'd said no because of you. He didn't want to be tied down because he couldn't miss this holiday or that holiday with his son."

"That's why you've scheduled the thefts for holidays. Because my father wanted to spend time with me?"

She smiled and it sent a chill up Gabe's spine. "Yes. I thought it was a nice touch. He used you as an excuse again when we invited him to join us in stealing the Cézanne from the Denver Art Museum. He wouldn't even help Dee with the security. That was his mistake. A fatal one. And Dee made hers when she told me that she could go ahead with the plan without him. She wasn't good enough to pull it off. They both paid."

Gabe stared at her. Why hadn't he seen it before? The coldness in her went so deep. "When Dee set off the alarm, you didn't have time to switch the paintings, so you left her there. You abandoned her. That's why she was shot. And then you framed my father with the Matisse."

"They had to pay. They were keeping me from being all that I can be."

When she glanced at the overhead lights, Gabe was certain that his time was running out. "But it turned out that you couldn't fulfill your potential without a partner after all. Even after you joined G. W. Securities, you couldn't pull off the kind of thefts that you'd pulled with Dee. That's why you visited Claire Forlani in Italy. And when you learned that she'd inherited her mother's talents, you gave her Dee's bracelet and persuaded her to follow in her mother's footsteps."

It wasn't surprise he saw this time, but shock. In spite of that, her gun hand remained steady.

"What I'm not sure I understand is why you tried to kill her. Was it because you feared betrayal? Or maybe you'd begun to sense that she wasn't going to *need* you. She was going to be able to make it on her own. Had she already threatened to leave you after this job?"

Bright spots of color stained Debra's pale cheeks. "No, Claire made a stupid mistake. She was supposed to steal the statue after tonight's robbery. Your signature and fingerprints would be found on it, and that would convince the FBI that you were behind all of the thefts. You'd be arrested and sent to jail, just as your father was. That was the plan."

"A good one," Gabe said as he prayed for time. He wanted to get that gun before the lights went out again. "But once Claire strayed from it, everything started to unravel. You couldn't use her for this job, so you had to come up with an alternate strategy. Then you found a second security system. And whatever your latest plan is, it won't work."

"Yes, it will. Did you think I wouldn't find a way around your system?"

Debra pulled a flashlight out of a pocket in the wide gown of her skirt. "The lights will go out again any second, and they won't come back on. You're going to disarm your new alarm and give me the Cézanne or Nicola Guthrie will be killed."

Fear hit him so hard that for a moment he lost his breath.

The muffled explosion and the blackout occurred at the same instant. Then came the sound of smoke alarms. The only light in the room came from Debra's flashlight and it glinted off her gun.

"I don't believe you have Nicola," Gabe said just as his cell phone vibrated.

"That will be her now." Debra set her flashlight on the small table with the silver bowl and aimed it at the painting. Then she pulled her own cell phone out of a pocket. "Mark Adams has a gun pressed to her gut. Not to her head or her heart. That would be too easy. If the trigger is pulled, she'll bleed out slowly, painfully."

He said a prayer to St. Francis, then spoke into the phone that Debra handed him. "You all right?"

"KEEP YOUR EYES ON ME and everything will be fine," Mark murmured softly.

Nicola badly wanted to glance around the table, to send a signal to Nash or her father. Several minutes had gone by, and the lights hadn't flickered again, but she was very much aware that Mark had his cell phone in his hand. She wasn't sure how much time she had. But her instincts told her that Mark was telling the truth about Gabe.

Even as a waiter set a filet in front of her, she kept her eyes on the agent who had worked so closely with her father. "Why are you doing this?"

His smile was wry. "I was given an offer I couldn't refuse. And the person I work with is very capable."

"Debra Bancroft."

Before Mark Adams could confirm or deny, there was the sound of an explosion. The floor in the ballroom vibrated, the chandeliers chimed. Then the room was pitched into blackness.

Mark's hand grasped her arm. She managed to snag her purse before he pulled her quickly toward the ballroom door. She heard her father's voice, telling everyone to be calm. But she figured Nash would be after her in a flash.

"In here." Mark shoved her into a storage closet right next to the ballroom. She heard the lock click and then felt the press of a gun into her side. "Don't make a sound," he breathed.

She didn't dare. They both heard footsteps running past toward the stairs to the lower floor. The room they were standing in was pitch-black. But she could picture it in her mind. The windowless room was used to store tables, chairs, glassware and china that her stepmother used in the ballroom. Very carefully, she slipped the strap of her purse over her shoulder. She wanted her hands free, and if she got the chance, she would go for her gun.

More footsteps rushed by.

She nearly jumped when Mark pressed a cell phone to her ear.

"Tell Wilder that you're alive and you'll remain that way as long as he does what he's told."

"You all right?" Gabe asked.

"Yes. He has a gun."

Then the line went dead.

17

"YOU WON'T GET AWAY with this, Debra." Gabe kept his voice calm in spite of the fear roiling inside of him. He had to push the image of someone holding Nicola at gunpoint out of his mind.

"I will with your help. Or Nicola Guthrie dies. Right now. All I have to do is punch one number into my cell."

"Why don't you fill me in on your plan? I'll be of more help if I'm not operating blind."

"Or you'll be more prepared to stop me. Turn off the second layer of security and get the Cézanne out of its frame. No tricks."

Gabe stepped closer to the glass case, pressed his thumb against the keypad and punched in a code. "I have to have some guarantee that Nicola Guthrie will be safe."

The glass slid open and Debra stared at it. "It's voice activated. I figured that much. But what else?"

"A certain combination of words." And he could lock the painting up again just as easily.

"Don't even think of saying them again. Just get it out of the frame. We don't have much time."

Gabe couldn't have agreed with her more. Time was not working in his favor. Jonah couldn't make a move, not with Nicola being held hostage. And once he handed the painting over to Debra, he would have nothing to bargain with.

"NOW WHAT?" Nicola whispered. She felt Mark ease away from the door. From the sound of his breathing, she knew that he was standing across from her. The gun was no longer pressed to her side, but it was close. No more than a foot or two separated them in the narrow room. She formed a mental picture of him in her mind.

"As soon as she signals me that she has the painting, we'll leave. That explosion you heard set off a fire in the kitchen area. They're already evacuating the ballroom, and we'll slip out with the others. As long as we have you and Wilder as hostages, they're not going to stop us."

The plan sounded good on the surface. And Mark might even take her along. But Debra wouldn't be taking Gabe. Once she had the painting, she'd kill Gabe and take off on her own.

Ruthlessly, Nicola pushed back the surge of fear. It wasn't going to help her a bit to keep thinking about how much danger Gabe might be in. She had to concentrate on Mark Adams. He was her only chance of improving Gabe's chances.

"You've surprised me, Mark. We suspected that some-one in the FBI office might be involved, but I didn't think it was you. You're a family man."

His short laugh held no humor. "Used to be. My family is breaking up. My ex-wife is about to remarry and start a new life. Debra has helped me through a rough time. With the money we've made on these robberies, we'll also be able to start a new life."

His belief in Debra was very strong in his voice. Nicola figured her best strategy was to chip away at that trust.

"What's taking so long? Debra has to have the painting by now. She's not going to call you."

"Shut up."

"She's going to leave you behind." In her mind, Nicola tried to imagine exactly where Mark's gun was. She pictured his height and exactly where the angle of his elbow would be. "If you kill me, there's no way you'll get away with it. My father will hunt you down. If you stop now, you can make a deal."

"She's going to call."

"No. She's going to cut her losses. That's the way she operates. Do you know that this isn't her first string of robberies? She's been at it for twenty years or more and she's never gotten caught."

"You're lying."

"She's good—so good she's never even made it onto Interpol's or the FBI's radar screen. No wonder you let her dupe you. There's a good chance she's been stealing art here in Denver ever since she went to work for G. W. Securities. That means she's got money tucked away. And so far the people she takes on as partners end up dead. This morning she tried to kill Claire Forlani in her hospital room."

"That's not true."

But the quaver in his voice was just what she'd been waiting for. In a very quick move, she lunged for his gun hand and used all her weight to shove it aside. There was a deafening explosion as she brought her knee up hard into his groin.

The instant she felt him slump, she let go of his arm, unlocked the door and raced out into the hallway.

Guests were still poring out of the ballroom. She pushed past them. At the top of the stairs, she spotted her father on the landing.

"Gabe," she shouted at him. But he couldn't hear her above the noise of the crowd. And they were slowing her down.

Taking out her cell, she punched in Gabe's number. It rang, then rang again. *Pick it up. Pick it up. St. Francis, make him pick it up.*

"IT'S TAKEN YOU LONG ENOUGH to get it out of the frame. Now roll it up."

Gabe did, taking as much time as he dared. When his cell vibrated, he reached to take the call.

"Keep your hands on the painting where I can see them," Debra said.

"It's my cell. It could be Nick Guthrie, Nash or Jonah. If I don't answer, they'll check here first."

"Okay, but watch what you say."

Gabe didn't have to say anything. He wasn't sure he could when he heard Nicola's voice.

"I'm okay. Take her down."

Then he drew in a deep breath and, shoving the painting back into the case, he said, "Nicola Guthrie is safe."

The glass slid shut.

"No. Make it open again." There was a thread of panic in her voice, but she kept her eyes on him, her gun steady as she pressed a number into her phone.

For a moment, Gabe let the silence stretch between them. "She got away. Nicola's safe."

"No." The coldness was gone from her voice. In its place was fury. "I want the painting."

In the glow of the flashlight, Gabe saw her hand was still steady on the gun.

"No," Gabe said.

The lights came on, and Gabe could see that there was

more than anger in her eyes. There was also a trace of madness.

In his peripheral vision, he saw the door to the salon open. Framed in it, Nick Guthrie and Nash stood, their guns aimed at Debra. And over her shoulder, he saw Jonah lift the grate aside and crawl out of the air duct.

"Drop the gun, Debra," Nick Guthrie said.

"No. You drop yours or I'll kill him. I'll blow his head off."

"You'll still be dead," Nicola said, stepping into the space between her father and Nash. "If you want to take someone with you, why don't you take me? I got away from Mark. I'm the one who spoiled your plan."

"You." Debra screamed the word as she swung the gun.

Gabe leapt forward. There was gunfire, a flurry of movement. Then Debra was lying beneath him on the floor, not moving.

He lifted his head to scan the room for Nicola. She was flat on the floor, Nash on top of her. But her eyes were on him.

"You all right?" she asked.

"Yeah. You?"

"Yes." Nash assisted her to her feet.

Gabe rolled off of Debra. Her blood stained his shirt. Jonah was checking for a pulse.

"She's breathing," he said. "Looks like a shoulder wound."

Gabe got to his feet, drew Nicola into his arms and simply held on. "She nearly shot you."

"She nearly shot *you*."

"Well," Nash said. "You're even then. Seems to me that the big mistake Debra made was tangling with either one of you."

As soon as Nick Guthrie finished talking with the rest of his team and calling for an ambulance, he joined Nash and Jonah near the Cézanne.

Still keeping his arm around Nicola to hold her close, Gabe met Guthrie's eyes. "Mark Adams?"

"He's in custody. After Nicola got away, he couldn't wait to turn himself in. He wants a deal. But I'm not feeling particularly generous. He tried to kill my daughter."

"Yeah."

"Well, he didn't succeed," Nicola pointed out.

"No, he didn't. I owe St. Francis for that one," Gabe said.

"Not just St. Francis." Nick Guthrie moved to pull Nicola into his arms for a long hug. When he released her, he said, "In this case, St. Francis had some help. You knew just what to say to distract her. My heart stopped beating when she swung her gun in your direction, but it gave us a chance to take her down. Good job."

"Thanks. Does that mean that you're going to let me work in the field?"

He studied her for a moment. "I'm going to need to replace Mark Adams. I can't think of a better candidate for the job than you."

Nicola was still hugging her father when the medics appeared at the door.

As they watched Debra being loaded onto a stretcher, Jonah said, "You know, Gabe used Nicola's name to open the glass case," Jonah said.

"Really?" Nick Guthrie asked.

Jonah nodded. "First and last names. He said them twice, and both times the glass moved.

"I've tried to tell him he's really stuck on her," Nash said.

Nicola looked into Gabe's eyes. "You used my name as the code?"

He framed her face with his hands. "Your name was what was in my mind while I was working on the system. For three months, I haven't been able to get you out of my head."

Then he pulled her close and simply held on for a very long time. There'd been that instant of helplessness he'd felt when Debra had swung her gun toward Nicola. For just that brief span of time, he'd felt the same way he'd felt when each of his parents had died.

As if she understood, Nicola ran her hands up and down his back. "I'm here," she murmured. "And so are you."

IT WAS WELL AFTER MIDNIGHT when Gabe and Nicola walked into his apartment. Debra Bancroft was in the hospital in stable condition. They were right about the forgery being concealed beneath her gown. Mark Adams had called a lawyer but was still hoping for a deal. Marcia had managed to resuscitate the chef after the filet mignon course had been ruined so that he could serve desserts and cognac in the ballroom. When they'd left Thorne Mansion, her father had been sharing some of his single malt Scotch with Nash and Jonah in his office.

"I wonder who the new owner of the Cézanne is," Nicola said. "In all the excitement, I forgot to ask."

"Your father told me that they received the highest bid that's ever been made this year. And it came from the Robineau family. It seems they couldn't bear to part with the painting."

"Nice." She tried for a smile and then yawned.

"You're tired," he said as he tucked a curl behind her ear.

"And you're not?"

"Yes, but I wanted…we haven't had any time together. I thought… Are you too tired for a nightcap?"

He was nervous, Nicola realized. And she'd never before seen him that way. "Do you happen to have a white wine in that magic cooler of yours?"

"I do." He moved away to select a bottle and uncork it. She followed and climbed onto a stool at the counter.

"I got some good news from Pete at the hospital while you were saying goodbye to your stepmother. Claire Forlani regained consciousness for a short time. The doctors believe she's going to recover fully."

"Good. I'm going to see if I can talk Marcia into hiring a defense team for her."

"You're going to what?" He turned to stare at her.

"Marcia likes to do that kind of thing. She's very generous with her time and with her money. And who knows what kinds of lies Debra Bancroft told that girl about her mother. She's so young. Maybe you could hire her at G. W. Securities."

"And you accused me of being a caregiver." He handed her a glass of wine. "I didn't even get you a Valentine gift."

"Good. One bouquet was enough."

Though she got a smile out of him, he didn't laugh. Instead, he lifted his glass in a toast. "To your new job. You got what you wanted."

She touched her glass to his and sipped. She had gotten what she wanted, a chance to work at her father's side. But as she looked into Gabe's eyes, she knew that it was no longer all she wanted. She was looking right at what she wanted more than anything.

She drew in a breath and let it out. She was no longer the Nicola who just worked hard and waited for things to happen. So in spite of the nerves tightening in her own stomach, she said, "You have something that you want to talk about. What?"

Fear. It danced up his spine. And it was every bit as sharp as what he'd felt when he'd thought Debra was going to shoot her. "I need time with you."

She raised her brows. "I thought we already agreed on that. We're going away. You can choose our destination. I have some vacation time."

"No." He set his glass down and ran his hands through his hair. "I want more than a vacation. I want…" He turned away, paced to the counter, then turned back to face her. "I stayed away from you for three months. I wasted all that time. That was my fault. And then I very nearly lost you tonight. That was my fault, too."

Nicola frowned at him. "And why was either of those things your fault?" She set down her wine and held up a finger. "Number one, I think it was St. Francis who was responsible for keeping us apart for three months."

He cocked his head to one side studying her. "How do you figure?"

"Father Mike said the statue was playing a part in all of this. If we hadn't run into each other in the church, if I hadn't been sure you were someone else, if we hadn't made love, we might not be where we are right now."

"And Debra might not have nearly killed you tonight. At least you can't argue that I'm not responsible for that. I hired her. I put her in a position to do everything she did."

She slipped off her stool, rounded the counter and grabbed his face in her hands. "Look at me. Debra Bancroft is crazy."

"Yes. She was with me for five years, and I didn't see it."

"She was crazier for a lot longer than that, and she was good at hiding it. Look at how many lives she ruined—your father's, Dee Atherton's, Mark Adams', Claire's and she very nearly ruined yours. How do you think I felt when I was stuck in that closet with Mark? I knew that the second you gave her the Cézanne, she was going to kill you."

Gabe pulled her into his arms and held on tight. "I've never been that afraid before."

"Well, the feeling was mutual. And you're really going to have to work on this 'I can protect everyone' gene."

He drew back and looked into her eyes. "And you're not guilty of the same? Who's going to see that Claire Forlani gets a defense team?"

With a sigh, he rested his forehead on hers.

"Maybe we can work on it together," she said.

"Yeah. But it's going to be a big job. It's going to take a lot of time."

"Eons," she agreed. "And there are other things, too. We both have very demanding jobs. We'll have to work on making time for each other."

"I do consulting work for the FBI. Maybe we could work together again."

"I'd like that." She met his eyes, saw the gleam in his. "Ready?"

"For what?"

"A lifetime of very hard work." She smiled at him. "And fun?"

"Yeah." He wound one of her curls around his finger. "What about you?"

"Very ready. And now will you please take me to bed?"

Laughing, he scooped her up into his arms and headed toward the stairs. "I thought you'd never ask."

"I didn't have to the first time." She nipped on his lower lip.

"Neither did I."

"Something else we'll have to work on," she said as they tumbled onto the bed.

"Forever."

* * * * *

**Look what people are saying about
these talented authors…**

JANELLE DENISON

"Kudos to Ms Denison for her fantastic, hot, steamy
love stories and the heroes that leave you
wishing you had one just like him!"
—*A Romance Review*

"No one does hot and sexy better!"
—*New York Times* bestselling author Carly Phillips

LESLIE KELLY

"*One Wild Wedding Night* features sexy and fun stories
with likeable characters. Oh, this one is definitely wild,
but even better, it also aims for the heart."
—*Mrs. Giggles*

"Filled with humour and heart, *Slow Hands* by
Leslie Kelly is a complete delight."
—*RT Book Reviews*

JO LEIGH

"Smart, funny, *Shiver* is exactly the type of book that's
needed to attract new readers under thirty to
contemporary romance."
—*RT Book Reviews*

"Jo Leigh's [book]…has that wonderfully rare
chemistry between hero and heroine that makes
you sigh with delight. Throw in deft humour,
and your enjoyment is guaranteed."
—*RT Book Reviews*

Janelle Denison is a *USA TODAY* bestselling author of more than fifty contemporary romance novels. She is a two-time recipient of the National Readers' Choice Award, and has also been nominated for the prestigious RITA® Award. Janelle is a California native who now calls Oregon home. She resides in the Portland area with her husband and daughters, and can't imagine a more beautiful place to live. To learn more about Janelle and her new releases, you can visit her website at www.janelledenison.com, or you can chat with her on her group blog at www.plotmonkeys.com.

Leslie Kelly has written dozens of books and novellas for the Blaze® and Temptation lines. Known for her sparkling dialogue, fun characters and depth of emotion, her books have been honoured with numerous awards, including a National Readers' Choice Award, an *RT Book Reviews* Award, and three nominations for the highest award in romance, the RITA® Award. Leslie resides in Maryland with her own romantic hero, Bruce, and their three daughters. Visit her online at www.lesliekelly.com or on her group blog, www.plotmonkeys.com.

Jo Leigh lives in a small, small town in Utah with a gorgeous view. She has far too many pets, but they do help to keep her sane and happy. A triple RITA® Award finalist, Jo has written more than fifty novels. She also enjoys researching her novels a little too much. The best place to catch her is on Twitter where she's Jo_Leigh, or you can write to her at joleigh@joleigh.com.

NOT ANOTHER BLIND DATE

BY
JANELLE DENISON
LESLIE KELLY & JO LEIGH

All the characters in this book have no existence outside the imagination of the author, and have no relation whatsoever to anyone bearing the same name or names. They are not even distantly inspired by any individual known or unknown to the author, and all the incidents are pure invention.

First published in Great Britain 2012
by Mills & Boon, an imprint of Harlequin (UK) Limited,
Eton House, 18-24 Paradise Road, Richmond, Surrey TW9 1SR

NOT ANOTHER BLIND DATE © Harlequin Books S.A. 2011

The publisher acknowledges the copyright holders of the individual works as follows:

Skin Deep © Janelle Denison 2011
Hold On © Leslie Kelly 2011
Ex Marks the Spot © Jolie Kramer 2011

ISBN: 978 0 263 89727 2

14-0212

Harlequin (UK) policy is to use papers that are natural, renewable and recyclable products and made from wood grown in sustainable forests. The logging and manufacturing processes conform to the legal environmental regulations of the country of origin.

Printed and bound in Spain
by Blackprint CPI, Barcelona

CONTENTS

SKIN DEEP

BY
JANELLE DENISON

To Brenda Chin, for always welcoming me back.
To my Plotmonkey Pal, Leslie Kelly—
thank you for the invite!
And to Don—thank you for the best
twenty-four years of my life!

1

SEX WITH A STRANGER was a fantasy Jayne Young had often entertained in her mind while she lay in bed at night, but she never in her wildest dreams would have believed that such a fanciful illusion would *ever* become reality.

She'd always been a quintessential good girl who took things slowly with a guy, and she'd never been tempted to indulge in a one-night stand with any man she'd dated. Yet here she was, allowing a gorgeous, smoldering hot pirate she'd met only a few hours ago to lead her away from the crush of people packed into the nightclub—all of whom were dressed in various costumes for Halloween—to somewhere more secluded where they could be alone and finally give in to the lust that had been simmering between them since the moment their gazes had met from across the room.

In a club full of scantily clad costumed women, she'd been surprised that he'd singled her out. With a slow, devastatingly sexy smile on his lips, he'd strolled toward her, a dashing figure in a billowing white cotton shirt that was halfway unbuttoned and gave every woman in the place a glimpse of his well-defined chest and washboard abs. Tight black breeches molded to his lean hips and hard, muscular thighs, and a royal blue sash cinched his waist.

He'd completed the look of a rogue with his tousled dark brown hair, and a black patch covering one eye. The other was a piercing shade of blue that made her heart flutter in her chest and raised the level of awareness thrumming through her veins.

Stopping before her, he'd executed a gallant, charming bow, his manner reminiscent of Orlando Bloom in *The Pirates of The Caribbean*. "You must be Jane."

That he knew her name had initially startled her, until she realized he was referring to the formfitting, one-shouldered, leopard print mini dress her best friend Darcie, had coaxed her into wearing in hopes of bringing out Jayne's wilder side for the evening. The sexy costume, complete with four-inch leopard print heels and a necklace of faux tiger teeth, had been an amusing and deliberate twist on her own name.

Darcie had glammed up her hair and make-up in hopes that Plain Jayne would find her Tarzan at the club. But even though her character's counter part was nowhere to be found, Jayne was sure her friend would be thrilled to know her efforts to transform Jayne had attracted such a smoking-hot hunk.

"I am Jayne," she replied, raising her voice above the loud music. It didn't matter that he believed she was playing a role—in fact, she preferred it that way. In this sexually charged environment, dressed so provocatively and way outside her personal comfort zone, she liked the fact that she was able to maintain her anonymity.

He straightened, then inclined his head and offered his hand in a sweeping gesture. "Care to take a whirl on the dance floor with a swashbuckling pirate?" he drawled.

She found his attempt to persuade her irresistible, and

the seductive look on his handsome face triggered a jolt of excitement unlike anything she'd ever felt before. Since Darcie had been enticed out onto the dance floor by a vampire, Jayne figured she might as well have some fun, too.

Exhaling a deep breath, she placed her hand in his. "I'd love to join you."

He gave her a flirtatious grin that made her stomach do a little flip, then led her into the throng of costumed revelers who were dancing without inhibition or modesty—a brash and bold attitude that Jayne didn't have much experience with. The atmosphere was electric, and for the first time in her life she threw caution, and her more reserved nature, aside and let herself enjoy the inviting beat of the music, and the pirate who'd picked her out of all the other women in the club.

It didn't take her long to get drawn into the suggestive scene around her, and since she didn't know anyone at the club other than Darcie, it was easy to relax and let loose. The next few hours were filled with heated looks and subtle touches between her and her pirate. The chemistry between them was undeniable, and what started as an instant attraction and flirtation quickly escalated to something hotter, sexier and oh-so-arousing.

The press of people forced her into close proximity with her hunk, not that she minded, and when she faltered on her too-high heels he caught her around the waist and brought her flush against him, searing her with the heat and strength of his body imprinting her breasts, her belly, her thighs.

That's when everything between them changed. With their hips pressed so intimately together, she could feel the hard length of him, could see the desire gleaming in his one dark blue eye. *For her.* A reckless thrill raced through her, and for what seemed like forever they stared at one another while everyone else continued to dance around them. Then his hungry, searing gaze dropped to her mouth.

Breathless with anticipation, her lips parted, and she dampened them with her tongue. That seemed to be the only invitation he needed to lower his head and kiss her... and she didn't even try to stop him. His lips were warm and soft and persuasive, seducing not only her mouth, but her senses. He deepened the kiss, his tongue tangling sensuously with hers, while one of his hands drifted over the curve of her bottom to haul her even closer. A hard thigh slid between hers, and his hips moved against hers in their own private dance—a slow, deliberate gyration that caused a pulsing, throbbing heat to settle between her legs.

She should have been mortified that she was acting so wanton in public, but she couldn't bring herself to care, not when he kissed her like a man who was dying of thirst and she was a tall, cool glass of water he couldn't get enough of. She'd never felt so desirable, had never experienced such an all-consuming sexual need.

And, oh, God, she didn't want it to end.

Too soon, he broke their potent kiss, and they were both breathing hard when he lifted his head, his gaze capturing hers in the flash of bright, colorful lights the deejay had aimed toward the dance floor. A silent, mutual acknowledgment passed between them—a bold, sexual invitation from him, and a too-easy acceptance from her.

He grabbed her hand and took charge, and she followed him as he navigated the crowd and the club, knowing that every smoldering look, every tempting touch and their deliciously drugging kiss had been building up to what they were about to do. She'd expected him to lead her down to the first floor of the club and outside somewhere, but instead he veered toward a door marked "emergency stairwell" and pulled her inside.

The door shut after them, enclosing them in a dim area that was as secluded as they were going to get for their hot, quick tryst. She had the fleeting thought that he probably did this kind of thing all the time, then immediately shoved the notion from her mind because right now, it didn't matter. Not when she was so turned on and aching for the kind of relief he could provide.

It had been a few years since she'd been with a flesh and blood man, and even then the sex had been lukewarm and nothing like the heat that was pooling in her belly and spreading like wildfire through her limbs. While she had zero experience with one-night stands, she was feeling impulsive and daring enough to let this incredibly hot guy have his way with her.

Darcie would be so proud of her for finally breaking free of the too-modest values that had been instilled in her from a young age and doing something outrageous to shake up her dull and boring love life. Having sex with a stranger in a darkened stairwell where the risk of getting caught was high was about as scandalous as she'd ever get.

With a sinful, I-can't-wait-to-have-you grin, he pressed her against the cool, concrete wall, then framed her face in his hands and locked his lips with hers and replaced every thought in her head with pure pleasure. Like the pirate he was, he plundered the depths of her mouth, using his tongue and teeth in erotic ways that made her moan and melt and primed her for so much more.

All around her, she could feel the loud pulse of the music rocking the nightclub, an encouraging beat that thrummed through her body and released something wild and wicked inside her. Determined to make the most of this onetime encounter, she slipped her hands into his unbuttoned shirt, his skin taut and blazing hot beneath the tips of her fingers. Her flattened palms boldly explored the hard, defined contours of his chest, and when her thumbs grazed his erect nipples he released a deep groan of approval that bolstered her confidence and gave her a sense of feminine empowerment.

As his mouth continued to devour hers, his hands moved, too, skimming down her neck and along her shoulders, leaving fire in the wake of his touch. His fingers caught the strap of her jungle-themed dress and tugged it down her arm to the crook of her elbow, then he pushed the cups of her strapless bra out of his way, as well. In the next instant, his mouth was on her bared breast, sucking hard, while his tongue flicked and swirled around her nipple.

Then she felt his hand between her widened legs, traveling up the inside of her thigh until he reached the elastic band of her panties. Undeterred, he slipped his fingers beneath the damp silk and stroked with such expertise and purpose that she raced quickly toward orgasm.

Pulling her breast deeper into his mouth, he increased the pressure on her clit, pushed a long finger inside her, and she plunged all ten of her fingers into his silky hair, her back arching and her breath hitching in her throat as her entire body convulsed in a shuddering orgasm.

He buried his face against her neck, the erotic brush of his breath against her skin arousing her all over again. "Jesus," he said in a voice that sounded like pure gravel. "I want you, but I don't have a condom."

Even though he'd just given her the most earth-shattering orgasm, she was still anxious to feel him inside her, and was eternally grateful that Darcie had tucked a condom into the small purse clipped to the leopard sash around her waist—in hopes that Jayne would get lucky. At the time, Jayne had humored her best friend, but as she retrieved the protection and handed it to her pirate she knew she owed Darcie a huge thank you.

The relief in her hunk's gaze spoke volumes. "You're amazing," he said, and kissed her lips again.

His compliment warmed her, spurred her, and she fumbled to open the top snap of his pants, then his zipper, to help him along. "Hurry, please."

"Impatient, too," he murmured with an amused chuckle, then groaned when she wrapped her fingers around his thick, impressive erection and gave it a squeeze.

He cursed beneath his breath and pushed her hand away so he could sheath himself. She took off her panties, unsure what to do with them until he grabbed them from her and tucked them into his pants pocket.

Suddenly, she was back against the concrete wall, his hands pushing up the skirt of her dress to her waist then hitching one of her knees over his hip. Both of his hands dropped to her backside, lifting her higher, until the broad tip of his rigid shaft found her entrance, teasing her with the promise of filling her completely.

Instinctively, she locked her ankles around his waist, and gasped in shock as he plunged inside her to the hilt. He was so large that the first thrust was almost painful, but as soon as he began to move, she softened around him and unadulterated pleasure began to vibrate through her in overwhelming waves.

She didn't think it was possible for her to have an orgasm during actual penetration, but this man and the skillful way he stroked deep inside her was proving her wrong. The slick length of him sliding in and out of her, the granite hardness of his body straining toward hers, the demanding passion of his kisses, all were designed to send her right over the edge.

Sex with him was raw and primitive, unleashing an

equally untamed side of her she never knew she possessed. She welcomed every frenzied lunge, every rough, driving thrust that pushed her higher. Fast and furious had never felt so good. Feeling as though she was spiraling out of control, she clutched at his shoulders, digging her fingers into the muscles of his back as an irrepressible tension spiraled tighter and tighter inside her.

Like a dream-fueled fantasy, her mind fogged with lust and need, and she gave herself up to what her body was chasing. As soon as she started pulsating around him, he stepped up the pace even more, then released a low, guttural growl as he came, too.

"*Wow,*" he murmured against her throat, and Jayne silently echoed his sentiment.

Long moments passed where they both tried to catch their breath, then he withdrew from her and she unlocked her ankles as he lowered her to the ground. The moment he stepped away from her, reality hit her like a slap in the face, and along with it came a heaping dose of embarrassment she could feel scorching her cheeks.

Self-conscious now, she looked away as she quickly pulled up the bodice of her jungle dress and tugged the skirt back into place. Now that their mutual itch had been scratched, she had no idea what to do or how to proceed, and he didn't seem inclined to dispel the awkwardness and uncertainty settling over her while he made some clothing adjustments of his own.

Jayne was smart enough to know that phenomenal sex did not equate to anything beyond this onetime fling, and the last thing she wanted to hear or face was a rejection from the hottest, sexiest man she'd ever been with. She refused to feel shame or regret for something that had felt so good, so before he could ruin her fantasy with some kind of lame brush-off line, she decided to leave with her pride intact while she had the chance.

"I've gotta go," she muttered, and turned toward the door and pulled it open while he was trying to zip up his pants.

The heat and noise from the nightclub hit her like a wall as she stepped back inside, and behind her she heard him call out urgently, "Wait!", but she didn't stop. Instead, she continued her escape, pushing through the crowd until the entrance was in sight. As soon as she hit the street, she hailed a cab, and once she was on her way back to her place she sent Darcie a text message telling her she had a headache and had gone home.

Now that she had time to think rationally, she couldn't believe what she'd done, how impulsive she'd been. Her behavior went against every ladylike lesson she'd ever been taught by her Aunt Millie, and she hoped she hadn't made a fool of herself with how eager and enthusiastic she'd been with him.

It was a good thing she'd never have to see him again.

2

Three months later...

"JAYNE, GWEN IS HERE to pick up her order."

Standing at the large wooden worktable in the back of her florist shop, Jayne glanced across the open area to the curtained doorway, where her best friend and store manager, Darcie, had poked her head inside.

"I'm just about done," Jayne said as she clipped the stem of a fuchsia Stargazer lily and added it to the arrangement of blue irises, white daisies, and purple statice laid out on the table. "Tell her I'll be out in less than five minutes."

"Will do," Darcie replied in a cheerful voice, before disappearing back to the store front.

Alone again, Jayne returned her attention to Gwen's bouquet. The older woman had been her first customer when she'd opened Always in Bloom four years ago. Gwen loved flowers as much as Jayne did, and every Thursday around ten in the morning she arrived to pick up whatever arrangement Jayne decided to put together for her.

Not only did Jayne appreciate Gwen's steady business, but she also enjoyed the woman's friendship. Gwen's warm and caring nature reminded her so much of her Aunt Millie, who'd passed away over five years ago after devoting her adult life to single-handedly raising Jayne.

Jayne had been orphaned at the age of seven when her parents had died in a car accident, and it had been her recently widowed Aunt Millie who'd provided her with a loving, stable home. Since Millie never had children of her own, nor had she ever remarried, Jayne had become the center of her aunt's universe.

Through the years, the two of them had bonded over the simpler things in life. Aunt Mille had taught her how to knit and sew, and made sure she learned how to cook from scratch. Instead of watching TV in the evenings, they'd read from the classics lining the bookshelves, or they'd invited Gwen over to play cribbage, rummy or mahjong. They'd spent many Sunday mornings baking pies, cakes and cookies, then took them down to the nearby retirement home for the residents to enjoy.

Growing up, Jayne had always been painfully shy and she'd been grateful for the many diversions her aunt had provided. But the hobby she'd loved the most was tending to the massive flower garden in her aunt's backyard. Together they'd planted everything from rare Victorian roses, to beautiful Ice Cream tulips, to the more vibrant orange and yellow freesia, and everything in between.

While her friends at school dated boys, or practiced cheerleading routines, and attended all the formal dances, Jayne preferred to have her hands buried in the earth's rich soil and that's where she spent most of her free time. What excited her the most was seeing the first bloom and reveal of stunning visual colors as the seeds she'd planted emerged into a breath taking botanical display.

She'd gone on to major in horticulture, and when her aunt died and left her with a sizeable inheritance, she'd decided to honor the woman who raised her by opening her own flower shop. Thus, Always in Bloom had been born, and the boutique had quickly grown into a thriving business that had consumed most of Jayne's time, but it was a labor of love she didn't mind.

Jayne finished off Gwen's bouquet with a sprinkling of baby's breath, then wrapped up the flowers in a cellophane sleeve and added a pretty violet ribbon bow. She carried the arrangement out to the front, where Darcie was ringing up a potted plant for another customer, and Gwen was sitting at the table Jayne had set up as a place for people to wait for their order.

Wearing black slacks and a patterned silk blouse accented with a string of pearls around her neck, the older woman looked well put together, as always. Her dyed-brown hair had been recently colored and styled, her make-up was immaculately applied and made her look much younger than her actual age of sixty-eight, and she sat in her chair looking every inch a lady who was used to the finer things in life.

"Here you go, Gwen." Jayne greeted her friend with a smile. "I received some beautiful Stargazer lilies this morning and couldn't resist using them in your bouquet. What do you think?"

"They're absolutely beautiful," Gwen said, her pale blue eyes sparkling with delight as Jayne placed the flowers on the table in front of her. "Then again, you've yet to disappoint me with your selections. That's why I gave you free rein. It's always a fun surprise to see what you put together for me."

"Good, I'm glad."

Gwen looked around the shop just as the woman who'd bought the potted plant left the store, then glanced back at Jayne. "Do you have a few minutes to talk?"

"Sure." She had nothing pressing to do, so she sat down in the chair across from Gwen, her curiosity piqued.

Gwen folded her hands on the table, her expression turning serious. "Do you realize that my wedding to Patrick is already next weekend?"

"Your wedding is on Valentine's Day, which is hard to forget," Jayne replied with amusement. Gwen was heading into her fifth marriage, to a man she claimed was "the love of her life", and she was doing it up big for the ceremony and reception. "Not only is it the most romantic day of the year, but I'm making all your flower bouquets and arrangements, so I know exactly how many days it is until you tie the knot."

Jayne suddenly wondered if there was a more pressing reason for Gwen to have brought up the short time frame of her upcoming nuptials. "Is everything okay with you and Patrick?"

"Everything is perfectly wonderful with Patrick. He is, after all, the man of my dreams." Gwen sighed like only a woman in love could. "Actually, I'm more concerned about *you*."

Startled and a little confused, Jayne pressed a hand to her chest. "You're worried about *me*? Why?"

"Because I received your RSVP card for the wedding in the mail the other day, and you only responded for a party of *one*."

Jayne didn't see why that was a cause for concern. "Yes. Just me."

"It's Valentine's Day, sweetie," Gwen said, her eyes as soft and caring as her voice. "You can't come to the wedding without a date. Even Darcie has a boyfriend to bring."

"Yes, I do," Darcie piped in enthusiastically from where

she was watering a nearby gardenia plant. "And, as you both know, he's absolutely *dreamy.*"

Darcie released an uncharacteristically besotted sigh to equal the one Gwen had just exhaled, and Jayne couldn't help but roll her eyes at all the lovey-dovey vibes the two women were putting off. Darcie's latest boyfriend, Josh, was the vampire she'd met at the Halloween party at the nightclub three months ago, and what had begun as a heated physical attraction between the two had gradually given way to a deeper interest, and just recently, love.

Jayne was truly happy for her best friend, who deserved a good man in her life, which Josh definitely was in spades. But sometimes, knowing that Darcie's relationship with Josh had begun on the night they met, after what Darcie referred to as the most orgasmic sex she'd ever had with a guy, Jayne was often left pondering a slew of "what-if" scenarios with her pirate. The most prominent one being, what if she hadn't let old securities get the best of her and had stayed that night, instead of bolted?

Unfortunately, and regretfully, she'd never know the answer to that question.

Having been raised by her reserved aunt and surrounded by Millie's older generation of friends, she'd always been swayed towards dating older, more stable men that her aunt approved of. The few relationships she'd been involved in had been comfortable, and while she and those men had been intellectually compatible, sexually she'd always felt as though something important was missing.

With her pirate, she'd had a taste of lust and passion and now knew exactly what had been lacking in her previous relationships—an undeniable physical attraction and burning desire. A part of her regretted that she hadn't been bold and confident enough to stick around and see if there could be something more between her and her pirate than a quick, heated encounter in a darkened stairwell.

Dressed as Jungle Jane in a place where no one knew her identity, she'd been able to let a more provocative persona take over and see where it took her. Their encounter had stemmed from the forbidden, and the illusion that she was this wild and wanton woman, but in her real everyday life, she was far from spontaneous or impulsive—and she was crazy to think she could have a relationship or future with a man as sexy and exciting as her pirate.

Yet knowing all that, it didn't stop her from laying in bed at night, her body tingling as she conjured up that night in her mind and recalled her pirate's kisses, his seductive caresses, and how he'd literally rocked her world as he pumped deep inside her, waiting for her to climax before he took his own pleasure. Her pirate had definitely set the bar high for the next man she slept with, and she often wondered if anyone would ever be able to live up to the standards he'd set for her.

"Earth to Jayne," Darcie said, her singsong voice jolting Jayne back to the present. "Are you still with us?"

Realizing her thoughts had drifted off to a place better left in the past, she shifted in her seat and smoothed a hand down her gauzy skirt, trying to quickly recall what they'd been discussing before she'd taken a trip down memory lane. Oh, yeah, Gwen was worried because Jayne was attending her wedding solo and didn't have a man in her life to celebrate Valentine's Day.

"It's not a big deal that I don't have a date. Really," Jayne insisted. She'd spent many Valentine's Days by herself, and was grateful that as a florist it was the busiest week, and day, of the year for her, so she never had much time to think about the fact that she didn't have a special someone in her life.

"I happen to think differently," Gwen said with a regal-like wave of her hand. The morning sun streaming through the window glinted off the massive diamond on her left hand, nearly blinding Jayne from the brilliant shine of her engagement ring. "And it just so happens that I have the perfect man in mind for you."

Jayne managed, just barely, to suppress a groan. "Another blind date?"

Darcie, who was standing behind Gwen plucking wilted blooms from a hanging basket of deep purple wisteria, smirked at Jayne. She knew all the disastrous details of Gwen's other attempts to set Jayne up, and she dreaded the thought of having to go through that torture again.

But Gwen loved to play matchmaker whenever she could, which Jayne found amusing considering Gwen had been married and divorced four times, and was getting ready to head down the aisle for the fifth.

In that regard, when it came to love and marriage, Gwen and Jayne's aunt couldn't have been more opposite in their views. Millie had never remarried because she believed there was only one love of your life, and she'd always disapproved of her friend's many relationships and unions. Jayne's aunt had always considered Gwen to be a little wanton and shameless when it came to men, and never hesitated to use Gwen as an example of the kind of behavior she refused to allow her young niece to emulate.

But secretly, Jayne had always admired Gwen's zest for passion and love and life, and her ability to go after what she wanted and not worry about what others felt or thought.

The older woman reached across the table and patted Jayne's hand affectionately, bringing her attention back to the present. "I know I might have missed the mark a tad last time, but I have a really good feeling about this man."

Truthfully, Gwen had missed the mark by a *mile* when she'd arranged a blind date between her accountant's son and Jayne. Sure, the guy had been good looking, but he'd also been way too cocky and arrogant when it came to his appeal to the opposite sex. They'd had absolutely nothing in common, and not only had he dominated most of the conversation for the evening—when he wasn't texting or talking on his cell phone—he'd left her footing the bill for dinner after his credit card had been declined. Then he'd had the audacity to kiss her, tongue and all.

Ugh. It was an experience she had no desire to repeat.

"Brian's incredibly handsome, and quite the gentleman which is hard to find these days," Gwen went on in her attempt to sway her. "And he's very successful and owns his own practice. He's quite the catch."

A smile lifted the corner of Jayne's mouth. "If he's such a catch, then why isn't he already taken?"

Gwen shrugged, as if the answer was a no-brainer. "Because he obviously hasn't found 'the one' yet."

Jayne was certain the reason why this Brian guy was still single wasn't that simple or sentimental, just as she was certain that she wasn't the woman of his dreams. "How do you know him?"

"He's Bella's veterinarian," Gwen said of the cute little Maltese she'd adopted a few years ago.

A doctor. She admitted to being impressed, but she just couldn't bring herself to go through another blind date of Gwen's choosing, no matter how good her intentions might be.

"I appreciate the thought, but I'm really not interested," she said, doing her best to gently turn her down.

Gwen wasn't having any of it. "How can you say you're not interested when you haven't even met him yet? I've known him for over two years now, and he's such a nice, polite young man. When I saw that he didn't have a date for my wedding either, I knew it was fate that I set the two of you up."

Jayne had to suppress the urge to laugh at the older woman's reasoning, but as much as she didn't want to agree to the date, she didn't want to offend Gwen, either. "Did you ever think that maybe he prefers to attend the wedding by himself, like I do?"

Gwen blinked much too innocently. "If that was the case, then why did he already agree to a blind date with you?"

Surprise rippled through Jayne. "He *did?*"

"Without hesitation," Gwen said, then pulled her wallet from her purse and withdrew a business card. "In fact, he gave me his personal cell phone number and he's waiting for you to call him to let him know when you're free for dinner."

It all sounded much too desperate to Jayne, like maybe the guy couldn't get a date on his own and was eager to take whatever he could get. Reluctantly, she took the card from Gwen, and read the imprinted name on it: Brian Reeves, DVM. She even recognized the name of his animal hospital, Advanced Pet Care, which was located a few miles away from Always in Bloom.

As if sensing Jayne was still trying to think up an excuse to avoid the blind date, Gwen tried a guilt tactic. "You wouldn't want to disappoint him, now would you?"

Jayne was very tempted to do just that.

"Give it up, Jayne," Darcie said as she straightened a rack of greeting cards and continued her eavesdropping. "Besides, it's one date, not a lifetime commitment."

"Exactly," Gwen chimed in, her gaze still optimistic.

Honestly, it wasn't the overly anxious vet Jayne was worried about disappointing, but Gwen. She really did adore her, and knew the older woman's heart was in the right place in wanting Jayne to find a man she could spend the rest of her life with. But after the last blind date Gwen had set her up on, Jayne didn't have a whole lot of hope that this one would end up much better.

Still, she knew she couldn't say no to a woman who'd been so good to her the past couple of years. "Fine, I'll go," she said, and the elation on Gwen's face made her agreement almost worth it.

She'd go to dinner with Brian Reeves, spend a few hours in his company, fulfill her end of the blind-date bargain, and at the end of the night pull the "let's be friends" card, which was the best way to avoid any hard feelings.

Friendship was good, especially since she'd have to see him again at Gwen's wedding.

3

BRIAN ARRIVED AT the oceanfront restaurant where he and his blind date had agreed to meet, thirty minutes earlier than the reservation he'd made for dinner. He checked in with the hostess to make sure that they'd have a table near the windows overlooking the water, then let the young girl know he'd be over at the bar until his date arrived.

The seafood restaurant was one of San Diego's most popular, and even though it was a Thursday evening, the place was quickly filling up. Since he wanted the advantage of seeing her first, Brian took a seat at the bar that gave him a direct view of the hostess stand, then ordered a Jack and coke to nurse while he waited.

As soon as the bartender delivered his drink, he took a sip, still unable to believe he'd let Gwen rope him into going on a blind date. He'd never had a problem getting a date on his own, and preferred to do so. But when Gwen had come into his office a week ago to get her Maltese updated on her shots, she'd caught him in a semi-compromising situation with another woman who'd spent the past few weeks attempting to seduce him, and was using a multitude of fake excuses about her dog's health to see him.

Shelly wasn't his type, not by a long shot. She had big

bleached blond hair, wore skin-tight pants with even tighter T-shirts that were so low-cut they revealed nearly half of her large, surgically enhanced breasts. Not only did he like his women all natural, with real curves and softer bodies, but he also liked them to possess a certain level of class and sophistication. Especially in public.

Numerous times, he'd gently turned Shelly down, but she clearly believed he was just playing hard to get and it was only a matter of time before he caved. He'd remained polite and professional, even as he'd grown increasingly annoyed over the fact that she was using her Jack Russell to get to him.

But her last visit to the pet clinic had been the clincher. Just when she thought the two of them were alone in the reception area, as soon as he delivered the news that the latest test results on her dog were negative and he saw no reason for Shelly to bring the Jack Russell in again, she'd plastered herself against him like an octopus in heat. She wound her arms tight around his neck, entwined one of her legs around his, and planted her lips to his in an aggressive, open-mouthed kiss.

Her attack had taken him completely off guard, and before he could diffuse the situation, Gwen had walked in on the two of them, her eyes wide with shock. He had to admit the scenario looked bad. Really bad. And it was more than awkward, to say the least, getting caught in such an embarrassing position by someone he liked and respected as much as Gwen.

It had taken a good amount of effort to disengage Shelly, but at that moment he knew what he had to do. He'd informed her that he could no longer treat her dog, and gave her the business card of another vet in town. She'd left in a huff, but at least he'd finally made his point that he wasn't interested.

Once Shelly was gone and he'd escorted Gwen and her Maltese, Bella, into a private exam room, the older woman hadn't wasted any time in chastising him for his behavior— even though it hadn't been his fault—like his own mother would have. If that hadn't been exasperating enough, she'd then insisted that she was going to find a *nice* girl for him because she didn't want him to end up with a hussy like Shelly. Better yet, Gwen knew a sweet woman who didn't have a date for the wedding either, and she was absolutely certain they would hit it off. And how great would it be that the two of them could attend the ceremony as a couple, instead of being alone and single on Valentine's Day?

The woman had been like a dog with a bone who wouldn't let go. While checking Bella's ears then listening to her heartbeat, he'd tried to gracefully bow out of the blind date by telling Gwen it just wasn't his thing, but she wasn't easily deterred. Instead, she'd enlightened him to the fact that the woman, Jayne, had already agreed to the date—which seemed a bit desperate to him—and he knew he'd look like a jerk if he refused.

So, reluctantly, he'd said yes. A day later Jayne had called his cell phone, and they'd agreed to a weeknight date the following Wednesday—something easy and casual since both of them had to work the next day. The arrangement was more than fine with Brian, and gave them both the opportunity to call it an early evening if they weren't the perfect match Gwen believed them to be.

Twenty minutes after first sitting at the bar, Brian spotted a woman walking through the doors to the restaurant, her black and purple outfit matching the color description Jayne had given him over the phone. She stood in line to check in with the hostess, giving him a few extra moments to finish his drink and observe her from a distance before they met face to face.

At least Gwen hadn't lied when she said that Jayne was pretty. Her silky, honey blonde hair was cut into a stylish, layered, shoulder length bob, and she seemed to be wearing minimal make-up—just enough to enhance her eyes, and some shimmery gloss on her lips. She was dressed more conservatively than the women he normally dated, in a purple blouse, a loose, flowing, black skirt and a pair of low-heeled shoes. There was nothing overtly flashy about her—she was the antithesis of Shelly in every way—and he found her entire appearance and ladylike demeanor a refreshing change.

Pleasantly surprised by his date, Brian slid off his bar-stool and made his way back to the front of the restaurant just as she reached the hostess stand. After a brief exchange, the hostess glanced back toward the bar and pointed at him. Jayne pasted on a smile and stepped toward him, and as he neared and got a closer look at her face, an overwhelming sense of familiarity washed over him.

Images of a woman in a sexy, one-shouldered, leopard print dress flashed through his mind, taking him back to that provocative night with her at the club. He'd seen up close and personal how those dark brown eyes of hers could turn hazy with desire, had tasted those lush lips and reveled in her uninhibited response to his touch. He also knew that the body beneath the simple outfit she wore now was soft and curvy, and fit his like a dream.

Three months might have passed, but he hadn't forgotten that night. Or her. She'd left an indelible imprint on his mind, and too often he'd wondered how things would have progressed between the two of them if only she'd stayed, instead of bolting while he still had his pants down.

But he'd just been given a second chance thanks to Gwen, and he planned to take full advantage of his lucky break.

Grinning, he stopped in front of her and held out his hand in greeting. "I'm Brian Reeves. You must be Jayne." He deliberately used the same line on her that he had when he'd first met her at the nightclub. Little did he know then that his Jungle Jane really *was* Jayne.

"I *am* Jayne," she replied, and as she slipped her hand into his to shake and looked into his eyes, the polite smile on her lips faltered.

He knew the precise second recognition hit her. Her eyes grew wide, her lips parted in shock, and a panicked look swept across her features. With her soft, slender hand enclosed in his, he felt her jerk back in startled surprise, but he didn't let go.

"Oh, my God," she said in a strangled voice. "You're the pirate."

"That would be me." He gentled his hold, but still didn't release her. Now that he'd found her again, he wasn't letting her go so easily. "So, we meet again."

Seemingly still in shock, she shook her head, the silky sway of her hair framing her delicate features. "This has to be some kind of mistake."

"A coincidence, definitely," he admitted with a smile. "But it's no mistake. You and I were set up with the best of intentions by Gwen, and I owe her big-time. I've spent the past three months wondering what I did to make you run off before we could even exchange names. I thought we had a strong connection." Holding her gaze, he rubbed his thumb over the pulse in her wrist and felt her shiver from his caress. Physical proof that there was still a level of heated awareness simmering between them.

"We only knew each other for a few hours," she said, her rationale thin and flimsy. "Hardly enough time to make any kind of connection."

"I'm going to have to disagree," he murmured, and knew

there was one thing she wouldn't be able to deny, no matter how hard she tried. He dipped his head toward hers, keeping his voice low so only she could hear. "Sexually, we connected quite well. Unless you were faking those orgasms?"

Her face flushed a bright shade of red, her embarrassment real enough to indicate that she wasn't the kind of woman who had a lot of experience with one-night stands. "I really can't do this with you," she said, the dismay in her voice matching the unsettled emotions in her eyes.

If he was an egotistical man, she would have crushed his male pride by now. But he was a confident and patient guy, one who believed that good things came to those who waited. A sexual attraction might have initially brought them together, but he'd dated enough women to know that there was a lot more substance to Jayne. Like that underlying vulnerability that intrigued and drew him, and a refreshing honesty he appreciated.

It was also difficult not to be aware of the obvious differences between Jungle Jane and this Jayne. Jungle Jane had been seductive and tempting. This Jayne was modest and far more self-conscious. It was an interesting contradiction. Ultimately, his gut told him that Jayne Young was a special and unique woman with a hidden sensuality just waiting for the right man to tap into. He'd had a taste of that wild eroticism, and suspected there was a whole lot more where that came from.

She was definitely a woman worth pursuing, for a variety of reasons, but getting her to agree was going to be another matter.

"Your window table is ready," the hostess said, interrupting their conversation as she came up to them with menus in hand.

"Come on, Jayne," he urged, and gave the hand he was

still holding a gentle, encouraging squeeze. "We're both already here. It's just dinner and I promise to be on my best behavior."

He watched her struggle with some inner conflict he didn't understand, then she released a deep breath and straightened her shoulders—which served to tighten her blouse across her soft, full breasts. "Okay. Let's do it."

Let's do it. He almost teased her over the double entendre, but didn't want to risk losing the ground he'd gained by embarrassing her again. The hostess walked into the dining area, and with a hand pressed to Jayne's lower back, Brian escorted her in the same direction, then held out a chair for her to sit facing the ocean view before taking a seat right next to her.

With Jayne's input on her preference of wine, he ordered a bottle of Pinot Noir. They were both quiet for a few moments as they perused the menu and decided what they wanted for dinner. Their waitress came back with the wine, poured them each a glass, and took their order. Once she was gone and they were alone again, Brian turned his attention to Jayne, who was smoothing her cloth napkin on her lap.

"Can I ask you something, Jayne?" he asked, keeping his voice light and neutral.

Despite his casual tone, a flicker of wariness crept into her gaze. "Sure," she said, not sounding certain at all.

He took a drink of his wine, and watched her do the same. "Why did you run out on me that night at the club?"

She set her glass back down, averted her gaze, and began fiddling with her fork. "Because I didn't want you to think that I'm *that* kind of girl."

He placed a hand over hers to stop her nervous fidgeting, and to force her to look back at him. In his estimation, the kind of girl she'd been with him, so sweet and hot and giving, wasn't a bad thing. But for some reason, she thought differently and he wanted to know why.

"What kind of girl is that?" he asked, genuinely curious to know her thoughts.

"You know…" Flustered once again, she pulled her hand from beneath his and waved it in the air between them, as if grasping for the right words to describe her behavior that night.

He found them for her. "Sexy? Desirable? Irresistible?" he asked, supplying all the adjectives that exemplified the woman he'd met three months ago. The woman he knew she still was despite her protective outer layers and demure demeanor that made her appear too prim and proper.

"I'm not *promiscuous*," she said, using a description that never would have crossed his mind had she not said it. "I don't go around sleeping with men on a whim. I'm sure you're used to that kind of thing with women, but for me, it just…happened."

He believed her, and wanted her to know that it wasn't a normal occurrence for him, as well. "I don't go around having sex with women I just met, either," he stated. "And just for the record, I'm very discriminate about who I have sex with. Like you, what we did that night at the club just happened. I didn't plan it."

She lifted a dubious brow, and he laughed at her skepticism.

"You don't believe me?" he asked.

She shrugged. "Your actions that night showed otherwise, not that I'm complaining."

It was a double-standard statement, and he didn't hesitate to point that out to her, grinning while he did so. "So did *your* actions, not that *I'm* complaining."

She blinked at him, and for a moment he thought she

was going to take offense. Then, unexpectedly, the lightest, sweetest laughter escaped her, the sound disintegrating the fine line of tension between them and immediately lightening the mood.

"Fine," she said on a sigh, even as a smile teased the corner of her mouth. "It just happened. For the both of us."

"And it was *amazing*," he added, wanting her to know exactly how he felt about her, and that night.

"Yeah, it was," she agreed softly.

He wanted so much to lean in and kiss her at that moment, to give her a physical reminder of what fantastic chemistry they had together. But before he could execute the move the waitress arrived with their dinner. She placed a dish of seared scallops and rice pilaf in front of Jayne, and grilled salmon and fingerling potatoes for him.

Now that they were on the same page regarding their attraction, he decided to take their discussion in a different, more personal direction in an attempt to get to know her better.

"Gwen tells me you're a florist, and you own Always in Bloom in town," he said as he speared his fork into a bite of salmon. "Tell me about that."

She didn't hesitate to talk about her business, giving credence to the fact that he'd chosen the right topic to get her to open up. She talked about her shop, her love of gardening and flowers, and how her Aunt Millie, the woman who'd raised her, was responsible for instilling a deep appreciation for nature and anything that blossomed from the earth's soil. She was animated and naturally endearing, and he was fascinated to see this whole different side to Jayne that completed the woman she was.

As they enjoyed their dinner and wine, he encouraged her to talk with questions of his own, and learned about the car accident that had claimed her parents' lives, and what her childhood had been like with her Aunt Millie. She'd had a stable, loving upbringing, but as she chatted about her aunt it became clear to Brian that some of Jayne's more modest and reserved traits had been due to her aunt's influence.

They talked about music, movies and books, and had a lot more in common than either of them would have thought. She seemed surprised to discover that some of the classics she'd read growing up, like *Call of The Wild* and *Treasure Island*, were some of his favorites, too. They both enjoyed jazz music, and while he would have pegged her for a romantic comedy kind of girl when it came to movies, she admitted to being a Hitchcock fan and loved thrillers as much as he did.

She asked about his family, and he told her about his parents, who'd been married for over thirty-five years and were still madly in love. He regaled her with amusing tales about growing up with his two older sisters that made her laugh, and how he was a total nerd in high school, which she said she found hard to believe.

"What made you decide to become a veterinarian?" she asked, right before she took a bite of one of her scallops.

"My father was a veterinarian," he replied as he refilled both their wine glasses. "As a kid, I spent my weekends at his clinic, cleaning cages and assisting him when he needed the extra help. I've always loved animals, so it was an easy, natural transition to become a vet like my dad. We worked together for a few years after I got my license, and when he had a heart attack and decided to retire, I took over the business for him."

"Sounds like we're both nurturers," she said with a smile. "Me with my plants and flowers, and you with animals."

"I guess so." He watched as she took a long sip of her

Pinot Noir, intrigued more than ever by everything he'd learned about her tonight.

By the end of their meal she'd relaxed and loosened up. She was smiling, her brown eyes were bright, and her expression was happy. He ordered a chocolate truffle cake for them to share, and she was now so comfortable with him that when it arrived she took her fork and went in for the first bite, which was followed by a deep, throaty moan of appreciation as she tasted the rich, decadent dessert.

Her enthusiasm made him chuckle. The rapturous look on her face made him hard. "I take it you like the cake?"

As if realizing how eager she'd been, she ducked her head and one of those engaging blushes swept across her cheeks. "God, I'm shameless," she murmured. "I love chocolate, and I love cake. Put the two of them together and I can't resist."

"Go for it." He pushed the plate closer to her. "It's nice to see a woman who isn't afraid to appreciate a good dessert."

She tipped her head. "Aren't you going to help me eat it?"

"I'll have a bite or two, but I'd much rather watch you enjoy it."

She didn't argue, and as a result she provided him with enough fuel for a dozen different fantasies, arousing him with the sensual roll of her eyes, a soft groan of pleasure as she swallowed a bite, and the slow glide of her tongue across her bottom lip as she licked away a smear of chocolate. He knew her seductive moves were uncalculated, which made it all the more of a turn on. He shifted in his chair to relieve the pressure straining against his zipper, and wondered if she realized the effect she had on him.

Probably not, but he intended to enlighten her before their date was over.

After eating the last morsel, she put her fork down and sighed contentedly. "That was *amazing.*"

Her comment was the same one he'd made about their hot night together at the club. He took in the glow on her face, and all he could think about was sex. With her. Again. "Yeah, it was."

His comment wasn't lost on her, and served to elevate the awareness that had been building between them all evening long.

He paid the check, and since they'd driven separate cars, he walked Jayne to hers. With every step they took toward her vehicle, she grew quiet and he suspected that a new batch of nerves was getting the best of her. When she turned toward him with her hand outstretched and a polite "Thank you for dinner," falling from her lips, he knew he was going to have to be a little more creative in order to make Jayne see that there was something worth exploring between them. He wasn't about to lose all the ground he'd just gained with her with a platonic handshake.

Slipping his hand in hers, he used it as an anchor to slowly pull her closer. "I'd rather have a kiss."

"I…I think we should just remain friends."

The longing in her golden brown gaze contradicted her too-formal request. He wasn't sure why she was so hesitant, but he was more than prepared to cajole her to his way of thinking.

Another gentle tug, and she was in his arms, her body pressed against his. When she didn't resist, he looped her arms around his neck, placed one of his flattened palms at the base of her spine, and threaded the fingers of his other hand through her softer-than-silk hair until he held her securely in his embrace.

Her breathing deepened, and her lips parted in anticipation. It seemed that all she needed was a little guidance, and he was more than happy to provide it.

"Yeah, we can be friends, too," he murmured, and set out to show her that while friendship was a good, strong foundation when it came to any relationship, the kind of hot physical chemistry they had together was an added bonus for both of them to enjoy.

The initial touch of their lips was soft and sweet, and when his mouth nudged hers in an encouraging gesture, she released a moan of surrender and made the first move to deepen the kiss, which he welcomed. She pressed closer, crushing her breasts against his chest as her fingers fisted in his hair. Clinging to him, she drew his tongue into her mouth, the slick heat and firm pressure of her lips on his spiraling straight to his groin in a rush of desire.

The guttural groan that erupted from his chest was an instinctive response to her seduction, primitive and purely male, and unlike anything he'd ever felt before. In a haze of lust, he realized this is what he'd waited three, long months for, and why no other woman since then had tempted him the way Jayne did.

She was, quite possibly, the one he'd been waiting for.

Every little thing he discovered about Jayne only made him like her more. They shared a lot of the same family values, and she was genuine, unpretentious and real. An intelligent, successful business woman who was passionate about what she did in life.

At this moment, he knew that passion of hers ran much deeper. She might be a lady in public, but in private…oh, Lord, he knew she had the ability to bring him to his knees, in the very best way.

Now that she'd given him all the ammunition he needed to coax her into giving the two of them a chance, he lifted his head and stared into her dark, hazy eyes. "You want me," he said, and grinned, knowing she'd be hard pressed to deny his statement after the hungry way she'd just kissed him.

She licked her damp bottom lip, as if tasting him again. "What woman wouldn't want you?"

Her opinion was the only one that mattered to him. "I like you, Jayne. A lot," he said as he stroked his hand up and down her back, wishing she was naked instead of fully clothed so he could feel her smooth skin beneath his palms. "And if it isn't already obvious, I want you, too."

She shook her head, a slight frown marring her brows. "No, you want the woman you met at the nightclub."

When she tried to pull away, he tightened his hold on her, taken aback by her comment and wanting clarification. "What do you mean?"

A soft sigh unraveled out of her. Her arms slid from around his neck, and her fingers played with the collar of his shirt—a sign he now recognized as a nervous gesture. "I'm talking about the daring, adventurous woman who had sex with you in a stairwell. But that was a onetime thing and isn't who I am. I'm actually quite ordinary."

She'd averted her gaze, and he tipped her chin back up so he could look into her eyes. "Trust me, sweetheart. You're far from ordinary." She fascinated him on all levels.

He'd also seen that daring, exciting, adventurous woman three months ago and knew she existed, but Jayne obviously didn't believe in her own sensuality. But now that she'd given him a glimpse of her upbringing with her staid, old-fashioned aunt, he had a better understanding of why she was so uncertain of her ability to seduce a man.

When she didn't respond, he decided to take on a different tactic, one that would be difficult for her to refuse and would give him more time with her without her feeling intimidated. She might be able to turn him down easily, but he had a feeling that for Gwen, she'd be more accommodating.

"Tell you what. Gwen set the two of us up because she thought we were a good match. I happen to agree." He feathered his thumb along her jaw line, then down the side of her neck until he felt her shiver from his caress. "She told me you were also invited to her rehearsal dinner Friday night, and she asked me to be there, too. So, let's make her happy and go as a couple to the dinner, and the wedding. We can enjoy each other's company for the next few days, then re-evaluate our relationship and where it might be headed after this weekend. What do you say?"

She worried on her bottom lip, and he could see the debate she was warring within herself. Should she, or shouldn't she? But somewhere along the way, their attraction won out over any doubts she might have harbored.

"I say...*yes.*"

4

She'd said yes.

Jayne lay in bed later that night, her mind replaying her response to Brian's proposition to spend the next few days together to make Gwen happy on her wedding day. While she'd originally agreed because she didn't want to let Gwen down, now, all alone, Jayne was forced to admit her reasons for saying yes to Brian went much deeper than pleasing her friend.

Jayne longed to please herself for a change, and if she was honest, she *wanted* to spend more time with Brian, even if it was only a few more days. Because unlike any other guy she'd ever dated, the undeniable attraction between them was hot and exciting, and for once in her life she wanted to embrace the erotic sensations he inspired and go with it.

Feeling sexy and desirable was all so new and different for her, and while she didn't have a whole lot of experience when it came to sexually confident men like Brian, she knew he was capable of giving her the greatest pleasure imaginable.

Unbidden, vivid images of the wicked things he'd done to her in that stairwell three months ago washed through

Jayne's mind, and her body responded to those provocative recollections. Brian's mouth ravishing hers. His clever tongue finessing her nipple before he sucked the tip deep and hard. Long fingers stroking her sex and bringing her to a shattering climax that made every orgasm that had come before pale in comparison.

And the entire time she'd responded so shamelessly—her hands tangling desperately in his hair, her body arching wantonly for more, her legs widening for his touch. Then she'd brazenly reached between them to take his thick shaft in her hand, shocking even herself with her bold move. But then he'd groaned his approval and desire had been quick to take over, and she'd instinctively stroked and caressed all that masculine heat and hardness, so eager to feel him thrusting deep inside her body.

And when he'd finally filled her up, she'd gone wild with a need so intense it was as if she couldn't get enough of him. For someone with little experience with such all-consuming ecstasy, the emotion had been frightening and overwhelming, and the wanton woman she'd become in that moment had been enough to make her bolt in the aftermath.

Closing her eyes, she shifted restlessly on her cool sheets as her trip down memory lane caused a rush of warmth to settle between her thighs, making her wish that Brian was with her now to ease the ache spreading through her. There was no doubt that he'd brought out a passionate side to her that she never knew existed, just as there was no denying that she'd liked how daring she'd felt with him. And for a few more days, she wanted to be the kind of bold and spontaneous woman who could keep a man like Brian satisfied.

She had nothing to lose, and everything, including immense pleasure, to gain.

THE NEXT MORNING at ten o'clock, Gwen arrived to pick up her weekly Thursday floral arrangement. As Jayne carried out a wrapped bouquet of Carnelian Mokara Orchids, the first thing she saw was Gwen's bright and eager expression. While Jayne would have liked to think the other woman's anticipation was due to the vibrant orange hue of the exotic flowers she'd chosen to put together, Jayne knew Gwen well enough to know she was more anxious to hear how her matchmaking skills had fared.

"Those orchids are gorgeous, Jayne," Gwen said, her polite compliment quickly giving way to the curiosity gleaming in her eyes. "So, how was your date with Brian last night? Did the two of you hit it off like I thought you would? Isn't he just the most handsome man you've ever met? And such a gentleman, too."

Gwen didn't have to sell Jayne on Brian's attributes. Jayne was already infatuated with the man, in a big way. "It was a very nice date."

"Just *nice?*" Gwen wrinkled her nose in disappointment. Obviously, she was hoping for the juicier results of their evening together.

While Jayne wasn't about to give Gwen a detailed report of her previous one-night stand with Brian, or their too-arousing kiss last night, she provided just enough to let the other woman believe she'd succeeded with this latest match of hers. "We clicked quite well, and I like him very much," she replied truthfully.

"And?" Gwen leaned across the counter, her gaze expectant as she waited to hear how the date had concluded.

Jayne smiled and gave her what she was angling for. A positive ending to last night's date. "And we'll be going to the rehearsal dinner together tomorrow night, and the wedding, too."

"I'm so thrilled." Gwen pressed a hand to her heart and

released a delightful sigh. "I just knew the two of you would make a perfect match."

Jayne wasn't so sure that she and Brian were perfect for one another, but the two of them had agreed to spend the next few days together to make Gwen happy on her wedding day. Being with Brian over the weekend certainly wasn't going to be a hardship considering how gorgeous and charming the man was, but everything about Brian made her want *more*.

More of him. More easygoing dates like they'd shared last night, where they'd connected on more than just a physical level and had enjoyed one another's company.

And, Lord help her, she wanted to experience more hot, spontaneous, unreserved sex like they'd had three months ago in a darkened stairwell.

As she charged the bouquet of orchids to Gwen's account, a flush of heat suffused her cheeks. When had her thoughts become so shameless? The answer came easily—the night she'd met her exciting, sexy pirate and he'd shown her just how good—no, how *phenomenal*—sex could actually be.

Since she was spending the weekend with Brian, she wanted one more night like the one at the club. He'd already made it clear that he wanted her, but she needed to give him the right signals to proceed, and she didn't know how.

Being raised by her sweet but old-fashioned Aunt Millie, Jayne had been instilled with a good-girl mentality from a very early age, and it wasn't an easy habit to break. But Darcie excelled in the art of flirtation and knew how to tempt and tease a man with the promise of pleasure, and Jayne hoped her friend could help her tap into her inner bad girl and give her the tips she needed to seduce Brian one last time.

That was Jayne's plan, anyway. It remained to be seen if she'd be successful.

"I can't wait to see the two of you tomorrow night." Gwen grinned, openly satisfied that her plan had worked like a charm. "Now I'm off to pick up my wedding dress."

Gwen gave Jayne a big hug, then gathered up her orchids and left the shop.

The rest of the day passed quickly for Jayne. Orders for Valentine's Day continued to pour in, and the extra help that she'd hired for the holiday was busy in the back of the shop putting together the various bouquets and arrangements for Valentine's, with Darcie supervising the process. Jayne worked on the delivery schedule, and double-checked floral displays as they were completed, then started on the arrangements for Gwen's wedding, which Jayne planned on delivering personally before the ceremony started since she'd be there, anyway.

Knowing she was going to be putting in a later night than usual so she could take tomorrow evening off for the rehearsal dinner, Jayne encouraged Darcie to take a late lunch with her at a nearby café. After their Cobb salads were delivered, Jayne gathered the courage to tell her friend about her plan to seduce Brian—and how she desperately needed Darcie's help to make sure she didn't fumble in her attempts to entice him.

An hour later, Jayne was armed with an arsenal of tantalizing tricks guaranteed to get Brian hot and bothered before the main event. According to Darcie, men were physical and visual creatures, and it was all about the slow build up of sexual tension, and arousing a man's five senses along the way. Her advice included Jayne wearing a light spray of perfume in strategic places that would tempt his sense of smell, and making sure whatever outfit she wore gave Brian plenty of skin, and cleavage, to look at to increase his awareness of her. Whisper intimate things in his ear, and don't forget the power of a subtle caress to raise the level of heat and attraction between them.

It all seemed simple enough…for someone who had experience. For Jayne, she knew she was going to have to stretch beyond her own personal comfort zone and ignore her more modest sensibilities in order to become that bold and brazen woman. If the pay-off was anything like that night at the club with Brian, she was willing to give Darcie's suggestions a try.

After lunch, Darcie insisted on accompanying Jayne on a quick shopping spree at the trendy boutique next to the café to find a new dress for her to wear—one that would make Brian's jaw drop when he picked her up for the rehearsal dinner. After giving a big thumbs down to Jayne's first three outfit choices, Darcie selected a sexy pink and black wrap around dress from a rack, declaring it the perfect dress to tease a man's imagination. Jayne also bought a new bra and panty set, and a pair of black heels that were higher and racier than anything she already owned.

Multiple bags in hand, they headed back to Always in Bloom and worked until after nine that evening. As soon as Jayne got home, she took a hot shower, put on a pair of cotton pajamas, and got into bed. She was too keyed-up to go right to sleep, so she reached for the novel on her nightstand and decided to read until she was sleepy.

At ten-fifteen, her cell phone rang. No one ever called her that late. When she checked to see who was calling, her heart skipped a beat, then resumed at a frantic, giddy pace when she saw Brian's name.

After inhaling a calming breath so she didn't sound too anxious, she set her book aside and connected the call. "Hello?"

"Hey, there," he said in that rich, smooth voice of his.

"I wanted to call you earlier today just to say hi, but things got a little crazy at the clinic and I just got home a little while ago. I hope it's not too late to call?"

"No, not at all." Was he kidding? Just hearing his voice made her feel all warm and fuzzy inside, like a teenager with a huge crush on the cute boy in school. "What happened at the clinic?" she asked, curious to know more about the things he did as a veterinarian.

"There were a lot of dog emergencies today, and two that were accidentally hit by cars, but nothing life-threatening, thank goodness," he said, his tone relieved. "Then, as I was getting ready to leave for the evening, a woman came in with a box of kittens that she'd found abandoned near her work. Normally I would have told her to take them to the animal shelter, but they were already closed and the woman was allergic to cats and couldn't keep them overnight, and I just couldn't turn the kittens away."

Smiling, she pushed her pillows against the headboard and settled more comfortably against them. "You're a softie."

"Yeah, I definitely have a soft spot when it comes to animals," he said unapologetically. "And I have to admit, these kittens were pretty darn cute. I could tell they were starving, so I took them to an enclosed pen I have in the back of the clinic and fed them. Then I went ahead and checked each one of them over to make sure they were healthy."

Of course he had. She could just imagine how gentle he'd been with each kitten, and she'd even bet he'd played with them, too. "Do you have any animals of your own?" she asked.

"No." A regretful sigh drifted over the phone line. "I'd love to have a Golden Retriever, but right now, my schedule at the clinic is so erratic that I just can't give a dog the kind of attention it deserves. When I get married and have kids, we'll definitely have a dog or two, and probably other animals, too."

Thinking about Brian being married with kids made her actually feel…jealous. A ridiculous emotion considering she'd just met him.

"How about you?" he asked, his question bringing her attention back to their conversation. "Any dogs or cats?"

Curling her legs beneath her on the bed, she glanced at the framed photo on her dresser that held a cherished picture of Jayne and her cat, and felt a pang of sadness that thankfully had eased over time. "My aunt gave me a kitten for my tenth birthday. She was white and fluffy and I named her Snowball. She died of old age about six months ago." Jayne still missed the feline every single day.

"I know it's hard. It's like losing a family member." His voice was laced with genuine compassion and understanding. "Have you thought about getting another pet?"

"Sure," she said, but knew it would be difficult to replace her furry friend. "I've thought about going to the animal shelter to adopt a cat, but I'm afraid I'll get there and want to take them all home."

"Now who's the softie?" He chuckled, the deep, masculine sound settling in her belly like a warm shot of cognac.

"Guilty as charged," she admitted.

"So, what were you doing before I called?" he asked, smoothly changing the subject, which she didn't mind.

She ran her fingers over the hardbound book on the comforter beside her. "Just reading the latest thriller from John Connelly."

"Mmm. Sounds exciting."

"Hardly," she said, recalling the gruesome murder scene

she'd been reading that he'd interrupted. "Homicide and serial killers aren't the kind of things that turn me on."

"Thank God," he said humorously. "So tell me, Jayne. What *does* turn you on?"

She wasn't adept at trading innuendos with men, so his flirtatious question caught her by surprise. Normally, she would have shied away from such an intimate discussion, but after Darcie's pep talk that afternoon, she realized this was her chance to test the waters, so to speak.

She plunged in before she changed her mind. "*You* turn me on."

"Good to know," he murmured, an unmistakably wicked note to his voice. "Tell me more."

She bit her bottom lip, feeling just a moment's hesitation. Could she go on and travel down the path this conversation was sure to lead? While engaging in phone sex was a foreign concept to her, the thought of exchanging provocative dialogue with Brian sparked excitement in her belly. Ultimately she trusted Brian and knew he'd never ridicule her attempts, and that knowledge gave her the courage to try.

"That night at the club…I think about it all the time." Her cheeks warmed, but knowing he couldn't see her reaction, she forged on. "It's my go-to fantasy when I need one."

"Mine, too," he said huskily.

His admission bolstered her confidence a little more. Laying her head against the pillows, she closed her eyes and summoned the sexiest memories of that night. "All I have to do is think about your mouth on my breasts, and your fingers touching me…"

"Where?" His voice sounded like crushed gravel. "Where are my fingers touching you?"

Her nipples tightened, and a rush of moisture dampened

her panties, right where she was imagining those long, skillful fingers. Their conversation was quickly turning erotic, her need for Brian building inside her like hot steam that needed release.

And it was easier than she imagined it would be to give him the answer he was waiting for. "Between my legs."

"Yeah," he rasped. "You were so hot and wet."

She pressed her thighs together to ease the ache building there, but it wasn't enough. "You made me that way."

He groaned, the sound vibrating over the line. "You're killing me, sweetheart."

In a good way, she knew. Knowing she could have such an arousing effect on him felt very empowering. "I loved the way you felt thrusting inside of me," she whispered intimately. "You were so hard and thick and I didn't want you to stop."

"You were so tight and eager, and I came a lot sooner than I wanted to."

She bit back a groan of her own and after only a second of uncertainty, she dared to ask, "Are you hard now?"

"Like granite." His breathing was heavy and labored. "And it's all your fault."

She smiled to herself. "I'd say that I'm sorry, but that would be a lie."

"You are so bad."

And bad never felt so good, she realized, surprised at just how easy it had been to be a little naughty with Brian. And how much she'd liked it.

"I need to go," she said reluctantly. It was after eleven and her alarm was set for five. "I have a ton of things to get done at the shop tomorrow and I need to get up early. I'll see you when you pick me up for the rehearsal dinner."

"I can't wait." He sounded anxious *and* impatient.

"Me, either." And she meant it, because as soon as they'd

fulfilled their commitment to Gwen, the rest of the evening belonged solely to the two of them and finishing what they'd started tonight.

5

Who was this woman?

The question tumbled through Brian's mind as he walked with Jayne to the garden area of the San Diego country club where Gwen's wedding rehearsal was taking place. Between the initiation of phone sex last night, and the sensual way Jayne was dressed now, he was beginning to wonder when she'd become such a self-assured version of herself.

When he'd arrived at Jayne's place to pick her up, he'd been stunned when she'd opened the door wearing a form-fitting pink-and-black dress that accentuated her curves. The top portion of the outfit came to a deep vee between her breasts, displaying a nice amount of pushed up cleavage, and the dress itself wrapped around her gorgeous body and tied off at the waist. The do-me heels were an added bonus that not only boosted her height, but seemed to give a lift to her confidence, as well.

Now, as they made their way to the gazebo where Gwen, Patrick, and a few other people were gathered, his body buzzed with awareness. The light, floral fragrance she wore filled his senses, and each step she took showed a flash of bare, slender leg that drew his gaze every damn time, and made him think about what she might be wearing beneath all that clingy fabric.

If he thought Gwen wouldn't miss them at the rehearsal ceremony and dinner, he would have ushered Jayne back to his car, driven her home, and as soon as they were alone the first thing he'd do was unravel that silky tie at her waist to unwrap her like the delectable gift she was.

But straight ahead, Gwen was waving at the two of them to get their attention. With her arm tucked into her groom-to-be's, she and Patrick both headed in their direction, making an unnoticed escape impossible.

"Jayne, you look lovely," Gwen gushed as she took in Jayne's statuesque appearance, then she glanced at Brian and gave him a once-over, too. "And, of course, you're as handsome as ever, Brian."

"And you are positively glowing," Brian replied to the blushing bride-to-be. He kissed the older woman on the cheek before shaking hands with her fiancé—a distinguished looking man with salt and pepper hair, kind blue eyes, and a likeable personality. "It's good to see you again, Patrick."

"Same here," the other man said with a friendly smile.

Gwen grabbed both of Jayne's hands and held them apart to get a better look at what she was wearing, then gave an approving nod. "I love your new dress and shoes. I think Brian is a good influence on you."

Jayne blushed, and Brian was glad to see that one of his favorite, endearing qualities about Jayne hadn't changed, despite the other transformations she'd made tonight.

"I had nothing to do with her outfit," he insisted.

"Oh, I'm sure you did." Gwen winked at him. "A woman only wears a dress like that to make sure her man's eyes stay on *her* at all times."

"Gwen!"

Jayne tried to admonish the outspoken woman, but Gwen wasn't dissuaded. "It's the truth. I've been around the block a time or two...or five," she admitted, and slanted Patrick a sheepish glance. "I've tried the tactic myself, and it's foolproof."

Brian laughed in amusement. "If that's the case, Jayne's ploy is working. I can't keep my eyes off how stunning she looks." He couldn't keep his hands to himself either, he thought as he slid an arm around her waist and pulled her closer to his side.

Jayne pressed her hands to her pink cheeks and shook her head in embarrassment. "You're both incorrigible."

"It's all in good fun," Brian assured her, knowing she probably hadn't anticipated just how much attention her makeover would draw.

Gwen smiled at the two of them, then shifted her triumphant gaze to Patrick. "Didn't I tell you they'd make an engaging couple?"

"You did." He patted the hand she'd tucked back into the crook of his arm, his eyes filled with pure, unadulterated adoration for the woman he was going to marry. "I'm always telling Gwen that she needs to stop with the matchmaking and blind dates, but she's an incurable romantic and insists that love sometimes needs a little nudge in the right direction to make it happen."

Gwen nodded in agreement. "I just don't ever want anyone to miss out on the greatest love of their life. That almost happened to me, and I'm just so lucky that I got a second chance with Patrick."

An unspoken, emotional look passed between the older couple, a private moment that only they understood and shared.

Someone called out that the rehearsal was about to begin, and Gwen and Patrick headed back to the gazebo where family members were waiting, along with the minister. Brian took a seat with Jayne on one of the white wooden chairs set up on the lawn. A half hour later the practice run for the wedding was over, and Gwen and Patrick introduced them to their children, who were actually older than Jayne and Brian with kids of their own. They mingled for a while and enjoyed a glass of wine and appetizers, then followed the rest of the group inside the country club for dinner.

There were over a dozen people seated at the table, and the conversation around Brian and Jayne was constant and lively, drawing them both into various discussions. But even as Brian talked with the man sitting across from him—who was Patrick's son, Collin—he was one hundred percent aware of everything Jayne said and did.

She was more flirtatious than she'd ever been with him before, and he didn't miss the oh-so-casual way she'd touch her hand to his thigh beneath the table as she asked him a question. Or how she'd purposefully lean into him as she reached for the bread basket, pressing her soft, full breasts against his arm. She whispered in his ear a few times, her husky voice like a caress straight to his groin, and even the way she ate her dinner was an erotic display of throaty moans of pleasure, a wet lick of her lips, and soft, sated sighs that made him think about sex. With her.

Every single move she made, every enchanting surge of laughter that escaped her, every look or touch she gave him, kept his libido at a fever pitch of need.

But there were times, when she thought he wasn't watching her—like now—that he noticed how uncertain and nervous she actually was, as if she wasn't quite sure of her ability to entice him. She was going through the motions, and his body was definitely responding to every single one of her attempts, but through it all he caught glimpses of the sweet, demure woman Jayne was at the very core.

And that was the woman he was ultimately attracted to and wanted.

She glanced up at him, a little startled to find him looking at her, watching her. She'd left her hair down in soft, loose waves, her eyes appeared dark and exotic, and good Lord, he ached for her in physical and emotional ways that defied his own logic or reason.

She tipped her head to the side and sucker punched him in the gut with a sensual smile she'd somehow perfected. "Why do you keep looking at me like that?"

"Because I'm enthralled by you," he replied honestly, and dipped his head closer to hers, to whisper in her ear the way she had in his earlier. "Gwen was right, you know. If your intent was to distract me the entire night with that sexy dress and the way it showcases all your best assets, then I want you to know that I'm totally and completely hooked."

She gave him what he could only interpret as an adorably coy look, but his comment definitely seemed to bolster her confidence. "Good."

Did she really say *good?* He almost chuckled, but didn't want to ruin the moment, or have her think he was ridiculing her. Far from it. He had no idea what she was up to, but he was curious and fascinated enough to go with it and see where it all led.

After dinner, they said their good-byes and Jayne promised to arrive early with all the flowers for the wedding and reception. Once they were sitting in his car with the engine idling, he decided to let Jayne decide what happened next—especially since she seemed to have some kind of agenda tonight. Whatever she wanted to do, he was game.

One hand on the steering wheel and the other on the gear shift, he glanced toward her side of the car. "Is there anything else you'd like to do this evening?"

He watched her take a deep, fortifying breath, then she met his gaze in the darkened interior of the vehicle, her eyes brimming with the same desire pulsing through him. "Yes. I'd like to go back to your place."

Where the possibilities were absolutely endless, he thought. "Sure." He kept his reply casual and nonchalant. No stress, no pressure, no expectations. Whatever happened between them once they arrived was totally and completely up to her. Absolutely nothing, or everything she could imagine—he was fine with either as long as it meant spending time with her.

He kept up a steady stream of light, easygoing conversation, mostly about the wedding rehearsal and how much he'd enjoyed meeting Gwen's and Patrick's families. By the time they arrived at his house she appeared much more relaxed, but that calm demeanor seemed to evaporate as soon as they walked into the entryway and he closed and locked the door behind them.

Gently touching his hand to the base of her spine, he guided her into the living room and switched on a lamp. "Would you like a glass of wine, or coffee?"

She shook her head, swallowed hard, and shifted anxiously on her high-heeled shoes. "The only thing I want is you."

Her words came out in a nervous rush of breath, and while his body was immediately on board with her idea, he was hesitant to jump right in until he was certain Jayne had thought things through. "Are you sure you want to do this, Jayne? Because we can just watch TV, or talk—"

"I don't want to talk." She tossed her purse onto the couch, then strolled toward him, the extra sway in her hips drawing his gaze like a magnet. "And I'm sure about *this,* about you and me. *Very* sure."

As he looked one last time into her eyes and saw the

want and hunger darkening their depths, he knew without a doubt her need for him was real and heartfelt, and that's what ultimately swayed him.

With her palm splayed on his chest, she guided him back a few steps, until he found himself pressed against the nearest wall. Immediately, he recognized her move as a role reversal that echoed the night in the stairwell, but this time she was the one in control. Obviously, she felt she had something to prove—to him or herself, he wasn't sure— and for now, for tonight, he was more than willing to let her have her way with him. But later, he intended to make it very clear that she didn't need to try and be something she wasn't with him, that she was everything he wanted and more without changing anything at all.

Then she kissed him, the exquisite feel of her soft, warm mouth against his making him forget everything but her and how much he wanted her. In his bed and in his life. For a very long time. Possibly forever.

The realization made him shudder, and she mistook his reaction for a physical one, instead of the emotional response it had been. He'd correct her error later, because at the moment she was a little busy deepening the connection of their mouths and chasing his tongue with her own while unbuttoning his shirt and pushing it over his shoulders and down his arms. He shrugged out of the garment for her and let it fall to the floor, and her hands quickly dropped to the waistband of his slacks to unbutton his pants.

Just as she started to unzip his trousers, he gently grabbed her wrists, pulled her hands away from his strain-ing cock, and murmured against her lips, "Let's go to the bedroom." He didn't want to do this standing up again. This time, he wanted things horizontal with a soft mattress beneath them.

But he'd forgotten that Jayne was the one in charge,

and she wasn't ready to do things the traditional way. "Not yet," she said, and treated him to a smile that seemed full of feminine secrets. "I want you to sit on the couch."

He reminded himself that it was her show, so he did as she asked. She moved to stand in front of him, and with her teeth grazing her bottom lip and her gaze flickering with a hint of unease that contradicted her next provocative move, she tugged on the tie securing her dress and let it slowly unravel, unerringly heightening the suspense of what lay beneath. Anticipation pumped through Brian's veins, and when the silky fabric finally slid down the length of her body and pooled around her high heeled shoes, his mouth went dry and his cock pulsed with lust and approval.

Her skin turned a rosy shade of pink as he openly and leisurely looked his fill of her, taking in the way the tops of her breasts nearly spilled from the cups of her black lace bra, and how those delicate panties framed her curvy hips and dipped between her supple thighs. He knew it had taken a wealth of courage for her to just stand there while he ravished her with his gaze, and he made sure she knew he liked what he saw. Every…single…inch of her.

Smiling, he forced his gaze back up to her face. "You are so stunning, you take my breath away."

She laughed softly as she knelt between his spread legs. "Darcie did say this lingerie would have that kind of effect on you."

"No, *you* have that kind of effect on me," he said, wanting to clarify the difference. The lingerie did not make her the woman she was on the outside, or even on the inside. She was beautiful, in every way.

She reached to undo his pants, and this time he didn't stop her. He toed off his shoes, then lifted his hips to help her remove his trousers and briefs. She dragged his socks off too, so that he was completely naked. Licking her lips, she shyly appraised his body, and eyed his erection with awe and fascination. Tentatively, she touched the broad head, ran a finger down the rigid length, then wrapped her hand snug around his shaft as she boldly explored that male part of him.

Jesus. His cock twitched and the muscles in his stomach rippled as he endured the overwhelming pleasure of having her hands on him…then her mouth as she unexpectedly leaned forward, wrapped her lips around him, and took him deep. A ragged groan erupted from his chest, and instinctively, his hips jerked upward. His hands fisted in her hair—at first to show her what he liked, then to pull her away when he discovered she was a natural at giving blow jobs and knew just how to push him to the brink of no return.

He tugged her head gently, and exhaled a relieved stream of breath when she finally released him. "I need a condom," he rasped. "They're in the bedroom."

"I have one in my purse." She reached for the bag she'd tossed on the couch earlier and retrieved a foil packet.

So, just like the first time, she'd come prepared. This all suddenly felt too familiar, like a repeat of the past somehow, but before he could analyze the feeling she was standing and skimming out of her panties and urging him to put the condom on.

As soon as the latex was in place, she straddled his hips and sank down on him, until he was buried to the hilt inside of her. Then she went utterly still. Eyes wide, she stared at him expectantly, hesitantly, every one of her doubts and insecurities laid bare for him to see.

He smoothed his palms up her thighs, then traveled higher, to the indentation of her waist. "There's no way to get this wrong, sweetheart," he murmured, and slowly guided her hips back and forth, again and again, so that she could feel the slide of his cock deep inside. "Just do whatever feels good. Slow and easy, or hard and fast, you're in charge," he reminded her.

Placing her hands on his shoulders, she adopted the same rhythm he'd created, slowly undulating her hips against his, then gradually picking up the pace until he was rubbing that sweet spot within her and she was completely lost in sensation. Moaning rapturously, she closed her eyes, tossed her head back and arched into him, taking him deeper still.

The straps of her bra fell down her arms, and her full, naked breasts spilled free, beckoning him with a temptation he couldn't resist. He palmed the weight of one warm breast in his hand, opened his mouth over the other, and used his teeth and tongue to finesse her nipple. She felt and tasted like heaven, and he couldn't get enough of her. Didn't know if he ever would.

She continued to ride him, and he knew the exact moment her orgasm surged through her. She cried out as her inner muscles clenched him tight, milked him, and he gripped her hips tighter, groaning as he came right along with her, his heart racing like a man who'd stepped off a very steep cliff with no net to catch him.

It felt like he'd taken a freefall...straight into love.

As he tried to catch his breath, he realized that the knowledge didn't shock him. Instead, he welcomed the feeling, and hoped she would, too.

Once he recovered, mentally and physically, he looked at Jayne to gauge how she was doing. Her head was tipped forward, but her eyes were still closed, as if she wasn't quite ready to face him just yet. But her expression was sated, and she had a small, pleased smile on her lips. Her bare breasts were still distracting as hell, and he slipped the straps back up to her shoulders so she was covered once again.

"Open your eyes and look at me, Jayne," he said, tucking her tousled hair behind her ear so he could see her face.

Her lashes slowly drifted upward and her gaze met his. An intimate warmth and affection glowed in the brown depths, and it was all he needed to see to know she'd been affected, too. She might have started out this evening believing it was all about sex, but she wasn't immune to the deeper connection between them.

He grinned at her. "I like this confident, sexy Jayne."

He'd meant it as a huge compliment, but instead of basking in the accolade the smile on her lips faded and the light in her eyes dimmed, and he wasn't sure why.

She moved off of him and he let her because he sensed she needed a few moments to herself. While she stepped back into her panties, he picked up his briefs from the floor, then made a quick trip to the bathroom. When he returned, she'd slipped back into her dress and was securing the tie at her waist.

Not a good sign, he thought.

"I should go," she said, and wouldn't meet his gaze.

In the short time he'd been gone the warm afterglow of sex had evaporated. She'd clearly withdrawn and erected emotional walls. Remembering the abrupt way she'd bolted on him that night at the club, a feeling of foreboding settled in the pit of his stomach.

Trying not to overreact, he braced his hands on his hips. "I'd like you to stay."

"I CAN'T." SOMEHOW, SOMEWAY, Jayne managed to remain calm as she picked up her purse, her gaze still averted. She feared once she looked him in the eye she'd unravel and fall to pieces, and that wouldn't be a pretty sight at all. "Tomorrow's Valentine's Day, and it's going to be crazy busy at the shop."

"I'm off tomorrow," he said, obviously hearing her reply for the excuse it was and calling her on it. "I'll come and help out at the shop with whatever you need until we have to get ready for Gwen's wedding."

"I'd rather you didn't," she said, and finally forced herself to look at him.

She saw the confusion etching his features, and sure enough, her heart clenched like a vise in her chest. A sure sign that she was in much deeper than she'd ever anticipated, and that scared her on a level so emotional it nearly stole the breath from her lungs.

As did his heartfelt comment about liking the sexy, adventurous Jayne who'd seduced him tonight. She'd heard the approval and awe in his voice, and deep inside she'd been unable to shake the lingering fear that *the real Jayne*—the one who'd been raised by an aunt who would have disapproved of her wanton behavior tonight—wasn't bold and daring enough to keep a man like Brian content and satisfied in the bedroom for the long term.

The truth was, she was way out of her league with Brian, and risking a relationship with him had the huge potential of leaving him disappointed with her, as well. Especially if she couldn't live up to his expectations of the kind of sexually experienced woman he thought she should be.

She'd wanted one more night with him, and it had been amazing—another hot memory to store away to fantasize about when she was alone. But she knew that ending things now, as difficult as it might be, was for the best and would undoubtedly save her a wealth of heartache later.

Brian stabbed his fingers through his hair in frustration, his brows creased into a dark frown. "I'm not sure what's going on here, Jayne. Was it something I said or did?"

She winced at the sharp note to his voice. "I can't do this," she whispered around the lump in her throat.

"Can't do what?" he pushed.

"Be with you." Swallowing hard, she pressed a hand to her stomach, a feeling of dread nearly overwhelming her, because she was about to push the most exciting man she'd ever met out of her life for good. "That confident, sexy Jayne you say you like so much isn't really me. And deep down inside, I'm not really the kind of girl who goes around having sex with strangers in a darkened stairwell."

"And I don't want a woman who has sex with every single guy she meets," he refuted with a shake of his head. "I know you're not *that* kind of girl. I knew the night we first met you were different, that you didn't do that kind of thing easily. And one more thing," he went on, clearly not done with his argument. "This is not about you having to be that confident, sexy, over-the-top person in order to hold my interest. This is about you and me and the connection between us. That's what matters, and we have *great* chemistry together."

Jayne wanted to believe him. She really, truly did. But when it came to the kind of scorching hot passion they'd shared, she found it difficult to trust that something so sexually phenomenal and emotionally gratifying could last into the future.

The burn of tears filled her eyes, and she hated that her emotions and fears kept her from taking the biggest risk of all with Brian. "I…can't."

He looked completely and utterly defeated. "You mean you won't," he said, his tone flat.

She didn't reply, because there was nothing left to say that could change her mind, and he seemed to sense that, as well.

He drove her back home in silence, but there was no denying that he looked angry and hurt, and she felt responsible for both. He walked her to her front door and made sure she was safely inside before turning and leaving without so much as a goodbye.

She knew she deserved Brian's cool attitude after the way she'd just cut him out of her life, and as she watched through the living room window as he drove away, she'd never felt so alone.

6

VALENTINE'S DAY was filled with love and romance, hearts and flowers, and secret admirers and passionate lovers. The moment Jayne opened the doors to her shop that morning she'd been bombarded by those sentiments, and was reminded with every flower, card, stuffed animal and balloon bouquet she'd sold that she was spending yet another Valentine's Day alone.

This year, by her own choice.

She'd had a lover and could have been basking in the knowledge that she had someone special to share the day with, but instead her heart felt empty, hollow, even. Like she'd lost something precious and rare. The pain of walking away from Brian was more intense than she'd ever anticipated, but her fear of rejection was even stronger and that was what had kept her from staying with Brian last night.

She'd honestly believed she could have a one-night fling with Brian and walk away with her heart intact, but that hadn't been the case. Because while she'd believed her seduction would just be about hot sex, she'd been flooded with emotions that were new and terrifying and had shaken her to the core.

Last night, she'd learned that she wasn't the kind of person who could separate the two into nice little compartments, and as soon as she realized that she'd fallen for Brian, and fallen hard, old fears had clawed their way to the surface and she'd panicked.

And now she was all alone. Again.

Sighing, she pushed the troubling thoughts from her mind and kept busy with the steady stream of customers that came into the shop throughout the afternoon. But there was no escaping the love, laughter and overall happiness everyone seemed to be feeling. Even Darcie's boyfriend dropped by to give her a large heart-shaped box of her favorite chocolates, and nestled inside had been a diamond engagement ring.

In front of everyone in the shop, Josh had gotten down on one knee and proposed to the woman he loved, and with a squeal of excitement, Darcie had said yes. Cheers and clapping ensued, and Jayne hugged her best friend and congratulated her.

While she was thrilled for Darcie, all the romance in the air made Jayne feel like she was suffocating. Needing a break, she went back to her office where it was quiet and pulled out some paperwork. A little while later, someone knocked on the closed door, then Darcie poked her head inside with a big, I'm-so-in-love grin.

"Guess what?" she asked, her eyes still sparkling with joy over her recent proposal.

"You're in love and engaged?" Jayne replied, her voice light and teasing.

"Yeah, I am. But that's not all." Darcie stepped inside, a pink box tucked beneath her arm. "Something just arrived for you."

Surprise and curiosity rippled through Jayne as she stared at the box, which had little cut-out holes in it and a heart on top with the words "Be Mine" written across. "Who is it from?"

"I don't know. A courier dropped it off." Darcie gently set the box on Jayne's desk. "Open it up and find out."

"Okay." Just as she reached for the lid, she heard a soft, mewling sound from inside, and her heart skipped a beat. She opened the box and staring up at her was the sweetest, cutest, fluffiest black and white kitten with the deepest green eyes. Immediately, Jayne knew who the feline was from, and as she lifted the ball of fur from the box she noticed there was a card attached to the big red bow tied loosely around the kitten's neck.

Cuddling the kitten to her chest, she read the bold, masculine print on the card.

> She needed a good home and I thought of you. I know you'll take good care of her. Her love and acceptance is unconditional, as is mine. Love, Brian.

"Oh, I am so in love," Darcie gushed as she scratched the kitten beneath its chin.

So was Jayne. With the cat and with Brian. She swallowed the huge lump in her throat and smiled as the cat began to purr—loudly. "You're already taken," she said to Darcie.

"So I am." She sighed and glanced at the diamond solitaire on her ring finger. "By the way, the courier also left a box of cat food and other supplies for your new friend. I'll have someone bring them back for you."

"Thanks."

Once Darcie was gone, Jayne played with the kitten for a while, then realized she needed to figure out a name for the feline, but nothing clever sprang to mind. She also thought about what Brian had written on the card, about the cat's love and acceptance being unconditional…as was his—despite the fact that she'd so carelessly, and selfishly, walked away from him last night.

Brian's words haunted her for the rest of the afternoon, until it was time for Jayne to leave. She boxed up the flowers for Gwen's wedding and reception, then went home to take a shower and change. She made a nice bed for her kitten in the laundry room and left her with a litter box, food and water, then headed to the country club on her own.

The fact that Jayne arrived for the wedding alone didn't escape Gwen's notice. As soon as Jayne was finished setting up the flowers and arrangements, she met with Gwen in the bridal room, the other woman looking concerned when she should have been happy and glowing.

"Where's Brian?" Gwen asked without preamble. She was sitting at a vanity table, dressed in white lace and looking like the beautiful bride she was going to be, while her bridesmaids continued to primp and get ready for the ceremony. "The two of you were supposed to come to the wedding together. What happened?"

Jayne knew the woman's questioning was inevitable, and she did her best to explain the situation without going into detail. "We decided to come separately."

"Why?" Gwen frowned. "Did the two of you have a spat?"

Jayne pulled a clear plastic container from her purse that contained a special something for Gwen. "More like a difference of opinion," she hedged.

Gwen waved a regal hand in the air. "Then talk it out and make it work."

"I wish it was that simple."

"It is," Gwen said matter-of-fact, then lowered her voice a fraction so only Jayne could hear. "And the best part is, the make-up sex is amazing."

Jayne laughed at the older woman's outrageous comment. At sixty-eight, Gwen was feisty as heck. "I made something especially for you."

Gwen wagged a finger at her. "You're changing the subject."

"Yes, I am." She didn't want to talk about Brian any more. It hurt too much. "It's a floral hairpin," she said, and showed her the cluster of fragrant roses and gardenias she'd designed.

"It's gorgeous," Gwen said, truly touched by the gesture. "Will you put it in my hair for me?"

"Sure." Smiling, Jayne used the attached comb to secure the flowers into Gwen's upswept hair, then pinned it in place.

Gwen looked into the vanity mirror, her expression softening. "Today I'm going to marry the man I should have married fifty years ago."

Jayne did the math and realized fifty years ago Gwen would have been eighteen. Gwen had always referred to Patrick as the love of her life, but Jayne didn't know the story behind their meeting and courtship. "What do you mean?" she asked.

"Sit down." Gwen patted the chair next to her, and once Jayne was comfortable, she went on. "I've never told you why I've been married and divorced so many times."

"It's really none of my business."

"I know that, but I want to tell you, because sometimes we lose sight of what's really important to us, like I did." Gwen glanced up, and her gaze took on a faraway look. "Patrick and I were both sixteen when we met, and we were young and madly in love and I thought we'd get married once I graduated from school. But my parents never approved of Patrick. We were wealthy, and his family was not, and my father wanted 'better' for me, and that's what he told Patrick when he went to my father to ask for my hand in marriage when I turned eighteen."

Jayne could only imagine how shocked and hurt Patrick had been, and by the pained look on Gwen's face, she'd been devastated, too.

"So, Patrick broke up with me and joined the Army, and I went on to be the dutiful daughter, and after a while Patrick and I completely lost touch." Gwen smiled sadly. "The first man I married was a doctor, but he wasn't Patrick. None of my four husbands were, hence the divorces. I spent all those years searching for that same connection I felt with Patrick, and even though we both went on to marry other people and have our own families, none of the other men I was with matched up. Patrick was the only one who accepted me for who I was inside, and not for my family's wealth, and I let him go and never even tried to fight for him and what we had together, and I should have. All those wasted years..." Gwen shook her head in regret.

The emotion in Gwen's voice prompted Jayne to take the other woman's hand in hers and give it a gentle squeeze. Obviously, Gwen's story had a happy ending, but it had taken many years for Gwen and Patrick to find one another again via a social networking site. But now Jayne had a better understanding of Gwen's need to play matchmaker and set people up. She wanted them to have their happily-ever-after, just like she'd gotten hers.

Jayne also realized that her Aunt Millie had been so wrong about Gwen. Gwen wasn't wanton...she was passionate and loving and hopeful. She was a strong, confident woman who enjoyed everything life had to offer and wasn't afraid of following her dreams, which included sharing the rest of her years with the man who'd stolen her heart fifty years ago.

"I know this sounds crazy, but I see myself and Patrick

in you and Brian. You two are slight opposites, but it's obvious to me that you also have a special connection, and that's worth taking a chance on."

Connection. There was that word again. Brian had used it, too. And they did *connect,* on so many different levels it was frightening to her. He was the first man to accept her completely, quirks and all, and as scared as she might be to hand her heart over to Brian, it was time to take a leap of faith and trust in Brian and what was between them.

Faith. She smiled, realizing what a perfect name that would make for her new kitten.

"The wedding is starting in five minutes," someone called out, and Jayne knew that was her cue to leave. She gave Gwen a hug, and before they parted ways Gwen shared one more piece of advice, and that was to follow her heart. Jayne promised her she would.

After leaving the bridal suite, Jayne took a seat on one of the white wooden lawn chairs just minutes before the ceremony music began. As the wedding party took their places in the lit-up gazebo, Jayne's gaze anxiously searched the small crowd of people, looking for Brian. She didn't find him, and a part of her wondered if he'd decided not to come tonight, then she discarded that idea. Despite what might have happened between the two of them, Brian wouldn't disappoint Gwen.

Once the ceremony was over, everyone filtered back into one of the country club's ballrooms for the reception. It was then, on the other side of the rows of chairs that she finally saw Brian. Her pirate. The man who'd swept her off her feet and hopefully still wanted her. He looked gorgeous, and her eyes ate him up, taking in his tousled dark hair, his crisp white shirt, and the perfect fit of his navy suit.

His gaze locked on hers, and her heart leapt into her

throat and her palms were suddenly sweaty. She forced her feet to walk toward him, and the sense of longing that filled her felt so, so right. Only with this man, she realized.

Because he was *the one*. From the depths of her heart, she knew it. And believed it.

She stopped in front of him, her stomach churning, because she had no idea what was going through that head of his after what she'd put him through last night.

"I'm so sorry," she blurted, needing to get this out before she lost her nerve. "I'm sorry I walked out last night. I'm sorry I was too scared to stay. All I know is that I'm following my heart now, and it's leading me straight to you." And she knew it always would.

"I don't want to lose you," she rushed on, her voice sandpaper rough. "And I don't want to spend years regretting the fact that I let you go. Can you forgive me for being so stupid?"

The corner of his mouth quirked up in a charming, relieved grin. "There's nothing to forgive, sweetheart," he said, his tone rife with understanding as he reached out and caressed the back of his fingers against her cheek. "I know you're scared and I figured you needed time to process everything. There was no way I was going to let you walk away for good, because you're worth fighting for."

She shook her head, wondering how she'd gotten so lucky with him. Oh, yeah, Gwen and her blind date. "Are you for real?" she teased.

"I think so." He reached for her and pulled her into his embrace. "But come here and you tell me."

Completely alone with him out in the garden area, she wrapped her arms around his neck, his body warm and solid against hers. And very, very real. "You are everything I've ever wanted, and more," she told him, and knew there was one request she needed to ask of him. "This connection of ours is all so new to me, so please be patient with me."

His hand stroked down her back and over her bottom, his eyes darkening with desire for her. "It's new to me, too," he confessed huskily. "I've never fallen in love with anyone so fast before."

"Love?" Shocked, the word caught in her throat.

"Yeah, love." For a moment, he looked uncertain, and his hold on her tightened, as if he feared she'd try and bolt again. "Are you okay with that?"

Hope formed in her chest, and she embraced it. "More than okay." She exhaled a deep breath, and trusting him to be there for her always, she returned the sentiment that had been blossoming in her heart. "I love you, too."

With an answering groan, he kissed her, pressing their mouths together in an intense, fierce meeting of souls. His tongue glided past her lips, and his hands slid into her hair to hold her steady so he could drink his fill of her. When he finally lifted his head, she was breathless and aroused and wishing they were alone.

"By the way. Thank you for my Valentine's Day gift. I already love her," she said of the precious kitten he'd given her.

He smiled, his hands still skimming her body, as if he couldn't stop touching her. "I knew you would. What did you name her?"

"Faith."

"Really?" He sounded surprised. "Any special reason why you chose that name?"

She nodded, her fingers undoing the first few buttons on his shirt so she could slip her hands inside and feel the heat of his skin against her palms. "Because every time I see her I'm going to think that I need to have faith in my life. Faith in you. Faith in us."

"I like that," he whispered. "A lot."

She bit her bottom lip and eyed the darkened gazebo behind them. Music poured out of the reception area, and they were still all alone. Dusk had turned to twilight, casting strategic shadows in the flowered arbor, and the romantic atmosphere gave Jayne a very naughty idea.

"Do you think anyone would miss us if we disappeared into that gazebo for fifteen minutes or so?" she asked huskily.

He arched a brow at her brazen suggestion, but the lusty grin tipping the corners of his mouth told her that he liked her way of thinking. "I think it's safe. Everybody's having too much fun inside."

Willing to take the risk, she led him into the white structure and proceeded to get acquainted with just how mind-blowing make-up sex could be. And how a bit of spontaneity could add a whole lot of spice to their love life.

Because with Brian, she felt daring and adventurous and wild. It wasn't something she had to force or pretend with him…it just was.

* * * * *

HOLD ON

BY
LESLIE KELLY

To Denise Damiano and all the rest of the "old gang"
at Answerphone—it was lots of fun!

1

SARAH HOLT'S JOB might not be the most exciting one in the world, but it sure could be sexy. Like right now, for instance.

She'd just heard personal details about someone else's sex life. Soon, she'd share those details with a rich, powerful man. They'd discuss private, naughty things. There'd be mentions of heat and odd sensations in personal areas. The word *intercourse* might enter the conversation, and *vagina* certainly would.

Sexy stuff.

Except for the fact that the man she'd be speaking to was sixty and married, that the heat was caused by fever and the odd sensations involved itching. Oh, plus, the intercourse was being had by—and the vagina belonged to—another woman.

Yeah, super-sexy, that. Only, *not*. But all in a day's work—if you worked as an answering-service operator for a company that specialized in taking after-hours calls for physicians. Or, in her case, if you were the co-owner of Call Anytime, who doubled as an operator during heavy shifts like this one.

Her business partner, Mindy, sat in their office doing

paperwork. Sarah, who had lost the coin toss, was here in the bullpen taking forty calls an hour. Which was why she had just had the pleasure of hearing an itchy, hot-crotched woman describe her symptoms…as if getting *that* personal would ensure a return call from her physician.

"So you'll get Dr. Emerson to call me back?" asked the woman who'd dialed her doctor's number on this busy Saturday. "Valentine's Day is Monday, and I've got a date."

Poor guy. Hope he practices safe sex.

Before the caller had finished describing her symptoms, Sarah had pulled up Dr. Emerson's after-hours instructions on her work station. As usual, he wanted to be paged to call the service to get all the gory details, rather than receiving them in a text.

"I'll page him and give him your message."

"So, he'll call me right back?" the woman persisted.

Knowing not to promise that, Sarah repeated, "I'll page him."

Hanging up, she sent the page, then eyed the dedicated doctor's line, which every operator could access but only senior ones were supposed to answer. She was the most senior person on the floor…and would almost certainly be the one stuck talking to Dr. Emerson about his yeasty patient. *Oh, yay.*

As Sarah waited for the doctor to respond—certain he'd call from a golf course—aka every Florida doctor's second home—she forced herself to remember it was good that she had to work the phones today. It meant business was thriving.

For the past two years, she and Mindy had worked sixty-hour weeks, both of them determined to succeed. Having been best friends since the second grade, when Mindy had rescued Sarah's Smurfette backpack from a classroom bully, they made a good team.

Mindy had always been the tough, ballsy, backpack-saver, while Sarah was the quiet, reasonable one who could be counted on to talk her friend out of doing something stupid. Going into business together had seemed like a no-brainer. Mindy provided the creative juices and Sarah the business sense. And after just two years, Call Anytime was a bona-fide success.

Of course, that business success had caused some erosion in other areas. Her personal life was in a stall. And her romantic one in a kamikaze death spiral.

Be honest…it wasn't like you had one to begin with.

"Doctors' line!" someone called, interrupting her musings.

She answered. As expected, it was Dr. Emerson, who listened, flirted, then hung up as someone in the background called, "Fore!" Sighing at how repetitive the days seemed, she decided to take a quick break, but paused when she saw an incoming call pop up on her work station.

"Somebody's calling Dr. Steve," she whispered. It was fitting that Steve Wilshire was a cardiologist—just seeing his name on the screen made her heart race.

Like Dr. Emerson, Dr. Wilshire liked to phone in for his messages. So, if this was a legitimate patient issue, he'd be paged, and somebody here would get to talk to him soon.

Her heart raced even faster.

Dr. Steve had the greatest voice, deep and calm, masculine and sexy. He'd made quite an impression on her during their very first conversation. He was incredibly friendly and easygoing when calling in, unlike a lot of other high-powered doctors. Never slimy, never inappropriate, never rude and abrupt—he was simply a gentleman. One who always sounded truly concerned about his patients.

From that first call, she had wanted to meet him in

person, something she'd never even considered before. Some devilish bit of curiosity had even made her look him up online.

Big mistake. Seeing his handsome picture on his website had almost made her too self-conscious to answer when he called. But, knowing they'd never meet face to face, she had let herself enjoy the brief verbal interactions—titillating highlights of some pretty boring days.

It was innocent and harmless. She'd never let on that she had a tiny crush on him, or that she fantasized that one day he'd ask if he could take her to dinner so they could meet at last. Their relationship was built on her lonely daydreams, she knew that...but that didn't mean it wasn't important to her. And though she knew he would remain in her daydreams, there was one thing she'd done differently when talking to Steve Wilshire. She'd let him hear the *real* her.

After surviving a shocking bout with esophageal cancer as a child, which had damaged her vocal cords, Sarah had been left with an unusual speaking voice. As an adult, the suggestion that she become a phone sex operator had grown so frequent, she'd considered changing her name to Desirée or Erotique. Yet, it was because of her voice that she and Mindy had come up with the idea for this business. Smooth and throaty could be sexy, but it could also be soothing, especially to frantic patients.

Soothing...except when she was talking to Steve Wilshire. Whenever *he* called in, she probably sounded like that vampy phone-sex operator everyone said she should be. She pretended she was the kind of woman who could *have* a man like that, rather than one who'd been so sheltered by her parents throughout her sickly childhood that she wasn't far past the virgin state. At twenty-five. Pathetic.

Four rings now. *Too long.* Unable to resist, she pushed

the answer button, saying, "Dr. Wilshire's answering service."

A woman's voice—airy, vapid—replied, "Hi. Uh, I have a problem. I mean, it's not a medical thing…it's personal."

Disappointment filled her. "The doctor requires any non-emergency calls to be made to his office when it opens Monday."

"He might wanna know I'm breaking our blind date tonight."

A blind date? The incredibly handsome doctor needed to be set up on a blind date two days before Valentine's Day? That was beyond wrong. And the very idea that someone was breaking that date, through an answering service no less, was even more so.

"But I guess you could leave the message for Monday, so he'll know why I didn't show up," the woman said, unconcerned.

Indignant, Sarah snapped, "I'll take the message."

"Okay. I met this other guy last night." Squealing, the woman added, "He's a rodeo clown and he's takin' me to Texas!"

A prize, indeed. "Okay."

"The doc won't care," she said carelessly. "We've never met. It was just a set-up through a friend of a friend."

Some friend. Sounded like Dr. Steve needed a new one. Stat.

Biting her tongue, Sarah took the whole message, sighing when she got the woman's name. Bambi. Just perfect. A bimbo named Bambi had definitely never been part of her sweet—and yes, a little erotic—daydreams about Dr. Steven Wilshire.

Sarah managed a somewhat polite goodbye before hanging up and paging the doctor. But she did not want to be the one to deliver this message. She might sound too personally upset on his behalf...because she was. Wonderful, handsome men like Dr. Steve shouldn't get dumped before the first date. It was against the laws of nature.

Pulling off her headset, she glanced at the operator in the next chair. "I'm going on break," she said, before heading into the glass-walled office she shared with Mindy.

Knowing Sarah better than anyone, her friend must have immediately noticed something was wrong. "What is it?" Mindy asked with a concerned frown.

"Some twit was supposed to meet Dr. Steve tonight for a blind date, and she canceled on him with two hours notice."

Mindy rolled her eyes, stating the obvious. "She obviously hasn't seen him."

No doubt about that, even if the woman hadn't confirmed it herself. "She said they never laid eyes on each other."

"Her loss." Mindy smiled that Cheshire-cat smile. "If I'd known he was on the market, I'd have made you take a shot."

Sarah sputtered a little, feeling heat flood her face. She had never said a word to anyone about her secret fantasies.

"You think I didn't notice you had the hots for the guy?"

"Oh, God," she groaned.

"You can't hide lust from me, chica. I invented it."

That wasn't too much of an exaggeration. Mindy had also likely invented, or at least inspired, the term *man-eater*. And yes, Sarah supposed there was lust to see. But what she felt went further than that. True, she was attracted to Steve Wilshire, but she also just liked him. A lot. A whole lot.

Maybe she'd built him up to be more than he was—like some kind of Prince Charming. But in her fairy tales, the charming prince didn't get ditched by some rodeo-clown-loving airhead.

"So, a blind date… You're sure they've never seen each other before?"

"I'm sure. Why?" Sarah asked.

Before Mindy could answer, the dedicated physicians-only line rang. To her surprise, Mindy answered it. "Doctors' line," she said, her eyes on Sarah.

Tensing, Sarah watched, wondering why Mindy had answered. Things weren't *that* crazy out in the bullpen.

"We did page you, Dr. Wilshire," her friend said. "But it's not a 911. The woman you're supposed to meet tonight called."

Closing her eyes, Sarah mentally filled in the other half of the conversation. *I didn't want to date her anyway. Where's that sexy-voiced angel who usually answers my calls?*

"She forgot where you're supposed to meet."

Her eyes flying open, Sarah mouthed, "What are you doing?"

"She asked me to text her the address. Oh, and she also wanted to know how you are going to recognize each other?"

Sarah leaned closer to whisper, "Are you crazy?"

Jotting something down, Mindy said, "Okay, doc, we're all set. I'll send her the info right away." Then she hung up.

"What are you thinking?" Sarah snapped. "Do you want us to lose one of our best clients?" The idea of losing even that small vocal connection with her fantasy man made her head hurt. Not to mention her heart.

"It's true, they've never met. He said he'd be wearing

a navy suit and she should look for him by the fountain."
Mindy shoved the paper she'd written on across the
desk. "Here's the address." She grinned. "You have two
hours."

Getting it, Sarah's jaw dropped. "You've lost your
mind."

"Oh, come on, it's perfect. He has no idea what the
woman he's meeting looks like. So, you take this chick's
place, have a great time, get laid by your dreamboat and
walk away."

Get laid by your dreamboat. The words echoed in her
head, even though "getting laid" by him had never even
entered her mind.

Making love? Well…she'd cop to that, if only to herself.

"Hell, I'd do it in a heartbeat," Mindy added.

All the more reason why she shouldn't. Mindy's love-
'em-and-leave-'em track record wasn't exactly stellar. "I
can't."

"You can. You're beautiful and sexy and smart… You're
the only one who doesn't know that yet." Smirking, she
added, "And if you don't do it, I will."

Sarah gasped. "You do and I'll rip your hair out."

The look on Mindy's face told her she'd been manipu-
lated into revealing how she felt about Steve Wilshire.
Damn.

But it was true. She did want him, even if they hadn't
met face to face. *Doesn't matter. You can't do it. You won't
do it.*

Only, as the minutes ticked by, Sarah began to suspect
that she could do it. And, more shockingly…that she
would.

STANDING BY THE FOUNTAIN in the lobby of an upscale
beachfront hotel, Steve Wilshire glanced at his watch. His

date was late—only ten minutes, but still, enough to make him worry.

What had he been thinking, letting Rick set him up? His old buddy had been married and divorced *three* times. That was two times more than Steve's pathetic attempt at matrimony. So what had compelled him to take the other man's advice and dive back into the shark-filled waters called dating?

Then he remembered. Dr. Graham Tate—older, proper, a bit stodgy…and his potential partner. The desire to form a partnership with another doctor—relieving the heavy weight of a solo practice from his shoulders—had led him here. Tate was a family man. And when Steve saw him tonight, he did not want to be asked, yet again, why he'd ever divorced that lovely Jenny.

Because lovely Jenny was a lying, conniving schemer?

True, but that wasn't a very good answer. Bringing a date would stop the questions and signal that he was not a sap pining for his ex-wife. Mainly because he *wasn't*…pining, anyway. Yeah, the break-up had stung, but looking back and being honest, he knew his own inattentiveness had at least contributed to it.

And if he ended up in bed with this woman, Bambi, who according to Rick would be the perfect person to get him 'back in the saddle,' all the better. No-strings sex with a party girl might be just what the doctor ordered.

Still, a blind date with a woman he'd never even spoken to? "You must have been out of your mind!"

"Excuse me, you're Steve Wilshire, aren't you?" said a woman, a *very* sexy-voiced one, who had come up unnoticed and had obviously overheard him talking to himself.

Great way to start the evening. She thinks you're loco.

Sighing, he turned to her. "Yeah, sorry, uh…"

The words died on his lips because she was *so* not who he'd been expecting to see. She was nowhere near the type of woman Rick would ever set him up with. She was too smart-looking, quietly pretty, not flashy enough for his old buddy.

Though she suited him just fine. *Very fine indeed.*

She smiled. And she went from pretty to breathtaking. "Hi."

"Hi," he replied, the breath sucked out of him by that warm smile, and the twinkle it brought to a pair of amazing bronze eyes.

Then there was the voice. God, that sexy, smooth, whiskey-soaked-velvet voice. He wanted to listen to her read pages from the phone book. And if he thought he might get to hear her whisper wicked, erotic words in his ear as he made love to her, he would happily lead her out of here to some place more private, to hell with the fundraiser, with Tate, with the partnership.

He'd never had such a strong, sudden reaction to a woman before, and he almost chalked it up to pure sexual deprivation. But he didn't think that was it. He met women every day, and since his divorce a lot of them had made their interest known. Some of them had been damned attractive, too. But not one had really gotten his juices flowing with just a few words.

Don't get too excited, jackass. Your real date's gonna be here any minute.

Right. She wasn't his date—she couldn't be. Frustration and disappointment washed over him and he forced himself to get his head out of his pants. Or her panties.

Mistake. Thinking of her panties almost put a tent in those pants of his. He clenched his teeth and willed his cock back into Idle. Hell, he was reacting like some fifteen-year-old kid meeting a hot college girl for the first time.

"You are Steve Wilshire, right?"

He nodded, wondering what she wanted. Because, as much as he might like to walk into the banquet with this woman on his arm, he knew she wasn't here for that. Obviously she recognized him from somewhere and had approached him for another reason.

Please don't be some surgeon's trophy wife.

The thought made him shift his gaze to her left hand. No ring. *Whew.*

Before he could ask her what he could do for her, she shocked him completely. "I'm your blind date."

He was momentarily struck dumb, all his expectations, his certainties, fleeing in a pleased rush. It didn't make any sense, but for just a second, he didn't really care. His pulse sped up a little, a pure adrenaline reaction to excitement.

Yeah. Excitement. Interest. Heat.

Intense curiosity.

She swallowed hard, lifted her chin, and stuck out a hand. Her plump bottom lip trembled the tiniest bit before she said, "It's nice to meet you."

"Uh, you, too," he murmured, taking her hand, still not quite understanding any of this.

She *had* just said she was his date, right? This petite, pretty rather than in-your-face-sexy woman with thick, honey-brown hair that brushed soft-looking bare shoulders, was his date? The woman with *that* voice was his date?

Wouldn't that be nice…if it were really true.

"I'm sorry I'm a little late," she said.

God, that voice. It brought forth every one of his boyhood Jessica Rabbit fantasies. It also sounded vaguely familiar…but probably because every guy dreamed of being set up with a woman who looked like sweetness and sounded like sin.

There was, of course, one problem.

"I didn't mean to keep you waiting."

"It's okay," he mumbled, still holding on to her hand, which she made no attempt to pull from his grasp.

Her fingers were soft, small, like the rest of her. But she was no waif. She had curves where a woman should be curved, and perfectly indented valleys that invited a man's hands. Those perfect curves and valleys were perfectly displayed in her strapless black dress.

He'd been expecting a tall, stacked, leggy, vapid blond bimbo and had gotten a short, curvy, brunette, whiskey-voiced mystery woman.

Not knowing what to say, or even what to think, he simply continued to stare, reaffirming his first impressions.

Yes, petite. Yes, adorably sexy. Yes, honey-brown hair, beautiful gleaming eyes, creamy skin, bare shoulders, amazingly sexy voice. Yes, incredibly hot.

And, no. She most definitely was not his date.

He'd seen a picture of the woman Rick had set him up with. Actually, he'd seen several. Bambi's Facebook page had contained a bunch of images. Many of them, he suspected, had been taken by her, courtesy of one extended arm—the new standard portraiture of the social-networking age.

This woman looked absolutely nothing like that collagen-lipped, platinum blonde, who, according to her profile, liked kittycats and words that started with the letter *S*.

Right now, looking at this imposter, a few *S* words came to mind. Words like *stroke*. *Slide*. *Squeeze*. And they grew even more graphic from there.

Funny, he hadn't had any of those wicked thoughts when he'd seen the pictures on his laptop screen. So, no, he was not disappointed at this last-minute substitution. Not one bit.

But he couldn't help wondering…if this *wasn't* the woman Rick had set him up with, who was she?

And what the hell was she up to?

2

You shouldn't have done this.

The words had been replaying in Sarah's head since the moment she'd spied Steve across the lobby. They had replaced the ones that had been rolling through her head during her drive home from work, her quick shower, her frantic search through her closet and the drive up the coast to this hotel: *You're not going to do this.*

Now, however, seeing the warm smile, the interest in his face, another phrase began to whisper. *This just might work.*

What that meant, what would define "success," she couldn't say. She'd been focused on just showing up and introducing herself, not much more than that.

Other than having the most romantic, exciting night of your life with a man you've been dreaming about for months?

Yeah, okay, that, too. But only way down deep in the most secretive recesses of her mind. Really, the main point had been to say hello, see if he called her a big, fat, lying imposter, and then wing it from there.

So far, so good. He was smiling, and there had been definite interest—attraction—in his expression for the first few seconds. At least, she *thought* that's what it had been. Of course, then there was the fact that he didn't seem to want to let go of her hand.

But she needed to take baby steps, to see if they made it through dinner before she dared dream that she might actually have a chance of physical interaction with this impossibly gorgeous man. Later, after the hors d'oeuvres, she'd think about a kiss. And if they made it through the salad, she'd contemplate his hands touching her in very sensitive places. With the surf and turf might come images of him surfing her turf.

As for actual intercourse? God, that was so far off her radar, she didn't know what she'd even say if he suggested it. The very thought of it would just have to wait until after some kind of decadent chocolate desert. Or at least a few drinks.

Speaking of which, she wished she'd stopped in the bar and had one. It might have steadied her nerves…not to mention her ankles, which wobbled in Mindy's borrowed, ridiculously high-heeled black shoes.

"I'm just glad you didn't stand me up," he said.

"Only a crazy woman would do that," she retorted.

Though he looked curious, he didn't question her vehemence. "Well, I have to admit, I was getting a little nervous," he said, sounding laid-back and friendly, though he continued to study her face closely. The gold flecks in his green eyes twinkled, and his sexy mouth bore the faintest hint of a smile. "I know a boring fundraiser isn't the ideal scenario for a first date, but I am glad I won't have to go in there alone."

First date. Not just blind date. The term jarred her…but also gave her hope. It was one thing to contemplate having a wildly romantic adventure on a one-time-only date. But he'd said *first*…implying there could be a second, or possibly more than that. She hadn't even allowed herself to go there in her head.

Was there a chance things might not begin and end tonight? Well, maybe. Everything depended on how well they hit it off and, of course, whether he was the forgiving sort. And if he had a sense of humor.

Oh, yeah, funny story, you see, my best friend, who's kind of easy, thought it would be a great idea for us both to lie to you, our client, and have me pretend to be somebody else for the night. Hilarious, huh?

The chances of him laughing, too, were pretty slim. Which just made enjoying every second she had with him all the more critical. Sarah had one shot, and she intended to make this a night she would never forget. She wanted to imprint every moment on her memories, to never forget that she had, just once, stepped out of her comfort zone and gone after a lovely moment with her own Prince Charming.

As for how far this went, how intimate those moments got? Well, that was still a big question mark at the end of the fairy tale.

Sarah had very little experience with physical intimacy, but what she lacked in experience, she hoped she would make up for in enthusiasm. And while she wasn't the most beautiful woman here, she knew her body had to be sending signals. Nature itself should be telling him she was attracted to him. There was a chemical reaction between them—she felt it, recognized it, even though she'd never experienced it before.

"I do have to say, I'm surprised," he said, finally releasing her hand, which he'd held on to for at least an hour. Or a minute. Same difference when it came to this man. "You're not the type of woman I'd have expected Rick to set me up with."

Rick. Rick who? Oh, God, she was so dead. What had she been thinking? There were so many details she hadn't thought through.

"Oh, wait. You've never actually met him, right? He'd said you were a friend of a friend."

Relieved, she nodded. "Right." *Just don't ask which friend.*

"Well, you're most definitely a pleasant surprise."

"Thanks," she managed to say, clearing her throat a little. Hoping to distract him, she added, "I'm glad you're not disappointed."

"Far from it," he said, still studying her intently. She felt the heat of that stare, not to mention the warmth of his tall, firm body, so perfectly clad in an impeccable blue suit.

He was, without a doubt, the handsomest man in the building. She'd spent a good five minutes eyeing him from across the ornate lobby, trying to work up the nerve to go through with this. During that time, she'd done some people-watching.

The hotel was bursting with travelers. There were couples here on Valentine's weekend getaways, pale, northern families with kids and au pair in tow, as well as a bunch of professional types who were heading toward a ballroom for what appeared to be a large, private function.

None of them were anywhere near as attractive as he was. With his dark-blond hair, sparkling green eyes, square jaw, broad shoulders, strong chest and the rest of that tall, lean form, he drew the eye of every female, from nine to ninety-nine, who walked past him. And for this night, this one amazing, *stolen* night, he was hers.

She tried to feel bad about stealing it. But to give herself credit, it wasn't really a theft, more like…a gift.

Actually, when it came right down to it, she was just

being a good citizen and recycling. Some other woman had thrown him away, and she'd picked him up.

Just like a Dumpster-diver. So classy.

"I hope you'll forgive me," he said, watching her closely. "But I've forgotten your name. This came about so quickly."

The word *Sarah* came to her lips, but she bit it back with a hard chomp on her tongue, and froze. Deer-in-headlights time.

If she gave him her real name, and he later remembered, she was doomed.

If she gave him the one he was expecting, and later forgot to answer to it, she was doomed.

Face it. She was doomed.

What on earth had she been thinking? She couldn't do this. She was *so* not a seductress. She'd only had sex with one other guy in her entire life—and, just like in that movie about the forty-year-old virgin, the longer she'd gone without, the more sure she was that she just didn't have the knack for it. Seduction, sex, romance, any of that stuff. She might have a sultry voice, and she might be pretty, but some sexy cell had been left out of her anatomy. She just didn't have what it took to *make* something happen with a man.

Coming here tonight had taken every bit of courage she had. And there were so many ways she could ruin this. Not the least of which was that she had to try to keep her voice as clear and un-throaty as possible, on the off chance he might remember the operator he'd spoken with once every week or two for the past six months. All these extra little details were bound to trip her up!

"Cat got your tongue?"

"Umm…." She seriously thought about just spilling her guts. She could tell him what had happened, throw herself on his mercy. Then, if he took it well, she could ask if he'd like her to continue as his date. The worst he could do was say no.

No, it isn't the worst he could do, he could fire you.

Not just fire her, but say a word or two to other doctors in the area. Blackballing really wasn't that uncommon in her business. Not that he seemed the type, of course. In fact, she couldn't imagine him being so vengeful.

But the business wasn't hers, alone. Mindy was her partner, and she deserved to be protected. Sarah was already taking an outrageous risk here. She needed to do whatever she could to keep Mindy out of it.

And honestly, of those two evils—him turning her down, or him firing her—Sarah couldn't say which was worse. Losing his contract, or losing her one chance to get close to him—either one was too depressing to contemplate.

He snapped his fingers. "Oh, wait, Bambi, isn't it?"

It seemed the decision had been taken out of her hands, at least for right now. Her throat painfully tight, Sarah swallowed her conscience. In a nod so quick and tiny it could have been mistaken for a reflexive hiccup, she confirmed the lie.

"Is that a nickname for something? Or your real name?"

Feeling like she was being thrown a lifeline, she breathed a sigh of relief at being able to tell him at least one truth.

"My real name's Sarah."

"That's better," he admitted, smiling down at her. "Sorry to say, you don't look much like a Bambi. Did you love the movie as a kid or something?"

She wrinkled her nose. "No way."

Dummy. She should have said yes. How else was she going to explain having the nickname Bambi?

"Not a fan, huh?"

"Well, I liked the first half when I was five. That was all

I was allowed to watch of it. I never saw the ending until I was in high school."

He grinned. "Let me guess. Overprotective parents?"

"You have no idea," she said, hearing the dryness in her tone. "I had to get a friend to show me how it ended during a sleepover. Believe me, nothing brings down a sweet sixteen party like a wimpy teenager crying off the two pounds of mascara she'd put on during the obligatory makeover session."

He chuckled, that same warm, masculine sound that had given her shivers through the phone. Now, in person, it made her legs wobble. Which made the stupid shoes wobble, too. If he actually laughed, she might pitch right off her shoes into the fountain like some high-dive performer off a pier.

So what? A handsome doctor will be right there to give you mouth-to-mouth resuscitation.

Huh-uh. When she pictured his mouth on hers, it was with both of them in a private, secluded place. And dry.

Well, mostly dry. Her panties had been moist since this afternoon when she'd first thought about spending a romantic evening with him.

"I never liked it, either," he admitted. "So, it was just one of those weird things that stick, huh? I get that. One of my aunts still calls me E.T. Apparently I looked like an extraterrestrial at birth."

"Well, you definitely grew out of that phase."

"Yeah, I'm glad the wrinkles, purplish skin and baldness didn't last past the age of twelve or so."

With every word he spoke, Sarah felt herself relax. Every sentence reinforced the impressions she'd had of him on the phone—he was incredibly easy to talk to. He had no pretensions, he went out of his way to put the person he was speaking with at ease. Just a really all-around nice guy, at least so far.

Again she had to wonder why on earth someone like Steve Wilshire needed a blind date. He should be able to stick his finger out his car window as he drove down the street, point to any woman of legal age, and name the time and place. *You. My bed. Tonight.*

Yes, indeed, you betcha!

"Listen," he said, "the official banquet doesn't start for another hour. Want to go into the bar so we can get to know each other a little beforehand?"

"What is this banquet?" she asked, before realizing that perhaps Bambi already knew. Duh. If she kept this up, she'd be exposed as a phony before they even ordered drinks.

He nodded toward the ballroom entrance. "It's a physicians' fundraiser. Good cause, but pretty boring."

Yikes, a physicians' event? Mingling with the medical set was risky. She had worked with a lot of the local doctors from Jacksonville down to St. Augustine for the past few years. Some she'd even met face-to-face.

If she was going to get busted, she'd prefer to do it with a drink or two under her belt. "Bar. Definitely."

Nodding, he put a hand on her elbow, lightly, like a gentleman. But the contact sizzled. Just as it had when he'd shaken her hand. She couldn't form a thought, much less a word as he steered her toward a dark, shadowy bar. Few people were in it, probably because it was too late for the afternooners and too early for the before-dinner crowd.

Gesturing toward a small, private table in a corner, he led her to it, holding out her chair as she sat down. "Okay?"

"Fine."

They ordered drinks from a flirty waitress who smiled a little too intimately at Steve. Sarah gave the other woman a hard look. It had taken everything she had to work up the nerve to do this—going out and trying to get something she really wanted didn't come easy to her. Especially when, this time, she was going after a magical night with a special man. So damned if some poacher was going to get involved this far into the game.

They remained silent until the waitress returned. When Sarah spied her big, minty mojito, she said, "Thanks," then stuck a straw in it and sipped deeply. She wasn't much of a drinker, but tonight she needed some liquid fortification. The drink was a strong one, the rum burning her throat and the mint tickling her nose. She knew she should slow down so the alcohol wouldn't go to her head, but she couldn't help taking one more deep sip.

"Nervous?" he asked, eyeing her over the rim of his glass.

She licked her lips. "A little. I've never done this."

He hid a smile behind his drink. "Been in a bar? Don't tell me your parents have never let you have a drink, either."

She rolled her eyes. "They'd probably prefer that. But, believe it or not, I did manage to escape from under their Bambi-hating thumbs."

"Gotta give them credit, they were right about that one."

"Yes. But, unfortunately, they still wanted to protect me from the big bad dangers of the world even after I grew up. Thank God they eventually retired and moved to North Carolina."

"That's a switch," he said, "given the snowbird population around here."

"I'm not looking a gift horse—or in this case, three gift states between me and them—in the mouth."

"Let me guess. Only child?"

"Uh-huh. You?"

"One of six."

She whistled. "And where do you fall in the mix?"

"Middle."

"Ooh, so you were the troublemaker, were you?"

A wry grin answered that question. "Maybe a little."

No wonder he knew how to deal with people, how to get along so well with others. Sarah had always imagined what it would be like to have a big family, a house filled with siblings. Sadly, she suspected it was her own childhood health issues that had prevented that from ever happening. Her parents hadn't been willing to let lightning strike twice.

"Uh, back to your original question, I meant I've never done this." She waved her hand back and forth between them. "Gone on a blind date."

"Neither have I."

Unable to help it, she asked, "So why are you here?" Swallowing, she tried to make that query sound a little less intrusive. "Sorry, I mean, I'm just surprised that a handsome doctor like you needs somebody else to fix him up."

"You might be surprised. I don't meet many people outside of my profession."

"So that whole doctor/nurse thing is just an urban legend?"

"It is in my case." With a shrug, he explained, "The nurses I work with all like to talk a little too much. I feel like I'm under a microscope and they're constantly dissecting me, talking about my private life, keeping score, whispering about who I might be interested in."

"That sucks."

"Especially for someone like me, who really likes his privacy."

She understood that, and felt a momentary twinge about having invaded that privacy by coming up here tonight.

"Anyway, I meant it earlier when I said I didn't want to show up alone tonight. I'm working on a partnership deal, but I've arrived stag at one too many events to please my potential new business partner."

Ahh. The light dawned. "You don't want him to look at you and see a free-wheeling bachelor."

"Something like that."

Then why in the name of God were you going to show up with a woman named Bambi?

Of course, she couldn't ask the question, but she couldn't deny being very curious. It just didn't make sense that this man couldn't get his own date for any function—from a fundraiser to a have-fun-between-the-sheets-raiser.

"Speaking of jobs, you're not a nurse, are you?"

Pleased that Bambi's occupation hadn't been previously revealed—especially since the woman sounded as though she worked as a stripper—she replied, "Hardly."

Then she kicked herself for being judgmental about Bambi. The woman had been pretty inconsiderate, calling an answering service to break a date, however, there was no indication that her job involved taking her clothes off. Look at all the people who'd thought Sarah should start a 1-800 number of her own. For all she knew, Bambi could be a scientist.

Though, if she had to bet between one extreme and the other—stripper or astrophysicist—she'd lay money on girl-who-jumps-out-of-cake-at-bachelor-parties.

He lifted his drink to his mouth again, but just before he sipped, he casually murmured, "So what *do* you do?"

Oh boy. Another one of those tricky questions. If she answered truthfully, he might put two and two together and come up smelling a rat. But she'd already had her fill of lying. Such dishonesty just didn't come naturally to her. Mindy probably would have invented some grand story about being a stock-car driver or something. Sarah just wasn't wired that way—to be either a stock-car driver *or* a blatant liar.

"Wait, never mind," he said, saving her from answering. "I'd rather maintain the mystery."

Sarah stared, glad he'd made it easy for her again, but also suspicious. Her luck wasn't often this good. That was okay, usually. After the whole surviving-deadly-cancer thing as a kid, she'd figured she'd shot her wad on good luck in one fell swoop, and the rest of her life would be about hard work and dedication. Could that phantom luck really have brought her to this moment, and kept him completely in the dark about it?

Hmm. Maybe she hadn't been as successful at carrying off this scheme as she'd thought. Perhaps she'd already done or said something to give herself away, and he was just toying with her.

Which left her wondering…just who was playing who here?

And more importantly—if she still got her once-in-a-lifetime chance with Steve Wilshire, did it really matter?

3

THROUGHOUT THE HOUR that they sat in the bar, sipping their drinks and talking, Steve kept a mental list of possibilities to explain everything about this strange turn of events. Not the date or the chemistry, the heat, the utter attraction. Those things were a given. But the mystery of just who this woman was that he was so attracted to. That had him stumped.

He had several theories about her and why she'd pulled a switch with Bambi.

Of course, the first possibility was that she really *was* Bambi, and that the pictures on her Facebook page were phony. But he didn't think that was it. Despite her explanation, she just didn't seem the type to have that nickname—not when Sarah, soft, sweet, sexy Sarah—suited her so very well.

Plus, she was obviously nervous, and it seemed to go beyond mere first-date jitters. Though she'd relaxed—especially after sucking down most of a second cocktail—he knew she'd been ready to bolt. That was why he hadn't challenged her on things like her name and occupation.

Bambi, from what Rick had said, was a dancer. At the time, Steve had been thinking ballerina.

God, he was gullible.

The major fact that ruled out a picture-switch, however, was that Rick had *told* him his date was a tall, stacked blonde. Which had sounded fine at the time, but now seemed a little unappealing.

This woman had only one out of three of those qualities. Not that he'd call her stacked, merely beautifully curved. And he simply couldn't stop thinking about stripping her out of that dress and touching every soft inch of her.

He shifted in his seat, not wanting to dwell on that thought, not when every damn time he looked across the table at her lovely face, his eyes were drawn down the long, slender neck, the soft shoulders and that tempting swell of cleavage rising out of her satiny black dress. Frankly, he'd always been a leg man, but, oh, he was on the verge of repenting and changing his ways.

Knock it off, he reminded himself. *Figure this out while you still have a brain cell left.*

Okay. Back to the list.

Another possibility was that the real Bambi wasn't interested and had changed her mind. But they didn't even know each other. So why the big deception? Why not just break the date?

Another idea. Maybe this one, Sarah, was so into him she'd kidnapped his real date and substituted herself. Far-fetched, obviously. But he kind of liked the idea that Sarah had done this because she wanted to be with him...not as a favor to a friend with cold feet.

He wanted her to want him. He wanted that a lot.

Whether she did or not, there were a lot of possible explanations for what was happening here. But no definite answers. Being honest, though, he had to admit that trying to figure out who Sarah was, and how she'd come to be here, sitting across from him, all soft-skinned, moist-lipped and wide-eyed, was the most fun he'd had in months. In fact, he couldn't recall the last time he'd enjoyed a woman's company more.

Though he really needed to stop thinking about that soft skin, those moist lips and wide eyes. Man oh man, was she a distraction. He found his stare drawn again and again to a tiny scar on her throat, wanting to lean across the table and nibble on it…and proceed down her body from there. Or up. Or both.

Definitely both.

"Would you like another drink?" he asked.

She shook her head. "Not if it means that waitress comes around and bends over in front of you again. I swear, it's a wonder she doesn't tip over the way she sticks out her chest."

"I hadn't noticed."

"How do they let you practice medicine when you have such rotten eyesight?"

Jaw dropping, he barked a laugh, liking the slightly disgruntled Sarah. Or the slightly tipsy one…he wasn't entirely sure which best described her right now.

"You should close your mouth," she said, her eyes gleaming with wickedness. "She might trip and accidentally drop a breast into it or something."

Eyes widening, he did as she ordered and snapped his mouth shut. *Tipsy.* Given her coyness and nervousness earlier, he suspected the rum had done a little something to loosen her up.

Not that he was complaining. Not at all. She had finally relaxed, let down her guard, and he looked forward to slipping past those last walls of her defenses, to find out what had really brought her here tonight.

"Sorry," she mumbled, nibbling on her lip as if she'd just realized what she'd said.

Though amused by her bluntness, it wasn't amusement that filled his head as he considered her words. A sultry image had taken up residence in his mind. Not of the waitress, of course. No. He couldn't stop envisioning someone else's perfect breast landing in his mouth, a soft, sensitive nipple tightening beneath his tongue and lips. Oh, he wouldn't be at all averse to having his mouth on Sarah's breast…or on anything else of hers.

He wanted her. Just plain wanted her.

It wasn't merely attraction, though, of course, that throbbed and hummed like a soundtrack beneath every word they said. Beyond that, though, he liked her. She was easy to talk to, blunt, had a great laugh and a ready smile.

They'd talked about the weather and the pros and cons of winter in Florida. He loved it, having grown up in Vermont and gotten his fill of snow by age two. She hated it, having lived here all her life and romanticized those hideous blizzards.

They'd touched lightly on politics—always a risky proposition these days, but had managed to agree more than they'd disagreed. They felt the same about movies—God love a woman who dug explosions and on-screen violence. She'd revealed a little more than she'd probably wanted to about her overprotective parents, and he'd mentioned the divorce.

And all the while, he listened to her words but had a hard time thinking about much more than the delightful way her voice rolled over him, affecting him head to toe. He felt as though he could step into the warm, sultry aura it created, as though it was a physical, tangible thing between them, waiting to wrap him in a sexy embrace.

You know that voice. You've heard it before.

But damned if he knew where. Maybe just in his most erotic dreams.

"So, your divorce," she said, coming back to a topic they'd only skimmed. Just as he'd figured she would. "Was it amicable?"

"I think lawyers invented that word," he said wryly. "But it wasn't *War of the Roses* ugly, at least, although people probably gossiped about it almost as much." His mouth twisting, he added, "Just FYI—I really hate being gossiped about. It's one of my biggest pet peeves."

"Noted. Why'd you split up?"

"I was a workaholic, and she was a deep-sea fisherman."

Her mouth dropped open.

Steve waved a hand. "Metaphorically speaking. Actually, she was a pharmaceutical rep. Now, those are some urban legends you should believe."

"And?"

"And she was trawling for the great white. I was the tuna that got caught in her net." Remembering his ex's romantic track record, he added, "But at least I wasn't the carp she caught first. I didn't even know about him until after we'd split up."

She gasped. "She lied about having been married before?"

"She lied about a lot of things," he said with a shrug, having long since gotten over the catastrophe that had been his marriage. "From big things like marriage right down to how much she spent on shoes in a month."

Across from him, Sarah looked away, her long lashes drifting lower over her eyes as she mumbled, "A real gold digger, huh?"

"It wasn't the money," he admitted, having realized that

for himself long ago. "It was the prestige. Her first husband was a dermatologist."

"And treating heart-attack victims is a step up from helping teenagers get rid of their zits?"

Laughing, he said, "You got it."

"Let me guess…her next one will be a neurosurgeon?"

He lifted a brow and feigned offense. "You're saying neurosurgery is more prestigious than cardiology?"

"Only on *Grey's Anatomy*," she insisted, holding her hands up in instant supplication.

"Okay, then. Yeah, you've got the gist. She remarried a couple of months ago…to a chief of staff at a big hospital down in Miami. I doubt he knows he's number three."

Rolling her eyes, she muttered, "I think the Surgeon General's wife better start watching her hubby like a hawk."

Funny how immediately she grasped the whole situation, all the while maintaining a genuine warmth. He had to add quick-witted and intuitive to the long list of things he liked about Sarah. Damned if he couldn't see himself falling for this woman, even if he didn't know who the hell she really was.

Not yet, anyway.

But the evening was still young. She'd let her guard down while engaging in light conversation. Soon enough, he'd get back around to asking the kinds of questions that might trip her up…or at least get her to drop the pretense and admit what was really going on here.

Steve didn't like to be lied to. In fact, he hated that even more than he hated being the center of gossip.

But so far, other than saying she was his date, he didn't think she'd outright lied. She'd looked relieved to give him her real name, and after that, he'd made sure not to put her in the position of having to make up anything. Every word she'd said since had had a genuine and natural ring to it. Real. Something about tonight—about Sarah—made him think that, no matter how this looked, she wasn't lying. She *wanted* to be here, with him. And she'd done something to make that happen.

He'd find out the whole story soon enough, he had no doubt. In the meantime, he was quite willing just to enjoy the mystery.

"What about you?" he asked her, after dwelling on what he could ask without making her so nervous she couldn't speak. There was one thing he wanted to know. "Ever married?"

She shook her head. "Barely dated, to be honest."

That he found hard to believe.

His skepticism must have shown itself. "I'm serious."

"Then the guys you went to high school with were blind."

"I was home-schooled. I went to community college for two years. But since I didn't have a driver's license, my father drove me."

"Your parents weren't just overprotective…"

"They were freaks," she said with a laugh. Then, as naturally as she would say *I'm a Libra,* she added, "I'm a cancer survivor."

Steve immediately frowned, watching her lift a self-conscious hand to her throat. That scar.

"My parents were crazy-overprotective, but only because I'd gone through a really rough time that lasted several years. I was diagnosed when I was nine, and it went on and off until I was a teenager."

"What kind?"

"Esophageal."

He whistled, truly surprised. The odds against a nine-year-old contracting that were huge.

"I know. It's rare."

"Incredibly."

"My mother blamed my father for having smoked a few cigars when I was a kid, and he blamed her for eating in restaurants where people smoked while she was pregnant. The fact is, sometimes things just happen." She shrugged. "It is what it is."

She was right, and the attitude wasn't an uncommon one amongst older cancer survivors. But he admired her for having realized it at such a young age. Then something else clicked.

"That explains your voice."

"Yup."

"Wow, now I feel like crap for being so turned on by it."

Instead of being offended, she looked positively delighted at his words. The sparkle in her eyes matched the pleased smile on her lovely face. "Really? You are?"

Like any red-blooded man wouldn't be? "Yeah. It's… very mysterious."

"It can be, I guess," she admitted. "I have received one or two suggestions about what kind of job I could get with it."

"What, doing narration for film or taping audio books?"

She nibbled her lip for a second, averting her eyes in embarrassment, then mumbled, "Uh…phone sex."

She was so damn cute when she said it—visibly self-conscious and embarrassed at having brought it up. Obviously, she hadn't noticed that he was already sitting over here trying to pretend he hadn't had sex on the brain since they'd touched hands out in the lobby.

"I've been told I would be a natural," she said, her cheeks pinkening even further.

A natural at sex. Oh, yeah.

Then he realized that wasn't what she'd meant. She'd meant whispering graphic, wicked things, telling a man what she wanted, how she was touching herself and how she wanted to be touched by him.

He grabbed his nearly empty glass, bringing it to his mouth to try to slurp up any last remnants of moisture left behind by the nearly melted ice. Because even talking about phone sex with this woman to whom he was already so attracted was very dangerous indeed. He needed to cool off and to occupy his mouth so he wouldn't just come right out and ask her if she wanted to blow off the fundraiser and get a room on one of the floors above them in this swanky hotel.

"The idea is pretty ridiculous," she said with a self-conscious chuckle. "Especially considering I'd have absolutely no idea what I was talking about."

Steve had just sucked a small piece of ice into his mouth. With that comment, the chunk went right down his throat, choking him for a second. He coughed into his fist.

"Are you okay?" she asked, wide-eyed and innocent.

Maybe too innocent. If that wasn't a hint of humor lurking on those lush lips, he'd be very surprised.

Rather than dance around it anymore, he came right out with what he was thinking. "Are you telling me you're a virgin?"

Clearing her throat, she gave a tiny negative shake of her head. "Not quite."

"Believe me," he said, "it's not the kind of question that can be answered with a 'kind of.' You are or you aren't."

"I can't believe I'm about to tell you this—it must be the mojitos," she said with a helpless shake of her head.

"To answer your question, technically, no, I'm not. But, uh, let's just say my first time was one away from my last…and neither one was enough to get me breathing hard, much less ready to comprehend what all the fuss is about."

He ran his fingertips over his damp glass, both stunned and incredibly turned on. Stunned because she was far too beautiful to be so inexperienced. Turned on because, oh, did he like the idea of helping her learn all she wanted to know. The chance to show this woman what all the fuss was about made that hotel room idea look better and better.

"So, even if I'd ever consider it, which I wouldn't, I'd be no good in the phone-sex game. Because I assume men who call those numbers are looking for a Baskin-Robbins sexual experience—lots and lots of flavors." She shrugged, looking unsure of herself, as if she had no idea how incredibly sexy she truly was. "They don't want *me*, who's so bland I don't know if I could even claim to be vanilla ice cream. Maybe I'm ice milk. Frozen yogurt, at most."

Steve could only stare. He'd never been so aroused at the talk of ice cream. Or any dessert. He had to shift in his chair as his trousers constricted around his rock-hard cock. Especially because he sensed Sarah was telling him these things not to engage in naughty conversation…but because she really wanted him to know. For some *specific* reason.

Suddenly, one possible reason occurred to him for her presence here tonight. Had she switched with Bambi—been so nervous and then flirtatious—because she wanted to move on down the menu from single cone to triple sundae with hot fudge and cherries on top? If so, did it make any difference whatsoever that *he'd* be the guy holding the ice cream scoop…or would *anyone* do just as well?

He didn't see how she could have been specific about

him, never having met him before. How could she? And
suddenly the idea that she would be sitting here seducing
any guy who'd happened to be standing by that fountain
in a blue suit made him a little nauseous.

You were ready to do the same thing.

Yeah. Maybe. He'd definitely thought about breaking his
dry spell with the woman he was being fixed up with.

But that was before he'd met Sarah. He now suspected
he wanted more than that…more than one night to blow
off steam. The only question was, did she? If he took her
upstairs now, would she be gone with the dawn, disappearing from his life as quickly as she'd entered it?

He couldn't know.

Which meant he couldn't take the risk. Not yet. Before he made love to Sarah, he intended to be very sure it
wouldn't be the first *and* the last time.

4

For the first hour of the banquet, Sarah spent her time studying the crowd, looking for a familiar face. She didn't see any, fortunately, but she sure saw a bunch of familiar names on table settings and in the program. Apparently a whole lot of doctors who had contracts with Call Anytime believed in this cause and had come out to support it.

Darn. If only she worked for skinflints.

Still, she didn't think it was going to be too much of a problem. Mindy handled most of the sales stuff, meeting face to face with customers. Sarah covered the books, the payroll, the business end. So she had met very few of their clients in person. And since she seldom worked the phones, she hadn't talked to many of them, either. In fact, Steve Wilshire was the only one she'd spoken with more than two or three times, and so far, he hadn't had an "Aha!" moment and unmasked her. Or, unvoiced her. Whatever.

"Doing okay?" Steve asked, an unspoken apology in his low whisper. The two of them sat with a large group, which included the doctor he was hoping to partner with. And frankly, all of them, while very nice, were so boring they could have made a kid hopped up on Red Bull and Twinkies drop for a languorous nap.

"Fine," she murmured.

"I owe you for this."

She smiled a little, liking the sound of that. "I'll hold you to it." Hmm. She liked the sound of that, too. Holding him to anything…especially herself. She'd been thinking of little else since their conversation in the bar.

Her frankness had probably taken him by surprise…but not as much as it had surprised her. She didn't know why she'd volunteered so much personal information. It could have been the two drinks, which had gone right to her head. Or it could have been the fact that he was so easy to talk to. Or just that she wanted him so much. Heck, maybe she'd been trying to proposition him in her own inexperienced, clumsy way.

Whatever the reason, the result hadn't been the two of them racing to the nearest room with a bed. As if the subject of phone sex and her inexperience had never come up, he'd simply paid for their drinks and escorted her into the banquet. He'd been the perfect gentleman. Which she found incredibly attractive, and terribly frustrating.

She'd wanted one night of romance with her dream man. Now she wanted…more. Just more.

Maybe not anything as blatant as getting laid, as Mindy had suggested. But a kiss on the cheek just wasn't going to cut it, not now that she'd shared intimate conversation with him, felt the warmth of his breath on her cheek as he sat beside her, experienced the brush of his strong hand on her skin.

You want to make love with him. Admit it. You always have.

It was true. Now more than ever.

"How about we get out of here early and go somewhere else for dessert?"

She sucked in a breath, feeling caught at having erotic

thoughts about him. She also wasn't sure if he was propositioning her, especially given their ice-cream conversation.

His sudden grimace said he realized that himself, and he clarified, "I meant, we could get coffee or something. It wasn't a sleazy come-on, I swear."

"Should I be relieved or offended that there was no double entendre in that invitation?" Honestly, she wasn't sure which she felt. Not that Steve was at all the cheesy/ sleazy sort—he wasn't—but she wouldn't mind thinking that he had, at least, given thought to making improper, but oh, so welcome, advances.

He lifted a curious brow. "Meaning?"

She could hedge, or change the subject, but the clock was ticking. She might only have this one night with this man, and with every minute that went by, she suspected that just a romantic date wasn't going to be enough.

She had tiptoed around her attraction…maybe it was time to be a little more forward. "I mean, I think I'd be pretty sad if you were *only* interested in coffee. Not…a hot fudge sundae."

"Thirty-one flavors?" he whispered.

"With whipped cream on top," she replied, wondering where she found the courage to be so bold. She licked her lips, knowing he couldn't take his eyes off them. "And a cherry."

He didn't say anything for a minute, just stared at her. His attractive green eyes narrowed the tiniest bit, and his mouth opened as he drew long, even breaths—in and out— as if thinking of a response.

Finally, he gave her one. "I'm interested. Very interested."

He didn't say another word, letting his tone and the heated expression on his face tell her everything she needed to know. His whole body was tight and aware, from the hard leg that brushed against hers underneath the table, up to his stiff jaw. He seemed to be fighting some inner battle…mind over matter. Or, in this case, mind over sexual response.

She bit her bottom lip, thrilled that he'd confirmed it. He wanted her. This handsome, sexy man who'd begun seducing her on the phone months ago without even knowing it, wanted her in his bed.

She felt like laughing, she felt like running. She felt like dancing, like hiding under the table. She wanted to slide over onto his lap, straddle him, twine her fingers in that thick hair and taste every inch of him. She wanted to apologize for being a bald-faced liar.

She wanted…him. Just him.

But they were surrounded by people—his colleagues— in a public place. So the tension that had been building in her for months, ever since their first conversation, couldn't be released. The steam just had to keep on building. She hoped her head wouldn't blow off before they finally had some time alone.

Or before he found out she was a fake and ditched her.

No. She couldn't think that way. This was going so well. They'd shared laughter and easy conversation. Absolutely the only thing wrong with this whole situation was that she wasn't the woman he had been expecting tonight.

So just make sure you are the woman he wants tomorrow.

The elderly woman sitting on Steve's other side suddenly asked him something, and he turned to address her. Sarah took the opportunity to grab her glass of water, taking a few long sips to try to tame her racing heart. Not to mention her raging libido.

She had barely set the glass back down when she realized she was being spoken to. "So, Sarah, what do you do for a living?" asked Dr. Tate, the cardiologist Steve was hoping would go into partnership with him. He seemed like a nice man—if a little dull. But his wife had been very friendly, and appeared very happy to see Steve walk in with a woman on his arm. Right now, though, she wished they were a little less friendly—and less apt to ask questions.

Seeing Steve still engaged in conversation with the older woman, she replied as truthfully as she could. "I'm in communications."

That was not a lie. She was more into communications than anybody here. You couldn't get something much more communicable than telephone work.

Communicable. Sounded sordid. Then again, to this very proper doctor and his wife, stealing somebody else's blind date probably was a little sordid.

Steve said he's happy you're here. And he'd sounded as though he'd meant it, so she really needed to try to let go of the guilt, at least long enough to see if there could be something more between them than one single date—or one amazing, perfect night in each other's arms. That anything more could only come after a moment of reckoning was something she didn't want to think about right now.

"And how did you and Steve meet?"

Not knowing how to answer that, since she wasn't sure how much Steve would want revealed, she was relieved when he jumped into the conversation. "Mutual friends," he said simply, dropping a light hand on Sarah's leg beneath the table.

She knew it was meant to be a reassuring it's-our-secret kind of contact. After their previous conversation, though, after he'd admitted he wanted her, she couldn't possibly take it as sweet and innocent. Regardless of how that warm, firm touch was meant, the reality was pure, sizzling excitement. Hearing his quick, surprised inhalation, she knew he felt the same way.

It wasn't as though he was touching her in a terribly intimate area—his hand was much closer to her knee than to anything that could be called the money-spot. But the strength of that hand, the possessiveness, the warmth…it took a simple touch up a notch into wicked intimacy.

His fingers were strong, hot against the bare skin of her thigh. He had a man's hands—not too smooth, just right, in fact. That, combined with the dessert-and-phone-sex conversation, had them both hyper aware of every look, word and, definitely, of every touch.

"Let's dance," he suddenly said in a low voice. He didn't so much ask as order, as if he, too, needed to get away from the table and probing eyes. Whatever their conversations had been, however pleasantly the evening had been going, things had just gotten a whole lot more personal. All because of a silly conversation about coffee versus dessert and a simple touch.

Heaven only knew what was going to happen when the touches became less simple. But oh, complications had never sounded so appealing.

Nodding wordlessly, she let him take her hand and help her up. He squeezed lightly, saying without words that he knew it had just gotten about ten degrees hotter in the room, but said nothing as they wove through the tables to the small dance floor. A band playing what she'd normally call old-people music stood on a small stage. By unspoken agreement, they moved past the other couples, heading for a far corner, near the door leading to the kitchens.

Then he stopped, turned and took her into his arms.

Sarah didn't even realize she'd been holding her breath until it slid out of her in a long, slow sigh at the feel of his tall body pressed against hers. Though she'd been cursing the high heels all evening, she couldn't deny that they helped everything line up very nicely. His trousered legs brushed against her bare ones and his hard chest pressed against her breasts, bringing their tips to rigid attention.

She had heard of people melting into someone else's arms, but had never really experienced it...until now. Her whole body went soft, accommodating all his hardness. Angles sinking into curves, two disparate forms conjoining into one.

"Mmm," she said, closing her eyes.

He made a similar sound, then rubbed his cheek against her hair. "Has this ever happened to you before?"

She didn't pretend to misunderstand. "No."

"I mean, we barely know each other."

That was true, even if she did know him a little better than he knew her. Still, she had the feeling that even if this had been a real blind date and she'd never heard his voice, never seen his picture, never half fallen for the calm, warm way he talked about his concern for his patients, she'd still be drawn to him the way she was right now.

"You just feel right. This feels right," she whispered.

He held her a little tighter, if that was possible. Sensing the ridge of heat pressed against her lower tummy, she knew he was losing the battle to keep control.

"All you have to do is open your mouth and I start to get hard," he admitted.

Rather than shocking her, his honesty thrilled her. Steve was bringing out the hidden side of her, the flirty, sensual woman who'd been repressed by her illnesses, her inexperience, her family situation, her job and her own insecurities. It was that side that responded. "You have some ideas about what you want me to do with my mouth?"

He groaned, his hands dropping lower so his fingertips

brushed the top curves of her bottom. Light, delicate strokes made her arch closer. Not really paying attention to anyone around them, she didn't even notice they were moving off the dance floor until she felt the hard laminate beneath her heels give way to softer carpeting. Quickly glancing around, she realized they'd ended up behind the raised platform where the band was performing, and were, in fact, hidden from view by both the stage and all the equipment on it.

Steve didn't have to tell her why he'd pulled her out of sight. Instead, he showed her. Without a word, he bent and covered her lips with his in a hot kiss. Sarah groaned in her throat, tilting her head and parting her lips, inviting him to explore deeper. He did, his warm tongue sliding into her mouth to meet hers in a slow, sultry mating.

They didn't stop dancing—or at least swaying. Their bodies were pressed together so closely not a sound could have passed between them. And the kiss went on and on, all the warm, spicy flavors of this man filling her up, sustaining her, arousing her to a fever pitch. Her nerve endings came alive, each strand of hair, every inch of skin. The connection was utterly electric and she felt it right to her core.

Finally, seeming loathe to do it, he ended the kiss, brushing his lips against hers one last time, then pulling away. He didn't go far; his jaw brushed her face and she could hear, by his shallow breaths, that he was every bit as excited as she.

"Nice," he finally murmured.

"Very."

Suddenly, against her stomach, she felt something thrum. "My God, it even vibrates?" she said, jerking her head back.

Steve let out a low laugh, then shook his head apologetically. "I'm sorry. It's hard to escape being on call when you're in a solo practice."

On call. The answering service. *Oh, God.*

"To be honest, I thought if tonight went really badly, I could have the service page me with a drummed-up emergency."

She raised a querying brow. "And now?"

"Now I really wish I'd gotten someone to cover for me."

So did she, and not only because she hated the thought of them being interrupted. The last thing she wanted was for Steve to start thinking about the answering service—and about one particular whiskey-voiced operator who sometimes relayed his messages.

Nibbling her lip, she watched him step farther away from the stage—out of earshot of the band—to check his pager. With an apologetic shrug, he then used his cell phone to call a number Sarah knew by heart.

It probably *was* an emergency, of course. Doctors had them all the time, and he wasn't the first to receive a page at the fundraiser tonight. Heck, he probably wasn't even the first to receive a page from Call Anytime.

Still, a tiny suspicion blossomed in her mind that Mindy could be meddling. Sarah had intentionally left her cell phone turned off so her friend could not call to see how the date was going. She wouldn't put it past the other woman to make up some call in order to get Steve on the line...to find out whether he was still out or had already called it a night.

Huh. If she had her way, he wouldn't be calling it a night until tomorrow morning.

Having kissed him, been held by him, Sarah was more sure than ever that she wanted to go to bed with Steve Wilshire. She wanted it desperately. Especially given how very much he seemed to want her, too. They had just clicked, the way she'd always suspected they would. The only thing standing in their way was the issue of the secret blind-date swap-out.

So tell him the truth.

She would. Soon. The few words he'd said about his wife—*the liar*—had rung loudly in her ears. Sarah hated liars, too, and God knew she didn't want to be one. Something deep inside just wouldn't allow her to go through with the entire plan—to steal one amazing, romantic night with him under false pretenses. Especially if that night ended up with the two of them in bed together.

Yes, he knew her real name, he'd spent an evening with the real woman; however, he needed to know the whole truth. And before they went any further, he would. In fact, she was going to tell him the very moment he returned.

Only, judging by the concerned look on his face after he finished his call, she might not have her chance.

"I'm so sorry," he said as he tucked the phone back into his suit pocket. "I have to go to the hospital. There's a serious problem with one of my patients."

Her shoulders sank in disappointment.

"Believe me, I'm not happy about it, either," he told her. "I had envisioned tonight ending a lot differently."

"I understand," she said. "Another time."

There was an emergency. She had to believe that, and didn't want to read any more into it.

You can ask anybody at the service if he'd called in and asked them to page him.

That was the inexperienced, unconfident Sarah's voice whispering doubts in her brain. It was that same Sarah who feared that if he said, *Sure, I'll call you sometime,* she'd probably curl up in a ball and die. She couldn't stand the thought of having misjudged him—them—so badly.

Too caught up in her own dark imaginings even to look in his face for the truth, she turned to leave their sheltered spot. But his hand on her arm stopped her. "Meet me for dinner tomorrow night."

Her jaw dropped open and her heart sang. "Seriously?"

"Absolutely." Grinning, he added, "Admit it, for a second, you thought that was a made-up emergency call, didn't you?"

She bit her bottom lip, not answering.

Rolling his eyes, he put a hand on her shoulder. "I *do* want to see you again, tomorrow night. There's a place a couple of miles up the beach, called Jolly Roger's. You can't miss it."

She knew the place. The name made it sound gaudy or touristy, but in truth it was a small, intimate seafood place loved by the locals. Sitting on a private stretch of beach, its views were beautiful and she couldn't think of a better spot to get things out in the open between them than on a lovely patio overlooking the churning waves.

"This isn't good-night." He lifted a hand to her face, tracing his fingertips across her cheek, then twining them in her hair. "It's just a twenty-one-hour break. Then we start over again. Seven o'clock tomorrow night."

Start over. As much as it pained her to stop now, with her mouth still tingling from his amazing kiss, she knew it was the right thing to do. Tomorrow would be the perfect time to come clean, to admit who she really was and how tonight had really come to be. Then they could start fresh. Besides, what was twenty-one hours when she'd been waiting for her chance with him for so long?

"Okay," she told him. "Tomorrow night it is."

5

By 6 p.m. on Sunday, Steve was beginning to worry.

By 6:45 p.m., to sweat.

And by 7:00 p.m., he was just about in panic mode. Because he was still at the hospital.

He was going to be late for his dinner date. Very late. And fool that he was, he hadn't gotten Sarah's number, so he couldn't call to tell her that. Hell, he hadn't even learned her last name!

He'd tried calling the restaurant only to be put on hold on the reservations line for what seemed like hours. In the middle of a crisis, he'd handed the phone to a nurse, begging her to relay the message. Then *she'd* been kept on hold and had to get back to work, too. So the message was never passed on.

"Damn it all," he muttered as he finally pulled off his scrubs and got dressed in the hospital locker room. He considered swinging by his house to change. It was only a half mile from the restaurant, one reason he'd suggested it. But he didn't want to waste even that much time. So he settled for wearing the khakis and golf shirt he'd put on before coming in this afternoon to check on the patient who'd gone critical last night in the middle of his date.

The patient was doing much better, and Steve should have easily been able to get home in time to get ready. But then an emergency case had come in. A seventy-year-old had keeled over on the golf course—yeah, like that was something different, here in The Sunshine State. Steve had been brought in to consult and it was seven-twenty by the time he flew out of the hospital entrance and hurried to his car.

Tugging his phone out of his pocket, he tried the restaurant again and, this time, when they tried to put him on hold immediately after answering, he wouldn't allow it. "No! Do *not* put me on hold, I've been trying to get through for an hour."

"Sorry, sir, but we're very busy," a young woman said, talking loudly to be heard over voices and the clank of dishes in the background.

"I'm meeting a woman there and I'm running late. I just need you to tell her I'm coming."

"Sure, sure, I'll tell her."

"Don't you want her name?" he bit out, getting annoyed.

She said something to someone else, then yelled, then finally responded, "Okay, sure, what's her name?"

"Sarah."

"Sarah what?"

"Uh, just Sarah. She's petite, gold-streaked brown hair just past her shoulders. Beautiful."

He heard the woman's sigh.

"Please, just try, would you?"

She hung up without even answering. Steve could only hope Sarah had enough faith in the hours they'd spent together last night to know he wouldn't stand her up.

Why would she? She barely knows you?

Not a comforting thought.

But at least she knew his last name. She'd called him by it last night. It was possible she'd gotten worried, looked him up and tried calling him. She wouldn't be able to get his unlisted home number or his cell, of course, but she could have tried the office and gotten the answering service.

The answering service that was directing all his calls—on his express, very firm orders—to Dr. Tate tonight. Steve had gotten the other doctor to cover for him, wanting to make sure he and Sarah had one uninterrupted evening together. He hoped it wouldn't be for nothing.

Be there, please be there, he thought as he headed down the coast. But when he got to the restaurant ten minutes later, frantically looking at every person and every table, inside as well as out on the deck, he knew she wasn't.

He strode to the hostess station. "I called a little while ago to leave a message for my date. Sarah."

The woman's mouth opened in surprise "Oh!" The hint of apology in her face told him all he'd needed to know, but she said it, anyway. "I'm so sorry, but we were slammed. It's Valentine's weekend. I just forgot." She came out from behind the counter. "I'll help you find her."

"She's gone," he said flatly, angry, though mainly at himself for not making sure he knew how to reach Sarah. He wasn't usually so careless. But he'd been off his game, off balance since the minute he'd laid eyes on her. "It's too late."

Shaking his head and thrusting a frustrated hand through his hair, he walked outside. There had to be a way to fix this. Racking his brain, he tried to think of possible ways to get in touch with her. He had the Facebook page bookmarked, but considering it hadn't really been hers, he didn't expect that it would do him much good. And Rick probably wouldn't be of much use, either.

His mystery woman might just remain a mystery forever. He might never see her again.

Feeling his head pound at the very thought, he reached his car, on the edge of the parking lot right beside a wooden staircase leading down to the beach. A strong gusty breeze blew sand and grit in his face, and he blinked, rubbing at his eyes. When he opened them again, something down near the water caught his attention.

A slight figure in a filmy, light-colored dress was moving along the shore, walking in the cold winter surf. The bright stars and nearly full moon overhead made her visible, but not recognizable. Still, something inside his optimistic heart wondered if it could be Sarah. Disappointed at having been stood up, might she have decided to go for a night walk on the beach?

Not giving it a second thought, he jogged down the steps onto the sand and walked toward her. "Sarah?"

She stopped, turned around. And as he drew closer, he realized Fate had been very kind to him tonight.

"I am so sorry!" he said, closing the distance between them in a few long strides. He stopped about two feet away, seeing the way she nibbled on her bottom lip. Her eyes were suspiciously bright. "I had an emergency at the hospital and had no way to reach you. I don't even know your last name."

She studied him, as if gauging his sincerity, then murmured, "Did the restaurant's phone not work?"

He quickly explained, hoping she would believe him.

Her mouth might have softened a tiny bit, but her tone didn't. "Are you sure you just didn't have second thoughts? I mean, we barely know each other. If you didn't want to see me again…"

"I did." He reached out and put a hand on her shoulder. "Look, if I intended to stand you up, why would I have come at all?" Taking the chance that she'd want him to, he moved even closer. "I wanted more than anything to see you again. I've thought about nothing else since last night."

She sniffed, then mumbled, "Bet your patient wouldn't be happy to hear that."

Smiling gently, he said, "I'll make it up to you, I promise." Tugging her even closer, he saw the indecision flash across her face. She was angry, still not quite trusting him, but wanting to believe. He saw that, and he understood it.

"I'm not used to this, Steve," she finally admitted. "It's all new to me, and I don't like how I felt, sitting there at that table, being stared at, pitied. I don't like feeling so vulnerable."

His heart twisted. "I'm so sorry," he repeated, picturing her waiting, her spirits crumbling. Every sweep of the minute hand must have convinced her she'd been stood up, and that she should never have trusted him to begin with. Sarah had laid out her inexperience last night; he knew she couldn't have a lot of self-confidence. He'd give anything to take that uncomfortable episode back. "Please forgive me and let me make it up to you."

Resisting for one more moment, she finally let him draw her into his arms. She wrapped hers around his waist, melting against him. They stood silently for a long moment, then, in a prim voice, she said, "I already ate."

"Even dessert?"

She tensed the slightest bit, then tilted her head back and looked up at him, those amazing eyes glittering in the moonlight.

They both knew what kind of dessert he was talking about. He wanted to dine on her, feast on her, have her in every way a man could have a woman. He wanted to pleasure her, show her what *"all the fuss was about."* Wanted to show her how sorry he was that he'd made her doubt him—made her doubt *them*.

And he wanted to do it right now.

Out here, on the beach, with the breeze whipping against their bodies and the sound of the surf churning, everything felt so much more...elemental. Primal. Including what he felt about her.

He just couldn't wait anymore, he was dying to taste her. Dipping his head, he caught her mouth and kissed her deeply. He plunged his tongue against hers, hoping to show her that he wanted to be here, wanted her, wanted *this*.

Reaching up, she twined her arms around his neck, not resisting when he lifted her, holding her tightly against him. When her slim legs rose and encircled his hips, he groaned out loud. Her filmy dress did nothing to conceal the womanly heat between those perfect thighs, and he reflexively ground his rock-hard erection against her.

When the kiss finally ended, he didn't let her down. Instead, glancing over his shoulder at the restaurant not too far behind them, then at the next structure down the beach, he said, "My house is right over there."

Her eyes widened. "Really?"

"Uh-huh. Call me overconfident, but I was hoping we'd end up there after dinner."

"You could have just invited me to your house to begin with," she whispered, leaning closer to nibble on his earlobe. "We could have started with dessert."

"Does that mean I'm forgiven?"

"You're definitely off to a good start."

Her fingers were twined in his hair, her soft breaths brushing over his skin. He felt encompassed by her, and so on fire he wasn't sure they would make it to his place.

But it wasn't as if they had much choice. Anybody could walk down from the parking lot.

"So, it's okay with you if we go to my house? Because I want you, Sarah. I want you badly," he said, making sure she knew what she was really saying yes to.

She didn't even hesitate. "Get me there now, or I'll get us both arrested for public indecency."

HER CAR WAS UP in the parking lot, and she suspected Steve's was, too. But when he said it would be faster just to walk up the beach, Sarah believed him.

Not that he let her walk. Not one step. As if she weighed nothing, he carried her, kissing her, stroking her, heightening her need to a fever pitch with every step he took across the sand. Sarah kept her legs around his waist and her arms around his neck, holding on to his big, strong body, knowing he would not let her fall.

Though she didn't think she'd soon forget how awful she had felt sitting at that table, surrounded by couples celebrating the romantic holiday one night early, she wouldn't trade the end result for anything. She was going to have a night of sensual pleasure with her fantasy man. It would be all she'd ever dreamed of, and more than she'd ever hoped to have.

You deserve this. You both deserve this.

She wasn't the same quiet, shy girl she'd been during her younger years. Now she was a woman, a desperately aroused woman. No more second-guessing herself. She wanted nothing more than to give and receive pleasure, to share erotic intimacy with the man holding her so strongly in his arms.

Needing to taste him, she slid her tongue down his neck, sampling a rippling cord of muscle. She nibbled lightly on the spot where neck met strong, powerful shoulder, and felt him shudder against her. He was rock-hard between her thighs, and every step rocked him harder where she most needed rocking. By the time they'd reached a wooden crossover leading up to his beachfront house, she was quivering, on the verge of something wonderful. Something she'd only ever experienced with the vibrator she'd bought when she'd first moved into her own place.

"Oh, please," she whimpered, feeling waves of sensation rise in her body as steadily as the waves were hitting the shore.

He kissed her again, deeply. He'd been holding her bottom while he walked, and now shifted one arm a little, so he could slide his other hand into far more intimate territory. She hissed at the feel of those strong fingers on her inner thigh, close to the elastic edge of her panties. Close, but not close enough. "More."

He obliged, stroking her, until his fingers moved under the filmy fabric to tangle in her soft curls.

Sarah groaned, gasped and quivered. And when that gentle, questing touch found the throbbing center of all sensation, she gave herself over to a consciousness-altering orgasm.

"Oh, my God!" she cried, throwing her head back to look up at the sky. She jerked, rubbing against him, wanting more. More pressure, more pleasure, more of everything. And the waves just kept coming like the steady, reliable tide. Over. And over.

Finally, when she could think again, she realized they'd actually made it up onto what must be his back patio. Steve didn't even try for the door, he simply walked over to a plush chaise longue and dropped her onto it. Arching and curving as the last effects of pleasure reverberated through her, she watched him strip off his shirt, then unfasten his trousers.

His chest was rippled with muscle, his body lean and strong, like a runner's. She lost her breath, unable to think about anything else except how those hips would feel between her bare thighs.

"You're beautiful," he mumbled, staring down at her.

Sarah didn't even hesitate, she simply began to pull her dress up, inch by inch, revealing to his eyes what he'd already experienced with his hands. Seeing him grab the back of a chair for support gave her so much confidence that she was smiling seductively by the time she drew the dress up and off.

She wore nothing but the panties underneath.

"Beautiful," he repeated before dropping to his knees beside her.

He ran one hand up her bare thigh, catching the panties with his fingertip, then drew them down. Now wearing absolutely nothing, she lay still, like a kid in that ice cream shop, not knowing what flavor she wanted to try, just sure vanilla would never cut it.

"Are you cold?" he asked, stroking his palm up and down her side.

"Not one bit." No, she was burning up, in fact. Everywhere he touched, a tiny ember erupted into flames, igniting every one of her senses.

He began to caress her, stroking her stomach, her hips, her thighs. Those big hands were capable of infinite tenderness and the barely-there touches soon had her writhing on the chaise. They were wonderful, but she wanted more. A lot more.

"Please," she cried, arching toward him, thrusting her chest up invitingly.

As if he'd merely been waiting for the invitation, he instantly moved his mouth to her breast, catching her nipple between his warm lips and sucking deeply. She felt the pull clear down to her toes and sighed happily, twining her fingers in her hair. He went back and forth, giving equal attention, using his fingers to tweak each sensitive nipple when his mouth was busy with the other.

Soon her hips were jerking reflexively, lifting, seeking the ultimate pleasure she knew he could give her. But there was one more pleasure she hadn't been prepared for. And when he finally moved his mouth away from her breasts and tasted his way down to her body, right to the curls of her sex, she let out another wavering cry.

"You taste so good," he muttered against her mound as his tongue tasted her clit.

Sarah had never experienced that particular intimacy, and she almost flew off the chaise. But that would mean he'd have to stop. And oh, God, she did not want him to stop.

He settled in, clearly with no intention of stopping, sucking her sensitive nub into his mouth, tasting, kissing. When his hand moved to tug at her thighs, she let them fall open to him, exposing herself fully. Steve moved his fingers up, testing the slick folds of her body. Carefully, gently, he slid one finger into her wet channel, going slowly, doubling the delight he continued to offer with his mouth.

Another orgasm swept through her. She began to shake, helpless against her body's response. Pleasure gushed through her, shocking at first, then slow and steady.

"You take my breath away," he told her once she'd finally floated back to earth.

While she'd been lost to bliss, he'd stood up, and finished unfastening his pants. Sarah watched with hungry eyes, desperate to see him, more desperate to have him—all of him. "Mmm," she groaned.

"You getting what all the fuss was about?" he teased. She nodded.

"No more vanilla?"

"I think I'm ready for the chunky monkey."

He said nothing else, just pushed his pants and boxer briefs down, revealing a thick, jutting erection. Every part of her that wasn't already dripping with want melted, and she parted her thighs farther, desperate to have him between them.

Before he knelt, though, he tore open a condom he must have had tucked in his pocket. God, she hadn't even thought of it. Some smart, contemporary woman she was.

Lifting her arms, she pulled him down to her. "Now."

"Now," he agreed as he began to ease into her, carefully.

She knew he was going slowly, treating her like the near-virgin he knew she was. But she didn't want restraint. She wanted the passion, the utter intensity that was making all his muscles bunch up, his face redden and the cords of muscle in his neck throb.

Reaching down, she grabbed his hips, arching toward him, trying to take what he wasn't giving. "More," she begged.

He resisted for a half second, then, with a groan, he plunged deep and hard, filling her completely.

This time it wasn't just a cry, it was a scream of pure pleasure that erupted from her lips. She probably startled the night birds winging over the water. Steve covered her mouth with his to swallow her joyful noises with a kiss.

They began to move, to sway, giving and taking, pulling and thrusting. Everything fell into place, as if they'd been made to do this with each other. Every stroke was answered, every offer of enjoyment accepted and reciprocated.

It lasted a long time. At one point, they shifted positions, so he was the one lying on the chaise and she sat on top of him. Her feet braced on the cool patio, she was able to ride him. Taking what she wanted, she drove him wild, judging by the look in his eyes as he stared up at her.

Finally, he grabbed her hips and held her tightly against himself, groaning as he finally climaxed. And then he pulled her down onto his chest, holding her tightly in his arms as the world gradually returned to focus.

"You okay?" he asked her, several minutes later, when it felt as though both their heart rates had returned to some semblance of normalcy.

"I am more fine than I have ever been in my life."

She meant that.

"I can't tell you how grateful I am for blind dates."

She couldn't help stiffening a tiny bit. God, with everything that had gone on tonight—from thinking he'd stood her up until they'd made wild, crazy love on his patio—she'd forgotten all about what had brought them together.

Her lies.

"I mean, talk about luck," he continued. "Who would have thought something this good could come out of a set-up?"

She swallowed, wanting to tell him. Needing to tell him. But unsure how to find the words. Naked and entwined also equaled vulnerable.

"How rare is it for two adults to find each other without having to play a lot of games or pretend to be people they're not just to find out if they're compatible?"

Playing games. Just as she'd been doing.

Steve traced a hand along her spine, sliding his palm down over her bottom. "I haven't felt this good in a long time. I wasn't sure I would ever be able to trust a woman again, but you, Sarah…well, I trusted you the minute I saw you."

"I felt the same way, from the first time I heard your voice," she whispered, meaning that.

He kissed her again, interrupting anything else she might have said. Then he sat up, carefully disentangling them and asked, "How about we take this inside?"

"Good idea." Inside. Clothed. In the light. Maybe then she could tell him how this whole thing had happened… and then see if he still thought blind dates were such a good thing.

Moving languorously, they pulled on their clothes, and she watched as he unlocked the back door. Once inside the house, she took a moment to look around, marveling at the beautiful place.

His house wasn't huge, certainly not a mansion—though, for a beachfront property, he'd probably paid as much as an inland mansion would have cost. All decorated in soft blues and yellows, the house seemed a perfect complement to the sun-drenched blue sky he probably saw out of these back windows every single morning.

"Drink?"

"Just water. I worked up a thirst."

"Ditto." He walked over to a wet bar area, opened a small refrigerator and pulled out two bottles. "Have I told you yet how glad I am that you went for that walk? I mean, I was getting desperate, trying to figure out how to reach you."

She liked the sound of that. She'd been feeling pretty desperate herself tonight. "Desperate, huh?"

"Yeah. Like I said, no last name, no phone number, I didn't know where you work, where you live. Nothing."

Which was exactly what she'd wanted. To think it had almost cost her this amazing, unforgettable night.

"Since I knew you knew *my* last name, I was hoping you'd try to reach me on my work number, which is published. I thought about calling the answering service to see if a sexy-voiced stranger had called and asked about me."

She tensed again as he handed her the bottle. "I didn't."

"Just as well," he told her. "Believe me, I did *not* want to call in there and give a bunch of lonely-hearts operators more reason to gossip about my private life than they already do."

Lonely hearts? That's what he thought of the women who took his calls—of her? She couldn't help stiffening a little. "You think they talk about you?"

Opening his water bottle, he dropped onto the couch beside her. "Of course they do. Everyone seems to, lately. I told you about the nurses. My own staff started giving me advice during the divorce." Sighing deeply, he continued. "And my *loving* ex had a habit of intentionally calling my work number when she knew I was unreachable. She'd leave messages with the answering service to cover where she really was and what she was doing."

Oh. Sarah began to get the picture. His ex-wife was not the only one who tried to use Call Anytime as an alibi. Cheating professionals actually did it all the time. Her anger rose as she realized that's probably what had been happening to Steve.

"Believe me, it's not pleasant to realize complete strangers are privy to your innermost secrets. You hire them to do a job and they end up holding your entire private life in their hands."

She swallowed, licking her lips, looking at it from his perspective. Sarah trusted her employees, and privacy issues were stressed as highly as efficiency. Yet she'd been the one to break those rules more than anyone else.

"I had to switch companies after the divorce because I was so damned humiliated when one of them started asking me if I was dating again yet. Another one told me I was better off without her."

Oh, God. She closed her eyes, feeling sick.

He didn't appear to notice. "I felt, I dunno...violated. Personal calls and messages going through complete strangers, knowing they were whispering about me the minute I hung up the phone, that was one thing. But people I'd never met speculating about my wife running around on me, and then feeling free to comment on it? Not my idea of fun."

Feeling dizzy, Sarah gulped her water. She was having a hard time focusing. Though at first, she'd been offended at being called a "lonely-hearts operator," she had opened up her ears enough to hear what Steve was really saying. To hear the tone in his voice—the embarrassment a proud, private man had felt. The humiliation. The hurt.

His wife must have been one piece of work. He didn't sound as if he was still wounded by having lost her, but rather by how it had thrown open his personal life to the world. While very friendly, he was obviously a person who liked to protect his privacy, and he'd been helpless to do it.

His trust had been violated...by her, most of all. She hadn't just eavesdropped on his private life, she'd inserted herself into it.

The magnitude of what she'd done last night really began to hit home. It wasn't just about lying anymore. There was no explaining this away as a little fib or a prank—*and oh, look how well it turned out, so let's just forget about it!* They were way past that because she'd done exactly what those others had done during his ugly divorce—she'd gotten involved in his private business, involving herself when she had absolutely no right to do so.

She could never forgive herself for being so selfish, so thoughtless. So how could she expect him to forgive her?

Feeling trapped, she eyed the back door through which

they'd come, and the front one on the far side of the house. There was no easy way out of here. No explanation he would accept. She couldn't possibly pretend she wanted to leave, not now that they'd proven in the most elemental way possible just how perfect they could be together. Nor could she get away without telling him her last name and phone number.

"Done?" he asked her, taking the empty water bottle from her hand.

Before she could say anything, not that she knew what she'd say, he reached for her hand and pulled her to her feet. "Outside was amazing. Now I want you somewhere a little more comfortable."

She hesitated, knowing it was wrong, knowing she had no business sleeping with him again under these pretenses. But she also knew he wasn't going to let her go.

Besides, this is your last chance to be with him.

That sad little bit of truth made her want to cry. But it was true. This was her last moment with the man of her dreams—the man she knew she could easily fall in love with. One last night before she disappeared out of his life as quickly and mysteriously as she'd entered it.

So, rather than making some excuse and leaving, she reached up, cupped his cheek, and whispered, "Then take me to your bed."

6

SHE WAS GONE.

Awakening at dawn, and rolling over to pull Sarah into his arms, Steve had been shocked to find nothing but an empty bed. The rumpled pillows, tangled sheets and a strand of silky hair were the only evidence that she'd been there.

Blinking, he sat up, immediately glancing toward the bathroom, even though the silence in the house—the emptiness—told him he wouldn't see her there. Nor did he think she was in the kitchen making coffee or something. The air was just too still. There wasn't the clink of a spoon, or even a whisper of sound above the inevitable churning of the waves outside.

"What the hell?" he muttered, getting out of bed to prowl the house, just to be sure.

Nothing.

Last night had been amazing. *Everything* had been amazing since the minute they'd met. So why would she just leave without waking him? It made no sense. If she had to go to work or be somewhere, she could have told him.

Then he groaned, remembering something else. "You don't even know where she works, jackass."

Nor did he know her last name. Even after almost missing her at the restaurant, he'd *still* neglected to get that basic bit of information. Or her phone number.

About to smack himself in the head for being so stupid, he suddenly spied a sheet of paper on his kitchen table.

Thank God. She'd left a note, probably to explain her departure and tell him how to reach her. But as he picked it up and read, he realized it wasn't what he expected to hear.

Dear Steve,
Please forgive me for skulking out of the house before you woke up. The truth is, I just can't face you. I've been lying to you. I'm not Bambi, I never was. I "stole" Saturday night's date with you...substituted myself in her place, all because I was selfish and wanted a chance with you.

I know you hate liars, and you hate having your privacy invaded, and I've done both. Hearing you talk about it last night broke my heart and made me feel like the worst person alive. I hope you can forgive me someday. Sarah.

He stared at the paper for a long time, then let it fall from his fingers to flutter back to the table, thinking about every word he'd said, every bit of conversation.

Yeah. He'd talked about those things, but not because he was trying to make her feel bad or coerce any kind of confession. The only time he'd been trying to do that was after they'd made love on the patio, and he'd told her how grateful he was for blind dates! He'd said it intentionally, opening the door to let her come clean about how she'd really come to be his date Saturday night. When she hadn't walked through that door, he'd figured she just wasn't ready yet. But with their intimacy and connection growing with every passing hour, he knew she would be soon enough.

He'd never—not once—equated her with his ex. Sarah wasn't a liar, and he'd never considered her to be one. Nor did he get the whole invading-his-privacy thing.

Yet, thinking about his words, he began to see how she would think he'd hate her for lying.

What a mess.

But one that he could fix. Because he wasn't willing to let her go, not without making sure she knew he wasn't angry that she'd "stolen" such a magnificent, wonderful weekend with him. He hoped like hell she'd want to keep seeing him afterward, but at the very least, she deserved to know he wasn't angry…and he deserved to hear her whole story.

"How?" he muttered. How was he supposed to find her?

He wondered about it as he made coffee, then showered and got ready for work. He was still wondering about it in his office later that morning, between appointments and friendly conversations with his staff, who were busily chattering about their Valentine's Day plans.

Just his luck. He found someone he'd like to spend the romantic holiday with…and he didn't even know her last name.

Finally realizing he did have at least one thing to go on, he tracked down Rick. Not wanting to get into the whole story, he merely asked his buddy to see if he could get in touch with Bambi—the real Bambi—to find out what had happened Saturday night. Why she'd backed out, and who might have known about it.

His friend called him back a half hour later. "Dude, Bambi's on the road, on her way to Texas. She met some other guy and took off. I'm really sorry, man. I had no idea she was gonna bail on ya."

"It's okay," he said. "What did she say about it? Did she send one of her friends in her place?"

"*Huh?* Somebody else showed up?" His friend was silent for a moment, then chortled. "Oh, I get it! And you want to know how to get a hold of her."

"Yeah, Captain Obvious, I do. So what exactly did Bambi say?"

"She didn't mention anything about swapping with some other chick," Rick admitted, sounding sorry to deliver bad news. "She said she was in such a rush to get out of town, she just called your answering service and asked them to tell you she wasn't gonna be there."

Steve quickly thought back to Saturday afternoon, remembering the message from the service about his date. But that didn't make sense, either. When he'd called in for the message, they'd made no mention about his date not showing up.

"Okay," he said, sighing with disappointment. "Thanks for checking it out."

"Let me know what happens. It's about time you get your membership back in the sexually-active club."

He was back in that club. Now he just wanted to get his membership card and *stay* there for a while. With Sarah as his club-mate.

Hanging up, Steve sat at his desk, the thoughts continuing to churn. Something was nagging at the back of his brain.

Some woman—not Bambi—had called the answering service, pretending to be her in order to get the information about the date. But, if that was the case, what had happened with Bambi's original message? He'd never gotten it.

The service. The answer had to lie there.

Reaching for his phone, he buzzed his office manager. "Would you bring me the information on the new answering

service company we hired a few months ago?" he asked,
still trying to figure it out. It wasn't that he needed the message retrieval number; he called it all the time and knew it
by heart. But somehow, he didn't think he'd get the answers
he wanted by dialing it now.

Then he thought of all those calls. Dialing that number.
Getting his messages. And he remembered something
else.

A voice.

"Son of a bitch," he whispered, everything starting to
click into place in his brain.

"Everything okay, doctor?" asked his office manager,
who'd just walked in carrying a few sheets of paper.

"I'm fine," he told her, shaking his head in disbelief.

"Okay, then, here's the info you wanted," she said, leaving the pages on his desk before walking out. He barely
even noticed.

Was it possible? Could the whiskey-voiced operator he'd
talked to on the phone several times while retrieving his
messages *also* be the whiskey-voiced seductress he'd spent
the past two evenings with?

It sounded crazy. But it also made perfect sense. And
when he glanced at the papers on his desk, including a
pamphlet for the company—Call Anytime—he knew it
was the truth. Because right there in black and white were
the names of the owners.

One of whom was Sarah Holt.

He'd found his mystery woman, knew who she was
and how she'd come to meet him Saturday night. Thinking about everything he'd said last night, he also now
completely understood why she'd walked out on him this
morning.

Now he just needed to figure out what he was going to
do about it.

"YOU ARE AN INSANE PERSON."

Trying to ignore her friend and partner, Sarah hunched deeper into her chair, wishing she'd never spilled her guts to Mindy about what had happened this weekend.

She should have just called in sick. Pulling the covers over her head and ignoring the world would have been a much better way to spend Valentine's Day. Having to come in to the office and listen to all her employees coo about their boyfriends and husbands, or, even worse, open the door to receive boxed roses or candy, was just plain painful when you had a broken heart.

Hers shouldn't be broken. She'd only gone out with the guy twice. Still, she'd known Steve Wilshire was something special before she'd set eyes on him. And those two evenings had been the most wonderful ones of her entire life. To think she would never get to sleep in his arms again, as she had last night, had her ready to burst into tears. Just like she had the minute she'd gotten back to her place in the pre-dawn hours this morning after sneaking out on him like a thief in the night.

"I mean, you tell me you're crazy about the guy, that you hit it off, that you actually spent the night with him last night…and then you just left?" Mindy was stalking around the room, railing, drawing the eyes of every operator on the floor. Considering the office she shared with Mindy was like a fishbowl, with glass walls, they had zero privacy. Everyone was paying attention, making no effort to hide it. "How could you do that? That is so not what nice-girl Sarah does!"

"Nice-girl Sarah doesn't lie her way into a guy's bed, either," Sarah snapped, sick and tired of hearing about stupid nice-girl Sarah. "I told you how he feels about liars, and about people who invade his privacy. Weren't you listening?"

"But none of that matters if he really cares about you. And it sounds like he could!"

They were going around in circles. The two of them had been having this same argument for a couple of hours, ever since this afternoon when Sarah had finally broken down and confessed why she was so miserable.

"Look," Sarah at last admitted. "He called operators lonely hearts and griped about them being nosy."

Mindy's mouth tightened. She took that personally.

"He can't stand liars, people who don't mind their own business…and answering-service operators. I am batting zero for three here, don't you get it? If he ever finds out the truth, he's liable not only to tell me off, but to fire us!"

Mindy opened her mouth to argue a little more, but Sarah put a weary hand up. "Would you just let it go? It's over. I took my shot, did what you wanted me to, had sex with my dream man and now I'm moving on."

Mindy glared, her mouth twisting in a frown. Throwing herself down in her chair, she said, "That's not what I wanted and you know it. That's what *I* would do. Not you. You're too nice for that. And you deserve to be in love."

"I think I *am* in love," Sarah replied sadly, touched as she finally realized Mindy's anger was generated by true concern for her.

"Oh, honey. I'm so sorry," Mindy whispered.

Yeah. So was Sarah.

Before she could say anything further, though, she saw Mindy's eyes grow wide. Her friend was facing the wall, while Sarah's back was to it, and something had obviously happened in the busy answering area.

"Stay here," Mindy snapped, leaping out of her chair.

Sarah began to turn around, but Mindy demanded, "No. Don't move. Just stay put. Let me see what's going on."

Then she hurried out of the office, slamming the door shut behind her.

There must be some drama happening with the operators, apparently. It wouldn't be the first time. Everybody's emotions ran a little high on holidays like this one. In a 24-hour-a-day, 365-days-a-year business, somebody always got stuck working when they didn't want to. So an employee who hadn't gotten the night off had probably said something snarky to someone who had.

Then she heard a man's voice, and Sarah's curiosity grew. They'd had a couple of male operators in the past, but none lately. Before she could get up to see what was happening, she heard Mindy respond to someone. Shockingly, her voice was raised, her tone angry.

"No, you're not going to talk to her until you tell me you're not here to give her a hard time. It was all my fault. If you want to blame somebody, blame me. You can even fire us, if you want. But don't take it out on Sarah."

Suddenly having a suspicion, Sarah leapt up and swung around. Staring through the glass, she saw Steve Wilshire. He stood in the middle of the bullpen, surrounded by operators, blocked from moving by a belligerent—protective—Mindy.

Their eyes met, hers, she knew, round and shocked, his…inscrutable.

Sarah's heart raced, her blood roaring as she understood the ramifications. He'd found her. Which meant he'd been looking for her. The only question was—had he come here to tell her off, and to fire her, as she'd told Mindy she feared? Or for some other reason?

Steve wasn't paying any attention to Mindy, or to anyone else. It was as if nobody other than Sarah even existed at that moment. His stare never wavered from her face.

Then he smiled that slow, tender smile, saying a million things without uttering a word.

"Oh, God," she whispered.

Her heart lifted, and a sense that everything was going to be okay washed over her, making her feel so hopeful, so happy, she didn't even recognize herself as the same woman she'd been an hour ago.

Still silent, Steve moved his arm, which had been behind his back, and lifted what he'd been hiding. A dozen roses. Beautiful, rich, crimson roses.

Mindy, finally noticing the flowers, not to mention the fact that Steve and Sarah couldn't take their eyes off each other, melted out of the way. Fierce mama lion protecting her cub—it was cute. Now, though, she and everyone else understood what Sarah had the moment she'd seen that smile.

He'd come here because he forgave her and wanted to be with her.

Still too surprised even to move, Sarah simply waited as Steve walked across the bullpen, skirting work-stations staffed by open-mouthed, wide-eyed women. When he got to her office and opened the door, she spared a moment to wonder woefully what her hair must look like and how red and swollen her eyes must be. But the warm, appreciative expression on his face as he stared at her said he honestly didn't care.

Entering, he pushed the door shut behind him, then took one step toward her.

She took a step, too. Then paused, saying what most needed to be said. "I'm sorry."

He lifted a hand to her face, brushing her hair back, then tangling his fingers in a few long strands. Pulling her closer, he whispered, "I'm not," then gently kissed her.

Sarah wrapped her arms around his neck, losing herself

to his embrace, somehow already knowing she would never—ever—tire of being in his arms. She kissed him back, again and again, silently repeating her apology with every soft, tender brush of their mouths.

Outside the office, there might have been some *oohs* and *aahs,* and she definitely heard clapping. But Sarah ignored everything else except the warmth of his body pressed against hers. She drank her own happiness from his lips, drowning in the tenderness of his hand on her face. And, most of all, the realization that he was here.

He'd come for her—knowing who she was, and what she must have done. And he still wanted her anyway.

The string of soft kisses finally ended, and Steve lifted the roses, offering them to her. "So, what do you say Sarah *Holt?* Will you be my Valentine?"

She nibbled her lip, wondering what on earth he'd gone through to figure out who she was. She looked forward to hearing the story…after she got finished showing him how very glad she was that he'd done it.

But that was all for later. Now, there was only this man, that smile, that amazing kiss. In his arms, she found everything she'd ever wanted and fantasized about.

Only, it was more than that. Because the reality was so much better than any dream could ever have been. She'd wanted one night of fantasy with her secret Prince Charming, but now suspected she'd landed in the most important relationship of her life with a sexy, wonderful man. A man looking at her with want and devotion in his eyes.

She'd never get tired of that look. Not ever.

"Well?" he asked.

"Yes, Steve Wilshire," she assured him, meaning it with all her heart. "I would love to be your Valentine."

* * * * *

EX MARKS
THE SPOT

BY
JO LEIGH

1

As much as Paige Callahan loved living in San Francisco, which was a lot, there were nights when climbing the hill to her apartment was a pain. Thing was, there was no convenient street parking, so there was inevitably a search that began with hope and crossed fingers, and always ended with her trudging up block after steep block, arms loaded with briefcase and tote, until she finally made it inside the building, where she then had to climb two sets of stairs.

Normally, the view from her living-room window made her feel instantly better, but not tonight. She dropped her stuff on the dining-room table, though she wanted to throw it across the room, and considered pouring a glass of wine. Too much trouble. Instead, she listened to her phone messages, surprised that there was more than one.

"Paige, I've left this message on your cell, sent you an email and now I'm resorting to the land line. We're still on for tonight, right? The restaurant is to die for, and I swear you'll love the club. It's been forever since you've been out dancing, and I know we can find the right number of drinks that'll make even you feel like shakin' your groove thang. I know you're going to meet someone fabulous tonight, I mean it. You know I'm psychic when it comes to hot guys, and, honey, tonight is your night! Seriously. Call me or face my wrath."

"Fiona," Paige muttered, as she deleted the message, "your wrath is a cupcake with sprinkles compared to the rest of my week. My *groove thang* is broken beyond repair."

The deal she'd been working on for six months had fallen apart today. As the senior director of major gifts for the San Francisco Museum of Modern Art, Paige was responsible for obtaining pieces for exhibit. The bigger the prize, the more complex the transaction, and this one, an outright gift of four Kandinsky major works, would have been a spectacular coup.

She'd poured her heart into this deal, only to have the donor decide at the eleventh hour that he'd rather give the paintings to his grandchildren who had no interest in donating or lending.

All this on a Saturday, her day off. A miserable, freezing February twelfth, which was supposed to have been spent hanging out with Fiona and Shelly at the day spa, followed by a long-awaited dinner at the Slanted Door. She'd even agreed to go dancing at Club 525, despite the fact that she really didn't care for the DJ scene. The only reason she'd said yes was because it had been a really long time since she'd met anyone even halfway decent, let alone someone she actually wanted to sleep with. But right now, all she wanted to do was crawl into her bathtub and stay there until the whole apartment complex ran out of hot water.

After a piteous sigh, Paige pressed the button for the next message.

"Don't hang up."

Paige stilled, her breath caught in her throat, instantly recognizing Curt, her ex-boyfriend. Curt, who hadn't called her in over a year, and that was only to accuse her of stealing his CDs, his portable DVD player and his Red Sox T-shirt. She reached for the delete button, but not quickly enough.

"I know you don't want to talk to me, and I don't blame you. I've been a…less than my best. Anyway, this isn't a joke or a trick and I swear to God I have no ulterior motives. I went to this gallery showing last night, and I ran into this guy I know from Berkeley. He's a good guy, divorced, has his own tech business, and he's got a significant private art collection, right up your alley. We had some drinks, got to talking. Long story short, I gave him your number. I know, I should have asked first, but I think you two might…"

There was a long pause, and Paige could picture Curt clearly. Sitting in his uber-expensive chair, his computer monitor cluttered with his stock tickers, accounts, sports scores. He'd be clicking away on his mouse, constitution-ally incapable of talking on the phone without checking his email.

"Anyway, his name is Noah. You can tell him to screw off if you want to, but I think…"

Curt cleared his throat. "Paige, I wouldn't have given him your number if I didn't think you'd be safe. He needs a date for Monday night, for a fundraiser at a gallery, and he's also interested in lending some of his modern-art col-lection, but I bet you could get him to donate some, too. Major pieces. And, um, I found the CDs. And the DVD player, and well, turns out I left the T-shirt at the gym. So, sorry about all that, but hey, maybe this thing will work out with you and Noah and we'll be square, huh?"

She heard the ding of his email alert.

"Okay. I hope this isn't too crazy. We should, you know, talk some time."

Paige's finger still hovered over the delete button, but

she didn't press it. What she did do was collapse on the couch.

Curt was setting her up on a blind date. Curt, her boyfriend for two years, who would have been *the one* if it hadn't been for his pathological need to manipulate everything and everyone in his life. *Curt* was setting her up on a blind date for Monday night. February fourteenth. Valentine's Day. Great.

And no, she and Curt wouldn't be square, even if Noah donated a damn wing to the museum. Okay, that would make her a lot less angry, but still. A setup by Curt. A setup she needed desperately, now that six months of work had gone down the drain. It was humiliating. Tragically pathetic. Especially because she was going to say yes.

SHIT, HE'D FORGOTTEN TO CALL the museum woman. Noah Hastings checked his watch, already knowing it was too late. She'd have been asleep for hours, and what the hell was he still doing up at three-thirty in the morning? That was the trouble with internet work, it was always there, hovering. A particularly vicious hack targeting online bank passwords had been detected, and his staff at White Hat Resources was working around the clock to stop it.

Noah had gathered a group of the best hackers in the world to his company, and it seemed as if none of his team ever slept as they held disaster at bay for banks, corporations and government institutions.

Noah trusted his people, but that didn't mean he could sit back and relax. He was one hell of a hacker himself, and this particular job presented an almost irresistible challenge. On the other hand, he wasn't just a hacker any longer and he had to sleep, eat regular meals, oversee and delegate. It was nights like this, hacks like these, that made him miss his lone-wolf days when he went mano a mano with some of the smartest bastards on the planet.

He stood, stretched his neck, his back. Turned off the parts of his computer system he could. His footsteps echoed as he crossed his dark living room, the lights of the city obscuring the stars. He forced himself to think of other things as he headed upstairs to bed. One glance at the print of an early Arshile Gorky painting that hung in the hallway and he forgot everything except his plan to protect his private collection of abstract expressionist art. It still stung that his ex-wife had gotten the original in the divorce.

He had no real desire to go to the fundraiser at the Channing Gallery, but at least meeting Paige Callahan would kill two birds. He'd be seen supporting the arts, and he'd find out everything he could about the benefits of setting up a private foundation versus outright museum donations.

Actually, inviting Callahan would kill three of those metaphorical birds. It also gave him an excellent Valentine's Day date. One who had no expectations, who cared nothing about the fact that his divorce was now final and that he was technically once again on the market. He most definitely was not. One divorce was all he was willing to experience. Monday night would be strictly business.

OF COURSE, PAIGE THOUGHT. Why wouldn't Noah call during the fifteen minutes she'd been away from her apartment? Why would Curt give the man her cell-phone number, even though he knew she was twice as likely to be with her cell than at home? She had no business saying yes to this date. Meeting. Interview thing. Not the way her luck was running.

She looked back at her phone. She still didn't know Noah's last name, and it hadn't shown up on her caller ID. But his number had, so she called him back. After four rings, she got his voice mail. Again no name, just his number.

"It's Paige Callahan from the museum. Sorry I missed your call. Try me on my cell, I've got that with me all the time." She gave him her phone number slowly, twice.

An hour later, he called back when she was in the bathroom, without her phone. After cursing her horrible luck and worse timing, she listened to his message.

"Damn, I thought we'd... I hate to do this, but I'm going to be hard to reach before tomorrow evening. Instead of playing phone tag, perhaps we can meet at the gallery? I'm normally not this informal, but work is problematic at the moment. Leave a message for me, either way, and I'll completely understand if the arrangement doesn't work for you."

That was it. Naturally, she called him right back, and naturally, it went directly to voice mail. "Paige again. I'll meet you at the Channing at seven. I'm looking forward to it."

As she disconnected, all the energy, which wasn't a lot, drained out of her. She still had no idea who the mysterious Noah was, what he looked like, or if he even had a collection worth thinking about. She'd called Curt to ask. Curt hadn't picked up or called her back, which was just the sort of thing Curt would do, confirming that she couldn't take anything that might happen at the gallery for granted. It would have been easier to cancel, but the fundraiser at the Channing was a very big expensive deal, and even if Noah turned out to be in cahoots with Curt, there would be other collectors, legitimate collectors, she could meet.

She listened one more time to Noah's message. He had a good voice. Deep. Sexy. He sounded tall, nice-looking. But who was she kidding? He could look like a hunchbacked troll, it wouldn't matter. This wasn't a date.

NOAH WASN'T FOND OF wearing a tux, although since White Hat Resources had taken off he'd collected four of the damn things. There was always some formal dinner, some gala, some fundraiser that required his attendance. He wasn't fond of those, either. But his company represented security and stability, and therefore he had to represent the same things to his clients.

Tonight's event was peppered with clients and potential clients, although he'd have to do some tap-dancing with personnel if he took on much more work. Great hackers weren't easy to find, and he didn't want to risk burning out his most valuable people.

He looked at his watch again. It was still far too early for the museum woman to have arrived. His arrival at six had been a favor to Leon, the gallery's owner, who was having trouble with his computer. It had nothing to do with hacking, which Noah had known beforehand, just some operating-system errors. He'd fixed things in ten minutes and had spent the next twenty looking at the auction pieces. There were two he'd liked from very promising young artists. He headed back to look at them again. Before he made a bid, he wanted to be sure.

2

SHE SHOULD HAVE TAKEN her car.

Paige stood in the middle of Timmons Street, watching as her favorite—her only—shawl disappeared around the corner. Carried away by the wind, aided by her tripping over her own feet, the shawl was currently stuck on the bumper of a Muni bus, being taken to places unknown, where it would most likely have a much better evening than she would.

It was freezing. Windy. Rain was imminent. She had to walk up a big honking hill and then another three blocks to get to a street frequented by cabs. Meaning her feet would hurt all night.

She should just go home. Go home, get out of the dress that had cost her a week's pay, put on her flannel pajamas and have herself a good cry. It was all going to be a disaster anyway. Valentine's Day. What idiot thought up that bit of torture? Sure, Curt had done a few nice things in the past, but before Curt, hell, during Curt, this so-called holiday had been as romantic as a vacuum cleaner.

As she started up the hill, resigned to her fate, she counted off just a few of the wonderful February fourteenths she'd had: She'd been stood up. Three different times by three different guys. Abandoned at a concert. In San Jose. Without enough money to get home. That had been a real treat. Oh, then there was the night her date, a Stanford man studying particle physics, had been violently sick all over her brand-new silk shirt. Sweet.

She should have just worn her damn coat. Her goosebumps had goosebumps and her teeth had started to chatter. She rubbed her bare arms, as if that would help.

If only the Kandinskys had come through. She'd never have agreed to go to this fundraiser. She'd have found out exactly who her ex had set her up with, do proper research first. She'd get recommendations, find out why, if he had major pieces, she hadn't heard of him.

Watch, this Noah character would turn out to be an international art thief who would bilk the museum out of millions. Yeah, that sounded about right.

The wind blew her hair into her face, and it was all she could do not to break down and bawl like a baby.

AT TEN AFTER SEVEN, Paige shivered as she shut the taxi door. She'd made it to the gallery, late but in one piece, for whatever good that would do. But she was here, so she might as well go inside. She squared her freezing shoulders and walked toward her fate.

The hostess of the Channing, Anna, whom Paige had met at quite a few fundraisers just like this, expected her, had known she was meeting Noah. The older woman informed Paige that his last name was Hastings and gave her an odd grin as she pointed Paige in the right direction.

"Oh," Paige whispered with a tiny gasp. He most definitely did not look like a hunchbacked troll.

Anna chuckled. "Have a wonderful evening."

"Well, things are certainly looking up," Paige murmured as she reminded herself that the night might feel romantic with the gorgeous art displays, the scent of the fantastic floral arrangements and champagne at her fingertips, but she wasn't here for canoodling, or even thinking of canoodling.

NOAH HAD ALWAYS DISLIKED mixing art with business. Art was his solace, his refuge. Music, too, but paintings, from famous works to street tags, if they hit him the right way, lingered, soothed and freed up the parts of his mind too concerned with computer code. His best ideas had sprung fully formed after indulging in his passion, losing himself in an artist's vision.

He glanced at his watch yet again. She was late. His gaze went to the gallery entrance. People were gathered near the door itself, so it was conceivable that she was already here. He had asked the hostess to send the woman his way, but perhaps Ms. Callahan hadn't spoken to Anna.

Curt hadn't described Callahan, not the physical part. He'd said she was smart, told him about her degrees and her work in restoration and authentication. That she was young to be as good as she was.

Noah knew Curt and Paige had been a couple, but no longer were. It hadn't seemed acrimonious, not from Curt's tone or from the fact that he'd offered her number. Noah hadn't asked any questions, not about the two of them. It hadn't seemed relevant. Now, though, he wished he'd looked up more than her museum biography.

A waiter came by with champagne, which Noah declined, and when he looked up again, a pretty woman stood at the front entrance. From her posture he knew she was searching for someone. He wanted it to be him.

The thought made him frown. The woman at the door was attractive, yes, but from a distance. He had no idea about the details and frankly, the details had always mattered to him more than the whole. But he was also a normal man and his brain often skittered to *want* when he saw *pretty,* usually for a second or two, then something else would catch his attention, or if he was in the mood and it seemed feasible, he'd make his move.

This reaction hadn't been a momentary blip, but a four-count beat, heavy on the resonance.

There was no real reason to think the beautiful blonde was Paige Callahan. In fact, the woman now standing next to the hostess was a more likely candidate with her laptop-sized bag and her nice but sensible dress.

His gaze moved back to the beauty. She wore bangs, her hair looked tousled and sexy. Her skin was pale and her face lovely. He moved toward the door, and she came more into focus with each step. Her dress wasn't the least bit sensible. The blue was the color of a Monet sky and it flowed around her curves like liquid.

Closer still, he saw the blue might just match the color of her eyes.

She smiled his way, raised her hand in a quirky little wave.

Let her be the one, he thought. It would make the whole evening so much more pleasant.

So, HE WAS GORGEOUS. Tall. Filled his tuxedo exquisitely. Tonight was all about the business of art, the part that had zero sex appeal. She had to woo him, all right, but for paintings. Donations. Lots of donations. But first, they had to meet.

"Paige?"

She nodded. She appreciated the fact that he extended his hand instead of going for an air kiss or, God forbid, a hug. She hated to do that with strangers, even men with chiseled jaws and great cheekbones. "Mr. Hastings."

"Noah," he said. Instead of the shake and release Paige expected, he held her hand in his, not moving, not squeezing, just…holding. "I'm sorry to do this to you tonight of all nights. Curt assured me it wasn't going to be a problem, but now that I see you, I imagine there are a lot of broken-hearted men in San Francisco this evening."

She felt herself blush, would have pushed her hair back if she'd had both hands free. "No, it's my pleasure. Actually, I would have been watching Netflix movies and eating microwave popcorn. This is much better."

He smiled. Nicely.

It hit her, what she'd said to him, and she died just a little bit. Microwave popcorn and chick flicks. She might as well have told him she wore granny panties under her flannel nightgown.

He looked down at their joined hands. His dark eyebrows rose as if he hadn't realized, and then he let her go. "What do you say we go get something to drink before we wander through the gallery?"

"Sounds excellent."

He touched the back of her right arm as he accompanied her to the main showroom. His hand was warm and it sparked a chain reaction that made her lose her step. Which made his grip tighten. Even though she'd caught herself before disaster struck, she knew her chest, her neck and most especially her cheeks were flushed, which was inappropriate and inconvenient as this wasn't the time or the place, and for heaven's sake, she was twenty-seven, not sixteen.

There was no way Noah hadn't seen her blush, but she hoped he attributed it to her clumsiness.

"Have you been to this fundraiser before?"

"Yes," she said, grateful for something to focus on besides the fact that his hold on her arm hadn't loosened at all. "The year before last. They raised over a million-five at the silent auction. I'm a big fan of supporting the arts, especially when so much of the money goes to education and preservation." She fought off a wince. Of course he knew all that.

"According to your biography, you were in preservation for what, two years?"

"That's right. Not at MoMA, though. At the Ryerson Museum in Santa Clara."

"I've never been there."

"Too late now. They've closed. Their collection is spread out all over the world."

"That's happening too frequently," Noah said. "Yet another reason for meeting you tonight. I want to share the pieces I have, and will have, but I don't want to put them at risk. From what I've learned, you know a lot about that."

"I do. I know we can come up with a plan that will be perfectly tailored to your needs."

He guided her gently toward a standing bar and they got into line behind a couple they both knew. He was a big shot at Skywalker Ranch, the George Lucas film facilities, and his wife was on the board of the Asian Art Museum.

Paige had known she would run into a great many acquaintances and colleagues, and that this was just the start of the socializing portion of the evening. She wondered again why she hadn't heard of Noah Hastings before tonight. If he had a substantial collection, it should have been on her radar. The only thing she could think of was that he'd just started collecting.

Drinks were finally secured, and she and Noah even scored some wonderful but small hors d'oeuvres before they began the tour of the exhibit pieces, all of which were up for auction. This particular fundraiser focused on the current art scene. Up for bid were pieces from the finest new artists from around the world. The buyers were willing to spend money based on their belief that this artist or that would end up being a superstar. In fact, for some lucky painters or sculptors, tonight's outcome could be the turning point in their careers.

"I'm curious," Paige said, hoping that if they kept moving they wouldn't be interrupted, because finally, *finally,* she felt herself. This was her world, after all, more important than a man whose touch could cause her to trip. "What brought you to collecting?"

Noah paused in front of a Georg Baselitz canvas. "Five years ago I was working on a project in Chicago, stopping a cyber threat attacking the stock exchange. I didn't have my current staff then, it was mostly just me and two other guys. I was thinking in circles, had to clear my head. I ended up at the Art Institute, and I got lost in a painting by de Kooning. I stared at it for a couple of hours and then I had it. The fix."

When Paige looked up, it was to find Noah looking at her, not the painting. He had blue eyes, but they were nothing like her own. His were the color of the sea and they were somehow disarming. She felt studied, but it wasn't uncomfortable. He should look closely. He needed to trust her.

Of course, she studied him right back, and it was in the small lines around his eyes, around his mouth, that she discovered more of him. Her first impression had been of a serious man, yet the history of his laughter was right there on his face. She guessed his age in his early thirties, but she could tell he was one of those men who would get better-looking as he got older. When she met his gaze again, she realized she wasn't bothered by his blatant stare because while it was calculating and yes, serious, she could tell that he was already leaning toward liking her, accepting her.

"What about you?" he asked.

"Pardon?"

"How did you come to art?"

She looked pointedly at the canvas. "I loved to paint, and wasn't half bad. But I don't have the magic. I've got an eye, though, and a reasonable talent for restoration. I found my place working on the business side."

He didn't respond, and she thought about glancing at him, but didn't. It would be easy to let herself get swept away by her physical reaction to him. The fact that she had responded to him at all was unsettling. She knew she was years away from being gobsmacked by looks, and she'd damn well better be past the stage where she got tongue-tied by wealth or power. She didn't even know if Noah had wealth or power. "You're a computer consultant?"

"White Hat Resources," he said. "My company specializes in neutralizing high-level computer threats."

"In other words, you're a hacker."

"Yes, exactly." He grinned. "We're the good guys."

"I imagine your services are in high demand."

He touched her arm again, in the very same spot. She did look up then. Excellent timing, as he led her to the next piece, by an artist Paige thought showed real promise.

"We're on the clock twenty-four/seven," he said. "It's a constant battle."

"And you're the boss, so all that pressure lands on your shoulders."

"Hence the need for art that moves me."

"I'd like to hear about your collection."

He turned to her, and she wasn't quick enough to glance away. Again, she was caught by him, drawn in. But just as he was about to speak, they were interrupted by a major donor to her museum. The man was the CEO of a huge corporation and had one of the great private art collections in the United States.

He shook Noah's hand, barely acknowledging her even though they'd had dealings. It was all right, though, as it gave her the opportunity to study Noah without being the deer caught in his headlights.

She wasn't the only one sizing up Noah. Mr. Saunders had skipped right over small talk and was asking about some foreign-sounding computer virus.

Noah frowned, took a half step closer to her, then very politely told Saunders that his company was aware of the threat, and that he'd be happy to set up a phone consult for Wednesday.

Saunders didn't care much for the brush-off, but made the appointment anyway. Noah graciously didn't gloat, in fact, he assured the man that his team would be in a better position to nullify the threat by Wednesday, so the timing was excellent.

It had been well-played, the whole encounter. She liked the way Noah handled himself. He was completely confident in his role and wore his power with elegance. Good to know.

"Sorry about that." He finished off his Scotch and looked at her wineglass. "Ready for another?"

She nodded, and they went in search of another bar. Unfortunately, they didn't get halfway there before they were approached by yet another titan of industry. He, too, wanted information and time with Noah, and the pattern continued over the next two hours.

Noah apologized, but there was little he could do short of being outright hostile. She'd have been a better sport if it had been easier to snack along the way, but carrying a tiny plate, a wineglass and her clutch while trying to look at art and be gracious when all she wanted to do was get Noah alone left her hungry and feeling cheated.

They'd almost finished the tour just as the auction came to a close. Noah stopped her before they left the annex, took her empty plate and almost empty glass and put them on a clearing tray. Then he took her hand in his and pulled her not toward the main showroom, but straight for the exit.

"This isn't working," he said, as he reached for the door. "I want to talk to you, and I can't here. Do you mind if we leave?"

She shook her head, glad to escape the interruptions, but a little nervous about their new destination.

He held the door for her and she went back out into the frigid night. They were at the rear of the gallery by the parking lot. He pulled a valet ticket out of his pocket. "The night hasn't gone quite the way I'd imagined. I don't know about you, but I'm hungry. And not for any more tiny food. How about we find something decent to eat? Somewhere quiet, where no one will know who we are."

As a shiver swept through her in the freezing night air, she grinned. "I'm in."

"Seafood? Steak? Italian?"

"Everything fancy's going to be booked to the gills. I vote for burgers."

"Good choice." He whipped off his tux jacket and put it around her shoulders, then pulled her close even as he walked them to the valet. "Then, after dinner, I'd like to take you back to my place."

3

As Noah gave the valet his tip, it occurred to him that his last statement left a lot of room for misinterpretation. As he walked around his car, he shook his head. He had this habit of leaping ahead in conversations, then neglecting to fill in the blank spots for the unfortunate person trying to follow along.

He slid on his seatbelt, then turned to Paige, wondering just how much trouble he was in. Her hand wasn't on the door, but her eyebrow was raised in subtle alarm, and her lovely lips had parted with the beginnings of a question. Such an expressive face.

He'd watched her closely in the gallery and her reactions to the art had been much more telling than her reactions to people. But that wasn't the point now, was it? "What I should have said was that if you're amenable, and it's not too late, I'd like you to come to see my collection, to get a feel for what I've got and what I'm hoping to do."

She continued to stare at him, but the eyebrow relaxed and she even managed a little grin. "Why don't we get some food. I'll be a lot more amenable after I have some fries."

"Great. Anywhere in particular you want to go?"

"Surprise me."

He released the Mercedes' brake, and merged into the smattering of traffic. "I'm something of a burger connoisseur, having lived off them for so many years. In between meals of mac and cheese and ramen noodles."

"Been there," she said. "College. And for a number of years after. They told me it built character, but I think that's a bunch of bull. All it did was give me lifelong cravings for food I swore I'd never eat again." She had relaxed into her seat, having apparently believed his explanation, and had even shifted her body so she could speak to him more easily. "French fries, though, they're my downfall."

He glanced at her, liking the way the city lights played over her face. "Am I contributing to the delinquency of an art specialist?"

"Yes. Completely. In fact, why don't you take all the guilt and let me eat in peace?"

"Done. I'll wring my hands at the first opportunity."

"Thanks. I appreciate it."

He turned on Van Ness, in no hurry despite his hunger. The evening so far had been…unexpected. It didn't exactly bother him that he'd found himself interested in this woman, but it did beg the question why. Paige was very attractive, there was no denying that. Maybe it was the combination of her blond hair and the vivid sky blue of her eyes. If he'd seen her across a room, he'd have never suspected that she was an art geek. It was shallow, he knew, but in his experience, women as beautiful as Paige preferred to look in mirrors, not at other people's art.

"Were you always a white hat?" she asked.

"I may have been a bit gray while I was finding my way," he said. "It's tempting, when you're a kid and you're good at code, to see what kind of mischief you can get away with."

"Were you ever caught?"

"Just the once was enough."

"Oh?"

"Nothing dramatic. I hacked into my brother's school and changed some of his records. He wanted to go to Harvard. I figured I could help."

"Did he get in trouble?"

"Nope. Just me. He did get into Harvard, without my assistance. I was without internet access for a year. Completely. It nearly drove me insane. Probably did, now that I think of it. I ended up designing code anyway. In my notebooks, by hand. I wasn't supposed to read magazines or books about computers, either, but I still managed to hear things. A year in the computer world is the equivalent of ten years in most other industries, and everything is life or death at sixteen, so I was terrified I'd never be able to catch up. I was better at computers than anything I'd ever done. I was scared spitless."

"And you've never crossed the line again?"

He smiled. "Not in any meaningful way. Certainly not with malicious intent."

"How come you weren't recruited by the FBI or CIA or something?"

"You watch too much television," he said.

"That was a non-answer."

He took advantage of the red light and looked at her full-on. "Yes, it was. I'm content with where I've ended up. For the most part. As with everything, there are compromises, challenges. Nothing's ever as perfect as we imagine it will be."

"That's true. Close is good, though."

"It is." He made the turn on Market, and in minutes they were parked in the lot for BurgerMeister.

"I thought this might be where we were headed," she said, the smile evident in her voice. "I love this place."

"I'm glad." He got out of the car and as he went around to open her door, he undid his tie and popped open the top two buttons of his shirt. Paige had let herself out, so he just locked up as she pulled his jacket tighter against the night. "You didn't bring a coat or…?"

"Funny story. I started out with a shawl. In fact, my favorite one. My only one. It met with an accident on the way to the gallery."

"Accident? You weren't—?"

"Only my feelings were hurt. It wasn't anyone's fault, unless you want to blame a particularly stubborn tree, the wind and the Municipal Transit System. I'll miss the shawl, but it wasn't a family heirloom or anything. You're probably freezing."

He put his arm around her shoulders again, more for her warmth than his, but he wasn't complaining. He liked holding her. The gallery had been full of the scents of flowers and perfumes, and now that he was close to her again, all he could smell was burgers. He wanted to know her scent, the feel of her skin, not his tux jacket. He also wanted to have her full attention when he told her something that mattered. It was crazy. Not like him, especially since the divorce. He'd have to be especially careful. Crazy had a way of getting him in real trouble.

They were able to get a table by the window. He sat across from her, as much to watch her as to keep a safe distance between them, although he supposed his precaution was futile considering he'd already invited her home.

To his surprise, neither of them needed menus, and Paige ordered his favorite meal, right down to the almost-burnt onions on the classic cheeseburger. She even asked for the strawberry shake. As far as deals went, this wasn't big, but it was a good sign.

The waiter left, and they were on their own again. There

wasn't much to see out the window, but the view from his seat was excellent. Not only could he look into her eyes, but her strapless dress showed off her lovely skin, including the enticing hint of her breasts above the blue material. He forced himself to look once again at her face, which was even more fascinating.

"I didn't ask," she said. "Did you put in any bids to-night?"

Noah nodded. "Two. Leon will call me tomorrow if I've won. They were both by an artist I'd only heard about. Daviel Shy. She's a filmmaker and illustrator as well as a painter. I'm impressed with what she does on canvas. I also donated a sculpture by Geoffrey Koetsch."

She narrowed her eyes. "You didn't mention that was your donation."

"I wanted your reaction without prejudice."

"How did I do?"

"Very well."

"As I recall," she said, "I didn't love it."

"No, you didn't. But you understood it. The reason I chose that particular piece for the fundraiser is because while I like it more than you, I have two other pieces by Koetsch that I prefer. I want to promote him, though. Not enough people know about what he's doing."

She leaned forward. He took another peek at her décol-letage, but only a peek.

"Tell me," she said.

He did. It was a conversation, not a monologue, and while it was broken up by food arriving and food being eaten, it was the kind of discussion that was yet another layer of what kept him fascinated by art. Just as with computers and hacking, there was an insider language to art and collecting, one he was still learning after five years. Paige was tremendously knowledgeable, and just as impressively, she wasn't afraid to acknowledge what she didn't know.

Then the conversation started winding. From movies to plays to books. It surprised him that she was into science fiction, although he wasn't sure why. That got them talking about graphic novels and comics, and she'd actually read a number of them. Again, a surprise, which she pointed out was sexist. He'd have to think about that. He had some great female hackers in his shop, but none of them had ever talked about comics. Then again, he'd never brought the subject up.

When he finally looked around, they were the only two left in the restaurant. Paige seemed just as surprised. There was a small struggle over the bill, but he won, and then they were back in the car, the heater on full.

"I can't believe it's after eleven." He turned the key all the way, and listened to the purr of the engine, reluctant to say good-night.

"I know. The evening went by so fast."

"Too fast."

"Yes," she said softly, a streetlight illuminating her face and the uncertainty in her eyes. "And we haven't talked at all about your options with your collection," she added, tugging his lapels tighter around her shoulders.

"Cold?"

"What? No." She relaxed her grip.

"We can make an appointment for later in the week."

She frowned, and then gave her head a small shake. "Right," she said, but then she shook her head again, frowned. "Absolutely."

"Or, you could take a look at it now." He enjoyed the advantage of sitting in shadow while he watched her moisten her lush lips in frustration. She was probably trying to be sensible, and while he admired that, he was glad to see he wasn't the only one still thinking about his earlier invitation.

"We could…" she said, slowly enough that he knew now for certain she didn't want to put things off. And not just seeing his collection.

He let the silence alone. Totally ungentlemanly of him, but he needed this to be her decision. God knew he wasn't inclined to be sensible at the moment, because Paige made him want things he hadn't wanted in years. He was sure that if he stopped to analyze the feeling, he'd find it quite unsettling.

She glanced out the window, then stared down at her hands, her blossoming smile telling him that she was fully aware that while his invitation earlier had been mostly about art, that had been then. Now, it would be difficult for him to show her his home without wanting her to see his paintings in the morning light.

"We should make an appointment," she said finally.

"You're right, we should."

"I think we'd work well together. I know I'd enjoy it. If I come up to see your 'etchings,' things may get tricky."

Noah smiled. "It's a risk, all right."

Her mouth twisted wryly and she slumped deeper into his jacket.

"I do want to work with you," he added quickly. "But I won't lie. I'm extremely attracted to you."

She looked down, and while he couldn't see it, he would bet she was blushing. But then her head came up and her gaze met his. "You know what's got me worried?"

"What?"

"The fact that I'm here because of Curt."

"I don't understand."

"He did tell you we were together for a couple of years, didn't he?"

"He mentioned you'd broken up quite a while ago. Are you still—"

"Oh, no," she said, quickly, her expression making it clear she was telling him the truth. "We're better apart, trust me. What's getting to me is that he set this up. He's a pretty astute guy. He reads people well. I can't help wondering if this was his weird way of trying to get you to…"

"Sleep with his ex?"

"Hire him as your broker."

"Ah." He hadn't gotten that feeling the other night, but Paige knew Curt a lot better than he did. "If it turns out it was that second thing…deal breaker?"

She took a moment, and he used the opportunity to tell himself that he wouldn't press the issue. He wanted her to come home with him, wanted very much to see her without the beautiful dress, but the part of him that wasn't his dick knew that taking her home might be the best thing to do.

"No. Not a deal breaker." Paige touched his arm. "I've enjoyed tonight more than I ever expected to and for all kinds of reasons, only some of them having to do with business. On the other hand, my week has been the worst. I mean epically bad. Losing my shawl was the least of it."

Noah tried to hide a smile. "So you're expecting us to be that bad in bed?"

She laughed. "I see one has to be single-minded to be a hacker."

"Yes, I get your point." He turned his attention back to getting the car on the road, somewhat annoyed with himself. She was being a good sport, and he wasn't generally pushy. Not with women. "Where do you live?"

She hesitated, then gave him her address. "I've put you off," she said after they'd gone a mile.

He glanced at her in surprise. "I thought it was the other way around."

"Not at all." She shrugged. "I'm flattered. And very intrigued."

"So?" Damn, he was doing it again. "Okay, look, no pressure. We get to your place. I walk you to your door. You either kiss me on the cheek and then lock me out, or you run in and get a toothbrush."

Paige's soft laugh filled his chest with warmth. "Deal," she said and kept her gaze straight ahead, giving him not even the slightest clue as to what was going on in that pretty head.

4

THE WHOLE WAY TO HER APARTMENT, Paige told herself going to Noah's house would be a colossal mistake. It wasn't just the bad-luck run she'd been having, although that was probably enough of a reason to crawl into her own bed until Mercury was either in or out of retrograde, she could never remember which one made life suck. It was the mixing of business and pleasure.

She needed his business a lot more than she needed to sleep with him. He smiled at her as he made a right. The automatic squeezing of her legs and her accelerated heart rate begged to differ.

Only, this wasn't just about sex. Because this was not an ordinary man.

Before Curt, during another long dry spell, she and her friends had gotten together one rather drunken night and written out their perfect-man lists. There had been but one ground rule: they were to be as specific as hell. He must like dry wit but not bathroom humor; he can't be allergic to pets; art needs to play a significant role in his life; good, but not great at shooting pool. Like that. She couldn't remember everything on her old list, but if she were to write one up now, Noah Hastings would have a whole lot of checkmarks to his credit.

If she did say no tonight, it wouldn't necessarily mean they wouldn't eventually get together. Pleasure should follow business, that was the wisest course. But the idea of postponing made her nervous. It wasn't logical, but then, intuition wasn't, was it? If it was intuition and not hormones in overdrive.

No. Intuition. This was a defining moment.

There were no guarantees. He might end up being someone totally wrong for her, or he could screw her both literally and figuratively and never speak to her again. The possibilities for a bad outcome far outweighed the chances for magic. Still…

"This is your street?"

She snapped out of her trance and saw it was, in fact, her street. There was her car, the one she'd decided not to take because she was certain not to find a better parking space. "You know what?" she said, as the car slowed way down.

"What?"

"I would like to go see your collection."

Was that a sigh of relief? Or wishful thinking? It definitely was a smile.

"Terrific," he said, and hit the accelerator.

"Wait." Laughter bubbled up past her lips. While it was tempting to tease him about his enthusiasm, she said, "Since we're here I'd like to run in and get some things."

"Right. Of course." He backed up the car.

"There's a spot on the right, see it?" She pointed.

He slid into the space that was directly in front of her front steps. "You want company?"

"Thank you, no. I'll just be a minute."

"I'll be waiting."

She moved to open her door, but stopped at the hand on her arm. She turned back, and then his lips were touching hers, softly, asking permission. Whether she gave it to him by a breath or her shiver, she didn't know or care because he deepened the kiss, letting her feel his intention. Her lips parted and he sneaked inside, tasting good and warm.

The last of her doubts fled as his hand slipped behind her neck, his fingers cool and sure. Although he kept the pressure light and his tongue hesitant, there was a banked tension in the shoulder she gripped that matched the way her chest had tightened. She wanted more, but not here, and not quite yet. The climax of the evening might be known, but the dance was still to come, and she didn't want to give up a single second of that.

When he pulled back, her eyes stayed closed until she caught her breath. When she did look, it was to see his gentle smile, his eyes alight from more than just the street-lamp. "I'll be waiting," he repeated, his voice lower and holding far more promise.

This time, she made it out the door, giddy with what she was about to do. Not the getting-her-stuff-together part, but spending the rest of the night with Noah. That was plenty to be giddy about.

She was up the building's steps in a dash, then in the elevator, her fingers tapping on her dress as she ascended, wanting the door to open, wanting to be done with tooth-brushes and makeup. Three words circled over and over in her head: "This is crazy." But it wasn't a warning. It was wicked, like smoking in the girls' bathroom or spiking the prom punch. She'd been in charge of the decorations at her own prom, and wicked was hardly part of her rep-ertoire, which she imagined was a large part of the thrill. As long as she was going to disregard a lifelong pattern, she couldn't think of a more delicious man to do it with.

Everything that was going in her overnight bag was in it, including an outfit for work tomorrow, and if she forgot something major, so be it. She thought about changing clothes, but only for a second. She did grab her coat so she could return Noah's jacket. Only because she had to, though.

She couldn't get over this *feeling*. Breathless, foolish, nuts, tingly, hyper. Everything she made a point not to be. This whole business was risky and stupid, and it was like a tonic, a cure for everything that ailed her. She wasn't quite so far gone as to think it was anything like love at first sight or destiny, but she didn't really need it to be.

She was about to break a whole boatload of rules. Damn the consequences. For her, that was saying a whole lot. She was all about the consequences, but even when she planned things out to the last detail—figured out every angle, made smart moves, did her homework—it could all end up in the toilet. Kandinsky anyone?

Her own giggle surprised her. She grabbed her purse, her bag and her jacket, and she was out of there. Her fingers shook as she locked her door. The elevator slowed on purpose, but then she was flying down the steps and he was still there in his sleek black Mercedes and the passenger door swung open before she hit the sidewalk.

Holy crap.

TALK ABOUT UNEXPECTED. As he watched her swing her bag into his back seat, Noah thought that of all the possible outcomes of tonight's fundraiser, Paige coming home with him was the least likely. But damn, he was pleased. She was ridiculously pretty. Better still, she was someone he could talk to. Not about computers, no, but then he had a lot of people in his life who wanted to talk about those. She knew art. She knew good cheeseburgers. She'd read

Watchman and *Locke and Key*. Better even than that, when he looked her in the eyes, there was a spark.

Maybe it was all about sex, and in the morning he'd be able to think more clearly. That would be a decision for tomorrow. Tonight, the moment he'd pulled out onto the street, he reached for her hand.

"Where are you taking me?"

"Pacific Heights."

"Really?"

He heard the layers of her comment. "Yes, I'm a decadent capitalist. No excuses."

"I'm not asking for any. I'd already gathered that thwarting hackers was lucrative."

"It is."

"Just so you know, I'm going to hit you up for a lot more donations than I'd intended. I hope you have a huge collection."

"Not yet. But some day I'd like to."

"Good. I'm quite ruthless. Not just for the museum, either. I'm tough when it comes to protecting art. Seriously protective."

"Yet another reason I want to work with you. I don't want to lose another painting."

"A theft?"

"A divorce. She didn't even like the work particularly. But she knew I did."

"Ouch. How long ago?"

"Just this year, although we hadn't lived together for the last three. She's in L.A. doing something in the recording industry, I'm not clear on it."

"I'm sorry."

"Don't be. It's better this way. I only thought we had a lot in common. I was young."

"I thought hackers didn't even date, let alone get married young," she said.

"I'm a rebel."

She squeezed his hand. "I'm still sorry. I know what it's like to have a broken heart." She paused. "On the other hand, I also know how good it can feel to leave when it's not working out."

"Curt."

"Precisely."

"I never knew him well, but we had some good times."

"That's pretty much how I felt just before I broke it off."

That made him glance at her, and sure enough, a wry smile and one lifted eyebrow let him know she wasn't kidding. He liked this woman.

His gaze went back to the road.

She leaned toward him. "I want to know more about you."

"Ask away," he said, only wincing on the inside at his recklessness.

"Okay. Tell me one of your favorite memories from childhood."

Unexpected. Again. He had to think about it. He'd had a good childhood. Not perfect, but none ever were. His parents, though, had been young and adventurous. They hadn't really been surprised that he'd been caught hacking. Or that he'd turned it into his profession. Ah. "My folks used to take spontaneous road trips. They'd wake me and my brother in the middle of the night from time to time, and we'd all climb in my father's ancient VW van. Someone would pick a direction, and off we'd go.

"West was out, as we lived near the beach, but that still left a lot of territory. They had no problem with us missing a few days of school, either. They considered the trips educational, and sometimes they even were. Once, we were gone for two weeks. We'd only packed for the night, so that was interesting. I was lucky. My parents are remarkable people, and they taught me a lot about independence and self-reliance."

"Wow. That's impressive. I like your folks."

He smiled. "So do I. They live in France now. I try to get out to see them at least once a year."

They'd made good time and were getting close to his place, but he liked this part, and didn't want it to end too quickly. "Your turn."

"Baking with my mom," she answered, quickly. As if she'd known her answer before she'd asked the question. "It was just us for most of my life. My father died when I was seven, and Mom worked a lot, but she found time for us. We would spend hours in the kitchen, making everything from bread to cakes to my personal favorite, cookies. Man, her chocolate chip cookies are still the best I've ever tasted. But that's probably because they're so full of good memories."

"Does she live near you?"

"Santa Clara. She works for the department of water and power."

"So you're close?"

"Yep."

Wrapped in comfortable silence, they climbed the hills in his neighborhood until they were almost at the summit. He slowed as he pressed the garage door open, and then pulled into the space, parking between his bike and the Jeep.

"I can't believe you have a garage. That is awesome."

"Spoken like a true San Franciscan." He turned off the engine and went around to open her door. She let him this time, even let him grab her bag. He liked it that even though she'd brought a jacket, she hadn't taken his off.

Then again, he wished she had when he touched the small of her back as they entered the house. Important information could be gleaned from that simple maneuver, and his data wasn't complete through the material. Had her skin shimmied? Would he have felt her heat? He needed to try it again, later.

Without a touch or the flip of a switch, the downstairs lights went on. Because he was and would always be a computer geek, he'd wired the place himself, making the most of automation. There were sensors throughout that would turn on lights, open or close blinds, lock and unlock doors and windows, pipe in music. A side benefit was the wow factor, which Paige demonstrated with wide eyes and parted lips.

They walked through the kitchen, her steps slowing as they passed the fancy stuff the designer added not for him, as he wasn't a particularly avid cook, but for his ex-wife. At the thought, he parted from Paige, putting her bag on the dining-room table while she was still checking out the deep-pot sink.

"You like wine?"

She nodded.

"Great. Why don't we find a bottle together. The cellar is next to the art room."

She stared at him more intently than she had at the sink.

"You have an art room."

"Temperature- and humidity-controlled."

"And a wine cellar."

He shrugged. "What can I say? Malicious hackers keep on coming."

"Show me."

He took her through the living room, where he removed his jacket from her shoulders, to the stairs, self-conscious now about the elevator. That had been installed for Mary's parents, who'd never ended up staying with them. Paige paused, staring back at the view. One whole wall was glass, and the city glittered below them. "We'll come back up," he said.

"Bet your ass we will," she said, her lack of reserve making him grin.

After a short wind down the circular staircase, he pressed his thumb on the biometric lock before he opened the cellar door. This room was all his. The redwood racks held over two hundred bottles, and the arches were all hand carved. Even the tasting table had been done to his specifications. "What's your pleasure?"

"Ogling."

"And to drink while you ogle?"

"I'm going to let you choose."

"Merlot?"

"Perfect."

She wandered as he picked out a particularly fine vintage. Before she'd made a complete tour, he'd poured them each a glass. She took hers, and he watched her face as she went through all the steps—the swirling, the sniff, added rolling her eyes in an expression of bliss—before she sipped. "Oh, man. This is amazing."

"I'm glad you like it," he said, stepping closer to her. He let her have one more sip before he took her glass and put it down next to his. Her surprise quelled as he pulled her into his arms. Now he could feel her body's reaction to his touch. The shimmy was there, all right, even before his lips came down on hers.

5

SHE TASTED THE WINE on his tongue, and decided that given the choice, she'd always order by the kiss instead of the glass. She clutched at his shoulder, not just in reaction to the way his mouth moved on hers, but because of the fact that she was here, that an hour ago they'd been eating burgers, that she was kissing this remarkable man at all.

It felt as if this were someone else's life. Hers was filled with lost shawls and long days and a lonely apartment. This was so unlikely, it made her think not of the man who was kissing her, but of the man who'd put them together.

He pulled away, not far. "Are you okay?"

She straightened, startled by his question. "Yes. Why?"

"I had you," he said, as his finger gently swept her cheek. "I had you, and then…"

"I guess I'm a little overwhelmed."

He stepped back and her hand dropped from his crisp white shirt. "I'm sorry."

"Why?"

He picked up her glass and handed it to her, then got his own. "I guess this wasn't such a great idea. We just met and—"

"I wanted to come."

He winced. "I got caught up in—" He looked up as if searching the ceiling for what he was trying to say. When he finally met her gaze again, it was only for a second. "This was inappropriate. I apologize. I should take you home."

He turned, his glass hitting the table too hard.

She didn't even think, she just grabbed his arm. "Wait. Stop. I'm here because I want to be."

First he stared at her hand, then at her. "We'll be working together, at least I hope we will. I can't promise that because I don't know everything I need to about the museum or what your proposal will be. But if it happens or it doesn't, it's not dependent on you being here. Staying here tonight."

"I figured that out before I said yes."

"I certainly never meant to overwhelm you."

She smiled, even though she knew the magic bubble had popped. "The overwhelm has nothing to do with your art collection. Trust me."

He looked around. "We should have stayed at your place. Mine is a bit much."

"It's fabulous. And the only wine I have is a perky little number from New Zealand that's not in the same universe as what you've got here. But it's not about the house, which is beautiful, by the way."

"Then what?"

Paige thought about what she should tell him, but after a few seconds she realized the only thing she could tell him was the truth. "The whole night. I didn't expect you."

"No?"

She shook her head. "It's difficult because it was Curt's idea. I don't know what your past with him was like, but with me, he had a real talent for manipulating me to get what he wanted. He was damn good at it, too. It took me a long time to catch on. But I did, in the end. Nothing is straightforward with him, and while he claimed he was just trying to apologize for some things he said, I can't be sure. He knows art, so I wasn't dismissing the idea that your collection would be great, but I never dreamed I would feel so…drawn to you."

He exhaled a big breath. "Now that I think about it, he did get a lot of help with his schoolwork. As I recall, some people claimed he didn't even take his own finals."

"All done cheerfully by women, I'm guessing."

Noah shrugged. "I don't know what his motives were in setting the two of us up. All I can tell you is that there is no hidden agenda on my part. I have several million dollars sunk into my collections, and I want to protect them and my investments. As far as being attracted to each other, I don't believe that's something Curt could manipulate."

"I don't know. He's pretty good."

"Not this good. I watched you walk into the gallery, and all I could think of was how much I wanted you to be Paige Callahan."

Her breath hitched. "Really?"

He nodded and his body relaxed.

"I was awfully glad you turned out to be you, too. And not just because you're pretty, either."

He chuffed out a laugh. "Pretty?"

"Fine. Handsome. If it had only been that, though, I wouldn't have come."

"So you really came for my etchings?"

"I'm trying to be serious and honest here."

"Sorry."

"I'm twenty-seven, Noah. I've been around the block a couple of times. I appreciate beauty, but it isn't nearly enough to entice me to bed."

"So, I'm more than just beefcake, huh?"

"The beefcake doesn't hurt, but yes. I haven't done anything like this in…well, ever."

"Never? What about college?"

"I was a stick-in-the-mud. Always studying. A wild night for me was going to the coffeehouse with my friends. I got too little sleep, worried too much, but I graduated summa cum laude. And…that tells you pretty much everything about me in a nutshell. Not terribly glamorous."

"No keggers?"

"Not a one."

"No boys?"

"A couple. Nothing noteworthy. Nice guys, though. I was more interested in school than anything else. My mother said I was a late bloomer. But then, she's my mom."

Noah touched her arm, but didn't move closer. "I believe you've blossomed into someone quite remarkable."

Her whole body flushed with a warm heat that started at her core. She cleared her throat, not wanting to derail the conversation, not when there was more to say. She wanted him to know who she was, and why staying wasn't a light decision for her. "The point is even when I was supposed to be reckless, I wasn't. I'm careful. With my safety and with my feelings. The only thing I'm impulsive about is shoes. Ask any of my friends. They're constantly trying to get me to shake loose. Get wild. I disappoint them so often, I'm surprised we're all still friends. I mean, I even hate my own surprise parties. So tonight is kind of off-script."

"I see."

She looked down, but he lifted her chin with the side of his hand. "No, I really see. You've just described me, fairly accurately."

"What?"

"It makes more sense now, this attraction. Except for the

shoe fetish and my friends trying to loosen me up, you and I are eerily alike. I back-up my work every twenty seconds. I don't like surprises. And I don't make a habit of bringing home beautiful women I've just met."

"Really?" she asked, but it wasn't a question. More a doubt.

"That surprises you?"

"With a bachelor pad like this? Yeah, it kinda does."

"I didn't build it as a babe magnet." He ran his hand over the tasting table. "This was supposed to be the last house I'd ever own. Where my children would grow up. Where I'd celebrate my fiftieth wedding anniversary. Didn't quite work out that way."

"You built it for her."

He took a sip of wine before he spoke. "I rushed things with Mary. We didn't sleep together on the first night, in fact, not for the first few weeks. But I didn't get to really know her. She didn't care for my hours. What had seemed exotic and a little dangerous in the beginning wasn't so pleasant when the blush was off the rose. She did like the money. I thought the house would bring us closer. For a while it did. She loved working with the architect and the designers. But when it came down to just the two of us in this big old house, there wasn't a lot to say."

"I really am sorry. At least you got a fantastic house out of it. I mean it, this is spectacular, and I've only seen a few rooms. I can't imagine what the upstairs is like."

He turned, got a bottle stopper out of a drawer and recorked the wine. "Still want to see my etchings?"

"Very much."

"Okay." He didn't move though, not for a long moment. "Let's just see where the night takes us, all right? Maybe it'll lead to the bedroom—and a large part of me hopes like hell it will—but I'd like it to be fine with both of us if it doesn't."

The butterflies in her stomach took her by surprise. She almost laughed when she realized she was having a major sexual response to a man telling her he wanted to be cautious. "I'm good with that."

"Also?" he said, still not moving along.

"Hmm?"

"You're stunning."

She felt the compliment all the way to her toes and had to bite back a huge happy sigh. Not because the words were so nice, but because the way he'd said them brought the magic bubble back. In spades.

NOAH WALKED HER ACROSS the basement to the art-preservation room, still a little shaken from their conversation. He understood Paige's concern about Curt setting this up, understood her all too well. It had got him thinking about just what the hell *he* was doing. He hadn't just invited her into his home, he was about to bare part of his soul.

He'd had almost the whole property redecorated after Mary left. Although he'd built it for a dying marriage, it had become his pride and joy. It startled him to realize how much he wanted Paige to approve.

He had iris-recognition on this room, which to his mind was superior to the biometric fingerprint systems. Once the camera scanned his eye, the door opened, and with some trepidation, he held it for Paige.

He wanted her to like his paintings, maybe more than he wanted her to like the house. Normally, he didn't give a shit. His taste was his own. But just as he'd been pleased when she'd ordered "his" cheeseburger, he wanted that same rush again. He wanted to see pleasure on her face.

"This is like a small museum," she said, entering the

space with careful steps, looking around at the walls, all painted the same matte white, the better to show off the intricacies and the colors of the paintings.

He walked with her, reading her as she slowed and studied each of his twenty-six canvases. They didn't speak, and that was good. Talking was for later.

This was how he viewed fine art. Quietly, in his own world. He loved the way his brain reacted to different paintings, skittering from sensation to memory to emotion.

But as she moved from the dark de Kooning to the vibrancy of John Ferren, she changed along with the tones of the work. He could see it not just in the set of her mouth, but her posture, the way her fingers held her wineglass. The cant of her head was extraordinarily telling.

If she didn't love the work itself, he already knew she understood it to her bones.

Dammit, he wanted her more than ever. That should be warning enough. He was behaving like a lunatic tonight. Running out on the fundraiser, sweeping this stranger away to a burger joint, bringing her here. Not his house—here. To this room. It was as intimate to him as his bedroom, sometimes more so. This was his passion unveiled. His heart. Some of his longest acquaintances hadn't ever seen the inside of this room.

In front of every canvas were two chairs. Incredibly comfortable chairs, placed at the optimal distance. She stood next to the chairs at each stop, then moved in front of them. He heard her sigh, more than once. Long, satisfied exhalations.

She *saw*.

When they were at the door again, she turned to him, studied him as she had his art. She touched the edge of his mouth with the soft pad of her thumb. "The collection is magnificent. I love your eyes."

This time, when he kissed her, she melted into him, and he into her.

6

THE WAY HE CUPPED the back of her head was almost as good as the way he kissed her.

He nibbled on her bottom lip, teasing her with his tongue until she whimpered. No, the kiss was better. His hand at her neck was wonderful, careful and urgent all at once, but his kiss made her stomach swoop and her knees grow weak.

But her stolen breath and wobbly knees weren't only from the slow slide of their tongues. She was knocked out by the house, the beauty of his art, the San Francisco night, the taste of merlot. The way she wanted him so much she ached.

Paige ran her hand down his long back, over his shoulder blade. His muscles bunched as he moved against her. He was hard all over. She was sure she couldn't really feel the heat of him through their clothes, but this wasn't reality. Not hers, anyway.

Noah pulled back. "Upstairs?"

She nodded, but he was already on his way to the wine room to gather the bottle and their glasses. Once back at her side, he offered her his arm. Together, they walked up the stairs. On the main floor, she retrieved her overnight bag. Her attention was pulled by the spectacular view, but only for a moment.

More stairs, beautiful artwork in the hallway, especially the Gorky. And then his bedroom.

She'd expected special but she got spectacular. Huge. Two walls were entirely glass, and the view of the city lights was captivating. She was vaguely aware that he slipped her bag from her hand, but she was already walking toward the free-standing fireplace that was nestled in a sculpture that would have been at home in her museum. The black-and-rust bedroom felt masculine, but not overly so. His bed rested on a platform that drew her gaze straight to the large canvas above it. It was an abstract, dark but dreamy, hypnotizing. The whole room was. Everywhere she looked, there was something wonderful, something astonishing. Especially when she looked up at Noah.

"Thank you," he whispered. "For being here."

"It's…" She didn't have the right words. So she kissed him instead.

His hands went to her shoulders, then skimmed down her arms in a feathery touch. When she shivered, he moaned. His fingers met at her back, at the top of her zipper. "Yes?"

She nodded quickly, anxious to get back to his lips. This kiss was short, as quick as it took him to undo her dress. She pressed her arms to her sides to keep the gown from falling. "The windows."

"No one can see in," he said. "No one can see you but me." He took hold of her hand and led her toward the junction of the two windows. Her entire field of vision was a panorama of the hills of San Francisco alive with light and motion.

Noah stepped back, slightly behind her. When she shifted her focus she could see him clearly in the window, herself as well. It was as if she were standing on the precipice of two worlds, the vast breadth of the stunning city at her feet and the breathless intimacy of the man about to touch her.

His hand rested warmly on her bare shoulder. His gaze met hers in the glass. She let go of everything but this moment. Relaxed her arms and watched as her dress slipped down her body, leaving her almost naked as if she were a piece of art herself, with swirls of blue puddled at her feet.

She heard his breath stutter, watched him look at her reflection. He brought his free hand to her other shoulder as he stepped just a bit closer. Close enough for her to feel his warmth.

The surreality was made even more intense by the fact that Noah was still dressed. She wanted him naked, yes, but something about this tableau felt more erotic just as it was. Naked would come, but right now she wanted to be here.

His hands brushed slowly down her arms. Not delicate enough to tickle, not hard enough to feel the texture of his skin. He moved slowly again, up the front of her arms to her neck then lower to her chest, watching carefully, as if he were sculpting her. His gaze didn't meet hers, and she wondered if he had been looking straight at her if she'd have seen the way he hungered.

He made her feel beautiful, extraordinary. She stood perfectly still as he continued to skim over her body, every angle, every curve. The only time he touched her was when he reached her hips. Carefully, as if unwrapping a rare gift, he lowered her panties, letting them fall to the tangle of her dress.

She refocused on her body. When was the last time she'd really seen herself? Months? Years? And never like this. As though she were looking through his eyes. The flaws had been the only things for so long. This was a revelation. She didn't look airbrushed or like the models in the magazines. She was fuller, less symmetrical. When he floated his palms over the soft roundness of her tummy, she didn't suck it in, paused but for a second to banish her inner critic.

He only went as low as his arms would reach. More, she thought, because his view would have been blocked than because he didn't want to.

Instead, he repeated the journey in reverse, only this time, he touched her. She gasped when she felt his hands on her upper thighs. He was warm, and big. Masculine hands so dark against her pale flesh. She couldn't see all of him, so she focused on his face. The term *lantern-jawed* could be used to describe him, but that wasn't enough. It didn't come close to describing how everything about his face worked. Of course, she would notice things like his symmetry and proportions. She'd been trained to look. But it was more than a surface beauty. There was intelligence in his eyes. He listened with his whole self. There hadn't been a moment when she'd thought he was simply waiting for his turn to talk. That shouldn't have made him better-looking, but it did.

She trusted him. It was too soon for that. She shouldn't. Hadn't Curt taught her anything? But there it was. She stood still as a statue and let him strip her after knowing him for mere hours, and she felt completely safe. Without doubt, if she said to stop right now, she knew he would. That he would take her home, and make an appointment to meet at the museum.

That made him gorgeous.

He drew her gaze back to the window when he lingered where her thighs met her torso. On each side, he drew a slow line, back and up, down to the edges of her pubic hair. Again. Defining that space, that line. And when she looked at his face, his lips had parted as he stared, his breath on her shoulder hot and needful. But it was his gaze that made her gasp. The want made her head swim, her body moist.

Dizzy at the sensory overload, she refocused on the distance. On the lights of the city. As she stared at the night it felt colder everywhere but where his hands held her.

He stepped closer, touching her, warming her now with his body against her back. The softness of his shirt belied the hardness of his chest. The cool shirt buttons were a tiny shock. The way his erection pushed at his pants was no shock at all.

"I want you," he whispered, his lips nearly brushing the shell of her ear.

"Yes," she said through a sigh, but she didn't turn. Not yet. She closed her eyes, wanting only to feel him for a moment. To sink below the water of darkness into pure sensation.

She wondered what her goosebumps felt like to his fingertips, to his palms.

But he clearly didn't want to wait, not for her to swim up again to light, because he turned her, pulled her into his arms. She opened her eyes just as he bent to kiss her.

7

NOAH CLOSED HIS EYES as he thrust his tongue inside her willing mouth. He was mad to get her in bed, to get rid of his clothes, to have her, and no one to blame but himself.

She was nothing less than exquisite, and seeing her mirrored in the glass had given him an experience he'd remember for the rest of his life. Odd that he'd never brought a woman here, to this spot, not even his ex-wife, when it was so obvious a thing to do.

Now, though, he didn't want to think of anyone else, not even in passing, not when the wealth of Paige was his for the taking.

He pulled back from her, met her clear, blue eyes. "I thought I was overwhelmed before," she said. "Now…"

"Do you want me to stop?" He knew even as he said the words that it might kill him if she said yes.

"No. I want to see you. All of you."

He smiled, more than happy to oblige. Perhaps it would have been more dramatic and more fitting for him to slowly disrobe, but he'd run out of patience the moment she'd pressed against him.

His cuffs gave him trouble, but it only lasted long enough for him to walk her to the edge of the bed. Then his shirt was on the floor, his pants undone with a bit more care, seeing as he was achingly hard. He pulled off everything else in a blur, but finally, he was as naked as she was.

Paige sat, her back straight, a small smile curving her lips as she took her sweet time giving him a once-over. He had to give her this. For God's sake, he'd just spent who knows how long studying her as if she were the Venus de Milo.

It wasn't comfortable, but he didn't really mind. He kept himself in shape, although he wouldn't be on the cover of *Fitness* any time soon. Though if it had been anyone else, he would have made an excuse, gotten on the bed, done something other than just stand there, not daring to look down. He knew his cock was sticking out like a flag pole, and that if her gaze dipped any lower, the flag might just wave. Her eyes kept him steady.

She looked at him the same way she'd looked at his art. As he'd looked at her. Not as a trinket but something worthwhile that deserved study. That brought heat to his face, and while he owed her a lot more time, he couldn't take it another minute. Just as she reached crotch level, he caved, and joined her on the bed. He'd meant to pull down the spread, but he needed to touch her now, arrange things later.

She laughed as she fell back, her hair spreading over the dark duvet in a halo of soft gold.

"Okay, fine. But come on. You're so much more interesting and beautiful to look at."

Her fingers brushed his cheek, then carded through his hair. "I beg to differ."

He looked down at her. "There's no contest."

"We'll have to agree to disagree. And thank you. But it wasn't just you enjoying the view. Standing there was an out-of-body experience. It didn't even feel like me reflected in the glass. I saw in a whole new way. That's not something that happens every day. So thank you for that, too."

He kissed her gently. "I don't think I'll ever stand in that corner again without seeing you in the window."

Her lips parted and her eyes widened for a second. The next second she moved, her fingers touching his jaw. "I want more," she said, as her nail moved slowly down his neck to his chest, where she flattened her palm near his heart.

The next kiss wasn't gentle. It was open-mouthed and needy, met with her own urgency. His hand went to her breast, cupping her, feeling the contrast between her hard nipple and the softness around it. Everything about her felt soft to him. Soft and curved, with none of his sharp angles or jutting bones. Even as he kissed her luscious mouth he wanted to move, to taste everything.

He gave in, sliding his lips down her delicate jaw and spending too little time on her neck, promising himself that he would return there later. But now he licked the flat of his tongue over her nipple before he took the edges of her aureole between his teeth and he swirled and sucked, moaning as his senses were filled with her taste, and finally, her scent.

Paige arched her back, shivering and gasping at his intensity. She was being ravished, and whatever her experiences in her past had been, this was something new. He was patient, clever, wicked. Very, very thorough. It was only after her heart stopped threatening to beat out of her chest that she was able to continue her own explorations. Her hand moved down his warm chest, up his side, down his cool back. Everywhere there was muscle just beneath the surface, tensing, releasing. The breadth of his chest was felt half by her body, half by her palm.

Even this, what should be just having sex, wasn't in

any way what she expected. It was layers of learning him, depths of perception as if she'd been given new and startling senses. She felt him tremble as if it was the only thing that was happening. At the same time her body was swept away by his lips and tongue and heat as if the entire world was him sucking her nipple.

Odd and perfect, she could hardly imagine what it would be like to have him inside her. At that thought, she had no choice. Her hand went from the top of his ass straight to his cock.

It was his turn to gasp, to arch, and she liked that she'd surprised him. He wasn't the only one who could shake things up.

"God, what are you doing?"

"I would think it was kind of obvious."

He looked at her, his eyes ablaze with a kind of delighted shock. "You... I was..."

She scooted down the bed until they were eye to eye. "I want all of it. I swear, I do. But I want you inside me."

He didn't blink, but his lips curved into a smile that was more than a little sinful. "I can do that."

"If it's no trouble."

His chuckle was a roll of soft wonder from her chest on down. Her hiss, when his grip abandoned her breast to thrust two fingers into her wet heat, made him laugh again.

"Touché," she said, although her voice sounded unnaturally breathy.

He kissed her as he shuffled them until he was looking down at her, his knees easing her legs farther apart. He'd gone for the missionary position. It seemed so normal after a night of surprises. But she was glad of it because she wanted to see him, watch his face as they made love.

And there was another revelation. Not many hours ago,

they hadn't met. They were complete strangers. She'd had no idea what Noah looked like. She'd felt too close to desperate about a potential acquisition and highly suspicious of Curt's involvement. That it was Valentine's Day had made everything worse. She'd been so sure it would all end in disaster. "Who'd have thought," she whispered.

He had braced himself on one elbow, his free hand meandering down her belly. "That this would happen?"

She nodded.

His smile was wry. "You were my safety date. Valentine's is a dangerous day for a man who wants no involvement. It's almost as bad as taking a date to a wedding."

His fingers brushed over her lower lips, a ghost touch that made her eyes close as she shivered. His smile had gone by the time she looked at him again. His gaze had darkened so much. He wanted her, it was all over the tense lines of his face, the way his chest rose and fell, how he dripped his hot excitement onto her inner thigh.

He pulled away, back. She gripped his arm, whimpered with the loss.

"One second. Two at the most."

He leaned over and reached for the side of the bed, and she realized. Condom. Important. But dammit.

"See. I'm already back." He ripped open the packet with his teeth.

"Would you like a hand?"

"No. Thank you."

He pushed himself up onto his knees so she had to lift her head to watch him as he rolled the rubber down. He winced as he did so; his penis jerked. He took advantage of his position to let his gaze roam. She couldn't blame him, as she did exactly that, but her impatience peaked with an inner pulse.

"Noah."

"Just torturing myself," he said. "I'm like a geek in an Apple store."

She grinned. "Wow. I've never been compared to electronics before."

He was over her, kissing her. "It's a compliment."

"I believe you."

"I want you," he said, his voice lower. Rougher.

"I believe that, too."

He thrust inside her, not stopping until he filled her. Even with him studying her, she didn't hide a thing. Not her moan, not the biting of her lower lip, not even her fingers digging hard into his back.

His slide soon quickened as he pushed and withdrew. Each time he came into her, he went all the way and each time, she lifted to meet him. It still wasn't enough. She wrapped her legs around his slim hips, let herself feel his muscles beneath her calves.

Part of her wanted to close her eyes. It flashed through her mind that she'd always closed her eyes, always focused on the sensations coursing through her body. Tonight she needed the connection more.

As she had at the window, she became a little dizzy with this heightened awareness. She'd naturally fallen into the rhythm of his breathing, so when his chest expanded, hers contracted. The smell of him, spicy and masculine, mixed with the scents of sex to make a new perfume that swirled in the heated air.

She loosened her grip on him but only so she could touch new places. She stole a bead of sweat from his temple. Tasted him, the salt sharp and intimate on her tongue. She touched his lips and he captured her finger between his teeth, rolling his tongue, sucking her.

With her free hand, she reached low, to the side of his

bottom just so she could feel the dimple when he thrust. He moaned low and long as she squeezed his cock.

Still their gazes held. He stared into her, releasing her finger as his hips moved faster, harder. Then, despite her resolve, the muscles in her body tightened, pulling her up and up, stealing her very breath…

Her eyes closed as she cried out.

8

HE GASPED WHEN SHE CAME. His body trembled in the war between watching her and finishing himself. He was close, so close. But she was incredible. Her pale skin flushed, her eyes danced beneath her lids, her mouth opened in a cry that tore at his chest.

Noah looked down, caught by the lines in her neck, but more focused now on the way his balls were tightening.

It was no good, he had to close his eyes. He'd think later.

His hips moved faster, he thrust deeper, harder, and there it was, the point of no return, the moment he wanted to freeze in time, to feel *this* forever. Everything tensed and his cry came from somewhere deep as he threw back his head, straining, stilling as the orgasm slammed. Starbursts flared as the tremors went on and on until he was empty, exhausted.

He wanted to let go, crash down, but she was under him, and she was smiling at him. One kiss, quick, because he needed air, to be continued when he stopped panting.

A hiss as he withdrew, not from discomfort but because he hated leaving that wet heat. Then he was on his back, next to her. Sweat cooled him down quickly, but didn't stop his gulping air. She was gasping, too. They were both grinning like fools.

"I should go clean up," he said, not surprised that he sounded drunk.

She nodded. "Probably."

"Can't move just yet."

"Uh-huh."

He barked out a laugh at how wrecked they both were. For a couple of minutes, they both just breathed. But he found her hand and she threaded her fingers between his.

"That was… Wow."

"Uh-huh."

"I mean," she said, turning to look at him, "unbelievable. So much happened."

His grin grew. He knew exactly what she meant. "It was a goddamned banquet."

She nodded, a bit of her hair falling from one edge of the pillow to another.

"I really need to get up. Before I fall asleep."

"Sucks to be you."

He laughed again, and that did it. He let her go and forced himself upright.

In the bathroom, he took care of business as his mind settled back into a more regular rhythm. He thought about taking a quick shower, but he was too tired, and he wanted to be back in bed. Next to Paige. Get them under covers, make sure she was comfortable. Sleep with her beside him.

Shit. He didn't like sharing his bed, not for sleep. He was doing it again. Wanting too much, too quickly. It had been the most intense sexual experience of his life, including his first time with his ex-wife. But this was when he needed to be careful. For all his logic, he could be a sentimental idiot. He'd let his dick do the thinking when he'd fallen for

Mary, and he couldn't do that again. Despite the fact that he wanted more, much more, of Paige.

He needed to pull back. Just take a step away, as hard as that would be. Not too far, though, because what if…?

They had the art to work on. Meetings. Lawyers. That would help, that would be great. They could still have lunch together. Dinners. Sex. He would take it slowly. Not jump into anything they'd both regret.

But he didn't have to step back tonight. She was still in his bed. Warm. Beautiful. Soft and sweet and God, the way she smelled and made him laugh.

With his hands full of soap, it dawned on him. He wanted to be careful with Paige. Not for his sake, but for hers. For *theirs*. There was a chance here for something important. He wasn't willing to screw it up.

He grabbed a towel and dried himself off, his smile back in place. He wanted her. More than he'd wanted anything in years.

PAIGE CURLED AROUND Noah's long, lean body, her head pillowed by his chest. She was wrung out and exhausted, but incredibly happy. She wanted the night to last forever. But sleep stole her away before the next breath.

When she woke, it was to light. To warmth. To Noah's body pressed against her back, his arm around her waist. The last of her dream skittered away, and she wasn't sorry, even though it had been a great dream. This was better.

He stirred next to her, grumbled something she couldn't make out. Then his hand moved on her tummy, a caress that made her sigh. She needed to see him, though.

As gracefully as she could, which wasn't very, she moved and shifted until they could look at each other from their respective pillows. His smile told her everything. She hadn't even known she'd been worried, but the relief was real. The night had been real. Given her record on Valentine's Day, that was something of a miracle.

"Good morning," he said.

"Morning."

"I'm glad you're here."

She touched his cheek. "Me too."

"So all that happened, that really did happen?"

She nodded. "Hard to believe, but true."

He just smiled at her, looking sexy with his hair all messed up and his eyes still half-closed. She even liked his five o'clock shadow. It made him look rugged, manly. Edible. But not until she brushed her teeth.

"Why don't you use this bathroom," he said. "Take a shower. It's a great shower."

"What are you going to do?"

"Wait for my turn."

"Hmm," she said, sounding as miffed as she felt.

"What?"

"It's a big shower."

He lifted his head and looked past her to the bedside table. "It's almost nine."

"What does that have to do with anything?"

"It's Tuesday."

"Oh. Yeah. I have a meeting at eleven."

"Which is why we shouldn't shower together."

She moved her hand to his chest, rubbed him right over his nipple, delighted with herself as it got hard under her palm. "We're both mature adults. We can control ourselves."

He glanced down to her hand. "We can?"

She nodded quite seriously.

His hand touched her upper thigh and before she knew it, his fingers were at her entrance. Then slipping inside. "But what if you drop the soap, and I accidentally—"

"Accidentally?"

"It could happen."

She grabbed his wrist as one sneaky finger found her clit. "It's Tuesday."

He frowned. "I have a meeting, too. At ten."

"We need to stop."

His frown deepened. "Fine. We'll stop." He pressed down just hard enough to make her jump. "Five minutes."

She tried to shake her head, but instead relaxed her grip. "We shouldn't."

"Four minutes."

"I have a presentation. I need to…oh."

"You certainly do."

It only took three minutes. She bucked into his hand, whimpered then cried out, shaken. Sated. And still wanting more.

"Of course," he said, letting the words trail. "We could play hooky."

Paige loved the idea, toyed with it for a moment. Especially when he brushed his very hard cock against her thigh. "I'd love to, I really would, but I can't."

He groaned his disappointment.

She lifted her head to stare down at him. "I thought you had a big horrible virus to fight."

Noah grunted. "Stupid computers."

"Terrible things. More trouble than they're worth."

"Damn straight."

She gave him a closed-mouth kiss, then threw back the comforter. "I'll be quick."

"Then I will, too," he said, turning away from her. They both got out of bed. She felt incredible, as if she'd spent a weekend at a spa. Watching him stretch was an added treat, but she didn't dare look below his waist.

"We'll meet back here in fifteen minutes."

"Where will you be?"

"Second bathroom."

"Ah. Okay. Fifteen minutes it is." She hurried to the bathroom, grabbing her overnight bag as she went.

His shower was just as spectacular as she'd imagined. She was careful not to get her hair too wet, and careful not to linger, as much as she'd liked to.

But she did let the water pound her back as she replayed moments from last night. There was still a chance that this was a one-night thing. She didn't want it to be. She couldn't remember the last time she'd been so curious about a man. Curious about everything. His childhood, his work, his friends, his hopes. There was no use calling it anything but what it was: infatuation. He'd swept her off her feet from the moment they'd met.

The first thing she would do when she got to work was call Curt. She would grill him, using force if necessary, to find out if there was any kind of hidden agenda. She prayed there wouldn't be, but with Curt…

It didn't matter, though, did it? She was smitten. She wanted more. Not just to work with Noah, but to be with him. This felt…different. Aside from the sex, which had been life-altering, there was more going on. She saw herself with him. It could be a colossal mistake, one that would leave her in shreds, but she didn't think so. Noah fitted in her life.

Time. She had to get dressed. Put on some makeup, do her hair. It was late, and they both had work. She hated it, but she got ready. All she wanted to do was crawl back in to that big bed of his.

It was after nine-thirty when she came out of the bathroom. He was standing on the other side of the bed, dressed in jeans and a mauve sweater she instantly wanted to touch.

His grin made her giddy, but there was also something expectant in that smile. His gaze darted to the bed.

Flowers. He'd somehow by some magic brought her flowers. Not an arrangement, nothing so studied. Pink-yellow daisies, purple-white mums and orange-fuchsia dahlias. A breath of spring in February.

"What's this?"

"Happy Valentine's Day," he said.

Her mouth opened, but she couldn't think what to say. "But how?" she asked, finally.

"State secret."

"You have a green house?"

"No. But my neighbor does."

"Are you going to be in trouble?"

He nodded. "It's worth it."

She gathered the flowers into a rather large bouquet. Sniffed and found a soft, gentle scent. Let herself shiver that he'd done this. For her. "Thank you," she whispered.

He walked around to her, lifted the flowers from her arms and tossed them once more on the bed. He gathered her close. Kissed her, a long, languid, peppermint-flavored kiss that curled her toes. When he pulled back, he looked at her in that way of his. "I want more. I hope to hell you do, too."

She smiled. "More sounds perfect."

"Perhaps we could start with dinner tonight?"

She kissed him again, rubbed her hands over that delicious sweater, then underneath. The best Valentine's Day ever.

* * * * *

Read on for a sneak preview of Carol Marinelli's
PUTTING ALICE BACK TOGETHER!

Hugh hired bikes!

You know that saying: 'It's like riding a bike, you never forget'?

I'd never learnt in the first place.

I never got past training wheels.

'You've got limited upper-body strength?' He stopped and looked at me.

I had been explaining to him as I wobbled along and tried to stay up that I really had no centre of balance. I mean *really* had no centre of balance. And when we decided, fairly quickly, that a bike ride along the Yarra perhaps, after all, wasn't the best activity (he'd kept insisting I'd be fine once I was on, that you never forget), I threw in too my other disability. I told him about my limited upper-body strength, just in case he took me to an indoor rock-climbing centre next. I'd honestly forgotten he was a doctor, and he seemed worried, like I'd had a mini-stroke in the past or had mild cerebral palsy or something.

'God, Alice, I'm sorry—you should have said. What happened?'

And then I had had to tell him that it was a self-diagnosis. 'Well, I could never get up the ropes at the gym at school.' We were pushing our bikes back. 'I can't blow-dry the back of my hair...' He started laughing.

Not like Lisa who was laughing at me—he was just laughing and so was I. We got a full refund because we'd only been on our bikes ten minutes, but I hadn't failed. If anything, we were getting on better.

And better.

We went to St Kilda to the lovely bitty shops and I found these miniature Russian dolls. They were tiny, made of tin or something, the biggest no bigger than my thumbnail. Every time we opened them, there was another tiny one, and then another, all reds and yellows and greens.

They were divine.

We were facing each other, looking down at the palm of my hand, and our heads touched.

If I put my hand up now, I can feel where our heads touched.

I remember that moment.

I remember it a lot.

Our heads connected for a second and it was alchemic; it was as if our minds kissed hello.

I just have to touch my head, just there at the very spot and I can, whenever I want to, relive that moment.

So many times I do.

'Get them.' Hugh said, and I would have, except that little bit of tin cost more than a hundred dollars and, though that usually wouldn't have stopped me, I wasn't about to have my card declined in front of him.

I put them back.

'Nope.' I gave him a smile. 'Gotta stop the impulse

spending.'

We had lunch.

Out on the pavement and I can't remember what we ate, I just remember being happy. Actually, I can remember: I had Caesar salad because it was the lowest carb thing I could find. We drank water and I *do* remember not giving it a thought.

I was just thirsty.

And happy.

He went to the loo and I chatted to a girl at the next table, just chatted away. Hugh was gone for ages and I was glad I hadn't demanded Dan from the universe, because I would have been worried about how long he was taking.

Do I go on about the universe too much? I don't know, but what I do know is that something *was* looking out for me, helping me to be my best, not to **** this up as I usually do. You see, we walked on the beach, we went for another coffee and by that time it was evening and we went home and he gave me a present.

Those Russian dolls.

I held them in my palm, and it was the nicest thing he could have done for me.

They are absolutely my favourite thing and I've just stopped to look at them now. I've just stopped to take them apart and then put them all back together again and I can still feel the wonder I felt on that day.

He was the only man who had bought something for me, I mean something truly special. Something beautiful, something thoughtful, something just for me.

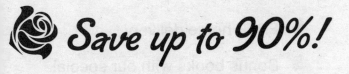

MILLS & BOON® Book Club

2 Free Books!

Get your free books now at
www.millsandboon.co.uk/freebookoffer

Or fill in the form below and post it back to us

THE MILLS & BOON® BOOK CLUB™—HERE'S HOW IT WORKS: Accepting your free books places you under no obligation to buy anything. You may keep the books and return the despatch note marked 'Cancel'. If we do not hear from you, about a month later we'll send you 4 brand-new stories from the Blaze® series, including a 2-in-1 book priced at £5.30 and two single books priced at £3.30 each. There is no extra charge for post and packaging. You may cancel at any time, otherwise we will send you 4 stories a month which you may purchase or return to us—the choice is yours. *Terms and prices subject to change without notice. Offer valid in UK only. Applicants must be 18 or over. Offer expires 31st July 2012. **For full terms and conditions, please go to www.millsandboon.co.uk**

Mrs/Miss/Ms/Mr (please circle)
_____

First Name
_____

Surname
_____

Address
_____

_____

Postcode
_____

E-mail
_____

Send this completed page to: Mills & Boon Book Club, Free Book Offer, FREEPOST NAT 10298, Richmond, Surrey, TW9 1BR

Find out more at
www.millsandboon.co.uk/freebookoffer

Visit us Online

0112/K2XEA

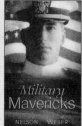